"Josh is dead, isn't he?" Patti heard Lorraine ask in her blunt manner.

"Yes, I'm sorry ma'am, he is. Do you think you can answer some questions for us?"

"As long as you answer some of mine," she replied.

The policeman glanced at Patti, and she saw the flash of recognition. She said, "Hi Robb. I'm Lorraine's friend. I drove her here. I don't know Josh-didn't know him, I mean." She blushed, for more than one reason now.

"Hi Patti. Good Lord, imagine seeing you here." He looked at her for a moment, and then said, "Perhaps you could wait here, then?" He opened the door and led Lorraine away. The last glimpse of Lorraine showed a strained, weary expression, like Patti had not yet seen on her friend's face.

The officer returned a few minutes later. He came to the driver's side this time. "How are you, Patti?"

"I've been better."

He nodded. "I understand, under the circumstances."

Patti thought of her surgery, now fading in importance. "It's not just Lorraine," she said, "but I won't bore you with it now. How are you, Robb?"

He took his hat off. "I'm pretty good. Better now that I've run into you."

This seemed like a dangerous thread of conversation to Patti, at this place and time. She felt their history rising between them. It was hard not to think of that clumsy first time for both of them, the awkward kisses and even more awkward embraces. She'd never forget that moment when they both knew they were about to take that last step as lovers. And so young, it seemed now.

Caught Holding the Bag

Booklocker.com, Inc.
2005

Caught Holding the Bag

Peter McGinn

To my wife Cindy,
shared memories, shared dreams,
and stuff like that.

Chapter 1

What she later called her "Great Adventure" started in early September for Patti Jo Lewis when she woke up in the hospital with an ileostomy and a bad case of denial. The anesthesia was slow to let go of her, so her brain was muffled enough to allow the denial to take shape. She imagined an accident of some kind, that she had saved the life of a child, but was injured herself. Her mind conjured up this fantasy and found it endurable only because the truth seemed less acceptable to her growing awareness of what had really happened.

By late in the day, the sleepiness receded and a cloak of pain, obscured by the drugs, surrounded her. She tried not to look at herself, tried not to think about what Dr. Regan had done to her; except that when she tried not to think of it, it became all she thought about.

That evening, a nurse named Amanda came in to help her. She moved the hospital gown aside, and Patti sighed, reality taking hold. She said, "It's there, isn't it?"

"What's there, dear?" Amanda said absently.

Patti thought, Is there anything else? If you woke up from surgery with a pouch on your body, you would not ask what is there. But she wasn't ready to put it into words just yet.

"Never mind," she said finally. A sob bubbled up inside her and escaped as a moan.

"What's wrong, dear? Did I hurt you?" Patti shook her head. Tears were beginning to obscure her vision, but she watched as Amanda removed the ostomy pouch, leaving the wafer on her skin. She caught a glimpse of the bright red stoma, and for a moment wondered if she was going to be sick. Fortunately, she thought sarcastically, she hadn't been allowed to eat yet.

"It looks great," Amanda said, repositioning the pouch.

"Not the word I would use," Patti said, half under her breath.

The nurse smiled. "It's a lot to get used to, isn't it? But you will. Dr. Regan does good work. You're looking pale. Are you okay?"

"I've felt better." She managed a weak smile.

Amanda touched her cheek, as if she were a little girl. Patti didn't mind. Right about then she wanted to be treated like a little girl. "Ain't that the truth," Amanda said. "Would you like your hair brushed before visitors' hours? It's gorgeous, you know. Here, let me help you." She shifted the pillows behind her and reached for the brush on the nightstand. "We'll wash your hair tomorrow. You'll feel a lot better by then." She sat sidesaddle on the bed next to Patti and brushed her hair in long slow strokes. "If my hair was this thick and black, I'd give up being a liquid blonde forever. I'd never look back."

Patti yawned, and Amanda set the brush down. "Listen, I'll come back in a while to check your vitals. You get some more rest now."

"That I can handle," Patti said, falling back against the pillow. She looked out her window, but all she saw was a patch of blue sky next to a corner of the hospital parking garage. She closed her eyes, but sleep didn't come. Instead a new roommate was wheeled in. Her name was Kate, and she was 87 years old. Patti knew her age because the woman said it four times during the time it took to get her settled into her bed.

A male nurse, talking to an apparent trainee, described the woman's rare condition, which caused her skin to peel off in strips if they weren't careful, so they could not use tape on her bandages. Patti still felt too sorry for herself to be grossed out by the description, as if it were being discussed on a television program instead of about a real person next to her.

What little compassion Patti felt for Kate evaporated through the night, as the old woman developed the habit of calling out for what she wanted instead of pressing her call button. "Tylenol!" she'd cry out five or six times, or "Ginger Ale," as if the nurses were huddled outside the door, waiting to be called. If Patti pressed her own call button and explained that her roommate needed something, by the time the nurse came in, Kate usually was asleep again, so the nurse would leave. Minutes later, Kate would wake up and the cycle started up all over.

Finally the next morning, before official visiting hours, Kate's husband Cal appeared. He pulled a chair up to his wife's bed and spoke to her in a soft voice. She seemed to stop needing things, and Patti fell asleep. Her dreams were a patchwork of confused images. The only part of the dream she remembered upon awakening found her sitting in her apartment, the IV still in her arm. The lines of the IV ran across the living room, and into the kitchen, stretching out like the oxygen tubes her great Aunt Roberta had required during the last years of her life. When Patti woke up, the image still fresh in her mind, she reached for the television controller. "That's it," she announced aloud, "No more sleep today."

Dr. Regan stopped by at noon and brushed aside her concern and dread. No, he hadn't thought it would come down to emergency surgery, but her body had decided things, and it would prove to be a relief for her after the years of illness, a time to heal. It could possibly be reversed down the road, though he couldn't make any promises. She should concentrate on mending and enjoying good health for a while. Good health, she thought, with this thing hanging off me?

Patti's father and brother visited her that afternoon, separately, as they weren't speaking to each other. Usually one of her familial duties was arranging her schedule so that the two of them didn't run into each other through her. They were on their own now, however. She figured she had her own problems.

They appeared before her, exhibiting the same awkward body language men often carry into hospitals, uncomfortable with illness. Dad came first, twisting his Red Sox cap as if squeezing it dry, searching the expressions of the nurses as they worked, as if he could pick up from them how Patti was really doing. Patti drifted in and out of sleep, so she was surprised when she looked up to find her brother now sitting at her side.

"How did you do that?" she asked him. He stared at her blankly. The way Tom slowly wrung his hands reminded her of Dad and the twisted baseball cap. Then Tom's partner Kelton swept into the room. She loved Kelton like he was another brother; he was as upbeat as Tom was sometimes morose. They balanced each other, she often told them. He kissed Patti's cheek and sat down. Their love seems so natural, so superior to what Dad and Mom had before Mom ran off: how could Dad disapprove? How could he let it split the family? But with Kelton present, Patti couldn't dwell on that.

"So," Kelton said once he sat down, "are you going to show us the piece of surgical pop art that saved your life?"

Of course, she wasn't about to display her pouch and scar like a proud war wound, but he made her smile for the first time since she woke up after the surgery. It was a good visit.

On Patti's third day after surgery, the W.O.C.N. stopped by to see her. She had stopped by right after the surgery, she understood, but she didn't remember it. The floor nurses had told her more than once to expect her again. Patti's question was, "What's a WOCN?"

The answer, Wound Ostomy Continence Nurse, hadn't been much help to

3

her except that word, ostomy, was there. "She can answer all your questions," one nurse told her, and Amanda said, "She will train you to take care of yourself."

"But I thought maybe you nurses could adopt me and I could stay here." Though she was kidding, the fantasy of others taking care of "that" was appealing to her.

Amanda laughed. "Sure, but once your insurance maxes out, this is a pretty expensive hotel. Besides, as far as insurance goes, as soon as something shows up in the pouch, you have to leave us. Carole will fix you up. She's a miracle worker."

"She'll have to be," Patti assured her. She began to imagine this WOCN in the flowing robes of a magician, strolling in and throwing the contents of a drawstring bag over her, magic dust that would transform her into...what? Her imagination, which her father claimed was even stronger than when she was a teenager, didn't take her that far. "You're twenty-two years old," he had said to her once, after she luxuriously imagined a problem-free idyllic life. "Sometimes you have to face reality."

Patti reached a hand down now, sliding it over the smooth plastic of the pouch. "Welcome to reality," she said to herself, "pull up a chair and stay a while."

Carole Stevens, the WOCN, didn't carry a magician's black drawstring bag, but she plopped a wicker basket down at the foot of the bed. There was a purple ribbon around the handle, and supplies and reading material jutting from it. Her hair was short, two shades darker than black, every strand in place. She oozed confidence as she swept around the hospital bed.

Carole shook hands with her. Her voice was soft and her green eyes kind as she asked Patti about herself. She seemed to know most of it already, but she gave Patti a chance to tell her tale of woe. When Carole took up the subject of the ileostomy and post-surgical care, however, she became more lively, her voice exuding confidence in Patti's ability to take care of herself. She helped her change the ostomy appliance, just for practice, she pointed out, as it could have gone several more days without changing. And she only helped; for the first time, Patti did most of the work herself. Patti's breath caught when she saw the stoma, but this time tears didn't flood her eyes.

Carole showed her how to remove the appliance to best avoid pulling on the skin, and how to prepare the area for the fresh wafer and pouch. She told her how to know when it needs changing, and she gave her a sheet of hints and tips for situations that might arise. When Patti was put back together again, Carole went through the contents of the basket: the extra boxes of ostomy equipment, the tape, powder, lotion, adhesive remover and other "battle gear," as she referred to it. She left her with a magazine, brochures, and a handbook, along with a promise to stop by again before she was released. Carole paused in the doorway.

"I hear you haven't been sleeping well," she said.

"What, is it in my chart?" Patti asked. Carole laughed.

"I have my spies here."

"It's just as well I can't sleep, considering what my dreams are like." She described her dream of her household movements being restricted by IV lines. Carole smiled.

"Well, that's original. But I guess you don't have to be Freud to figure it out. You are obviously concerned about being able to continue your normal life after you get home."

"Silly of me, I suppose."

"Not silly at all, Patti. It's about as natural a worry as you could have, under the circumstances. And that reminds me, if you are willing, you are going to be visited by a free spirit."

Something about the way she said it reminded Patti of Dickens and The Christmas Carol, "You will be haunted by three spirits."

"Who?" she asked.

"You'll like her, I think," Carole said. "A visit by someone who has had the same surgery you have had. It will be good for you. You can see for yourself that people do thrive after this surgery. What do you think? You have to give permission."

"I guess it will be okay."

Carole smiled. "You don't sound sure. With today's privacy laws, I need you to be sure, maybe even in writing."

Patti wasn't sure what she thought of it, but she said, "It may do me good. I'll sign a paper if you want. Thank you." Carole waved and left.

"Something else to look forward to," Patti muttered, but she was intrigued all the same. By day three of captivity, she was looking forward to a little excitement. But she had no idea how much excitement was headed her way because of her next visitor.

Chapter 2

The free spirit breezed in just after the supper tray was cleared away. Her name was Lorraine Simoneau, she announced in a loud voice. She was a big woman, big as in tall, full-bodied, but muscular. Somewhere in her late thirties, Patti guessed, though she wasn't sure. As Lorraine strode over to shake hands, Patti took in her tight jeans and dazzling white sweater in a glance and thought, Does this mean I will still be able to wear jeans? Then she got swept up in Lorraine's personality, which proved to be just as strong as her voice and her handshake grip.

"How are you doing, lass? They taking care of you here?" Patti wondered if the thundering voice was turning heads way down at the nursing station.

"I'm fine, they're real good to me," she replied.

Lorraine noticed the basket, still on the bed. "I see Carole has been in to see you," she boomed.

"Yes. She's great."

"Isn't she though? She has saved my butt more than once. Some hospitals still don't have ET nurses, never mind WOCNs. They send patients home with just the clothes on their backs. So tell me, are you married? Carole didn't say."

Patti blushed for no particular reason. "No."

"No? Engaged? Serious about anyone? Just tell me to mind my own business if you want. Otherwise, I'll keep asking."

"No, that's all right. I don't mind. I'm not serious about anyone right now." She watched as Lorraine sat in the lone chair near the bed. It was too small, and she smiled at the sight.

Lorraine noticed the smile. "Isn't this ridiculous? They must think tall people don't need to sit down." She set her pocketbook down by her right leg. "Patti, would you believe me if I told you that your social life will be every bit as good after this surgery as it was before? Or even better if you were sick before. Were you very sick? IBD, wasn't it?"

Patti nodded. "That's what they said, finally. It took years and a really bad outbreak for them to figure it out, it seemed. I think it was an ER doctor who first suggested it."

"Cramps, diarrhea..." Lorraine began.

Patti took up the list. "Yeah. And weight loss, no appetite sometimes. Finally blood in the stool. I was sure it was cancer but they never found it. And there were times when it wasn't so bad, when it felt like the meds were helping. My friends thought I had an eating disorder. It was horrible."

Patti noticed Lorraine smiling at her. "What?"

Lorraine shook her head. "Nothing. But did you notice you said it was horrible? Not is, but was?"

Tears seemed to spring up out of nowhere again. She fought them off. "Is it going to be better then, Lorraine?"

"Lots better, girl. You wouldn't believe me, so I'm not telling you how much better." A short silence developed. "Do you want to ask me anything, Patti? Anything at all?"

Patti shrugged. She knew Lorraine wanted questions about her recovery, but she was curious about the woman. "Are you married, Lorraine?"

"Not any more. I was up until last year. A real hunk, football coach, great buns."

Patti smiled. "What happened?"

"We were unlucky, I guess."

"Unlucky?"

"Well, sort of. It all started on Super Bowl Sunday a couple of years ago. A dozen of his nearest and dearest friends helped him decimate my house while I was gone. Seems they wanted to play some football during half-time, but they were too lazy to go outside, or else they didn't want to miss a single beer commercial. I came home and they took off. They scattered like dry leaves. "

In a strong wind, Patti thought, contemplating the men faced with an angry Lorraine. "He was sleeping in the easy chair," Lorraine continued. "The place was wrecked. It was all downhill after that. A downhill plunge to the divorce."

Patti thought for a moment. "Okay, but I don't see where that was bad luck. You mean that you came home before he had a chance to clean up?"

"No, he wouldn't have thought of that. The bad luck was that while he slept, he started his loud open-mouth snoring, and just when I had picked up his dirty, rolled up socks that they used as a football."

"You didn't!"

"I did. If I'd thought about it, I wouldn't have, but I was livid, and it looked like a perfect fit. He never woke up so quick, let me tell you."

Patti laughed, then gripped her stomach. "Ow."

"Only hurts when you laugh, right? I remember that."

"I guess I haven't laughed much since the surgery."

"I don't wonder," Lorraine said. "You haven't had much to laugh about, have you? But you'll soon get back into the habit."

"Not too soon, I hope. Ouch."

Lorraine's face clouded up for a moment.

"What's wrong, Lorraine?"

Lorraine shook her head vigorously. "Nothing. I've got myself thinking about Josh with that story. He wants to talk to me. He hasn't handled the divorce well at all," she added.

"How so?"

"This isn't the time for that story, I think."

"No really," Patti persisted. "I want to know."

"Well, at first he pretended that I just needed a little freedom. He told our friends I would be back in the fold any minute. Then he got angry, impatient. When was I going to come to my senses? Then he claimed he accepted that I wasn't coming back, and he started dating every woman he could. I figured once he got through that stage, he would work through to real acceptance. But over the past few months he has gotten morose, morbid almost. He keeps hinting at some trouble he's in."

"What kind of trouble?"

Lorraine shrugged. "He doesn't say, only that it's big enough to sweep him away. Those were his words last week." Lorraine stood up quickly and walked the few steps to the window. "I'm sorry, Patti."

"For what?"

Lorraine was shaking her head again. "I'm standing here telling you my problems. I've broken rule number one; this visit is supposed to be about you. I guess I'm more worried about him than I realized."

Patti reached for the control to raise the head of the bed. Over its hum she said, "You don't have to apologize, Lorraine. I need the distraction so I don't dwell on my own morose thoughts."

"It's sweet of you to say so," Lorraine said, "but it's still a no-no for an official ostomy visitor."

"Is that what you are?"

"Yes. I went through training and everything. Want to see my official certification card?"

Patti wasn't sure if Lorraine was serious or not, but she played along. "Sure, I'd love to."

Her visitor pulled a wallet from her purse, and extracted a yellow business card from it. She passed the card to Patti. "Now aren't you impressed?"

"Very," Patti answered, passing it back. "Do you have a secret handshake, too?"

"Yes, but you'll have to wait for those stitches to heal before you try it."

Patti smiled, playing with the ribbon on the basket with her toes. She blushed when she saw Lorraine watching her. "Lorraine?"

"Yes?"

"Are you dating again?"

"God help me, yes, I weaken occasionally. Are you worried about that?"

Patti half shrugged. "A little."

"Don't. Think of it this way: if a guy likes you- I'm sorry, are guys your preference?" Patti nodded, and Lorraine went on. "If a guy likes you but he loses interest because of how your internal plumbing is hooked up, which could have saved your life, by the way, how shallow does that make him?"

"I guess so."

"Darn tootin'. Think of it as an early warning device, a jerk detector. It could save you weeks or months of trying to wean out the pinheads from the good ones."

Patti smiled. "Wow. Every woman should have one."

"That's the spirit." A slow smile spread across Lorraine's face. "You're afraid I'm going to talk about sex now, aren't you, Patti?"

Patti twirled a lock of hair around a forefinger and pressed the finger to her lips. "Petrified."

Lorraine threw her head back and laughed, a startling sound. Patti looked towards the door self-consciously, half expecting a nurse to check out the sound.

"Well, maybe next time we will, if there is a next time."

"I'd like that," Patti blurted out. "Seeing you again, I mean, not talking about sex."

Lorraine laughed again. Patti began to realize how good it might be to have a dynamo like this woman on her side. Lorraine stood up. "Thank you, sweetie. I feel the same way. You've got potential, and we all have to look out for each other, after all. A woman visited me after my surgery, and was a big help, so I figure I can give back a little of it. Would you like me to stop by here again before you go home?"

"Yes, please."

"You got it. And after you get out, I'll take you to the next ostomy chapter meeting, if you're interested. We have an interesting bunch, and you'll be with people who know what you're going through."

"I'd like that. Carole suggested it while she was here."

"Great. She's supposed to. Here, while I'm thinking of it, write your address and phone number on this." Lorraine passed a small spiral pad and a pen over to Patti.

Patti wrote her name and phone number down, and handed them back. Lorraine said her goodbyes, blowing Patti a kiss as she left the room. Patti couldn't say exactly why, but she felt her life had taken a small turn for the better with this visit.

A nurse came in right after Lorraine left, a nurse Patti hadn't seen yet. "She isn't the comforting type, is she? Not that I'm being critical, mind you."

"Of course not," Patti said. She pondered Lorraine's visit. It wasn't about sympathy or pity. She realized that it hadn't occurred to her after the first impression of the jeans that Lorraine even had an ileostomy, like she did. Maybe this surgery wasn't the end of the world for her.

After Lorraine left the hospital, she sat in her car in the parking lot for a few minutes and took notes while the visit was fresh in her mind. She sometimes used them to compare notes with Carole afterwards. When she made mistakes, she liked to know about them and correct them for the next time. And as she had said to Patti, dragging her own sordid personal problems into the conversation had been a big mistake. Patti had been sweet about it, but that didn't alter the fact that she had gone off course.

A part of her was still connected to Josh, despite the divorce. Sixteen years of marriage did that to you. Sometimes she felt she had taken the easy way out, leaving him after his drinking got worse. He had never hit her, of course, and he still functioned fairly well in his sports-oriented world, where drinking was both honorable and expected. Lorraine's grandmother had put up with drinking all through her 41 years of marriage, and Lorraine had always sworn she wouldn't let it happen to her. "It is part and parcel of marriage," her grandmother had told her once. "It won't be for me," Lorraine had shot back with all the wisdom a teenager can muster.

She still worried about him, and not just because of the drinking. He kept making references to this calamity overtaking him, hinting the only solution to his problems might rest in the top drawer of his bureau. Of course, the German World War II knife his father had given him rested in that top drawer. Josh had stopped her in the hallway that very afternoon, anxious to talk to her. She begged off, saying she had to visit someone in the hospital; surely this could wait. "He said, "Lorraine, I'm a freight train heading over a cliff. I would think if you don't want to help me, you'd at least want to stand and watch."

Lorraine had rolled her eyes and rushed on to her visit with Patti. Now she wondered, though, was he being melodramatic, or could he really be in deep trouble? Should she call him? On an impulse, she dug into her purse for her cell phone and punched in his number, their old number. While it rang, she rolled her window down a few inches to let some air in.

"Yeah, hello?"

"Oh, God," Lorraine said. She could tell even with the brief greeting, Josh was drunk, or at least well on the way.

"Who is it?"

"Josh, it's me."

"You say that like it's supposed to mean something to me."

"Have you been drinking? Don't you have a practice to run?"

"Here's your chance to do me a favor and get my ass fired out of that thankless job and ruin my life some more."

"You're doing that just fine on your own, Josh." This was going nowhere. She gave it one last try. "Josh, you wanted to tell me something important this afternoon. I regret I had to run. Do you want to tell me now?"

"You have some time to spare now, do you? Your concern touches me. Forget it. You can read about it in the goddamn paper like everyone else." He hung up on her, with gusto, by the sound of it.

Lorraine turned off her phone and dropped it back into the purse, muttering, "That was a great idea." She started the engine and, shifting into reverse, decided she would talk to some of the assistant football coaches. Maybe she could find out what was brewing in Josh's life. It can't be that bad, she thought, I would have heard something. She wished she could be sure.

That same afternoon, Tom, Patti's brother, stopped by her room again. She had just taken her first walk around the ward without her IV. He kissed her forehead and sat down.

"Okay, Sis, this is okay, but it has been several days. Don't you think you should be getting over it and going home?"

Patti smiled. "Thanks for the sympathy."

He shrugged. "Hey, sometimes tough love is what is needed." He looked out her window. The hospital employee parking garage loomed. "Well, you're paying way too much for that view. How are you feeling?"

"Better than I look."

"What a relief. You look like hell. I'm kidding," he added, standing by her side. "You look much better. You were out of it last time I was here."

She reached out and squeezed his hand. "Yeah, it's a shame they only

11

waste morphine on you when you can't fully appreciate it. Yesterday is a blur to me now. I'm pretty sure both you and Dad were here, but beyond that, I couldn't say. You didn't run into him here in the hospital, did you?"

"Hell, no. I arrived with a plan. First Kelton and I checked the parking lot for Dad's truck. We found it, so we knew he was up here with you. I posted myself in the cafeteria near a window facing the parking lot, and Kelton stood out in the hall keeping an eye out. Kelton came in after twenty minutes or so and said he had spotted Dad leaving. So I hustled my bustle up here to see you while Kelton stood guard to make sure Dad didn't come back up."

"Hustled your bustle?"

"It's an expression. All so I could come up here and visit my Pitti-Patti."

"Don't use that name. How many times do I have to tell you?" Tom had saddled her with that nickname when she was a toddler.

"You're still my baby sister."

"Am I? I don't think so, and I can prove it. Exhibit A: I'm 22 years old, only a year younger than you are, in case you need reminding. Exhibit B: My father and my older brother are acting like 10-year-olds, and expect me to step in and settle their differences."

"I'm not acting like a ten-year old."

"Yes, you are."

"Am not!"

Patti smiled. "Hiding in the cafeteria and playing spy with Kelton is not typical adult behavior."

"Okay, I never said I was typical." He stared at a minor commotion in the hallway outside her room. He glanced back at Patti. "So what did Dad say about me?"

She laughed, until the pain cut it off. "Ow. Don't do that." That question was a running joke between them, since their father refused to even mention Tom's name nowadays.

Tom reached for the television remote. She grabbed it out of his hand. "Nice try, pal. We're going to have a conversation here. I'm not recuperated enough to listen to you make fun of TV shows. My stitches aren't nearly secure enough yet."

He crossed his arms. "Okay, we'll talk instead. Has the doctor told you if the surgery can be reversed someday, or changed to one of those continental surgeries?"

She laughed again, grabbing her abdomen. "I told you not to do that. You know it's called continent surgery. No, it's too soon and I shouldn't get my hopes up."

"I'm sorry, Patti."

"It may be fine, Tom. After I heal, I should feel better than I have in years. I must confess, I felt plenty sorry for myself before, but I'm better now. I met an interesting lady today, a real whirlwind, and she had the same kind of surgery I just had."

"You're kind of a whirlwind yourself. Will you be seeing her again?"

"Yes. And I have a feeling my life will be more interesting because of it."

"Interesting? Is that what you're looking for? I would think Kelton, dear old Dad, and I have made it interesting enough already."

That's getting old, Tom. You have to move over, there's a new game in town."

Chapter 3

Three days later, Lorraine drove along an unfamiliar street on the outskirts of town. This was a newly developed area, former cow pastures and woods transformed into neat, expensive developments. Lorraine slowed the car down as she approached a large white sign near a turnoff. She shielded her eyes against the afternoon sun. The sign depicted a map of the development, not yet completed, called White Birch Estates.

"Finally," Lorraine intoned. She turned off and drove up the stretch of access road. She glanced around as brand new houses popped into view. "Figures; no white birch trees and no estates."

Lorraine passed a block of mailboxes for the residents and turned left. So far so good as far as the instructions were concerned. Second left, third house on the right, a circular driveway and a small wooden lighthouse near the road. She spotted the powder blue house up on the right, and slowed down. A small sign near the driveway said, "No U-Turns Please." Lorraine pulled in behind a Lincoln Continental. She got out of her car and looked into the windows of the Lincoln as she walked past. "The car is almost as big as the house," she muttered as she approached the steps. She rang the bell. A small dog barked frenetically inside. After another 30 seconds, a woman opened the door.

"Hi, I'm Lorraine Simoneau. I think we spoke last night."

"Yes, good afternoon. I'm Alicia Turner. Come on in, please." The woman didn't offer to shake hands, but stepped aside, opening the door wider. She closed the door behind Lorraine and motioned towards the sofa against the wall to their right. "Please, sit down."

Lorraine glanced around the room as she sat down. A doorway opened into what was most likely the kitchen and dining room, and straight ahead was a flight of stairs. The room was immaculate: no toys, so no kids, Lorraine figured. The aroma of coffee and something baking reached her. She had hurried out of the house that morning after eating just a bagel, and her stomach lurched appreciatively.

"Thanks for coming to see me on such short notice," Alicia said. She was a tall woman, almost as tall as Lorraine but more petite in build. She carried herself with a grace that made Lorraine think of royalty. Her clothes, the jewelry, her made-up hair, contributed to a look that spoke of money, a look that didn't seem to go with the smallish house, however nice it was inside. She looked to be 35 or so, but Lorraine suspected she was one of those women who fought to look younger than she was. She wore plenty of makeup.

Before Alicia could sit down on the other end of the sofa, a man came down the stairs. "I put her in your bedroom," he said. As if to explain the statement, the dog's yipping could be heard again, muffled this time.

"She'll calm down," Alicia said. "Ned, this is Lorraine, from the ostomy group. This is Ned, my uncle."

Ned forestalled any thought of a handshake by lifting a hand in a sort of wave before sitting down in the glide rocker. "Hi Lorraine."

"Glad to meet you." Lorraine thought of her great Aunt Meg, so many years ago, a legend in the family for all of the "uncles" who lived with her at different times of her life. Surely nowadays relationships didn't need to be covered up with such euphemisms.

"Can we offer you some coffee?" Ned asked. He glanced at his niece.

Alicia stood up again. "Yes, of course. Lorraine?"

"Well, sure, that would be great."

"Cream and sugar?"

"No thanks, straight up."

Alicia walked over, pausing in the doorway. "Ned?"

"No, I'm fine, thank you."

"How many people are in your organization?" Ned asked, after Alicia left the room.

"Our local chapter? We have about 200 members right now. Some are medical people, but mostly members."

Ned nodded. His hair was so thick and full, for a man apparently in his fifties, that Lorraine wondered if it was a wig, or if he belonged to one of those hair replacement clubs that advertised endlessly late at night. He was tending to being overweight, but still carried it well.

Lorraine heard the tinkling sound of stirring from the kitchen. Alicia appeared again, crossing the room to hand a dainty cup on a saucer to Lorraine. In her other hand she held a plate of cookies. "Would you like a spice cookie? My favorite recipe, reheated from The Whole Grain." At Lorraine's questioning look, she added, "It's a marvelous bakery intown. You must go there sometime."

"They look and smell irresistible," Lorraine said, taking one. "Thank you." She set the cup and saucer on the coffee table, and then picked up the cup by itself.

Alicia smiled and went back to get her own coffee cup before sitting down.

Ned cleared his throat. "We read in the Weekly Shopper that your group pays for children to attend an ostomy camp every year. Very laudable."

"Thank you," Lorraine said. His use of the word "we" irritated her. It was Alicia who had called and asked her to come out. Why wasn't she talking? Besides, the article had appeared in the free shopping newspaper over a month before. Still, she'd consider forgiving a lot of a man with piercing blue eyes and the confident direct manner he seemed to possess, as long as the confidence didn't inflate to anything worse.

"And you provide other services, I understand?"

What was this leading up to? Lorraine wondered. But she said, "Yes, we visit people who have ostomy surgery, so they can see someone who has been through it. We distribute literature and other instructional materials, and we hold meetings and invite speakers."

"I see."

The dog's yipping started up again. Alicia stood up. "Excuse me; I'll go give him a Valium." She left the room.

"She's kidding, I think," Ned said.

Lorraine smiled and nibbled on the large cookie. She tasted oatmeal and brown sugar, almost overcome by spices.

"Your husband is the coach of the football team." The observation was somewhere between a question and a statement.

"Ex-husband."

He looked at her. "Really?" The yipping from upstairs ceased. "For how long?" he asked.

"A year now, officially. Why?"

"I've spoken to your husband many times. He always referred to you as his wife. I assumed you were only separated."

"That's funny," Lorraine said, "he never called me his wife when we were married. I was his old lady." She said it without rancor. When they first married, Josh had started calling her that, using an outward nonchalance to cover his strong feelings for her. But that was all for nothing now. She winced as she thought of what he might be calling her to his pals now.

"Come to think of it, he did say 'old lady.'"

"I guess ex-old lady doesn't work."

"He's in a bit of trouble now, isn't he?"

The question caught Lorraine off guard. She covered her confusion by leaning over and setting her cup back on the saucer. "Is he?"

"That's what the dirt on the street says. Seriously, we're a little concerned."

"Who is we?"

"I belong to the football boosters. We supported giving Josh the job in the first place two years ago."

"And now you regret it?"

He smiled. "Not at all. We think he has the kids primed and ready to win the state championship. We'd hate to see him get in his own way. Our first priority is the team, the kids."

"Very laudable," she said, purposely repeating his earlier phrase. He seemed not to notice.

"What kind of trouble is Josh in?" Lorraine asked, "according to the dirt, that is."

He shook his head. "We shouldn't go into that. I'm sorry, Lorraine, but I didn't realize you were no longer married to him. Perhaps you could suggest to him that he come see me. I can help him."

"Can you? How?"

"I know a lot of people. His goals and mine are the same: a state championship. All he has to do is ask."

"For what exactly?"

"Again, I'm sorry. I'm being deliberately vague. Please just let him know that I'm anxious to help him out."

"Why can't you tell him yourself? He's in the phone book."

"I'm afraid we haven't always seen eye-to-eye, he and I. Sometimes a third party can clear the way for a discussion. I have kind of a reputation for being a hard-ass. You may be surprised to know that."

"Then again, I may not be."

He tilted his head back and laughed. Lorraine was attracted to his open manner, the way he could apparently laugh at himself. Or was it an act?

"Why are you interested in the ostomy group, Mr. Turner?" She hoped to surprise him with a direct question of her own.

"Ned, please."

"Okay, Ned, why are you so interested? Are you having surgery?"

"No."

"Then why? Or do you need to be purposely vague again?"

"I like you, Lorraine. I hope you don't mind me saying so."

"If it's true I don't mind."

"Do you doubt my sincerity?"

"Not yet. Men have liked me before. I don't find it too unbelievable."

He laughed again. "Damn it, you shouldn't. But as for your question, there are a couple of reasons I am interested in your organization. The most important is that my niece is facing that type of surgery. I'm trying to talk her out of it, to be honest, but never mind. It's not my place to discuss that with you. But there is another reason I am interested. It has to do with something that happened a few years ago."

"I see."

"I'm hesitating because I don't come off looking too good in the story." He stood up and paced across the living room. It occurred to Lorraine that this was someone used to giving orders and throwing himself into his work, not one to stand around a water cooler and tell a story. Another Josh, she thought. Should she take that as a warning not to get interested in him? Was she getting interested in him?

He paused by the window. "Gotta get my car washed," he mused. "Is that a Taurus?"

"Yes, I'm a Ford man," she said. Ned smiled, and she added, "You're stalling."

"Yes, I am." He turned away from the window. "A few years ago, I was staying at a resort down in South Carolina. Actually, a friend of mine owns it. I put up some money for him, and he invited me down when it opened. Nice golf course. Lousy food. He's says it's better now." He shook his head. "Anyway, I got to know this couple, and he'd had surgery a few months before." Ned looked at Lorraine, holding her gaze for a moment before glancing away. "Ostomy surgery."

"Really?"

"Yeah. Cancer. Anyway, it played on my mind, and..." He shoved his hands into his pockets. "Damn. I'm sorry. Now that it's coming right down to it, it's harder to form the words than I thought. I'll just say it. In my continuing efforts to be as big a jerk as possible in every social situation, I told my friend I didn't want the guy swimming in the pool, as if he might pollute it or something."

"Oh."

"I know. You don't have to say it now. It put my friend in a bad place. I helped finance the place, after all. He spoke to the guy, who was outraged, as you might expect. His wife threatened to sue Ron. It was a mess. By the time my companion convinced me to withdraw my objection, the other couple had gotten their money back, plus a little extra, and left. It has played on my mind."

"And well it should," Lorraine said.

He smiled again. "I deserve that. I make mistakes, more maybe than most

18

people, because I'm what my first wife called a man of action."

"What does she call you now?"

"Let's not go there. But I tend to act first and think of the consequences later. It often works in my business dealings. I accomplish things advisers try to talk me out of attempting. I find it doesn't work so well in social situations."

"So what does your second wife call you?" Lorraine picked her cup back up, pleased that she felt in control of the conversation again, unsure why she found it pleasing.

"How do you know there was a second wife?"

"There always is. Right on the heels of the first, I bet."

"God, yes. I married her too soon after my divorce. I'll never make that mistake again."

"You'll make different ones."

He leaned back and laughed again, which was what Lorraine had aimed for. "I already have," he said. "What about you? Are you serious about anyone right now?"

She heard the hope in the question. Even someone as confident and glib as he was couldn't ask it without exposing a hope behind it.

"No, I'm too generous a soul to restrict myself to just one man."

"Kind of you, I'm sure," he said.

Alicia came back into the room, holding a small brown poodle.

"How adorable!" Lorraine said.

"Isn't she? I'm sorry, but if we get this over with, she'll settle down and be quiet. Are you up to it?"

Lorraine set the cup back on the saucer. "Sure, let her rip."

Alicia set the little dog down. "Aspen, be good."

Aspen apparently defined good as friendly, for she tore across the room and leapt into Lorraine's lap. Lorraine absorbed several licks before the dog jumped back down and ran over to give Ned the same treatment.

"What a ball of energy," Lorraine commented, guarding her coffee cup as Aspen sprang down from Ned's lap and approached her again.

"Isn't she? She loves everyone she meets." Aspen licked Lorraine's free hand, circled the living room twice and then settled into a bed next to a stereo speaker near the window.

Alicia sat down on the couch. "There. That's all it took. But I don't like to inflict her on strangers the moment they come through the door. Now I suppose I've missed everything."

Ned stood up. "Well, you missed me admitting to a huge lapse in judgment. Does that count?"

"Oh, another chance will come along soon."

"Very droll." He stepped over to where Lorraine sat. Reaching into his shirt pocket, he pulled out a check, folded in half. "Please take this, Lorraine, for your chapter to use as they see fit." He stood up and came over to her.

"There's no need, really," Lorraine said.

"Please. It's nothing. Writing this check was a lot easier than telling you my sordid story, believe me."

"Oh. That story," Alicia said. "You do know how to impress someone you've just met, uncle."

Lorraine took the check from him, watching him as he moved away again.

"Would you like more coffee, Lorraine?" Alicia asked.

Lorraine struggled to her feet. "No thank you, really. I have to go drive a friend home from the hospital. Unless you have any other questions for me?"

Ned motioned to the door. "No, not yet. Will you mention to Josh that I'd like to talk to him?"

"Yes, I'll tell him."

Ned stood in the doorway after Lorraine passed through. After she opened the car door, he said, "I do have one more question. May I call you? I'd like to see you again."

"Sure. Why not?" She held up the folded check he had given her. "I won't charge you next time."

He laughed and waved. Lorraine started the car and drove slowly out of the driveway. She glanced at the check still in her hand. She had assumed it would be a hundred dollars or so. In neat script was written "One Thousand and Zero Dollars." She set the check on the passenger seat. "They won't believe this at the executive meeting," she said under her breath. If Alicia was potentially having the surgery, why hadn't she asked any questions? She decided to find out more about Ned if she could.

Dressed in her street clothes at last, Patti sat in the chair with her feet tucked under her. She held a paperback romance novel in her hands, but she was staring at the pain pill on the rolling table in front of her. She wondered how long she would have to take pain medication. "As long as you need to, but no longer," Nurse Amanda had told her unhelpfully. "You'll know when to stop," Lorraine suggested, when Patti had called to ask her to take her home.

"Not yet, for sure," Patti muttered, reaching for the pill and downing it with a swallow from her ice water. The room was quiet. Her roommate had just been swept off for some sort of test or x-ray, and it felt strange to Patti to be ignored after days of being the center of considerable medical attention. Her overnight bag and the basket of ostomy supplies from Carole were packed and ready on the bed. Carole's last visit to her had almost been a social call, with just a review of what they had gone over before. Patti was anxious to leave, but she was enjoying this quiet moment at the same time. All that ended a few minutes later when Lorraine swept into the room.

"Hi sweetie, are you ready to blow this joint? I'm not holding you up here, am I?" she added without waiting for an answer to the first question.

"No, we seem to be waiting for a doctor or someone in power to sign me out."

Lorraine walked over and kissed Patti's cheek. "There, you're not healed enough for one of my hugs. Have they paged the good doctor?"

"I don't know."

"Well, never mind. I'll go check into it. Go back to your book. I'll be right back."

Patti looked at the book in her hand. The heroine, fiercely independent yet yearning for love, hadn't quite grabbed Patti's sympathy. She dropped the book into her purse on the floor. Where were the heroines with ostomy pouches on their perfect, slim bodies?

It soon occurred to her that Lorraine was quite a catalyst for action, for a half hour later Patti was being wheeled through the corridors of the hospital for her discharge. The basket of supplies and her purse rested in her lap, and Lorraine carried the overnight bag.

Lorraine glanced back at Patti. "I'm surprised your father and brother aren't here to see you off, or did you order them to stay away?"

"More or less," Patti admitted. "They both wanted to be here, but not if the other was here too, so it became my big decision who should have the honor. I told them I'd compromise and have you bring me home. No one was happy about that decision except me, which was nice for a change."

"Good girl. You're learning."

Now at the front entrance, Patti stood up, holding her purse and the basket. The orderly wished her good luck and moved away with the wheelchair. Lorraine and Patti went outside.

Patti stood in the sunlight, shielding her eyes and feeling slightly off balance after spending so many days indoors. The noises seemed louder than she remembered, the sun brighter, the breeze fresher. "Wow, I feel almost dizzy under the wide open sky. Was I really only in there less than a week?"

Lorraine looped an arm through Patti's and guided her to the left. "It should have been longer, but don't get me started on insurance companies. I'm illegally parked over this way." Patti allowed herself to be led to the vehicle and installed in the front passenger seat, the basket and purse at her feet. She lay her head back as Lorraine tossed the overnight bag into the back seat and got in to drive. Lorraine started the engine but paused a moment before shifting gears.

"How do you feel, Patti?"

"Scared. I'm glad I'm out of there, but I don't know how I'll cope. Dr. Regan says I'll feel better than I have in years."

"He's right," Lorraine confirmed.

"Okay, I'm all for that, but still, I've got this strange thing on my body I didn't have a week ago. What about that? How will I manage?"

Lorraine shifted into drive and eased into traffic. "At first you'll manage a day at a time. And then, believe it or not, it will all become second nature to you. What you're feeling is totally normal, Patti. It's a big adjustment, but it will be made easier by the fact that you'll feel so much better. You said you live on Spring Street, right?"

"Yes."

"You'll see. You have strength inside you that you haven't begun to use until now."

"I hope so. It's time for me to unwrap it and try it out."

Lorraine laughed. "Besides," she went on, "you'll have me and Carole to fall back on when you have problems or concerns."

"Thank you. You will be getting calls, I'm sure." Patti felt something under her leg. She reached down and picked up the folded check. "What's this?"

Lorraine glanced over. "A contribution to the ostomy chapter. Check it out."

Patti unfolded it. "Wow. Impressive. Hey, this is the guy who owns that chain of pharmacies. Value Plus."

"Really?"

"Yeah. Talk about deep pockets. My brother's partner used to work for the guy."

"What do you know about him?"

Patti tilted her head and shrugged. "Not much. I gather he can be rather ruthless in his business dealings. But you can probably say that about anyone with a wad of money. Why? Do you doubt his charitable motives?"

"Maybe, but not just that. He was coming at me from multiple angles. I didn't quite know what to make of him."

"What angles? Did he come on to you?"

"Not directly. He says he'll call me, though."

"Wow, you move fast."

"It's my aloof attitude. It turns certain men on."

"Is he not married then?"

"I don't know for sure. He acts single, and he talked about an ex-wife, or ex-wives. I was left to draw my own conclusions. But that's a side issue. He also says he knows Josh is in some kind of trouble and wants to help him."

"What kind of trouble?"

"He was vague about that. He had been under the impression I was still married to Josh; once he found out otherwise, he didn't want to enlighten me."

"That's odd." They waited at a light. When it turned green, Patti said, "If it made a difference to him that you aren't married to Josh anymore, he must have planned all along to ask about him, in addition to giving you the check for the chapter."

"That has occurred to me."

"So what are you going to do?"

"What do you mean?"

"I mean, if he calls you. What are you going to do?"

"Well, I'll answer the phone."

"Don't be cute. Will you go out with him?"

Lorraine thought about it. "Sure, if he asks me the right way. He intrigues me, and I'm not easily intrigued. Besides, he was pumping me for information of some sort, and I want him to see that two can play that game." She stopped at another intersection. "Hey, this is Spring Street. Which way?"

"Take a right. It's number 101, that green monstrosity up there across from the pizza place."

Patti pointed out where to park and led Lorraine inside her first floor apartment. "Tom has been here," she said after looking around. "I left the place in a hurry, so it was kind of a mess." The living room was large and open, and very neat. "He knew I would have hated to come home to clutter and would have been tiring myself picking up. I love a clean living space. It's almost an obsession with me."

"That will have to end when you have kids. If you have kids," Lorraine added.

"You're probably right." Patti set the basket down on the coffee table and dropped her purse on the couch. She sat down next to it. "Riding home was hard work. I need to sit and collect myself, as my mother used to say."

"I think that's the first time you've mentioned your mother, Patti. Is she dead?"

"No, she's in Thailand. She ran off with a snake charmer." Patti glanced at her friend. "I'm sorry; that's an old joke of my dad's. I used to think it was funny when I was younger, until I realized the pain the joke grew out of. My mother lives in London, with a journalist. She fell for him when he was here covering President Bush down in Kennebunkport. The first President Bush, that is. My mom rented a camp for a month down there, to paint. Took me with her. They had a torrid affair, and she went back with him."

Lorraine settled into the wicker chair near the window. "She had a torrid affair right in front of you?"

Patti blushed. "I didn't know that then. I was pretty young. But yes, she pretty much did. I had my own bedroom, so it's not like she...well, never mind. Dad was supposed to spend the last week there with us, but Mom asked him to please not bother. She was in a painting rage and didn't want to stop. That was her story. She wanted to send me home, but I cried and she relented. I loved it there, even though she practically ignored me. Chad, her lover and now husband, was kind to me, and I loved playing on the beach. On the last day, Dad came to get us, but it was just me. Mom left ten minutes before he got there. He never forgave her for that. It took three years, he told me, to pay for the camp rental. He's still paying emotionally, though."

"That's terrible. What a way to leave someone."

"Yeah. She only took one suitcase. Even left her paintings behind. I wonder now what Dad did with them, but I've never dared to ask. He is reserved, and very slow to show emotions. When he does, it can be a terrible sight. I talk to Mom often now, and she told me once she never knew how Dad felt about her, about anything. She claims it's different with Chad. Do you have any children, Lorraine?"

"No. Somehow the kids I've taught have always been enough for me. Virtual parenthood." Patti noticed she was staring at her hands.

"What's wrong, Lorraine?"

Lorraine shook her head. "I'm just worried about Josh. It's a lifetime habit I can't seem to get out of."

"Give him a call."

"It's not that easy. In the seven steps of divorce, he seems to be frozen on the step where he blames me for everything wrong with his life, and yet still expects me to return to him."

"I thought the seven stages have to do with death," Patti observed.

"The death of a marriage is pretty much the same. I finished mourning a long time ago, though I still miss him at times. The old him, that is, before his jerk genes took over. He still wants to talk to me, but he seems incapable of doing it in a rational manner. He was ready to talk to me a few days ago, but by the time I called him back he'd been drinking. Now I have to wait for him to call again. I refuse to take his verbal abuse, no matter how concerned I am."

"That's like my dad," Patti said. "It makes all the difference in the world which of us brings up a touchy subject. Like Tom being gay."

"What's going to happen between them?"

"Between Dad and Tom? What do you mean?"

"I mean long-term. How do you see them getting along with each other?"

"What an odd question. I have no idea. Five years ago I had no idea Tom was gay, though he tells me I should have known. And I didn't know Dad was homophobic. Perhaps I should have known that, too."

"What about five years from now?"

"What are you fishing for, Lorraine?"

"Could I get some water, Patti? Stay where you are. I'm getting it myself."

"I'm sorry, I should have asked, even in my sorry state."

"Don't worry about it. Do you want some?" Patti shook her head, and Lorraine went into the adjoining kitchen. Patti heard a couple of cupboard doors open and close, and then heard the faucet running. Lorraine returned to the living room with a half glass of water.

"That hit the spot." She sat back down in the wicker chair. "What do you want for your father and brother, specifically? It isn't a trick question; I just want you to say it."

"I want them to get along with each other, obviously." Patti felt an edge of irritation in her voice and added, "I want Dad to get a clue, and I want Tom to forgive Dad for taking so long to get a clue. And then Tom can come back and work with us again."

"What are you doing about it?"

"What am I doing about it?"

"Yes, what are you doing to make it happen?"

"I don't know. What can I do? I keep bringing it up, when I can. They are both quite stubborn. There's not much I can do."

"I wonder."

Patti raised her feet up on the couch. She stared at her friend. "Okay, this is maddening. What are you getting at? Just come out with it."

"I just feel that you have more power with them than you might think." She downed the rest of the water and leaned forward to set it on the coffee table. "They both love you a lot, I'm sure, even though you haven't said so. You're on Tom's side, but your father doesn't hold it against you. You still work with your father every day, but Tom doesn't hold that against you. They both love you. Use it, that's all I'm saying. Apply some pressure."

"You mean issue some sort of ultimatum? I've thought about it."

"No, anything but that. Ultimatums don't work on stubborn people. That would just harden them against you, and you'd lose both of them. But you've been working too hard at running interference between them. They are big boys. Let them know how important their getting along is to you, but let them handle it themselves."

"Can I do that?"

"I think you can, and should, but my vote isn't the important one." Lorraine stood up again and walked around the coffee table. "And now I should leave. You need to rest and get used to being home again."

"I could use a nap," Patti admitted. "How decadent. Could you open this window? I think I'll settle down right here on the couch."

Lorraine stepped over and unlocked the window above Patti's head. She slid it open about eight inches. "Is that enough?"

"Perfect. I love feeling the breeze on my cheek."

"Do you need a pillow or a blanket or something?"

"No, the couch pillows are fine." She tucked a pillow beside her and looked up at Lorraine. "Thank you for bringing me home."

"It's all part of the service." She leaned down and kissed Patti's cheek. "Take care of yourself. Are you coming to the chapter meeting Saturday night?"

"Yes. I'll be mad to go out somewhere by then, I'm sure."

"Great. I'll give you a ride."

"Okay. I suppose I should call Tom and Dad, or they'll call and wake me up anyway. I need to get my cat back from Tom. Could you pass me the phone?"

Lorraine handed her the cordless phone before leaving the apartment, waving as she went through the door.

Patti pushed the speed dial number for her brother and tucked the phone up under her ear. Kelton, Tom's partner, picked up after the first ring.

"Hi Patti," he said, obviously having checked the caller ID. "You're in for a treat. Poor old Tom has been disassembling and reassembling his moods all day. Me, I'm just staying out of his way. How are you?"

After an exchange of concern and assurances, Kelton gave the phone to Tom.

"Hi you," he said.

"Hi yourself. Can I judge from your tone that you are still miffed at me?"

"I'm miffed at a lot of people right now. Let me check my list; yeah, you're on it, I'm afraid."

"Very funny. You and Dad put me in a rotten spot, you know, making me choose which of you should pick me up at the hospital. Now tell me that was fair of you guys."

"No, I admit it wasn't fair. The only reason I wanted to make you choose was that I was sure you'd pick me."

Patti laughed and then cut it short. "Ow, that still hurts."

"Now you know how my inner pain feels."

"Give me a break. Don't expect sympathy from me just yet. I'm still feeling sorry for myself. I'm supposed to be the center of attention for a while longer. Which reminds me, when can I have my cat back?"

"Cat? What cat?"

"Tom, there are some things we just don't joke about."

"Okay, I'll bring the wretched thing home to you."

"How was she?"

"Passive aggressive, as always. She loved up to us by day, but at night she ate our paperbacks."

"You're making that up!"

"No, I'm only exaggerating. She mostly used her claws to shred Kerouac, I'll admit, but I swear I saw tooth marks on it too."

Patti heard a voice in the background on the other end of the line. "What did Kelton say?"

"He commented that even dead authors are not safe from cruel critics."

"And neither are brothers who hold poor kitty cats hostage and keep them on a diet of paperback novels."

"All right, I'll bring her over. Is now soon enough?"

"It will have to do. No wait, I want to take a bit of a nap. Bring her over in a couple of hours."

"Okay, I suppose I could feed her a short story to tide her over. Hey, is you-know-who going to be there?"

Patti thought about Lorraine's advice, and she resisted the urge to reassure him. "I don't know; I haven't talked to Dad yet. If he shows up while you're here, you'll just have to deal with it. My doctor says I shouldn't lift anything heavier than a breadbox for eight weeks, and this feud between you and Dad is the heaviest burden I have right now. I need to not run interference between you two for a while. Will you let me do that, please?"

"I'll let you, but will he?"

"Tom, you're doing it again. I'm asking you right now, not him. Do I have your permission not to play middle man between father and son for a change?"

"I suppose, but what do I get out of it?"

"Blond brownies, warm from the oven."

"Why didn't you say so? It's a deal. I'll bring the amazing book-eating cat over in two hours or so, Dad or no Dad."

"Thank you. You're always good to me, eventually."

They said their goodbyes and Patti pushed the button for the dial tone. Did she really dare to arrange for their father to come over at the same time as Tom? Clearly she'd have to handle him differently to get the same result, more obliquely. She'd appeal to his softer side, as narrow as it was sometimes. She punched in his speed dial number.

"You made it home all right, then," he said after their greetings.

"Yes, Lorraine got me home safe and sound. It seems strange to be home again. Strange and wonderful."

"Do you need anything?"

Patti smiled. Here was the difference between father and son. It was just like Dad to ignore the emotional needs she might have and focus on common sense: what did she need? Tom tried to cheer her up with his humor, but wouldn't think of physical needs until after he got here and talked to her for a while.

"I could use some milk, Dad. I'm sure mine has lost its charm along with its smooth white color. Whole milk will be fine. Eggs, too. And orange juice would be great. Are you sure you don't mind?"

"No, of course not."

"Thanks, Dad. Listen, wait a couple of hours before you come over. I'm going to take a nap."

"That's a good idea."

"I thought so. I'm exhausted." She drew in a deep breath. "And Dad? Tom is coming over with Spring later on, too. Can you handle it? If he's here when you are, can you pretend you know him as a favor to your poor weak daughter? Please?"

After a pause, during which Patti didn't breathe, he said, "I'll meet him halfway," he said. She heard the reluctance, but it was still more than she had expected. Could it be this easy? Could her recuperation operate as a bridge between the two stubborn men? She shook her head. Her life just wasn't that simple, she suspected.

Patti's late afternoon became surreal when a phone call woke her from her nap, and a voice she knew well but which always surprised her called her out of her sleep.

"Mom?"

"Darling, I'm so glad I've caught you. How are you feeling?"

"Like crap, mostly," she replied, finding the lure of international sympathy and even ancient maternal guilt too irresistible.

"Oh Patti Jo, I knew I should have flown in to be with you."

For a moment the horrifying image of juggling the visiting hours of a feuding father and son and the father's ex-wife rose before her eyes.

"Oh no, Mom. It's better this way. I see you so seldom, I want to be able to appreciate it."

"Yes, so you told me. You'll have to remember my other idea. You must come out for a visit as soon as you are well enough, before you start working again in that horrid garage."

Patti passed over the reference to her working in her father's business, long a sore point with her mother. "I'll give it some serious thought, mother. It's tempting."

"I insist on it. Listen, do you need anything, dear?"

"What do you mean, like magazines? Are you going to Fedex them to me?"

"Don't be impertinent. You know what I mean. Do you need any money? The bills..."

"No, thank you, mother. Dad took care of all that. I'll let you know if I need anything."

"Fine. This surgery, Patti, are you...are you going to be okay with it?"

"I think so, mother. It is a lot to get used to, but I have people helping me, and they say I will feel better than I have in years."

"Oh, I hope so. Chad did a little research. Sometimes these things can be reversed, so you can be..."

"Normal?"

"I just want what's best for you, love."

"I know, mother. They don't know if I could ever have a reversal or a continent operation. My job is to recover from one surgery and enjoy relative good health before contemplating more surgery."

"Of course. I understand. I just don't want any option overlooked in the long run. How is Tom?"

"Call him and ask him, mother."

"I will, Patti Jo. Don't give me another lecture on that subject. He's always so sarcastic and monosyllabic when I speak to him, like your father used to be. I really must fly, sweetheart. We're going to a thing tonight. We're going to meet the Queen's plumber."

Patti hung up a moment later, unsure if her mother was serious or not. Her nap shattered, she got up to fetch her recipe for blond brownies. She'd have to wait for the eggs, but she could get the other ingredients out. She pulled out her mixing bowl and a wooden spoon. She set the bowl down and then began looking for ingredients. The flour canister, brown sugar, vanilla, chocolate chips, chopped nuts, baking powder, salt; she lined the containers up along the counter. The butter was in the fridge and eggs were on the way. What else was there? She was forgetting something. A knock on the door prevented her from peeking at the recipe. Still holding the spoon, she walked quickly into the living room and opened the door. Tom had arrived first.

After an exuberant greeting, on Patti's part anyway, with her cat Spring, Patti settled onto the couch. Tom sat in the large wicker chair near the stained glass window. Spring rubbed against Tom's legs.

"Now she acts like she likes me," Tom complained.

"She would like you a lot more if you stopped telling cruel lies about her."

"Whatever. We'll get along fine if I keep the bookshelf well-stocked."

They watched as the cat walked over and jumped into Patti's lap. "Reunited at last," she said, and this reminded her of what she had to say before they had more company. After Spring settled into a ball in her lap, Patti said, "Speaking of family, Dad is bringing me some supplies. He should be here soon."

"Really?" He glanced at his watch. "My, my, look at the time." He made a move as if to get up.

"Don't you dare. You promised you'd make an effort."

"I'd love to, Sis, but the man's hopeless. The old man is like a raging river. Short of damming him, with either spelling, you can't hope to change his course. You can only settle in and admire from afar, maybe stick your feet in and feel the cold power. Try to change him, and he'll cast you adrift, and you'll feel the waters close over your head."

"Okay, okay, you've worn out that metaphor. But he said he'd make an effort too."

"He'll take one look at me, turn on his heel in a perfect military about-face, and leave again. He may linger long enough to mumble something with the word 'homosexual' in it. And he'll swear later that he made all the effort he can be expected to make."

"It won't be like that," she asserted, feeling on shaky ground.

"No? Well, maybe not. You're the one making the blond brownies. I won't argue with you."

"Baking soda!" she said, excited.

"What?"

"Nothing. I just remembered something. Just please, don't provoke Dad, okay?"

"But it's fun, in a sick way."

She pointed at him. "I'm warning you."

"That's a wooden spoon you're threatening me with there."

"Tom, you've never broken a promise to me yet."

"I didn't promise..."

"Tom..."

"All right. Maybe I said I'd be on my best behavior, so I will be. That's all I can promise. If he asks me again to join that religious support group that cures homosexuals, I will have to respectfully decline."

"He won't bring that up again. I already had a talk with him about that."

"You did?"

"Yes. I'm on your side, bro, I keep telling you. But we have to bring him along slowly."

"Slowly is right, Patti. There are glaciers that move faster."

"Glaciers move faster than you think."

"That makes me feel a lot better. Thank you."

Patti didn't answer, but rather sat looking at the spoon in her hand.

"Patti, you have a look on your face. You're thinking again."

She set the spoon on the arm of the couch. "I just had a crazy idea."

"This is where a terrible fear takes hold of me."

"Oh hush up and listen. Mom wants me to fly out and stay with her for a while, but the doctor doesn't want me to fly for a while. In fact, by the time I can travel like that, I can also start working again and going to school. So instead, why don't I ask Mom to come spend time with me here?"

"In this apartment? It is surely beneath her."

"Okay, in a B&B on the ocean or something, The concept is the same. Here in Maine, anyway."

"Fine, so far. I'm waiting for the other shoe to drop. What does this have to do with Dad and his homophobia?"

"I'm working around to it. Maybe I can figure out a way to get Mom to talk to Dad about it. When he hears her spouting the same kind of garbage, he'll be obliged to disagree with her. Don't look at me like that. It's not as crazy as it sounds."

"Hold on, Patti. Mom is a lot of things, God knows, but she isn't homophobic."

"Of course she is, isn't she?"

"Why do you say that?"

"It's just, you and she, I mean, you don't get along with her either. And especially lately. I assumed..."

"No, it goes back further and deeper than that."

"Oh."

After a moment, he asked, "But will you still invite her here?"

"I should. I don't want to go there so close to my surgery. It's a good time for me, since I can't go back to work. I feel patient enough to have her around for a week or so."

"Than you're a lot stronger than I am."

"Why? What is it between you two, if not your being gay? Did I miss something?"

"It's genetic."

"That's no answer." Patti tried to form a new question, but there was a knock at the door. "That'll be Dad."

Tom straightened up in his chair. "Great. Time to put on my battle gear."

"Tom..." Patti said, getting up. Spring jumped out of her lap.

"I'm kidding. Look at me, telling jokes and relaxing over here. You should be glad."

She moved towards the door. "You're impossible. If you say the wrong thing and set him off, I shall cheerfully bludgeon you to death with that wooden spoon."

"Cheerfully, Sis? That's seems kind of harsh."

Patti opened the door. Their father stood on the landing with a paper bag. "Dad, you're the only person I know who actually asks for paper at the grocery store." She took the bag from him and leaned in for a hug. "Come on in. As you can see, someone else is here. Thanks for picking this stuff up."

"I could put those away for you."

"No, I'm fine. This bag is under the weight limit for what I can carry."

She walked to the kitchen, determined they would get along without her continual guidance. She heard an exchange of low-key greetings. She remembered what her mother said about the sarcasm and monosyllables. Patti unloaded the bag, smiling when she noticed the milk, skim instead of whole. It reminded her of when they had all lived together, and she never dared to send father or brother to the grocery store alone. Her smile widened when she saw the Ring Dings at the bottom of the bag. She didn't eat them anymore, but it was sweet of him to remember them, a throwback to her childhood. As she put away the milk and eggs, she heard Tom initiate conversation out in the living room.

"Patti's looking pretty good."

"Why shouldn't she?"

"Well, I don't know. I guess because she had major surgery, is all."

"She'll come through with flying colors," Dad said. "She's a fighter."

Patti expected her brother to come back with something like "And I'm not, right?" But he apparently remembered his promise. She wondered if she should linger here or go out and try to help the conversation limp along. She lingered.

"How are things at the shop?"

"Fine."

"Are all the guys still there?" This was strictly small talk, for Patti kept Tom up to date about the garage.

"Nothing much changes there," Dad said.

Well, of course, things changed a lot when Tom left, Patti caught herself thinking.

Tom went on, and Patti could have hugged him for his efforts. "It's different working in a dealership, let me tell you."

Patti tried to will her father to casually mention missing Tom in the garage, but even as she willed it, she knew he wouldn't say anything of the sort.

"I wonder they get any customers at all, for what they charge an hour. Flat rate shops. Outrageous."

Tom refrained from pointing out what occurred to Patti, that they charged a flat rate for certain jobs in Dad's garage too. Instead he said, "There are a lot more expenses involved in the dealership, some relating directly to improving service. They're sending me to New Jersey next month for specialized training."

Their father made a rather guttural noise to indicate he wasn't quite conceding the argument. Patti decided it wouldn't get any better, and she reentered the living room.

"If you guys want to stick around for a while, I am making some blond brownies, just like the old days."

Tom stirred in his chair. "You don't have to ask me twice. I promised Kelton I'd bring him home a couple."

"Kelton," their father said dismissively.

"What?" Tom asked. "I'm allowed to say his name, aren't I?"

Their father moved toward the door. "You can say anything you like, because I'm leaving now."

"Dad," Patti said.

"Don't 'dad' me. We've gone round and round on this. Another go round isn't going to do us any good. When you told me about this decision..."

"It wasn't a decision," Tom said. "If you don't understand that-"

"When you told me," their father said louder, "You told me I didn't have to like it; I only had to accept it."

"He said that?" Patti threw in.

"Well," their father continued, "I've accepted it, but I don't have to like it. And I'm damn well not liking it. Not another word!" To Patti he said, "Let me know if you need anything, but no more family reunions." He left, closing the door behind him.

"That went well," Tom said into the teeth of the silence following their father's departure.

"It could have been worse," Patti said. "He said no more family reunions, so he's admitting now that you're a member of the family. That's something to build on."

"So was the land around Pompeii," he said. She looked at him. "A joke," he added.

"I figured that out. Did you happen to see where I set that wooden spoon down? See, I can tell jokes, too."

"Are you okay, Sis?"

"Yes. No. I don't know. I'm feeling tired, mostly."

"Of course you are. Listen, forget about baking. I'll take off and you can get some rest."

"No, I didn't mean it that way. I'm mentally tired. Dad has got to come around someday."

"We'll wear him down eventually. We'll be a warm family again."

"I bet a lot of people said that in Pompeii."

"Patti! Another joke. Not a good one, but a joke. I'm proud of you."

"Thanks. Now stand back and let me bake. That's what I do best."

"Are you sure you're up to it?"

"I'll do it in stages, and sit down if I need to."

"Cool. I'll watch. That's what I do best."

She started measuring dry ingredients and dumped them into the bowl. "You know, I missed Mom after she left, but really, some of my fondest memories involved us, just like this, with me cooking for my big brother."

"You mothered me like I was your little brother. I think Dad missed Mom more than either of us. I got so I could tell when he was seeing Mom in you. This mixture of pride and pain would come into his eyes."

Patti's eyes stung for a moment. It had never occurred to her that she might have reminded Dad of Mom. If it pained him, he never let on to her. She yanked a paper towel from the holder and dabbed at her eyes.

"I tried not to hate her for leaving," she said. "I tried to think it was romantic, her wrenching herself away from us for love."

"Oh, please."

"What?" She measured the brown sugar.

"She didn't go with him until after he wrote a best seller about one of the Royals and got promoted at his newspaper."

Her hands paused holding the salt shaker. "I thought they fell in love for the first time that summer I stayed with Mom at the camp."

"No. They had started their fling before, but broke it off once. Dad knew about it before, and took Mom back anyway. Though he probably didn't let her forget it."

"I had no idea."

"I'm not surprised. Dad hasn't wanted to talk about it."

"That's an understatement. I guess he wanted to protect me."

"And himself. Hey, are you ever going to stop chatting and actually make some brownies at some point?"

Patti rolled up her sleeves, gave her brother a look, and then went out into the living room in search of the wooden spoon.

Chapter 4

On the following Saturday, Patti straightened up and looked at herself in the mirror. She was finished with what she called in her mind "The Changeover," replacing her ostomy appliance and pouch. Patti checked her watch. Twenty-five minutes. The minor struggle to fasten it securely had seemed much longer than that to her. She remembered Lorraine telling her that within a few months, she'd be done with the weekly process in five or ten minutes. She couldn't imagine it.

Still, it was lovely to be home again. She didn't feel as safe as she had in the hospital, however, and every so often she'd reach down and brush her fingers or palm across her slacks where the pouch rested, as if it were in danger of falling off or filling up so quickly as to require constant vigilance.

She took one more look at herself before dressing. When she was growing up, Patti had always dreamed up punishments she would suffer, at the hands of her parents and others, for all of her minor childhood sins. Some of the punishments she imagined were off the wall and unique, but her fertile mind had never produced a punishment quite like having to wear a pouch on her body full-time. "Once again truth is stranger than fiction," she said aloud.

She sighed, with a silent admonition to stop feeling sorry for herself. So she was a bag lady now; people had worse problems. Her reflection didn't look convinced. She washed her hands, using plenty of soap and hot water.

Emerging from the bathroom, she smelled the chocolate chip cookies cooling on the counter. She walked into the kitchen and lifted the clean dish towel she had placed over them to protect them from her cat's interest. The black and white cat eyed her from her perch on one of the kitchen chairs, casually licking her paws, chiding Patti for her mistrust, it seemed.

Patti retrieved the bowl from the refrigerator and dropped spoonfuls of batter onto the final cookie sheet. She slid it into the still warm oven, and then nibbled on some raw dough, a habit left over from childhood. The doorbell rang; Lorraine, no doubt, a few minutes early.

Patti let her new friend in. Lorraine took off her windbreaker and lifted her nose in the air, which immediately reminded Patti of her cat. "Mmm, there is baking going on here," Lorraine said, setting the jacket on the couch. She followed Patti into the kitchen.

"Yes, well, you said people brought in snacks. I thought I would try my hand at it. I've never baked so much in my life like I have the last few days."

"It smells great."

A high-pitched beep sounded behind them, and after a few seconds, another. Patti grabbed the dish towel and stepped over, fanning the smoke detector near the doorway. "Isn't this ridiculous? The landlord must have bought stock in the company that makes these. They're everywhere in the apartment. This one's always going off when I bake."

"It seems strange to install one so close to the stove," Lorraine conceded. "Might as well have stuck it in the oven. At least then the sound would be muffled."

Patti smiled. "I suppose I could disable it."

"Or clean your oven," Lorraine suggested.

"Anything but that. I'd buy a new stove first."

Lorraine laughed and sat down at the kitchen table. Patti began rummaging around in a lower cupboard. The noise drew her cat back into the kitchen after she had gone into hiding at Lorraine's arrival. "Pretty cat," Lorraine commented.

"Her name is Spring." Patti pulled a plastic container out. "This will hold enough cookies."

Lorraine held out a hand. The black and white cat sniffed at it, then unceremoniously leapt into Lorraine's lap. "I see why you named her that," Lorraine said. "Spring has sprung."

"You know," Patti said, "she does jump up on everything: the counter, the table, and I even caught her sitting on top of the fridge once, looking rather pleased with herself, I might add."

Lorraine began petting Spring, who immediately started purring.

Patti took out some squares of wax paper. "Actually, I named her after the season. When I was five, I had a white cat that I named winter. Then after she died, I had a money cat with wonderful fall colors, so I named her Autumn. She ran away."

"I see." Lorraine watched Patti load cookies into the container. "Of course, here in Maine, if you keep naming them after the seasons, someday you'll have a cat named Mud. You precut your wax paper?"

Patti blushed slightly. "I reuse the wax paper bags from boxes of cereal."

"Well, aren't you thrifty."

Patti layered the cookies and wax paper until the container was full. "My father taught me to do it. Or did I teach him?"

The cat jumped down from Lorraine's lap. Lorraine watched her run out of the kitchen. "Guess she's had enough. Have you been getting out much, Patti?"

Patti shrugged. "I don't know. I go to the store, and I run other errands. But I still feel self-conscious, so I come straight back. Sometimes I feel sure people notice the shape of it under my clothes, or the sounds it sometimes makes."

"That's a normal feeling. Listen," Lorraine interrupted herself. "How are your father and brother doing?"

Patti remembered the tense little scene in her apartment. "Somewhere between detente and open warfare."

"That's a start. Rome wasn't dismantled in a day. Hey, could I try one of those cookies that you've been waving under my nose?"

"I'm sorry." Patti stepped over and held a cookie out.

"Thanks. Half the game is confidence, Patti, and knowing that we don't all have a scarlet 'O' branded on our foreheads, for ostomy. It's natural to think that people have some way of knowing. But we're all too self-absorbed to even have a shot, even if it were possible to tell. When you're out and about or in the store, do you suspect others of having an ostomy?"

"Well, no."

"There you are. Why would anyone else? You have to have confidence in your appearance."

"You're right. I'll try." Patti sealed up the container. "I guess I'm ready."

"Is that what you're wearing to the meeting?"

Patti glanced at herself. "Why, what's wrong with it?" She saw Lorraine's expression. "Okay, I get it. I look great. Confidence."

Lorraine grabbed her windbreaker. "Right. Let's go."

During the drive to the medical building where the meetings were held, Lorraine asked, "What did you say you do for work?"

"I'm the service manager for a garage intown."

"A lady shop manager at your tender age? I'm impressed."

"Don't be. It's a small garage, and my dad owns it."

"That's right. You mentioned you work with your father It still seems like a lot of responsibility."

"Yeah, I guess it is. I've worked there since I was 13, though, so it almost seems like home to me. A lot of the customers are like extended family. The days sure do fly. While I was in the hospital, Dad and one of the mechanics worked the desk for me, so at least now I know I won't have to be there all the time. I was kind of possessive about the responsibility."

"Sounds like you love it."

"Love is a strong word. I like it okay, but..."

Lorraine put on her left blinker. "It's that brick building. We park near the back. You were going to say?"

"Oh, just that I enjoyed it more when Tom worked with us. The camaraderie was great. Now the other mechanics avoid talking about him when Dad is around. Tom is working at the Lincoln-Mercury dealership across town." Lorraine pulled into a spot and shut off the engine. They got out, with Patti stopping to reach into the back seat for the cookies.

Lorraine led the way to a short set of stairs. "It's up here in a sort of mezzanine."

Patti followed Lorraine. "You teach, right? You didn't say what you taught."

Lorraine paused at the top, half-turned to wait for Patti. "Gym, to wave after wave of monstrous teenaged girls. I can't begrudge them. I was monstrous at that age. Here we are."

It wasn't your average conference room. Large windows along the rear of the room overlooked a plaza of stone walkways and benches, and small shrubbery and trees. A tall hedge bordered the plaza, screening out the busy street beyond.

"Nice room," Patti said appreciatively.

"Isn't it, though? Here, let me put your cookies over with the rest of the treats. I need to go see our president for a moment. You mingle, or fade into the wallpaper, or whatever strikes you."

"I know one thing; I'm going to grab a seat facing that view," Patti said, but Lorraine had already left. Patti heard someone else come into the room. A rather cute little old man in a white shirt, black bow tie, and pressed black pants, stood in the doorway, looking rather lost.

"Where is she?" he asked, to no one in particular, it seemed.

Patti smiled. "I can't help you, I'm afraid, unless you're looking for Lorraine. She is the only person I know here."

"Where is Rose?" the man asked. Then his face brightened, and he walked past Patti towards a woman standing near a window.

"Nice meeting you," Patti said under her breath, unable to suppress a smile of chagrin. She looked around. As Lorraine had predicted earlier, all of the attendees so far were older than Patti; some much older. Lorraine appeared to be the closest to Patti's age, and she was a bit older than Patti had originally guessed. When Patti had teased her about pushing forty, Lorraine replied,

"Honey, if I'm pushing forty then I'm doing it from the other side."

A tall man with most of his hair underneath his chin made noises about bringing the meeting to order. Patti sat down. A moment later, Lorraine dropped into the seat beside her. The president, Clifton Royce, introduced himself and proceeded to read the meeting's agenda. The minutes of the previous meeting would be read by their lovely secretary; the titter that went through the group suggested to Patti that the secretary must be the president's wife. That would be followed by the Treasurer's report from the Venerable Clay Wilkes. After that would come introductions around the table and then the presentation by their featured speaker. After a short break for refreshments, the rest of the business meeting would ensue, with all its calamities and pitfalls, Clifton finished up, with a wink that struck Patti as being aimed in her direction. Lorraine confirmed that when she muttered, "Old goat."

Patti spaced out for a while after that, studying the faces around the table, trying to imagine what this or that person did for work, or what it was in their life that kept them going. This was a variation of a game she played as a girl, whenever she was in church or at any kind of gathering of strangers. She liked to think her attention span was much longer as an adult, but she still fell into the game at odd times. Like now. Times of stress, she wondered?

She realized that the introductions had begun. The woman sitting with the bow-tie man introduced herself as Shirley, and added that this was her husband Lester next to her. Patti leaned towards Lorraine. "I thought her name was Rose."

Lorraine smiled and whispered back, "That's what he told you, but he is forgetful. Rose is the name that Shirley gave to her stoma years ago. Lester has trouble remembering that, poor dear."

"She named her stoma?"

"Yes, some people do. It helps sometimes to be able to speak of it in the third person."

Patti glanced at Lorraine. She seemed to be serious, but she knew Lorraine would make a great poker player.

A skinny balding man stood up when it was his turn. "Hi, I'm Hal Trent. I've had my colostomy since roughly the time Joshua blew on his trumpet. We had to use the bladders of large animals instead of plastic pouches back then, but that's another story."

"There's always another story, isn't there, Hal?" Lorraine asked good-naturedly.

Hal held up a hand to acknowledge her comment. "That's right, lass. And I bet you have some tales to tell, too. Anyway, I am retired now. I finally retired for real last month, after figuring out that I was busier semi-retired than I had been working full-time. They held a dinner for me, but they couldn't seem to convince the caterer to show up. I hope that isn't a sign of how my golden years are going to go. I'm done," he said abruptly, and sat down.

Patti turned to Lorraine and asked barely above a whisper, "Have you named your stoma?"

"No, I've never gotten on a first name basis with mine. Although once, back when I was married to Josh, I threatened to name it after him, because he was full of it too."

Patti smiled, but now it was her turn. "Hi, I'm Patti Jo Lewis. Please call me Patti. Actually, I just came in to get out of the rain." A couple people laughed, a few more smiled. "Sorry, bad jokes pop out when I'm nervous."

"What's your excuse, Hal?" Lorraine chided from beside Patti. Hal managed to slightly bow from his seat.

Patti took a breath and dived in again. "I have a brand new ileostomy. Lorraine visited me in the hospital. She has been great. I'm doing pretty good, when I don't think about it, but I think about it all the time." She felt herself blushing. "Sorry, another joke. I feel better than I have in years, but still it is hard for me to deal with sometimes. I've tried to talk to people about what it's like for me, people besides Lorraine, I mean. Friends my age just say yuck, and can I talk about something else."

"You need better friends," Lorraine put in.

"I'm working on it. And older friends and relatives tell me I should be grateful to be alive, which of course I am. I was pretty sick a few times. But it's hard to be grateful 24 hours a day, which is when it seems like I am aware of this change in me. I know it is shallow of me, but-" the tears seemed to come from nowhere. Patti didn't think she was that upset. Lorraine passed her a tissue.

"It's harder for young people," Hal said, but he stopped talking when Carole Stevens raised her hand from where she sat at the end of the table. The ET nurse stood up and started walking around the table. Patti assumed she was heading for her, but she stopped behind a woman with long reddish hair.

"It's not harder for young people," Carole said. "But it's hard for different reasons, perhaps. Julia, maybe you can go next." Lorraine shifted her position slightly so Patti could see Julia better.

"I'm Julia Mannix. My name used to be Julie, as some of you know, but I changed it to Julia because that is more glamorous. I've had my ileostomy for

34 years, since I was 21." She was looking at Patti now, and Patti at her. "The first year after the surgery, I was a mess. I put my family and friends through hell and said 'why me?' a lot. I broke things. I even broke up with my boyfriend because I was sure he couldn't possibly love me after the surgery. He said he did, but I knew that he just said it because that's what people say in those situations. I knew everything, you see, even at 21." Lorraine and a few others laughed.

"So what happened?" Patti asked.

"Well, once I broke up with Frank, I decided I wanted him back."

"Ain't that the way it always is," Carole said, now working her way back to her chair.

"Well, it was with me. I saw red whenever I saw him talking to another girl, even though the breakup was my idea. I loved shopping, still do, in fact, so I decided that a new wardrobe would win him back. If I couldn't wear bikinis after the surgery, then I would find one-piece suits that would knock his socks off. Shopping saved me, girls and boys. Very therapeutic. I recommend it highly. It helped me become a whole person again."

"Good thing your parents had some money," Hal said.

"Well, they did when I started, anyway."

"Did you win him back?" Patti wanted to know.

"Sure, but a year later we split up again, for a real reason."

"Tell her the rest of the story," Lorraine suggested.

Julia obliged. "I met Frank again, let's see, seven years ago, both of us in between spouses. We got married, after all that time."

Patti smiled. "That's a great story."

"I know. It would be even greater except we got divorced later. Four years were all I could stand of him." Others in the group laughed, and Patti realized that this story had been told so many times, to new members like herself, that it was almost like a shared experience for the group now. The introductions continued.

Patti felt tears spring into her eyes again, and she wasn't even sure why. Maybe because this was the first time she was out of her apartment without feeling nervous. She reached for another of Lorraine's tissues. Lorraine pushed the small package of tissues over to her. "Keep the change," she said, meaning the whole package. Patti took one of them and dabbed at her eyes again.

"Maybe I should go," she said softly. "I thought I would handle this better."

"You're handling this just fine. Besides, if you leave, you'll get fifteen calls tonight from everyone here, asking how you're doing. Do you really want to waste your evening that way? You have a bit of a cry and let us all keep an eye on you."

Patti stared at the benches and the stone paths outside the window, imagining walking along arm in arm with a man who didn't care if a woman had a bit of extra plastic attached to her body. The introductions finished up. Clifton Royce sonorously said that he would read the announcements of upcoming chapter events and member birthdays, and then they would take a break before calling on their honored speaker.

At that moment, a phone rang behind them. Patti twisted her head around and saw a wall phone outside the meeting room. Carole stepped outside to answer it. Lorraine noticed Patti's interest.

"That's probably for Carole. She's the only ET nurse at the hospital, so she's practically always on call."

Carole spoke a few words into the receiver, and then set it down so it hung dangling by its cord, rotating slowly. She walked back towards the meeting room.

"Not for her, by the looks of it," Patti observed.

Carole strode over and whispered in Lorraine's ear. Lorraine got up and hurried out of the room to the phone. Patti watched her friend for a moment before turning her head to look at Carole. The nurse handed Lorraine's purse to Patti.

"Patti, I have to introduce Dr. Groves, our speaker. Please go out there with Lorraine, and close those double doors behind you."

"What's wrong?"

"I don't know, but it's serious, that's for sure."

Patti grabbed her own purse and headed for the doorway. She eased the doors closed behind her, leaning back slowly against them until she heard the click of the latch. She remained there so as not to intrude upon her friend's conversation. Even at that she heard enough to know this was about Josh. The tone Lorraine used when asking, "How is he?" confirmed that it was, as Carole surmised, serious indeed.

Finally Lorraine hung up the phone, wiped under her eyes with her fingertips, and leaned back against the wall. She noticed Patti.

"Jesus, Mary and Joseph!"

"Lorraine, what's wrong?"

Lorraine shook her head. "It's impossible. That was Raines, the principal. Something is going on with Josh. 'A situation has developed,' Raines said. Josh; God, I'm having trouble forming the words. Josh may have been holding some of his players hostage in the field house, and holding the police at bay."

Patti walked over in quick steps and took Lorraine's hands. The small action seemed to spur Lorraine on to say more.

"Raines isn't sure what's going on; the police aren't telling him anything in the way of details, but at least one shot has been fired. I have to get over there."

"Of course. Shall I drive?"

Lorraine pushed herself away from the wall, distracted by her own thoughts. But she glanced up at Patti. "I'm sorry, what did you say?"

"Maybe I should drive you over? You're not in any condition, are you?"

"Yes, please drive. Thank you."

Patti didn't know what to say during the short walk to the car. As they approached the car, Lorraine said parenthetically, "I'm glad I left that number with Connie. I always switch off my cell phone for these meetings."

"Connie?"

"She runs a maid service. She does my place on the weekend, off hours, because I helped her daughter get into Boston College."

"You have a maid?" Patti asked as they climbed into the car.

A bit of Lorraine's spark seemed to return to her voice. "Yes, aren't you impressed?"

"I'm dazzled." Patti started the car and drove out of the parking lot. Lorraine fell quiet, her mood apparently turning serious again after that brief interlude.

"It may be all right," Patti suggested after a silence, though she didn't believe it. Lorraine didn't respond. Even with a brilliant sunset reflecting off the windows of houses they passed, even as the brave words were spoken, Patti knew they were false, that a tragedy of some sort awaited them at the high school field house.

Patti turned right onto School Street. Passing the elementary school, they saw the police roadblock ahead of them. Further ahead, past the middle school and close to the high school itself, an ambulance and several more police cars were clustered where the school buses usually swung in to load and unload twice a day. There were clumps of students and smaller groups of teachers everywhere. Patti pulled up in front of the saw horses and rolled her window down for the policewoman who approached their vehicle.

"Hi Officer. This is Lorraine Simoneau. She was asked to come down."

The woman leaned down to peer inside. "Yes, hi Coach. You had my daughter in gym last year. Judie Mills."

"Yes, I remember her," Lorraine said, "Quite a volleyball server, as I recall. What's going on here, anyway? Can you tell me?"

The officer shook her head. "It's not for me to say, Coach. I don't know all of it anyway. But it's a hell of a mess." She looked at Patti. "Please drive up to where the ambulance is and ask for Officer Robb Turner. I'm sorry, coach."

She moved the saw horses to the side, and Patti eased the car through, feeling a half-smile creep across her face, despite the situation.

"Sorry?" Lorraine repeated. "Sorry for what? Sorry for what?" She glanced over at Patti, and saw her expression, the slight smile. "What's up with you?"

"Oh, I used to know a Robb Turner, in high school."

"You're blushing. Just how well did you know him? Heavens, now you're really red. I guess I can draw my own conclusions."

Patti parked close to the ambulance. The strobing blue lights of the police car increased the air of tragedy for Patti. She looked around after shutting off the engine. Two local television news vans were parked twenty yards away. Patti glanced at Lorraine, who had glimpsed them too.

"God. An hour ago I was living close to a normal life. Now I'm going to be one of those ghastly, stunned relations you see on CNN, shoved in front of a spotlight mumbling sacred truths about a loved one."

Patti leaned over and hugged Lorraine as best she could, words of encouragement and hope stuck in her throat. Another police officer came over to them. Patti recognized him: same baby face and jet black hair. He leaned in on the passenger's side.

"I'm Officer Turner. May I help you?"

Patti stared all around, everywhere except at Robb, as Lorraine introduced herself. They of course were now the main object of attention. At this moment, it struck Patti as impossible that this school could ever return to normal.

"Josh is dead, isn't he?" Patti heard Lorraine ask in her blunt manner.

"Yes, I'm sorry ma'am, he is. Do you think you can answer some questions for us?"

"As long as you answer some of mine," she replied.

The policeman glanced at Patti, and she saw the flash of recognition. She said, "Hi Robb. I'm Lorraine's friend. I drove her here. I don't know Josh-didn't know him, I mean." She blushed, for more than one reason now.

"Hi Patti. Good Lord, imagine seeing you here." He looked at her for a moment, then said, "Perhaps you could wait here, then?" He opened the door and led Lorraine away. The last glimpse of Lorraine showed a strained, weary expression, like Patti had not yet seen on her friend's face.

The officer returned a few minutes later. He came to the driver's side this time. "How are you, Patti?"

"I've been better."

He nodded. "I understand, under the circumstances."

Patti thought of her surgery, now fading in importance. "It's not just Lorraine," she said, "but I won't bore you with it now. How are you, Robb?"

He took his hat off. "I'm pretty good. Better now that I've run into you."

This seemed like a dangerous thread of conversation to Patti, at this place and time. She felt their history rising between them. It was hard not to think of that clumsy first time for both of them, the awkward kisses and even more awkward embraces. She'd never forget that moment when they both knew they were about to take that last step as lovers. And so young, it seemed now. "God," Patti said, before she could squelch it.

"What's wrong?"

Patti was relieved. Wrapped up in his official capacity, he was oblivious to her state of mind. She motioned a hand towards where Robb had taken her friend. "Is Lorraine all right?" She asked him.

"She's doing okay. Really, it will just take a few minutes. We have a few questions for now, plus we have to tell her what she needs to know."

"What do you mean?"

The young officer shrugged. "She needs to be prepared for what the newspapers and the TV news will say."

"What will they say?"

He looked back towards where he had come from a moment before. "Well..."

She smiled her brightest smile. "Come on, are you going to make her tell me, so soon after hearing herself?"

"I can tell you the basics, I guess. Josh Simoneau died from a single bullet wound. The investigating officer feels it might be a suicide."

Patti heard an unspoken 'but' in the statement. "Okay, but what is it you're not saying?" She asked the question assuming he wouldn't answer, screening himself behind an official need for investigative secrecy. As he looked at her, however, she became aware of his attraction to her. It was still there. She tested it by smiling at him and watched his expression change. She was about to assure him he didn't need to tell her if he wasn't supposed to, when he spoke.

"Actually, I can't say much, because the investigating officer is my father. But I'll just say that right now three theories exist, one that it was suicide and the others that it wasn't. That much will be public record soon enough."

"I see. And the other theories?"

"Well, accidental death, through a struggle, or murder, I'm afraid."

Patti swallowed. She hadn't expected that. "Wow." She reached out and touched his arm. "Thank you for telling me. Knowing that will help when I'm with Lorraine again. You don't have to say any more."

He appeared grateful. After a moment, he said. "Patti. My God."

"Yes. Just what I was thinking. You still go by Robb, then? Two 'b's?"

"Yes. There is only one Robert in my family, and that's my father."

From his tone and facial expression, Patti remembered the turmoil between father and son. She'd only met the man once or twice. Did every father and son have such problems? "Maybe one Robert is enough for any family," she joked. He smiled.

"It's enough for my family, that's for sure. Would you excuse me, please? It's wonderful to see you, but I have to tear myself away. I'm supposed to be in charge of crowd control."

"Really? What does that entail?"

"I'm not sure. My father didn't go into details, and this is my first real crowd on the job."

"How exciting. Would you like to practice on me? Maybe order me back behind the barricade?"

"No thanks. I'd rather have you where I can easily find you again. Excuse me. I'll be back."

Patti figured cop time was sort of like dog years, and she'd be there for a while, so she settled into Lorraine's car to wait. The ambulance started up its large, rumbling engine and pulled away. God, she thought, what is happening with Lorraine?

Officer Robb Turner led Lorraine to the field house. "This is a terrible thing," he said, glancing back at her. "For you, of course, ma'am, but I mean for the whole community too."

"Yes," she agreed, grateful for his effort, but not up to normal conversation.

He settled her in a small office shared by the soccer and field hockey coaches. Football being big in this town, Josh had his own office in the high school itself, and one in the field house that he shared with the assistant coaches. Lorraine assumed the shared office was where the body was found. She shuddered at the thought of it.

"Please wait here a moment," the young officer said, and he left the room.

Within a few seconds, the door opened again. Two men entered, both wearing dark suits. Lorraine recognized one of them as Sam Ripkin, the town chief of police. He used to meet with Josh periodically and talk about security at the high school games for five minutes, and then spend a half-hour discussing the team's chances of winning the next game on the schedule. Of course, Lorraine had more history than that with him, even if he didn't seem to remember. He shook Lorraine's hand warmly, pressing her hand in both of his.

Concern was pressed into every line of his rugged face. "I am very sorry about your loss, Lorraine. It is a tragedy."

"Thank you, Sam. I can't believe it."

"Of course you can't. This is Detective Lieutenant Robert Turner. He is in charge of the investigation. It was his son that brought you here."

The detective stuck out his hand, and Lorraine took it. His handshake was brief, less personal. The odd thought struck Lorraine that the man seemed to have a square head. She was reminded of a cartoon character where the artist hadn't taken much trouble for realism.

"The death of your husband is a tragedy for the entire town," the detective said.

"Ex-husband," Lorraine corrected.

"Excuse me?" The question came from the chief of police.

"Josh and I were divorced, Sam. I assumed you knew." If the situation weren't so grim, Lorraine could have laughed at the look exchanged between the two men. Their investigation wasn't off to a great start.

"This is very awkward," he said.

"Does this mean you don't have to interrogate me?"

"Please Lorraine," Sam said, "I hope you are joking. It was never going to be like that, just a few background questions."

"I think the questions still need to be asked," the detective said.

"Of course," Ripkin agreed. "Lorraine, believe me, I have spoken to your- to Josh many times, and I was led to believe you were separated, but still married."

"I'm not surprised, Sam. Josh was in denial, I believe. He gave a lot of people that impression. It never made the newspaper. I don't know how he managed that, except the sports editor probably had something to do with it."

"I see," Ripkin said. He cleared his throat. "Forgive me, I'm still a little off balance here. This dreadful business today began with an anonymous phone call saying that Josh was holding some players hostage here in the field house."

"Anonymous?" she asked.

"Yes. We think the call was made by one of the football players. Anyway, the dispatcher took the call very seriously, and hustled someone out here. When the initial officers arrived, however, there was no hostage situation. They found Josh's body; I'm sorry, Lorraine," he said when he saw her flinch.

"That's okay, I want to know it all."

"Of course. We found his body in his office at the other end of the field house, shot once. There was a pistol nearby. The room is in slight disarray, indicating a possible struggle."

"Or to make it look like a struggle," the detective threw in.

"Yes," Ripkin said, "we can't know for sure at this point. A few of the players were probably here before us but left again. Let me make this clear, Lorraine. Anything could have happened. It might have been an accident, leading one or more players to panic, disturb the room and leave. It could have been suicide or-."

"Murder?" Lorraine said.

Ripkin shrugged, as if he would have preferred not using the word. "The scene is, shall we say, open to interpretation."

"I see," Lorraine said, though she wasn't sure she saw at all.

"Tell me please," the detective began, "was your husband; I'm sorry, was your ex-husband upset lately?"

"Upset?"

"Yes. We found alcohol in his desk, and we have heard that he was to be disciplined by the school."

Lorraine's eyebrow rose. "I hadn't heard that, though he has hinted about a problem. As for the alcohol, he has at times had a problem there. It comes and goes. It's hard for me to know how serious it is, I'm afraid. Drinking goes quite naturally with sports, it seems. Plus we haven't spent a lot of time together since the divorce."

"I understand," Detective Turner said. "You haven't addressed the other portion of my question, so please forgive me for being more explicit. We are trying to get at the truth behind this tragedy. Has your ex-husband spoken at all about harming himself?"

"It has come up in the past," Lorraine admitted, "but..."

"Yes?"

"I was just going to add that I've never taken it seriously. That sounds terrible, I'm sure. He always referred to a German knife given to him by his father, obtained during World War II. It could solve all his problems, he'd say. Mostly he was kidding, I think, or trolling for sympathy, because he prided himself on being the sort of man who would fight against any odds and never take the easy way out. So suicide is one of the interpretations the scene is open to?" she asked, referring to his earlier comment.

"We have to consider it at this time," Ripkin said. "But it wouldn't be proper for us to speculate this early in the investigation. It is proper for us to consider every angle," he went on, more to his subordinate than to Lorraine, it seemed to her, "but we don't want to give the impression that we favor one over another until the facts and evidence are gathered."

The detective turned to Lorraine. "I am being chastised, properly so, I might add, for having a hunch, Ms. Simoneau. But let's set all that aside for a moment."

Lorraine looked back and forth at the two men, developing her own hunch on the spot: these two didn't like each other one little bit.

"You said, Ms. Simoneau," the detective began, "that you hadn't been able to talk to your ex-husband about what was apparently bothering him?"

"That's right, we never did get around to it."

"And you have no idea what it might have been about?"

"No, except that since he ate, drank, breathed and lived for his team, I thought it must have to do with that. If he put as much energy into our relationship as he did into the team, we'd be together still, I imagine."

"Do you know of anyone else who might know what was bothering him?"

"Well, if it did have to do with the team, perhaps the assistant coaches might help you. He was a micro manager, though, so he may have kept it to himself. If it doesn't have to do with the team, his mother could know, though Josh tended to gloss over his difficulties to his mother and me. That was a pet peeve of mine, actually. He didn't open up very easily in the best of times." Lorraine realized how easily she had slipped into the past tense, and she found it hard to breathe as she thought about it.

"Are you all right, Lorraine?"

"Just a second, Sam. I'll be fine."

"Speaking of assistant coaches," Turner said, "one of them resigned a year or two ago, didn't he. Health problems?"

"Yes, that's right."

"Was it really health reasons?"

"I don't know. I sensed more at the time, but Josh never confided in me then, not like he used to years ago."

"I think this is enough for now," Ripkin said to the detective.

"I'm almost done," the detective said. "I'm sure Ms. Simoneau wants to be of as much help as possible. You and Coach Simoneau never had children, I believe?"

"That's right. I didn't want to raise them alone, plus the players were like a flock of sons to him."

"Quite so. Were you aware that he had kept up a long-term relationship with another woman dating back many years?"

"What an interesting question," Lorraine said, momentarily stunned.

"That question is quite inappropriate," Ripkin said sternly. "I'm sorry, Lorraine, you don't have to respond to that."

"I don't mind, Sam, though I confess it took my breath away for a moment. I heard rumors before we moved to Vermont many years ago, rumors that he was involved with someone in this area. He denied it, of course. After we came back here for this job, the rumors resurfaced. They probably contributed to the divorce, but I never confronted him on it."

"Why not?"

The detective's question caught Loraine off guard. "I don't know. I guess I don't enjoy confrontation as much as some people do."

"Funny," he mused. "I would have guessed you do. If I may indulge in one follow-up question, then," the detective went on, sailing through his chief's disapproval, "I assume, then, that you haven't heard that his son from that relationship is on the football team this year?"

"You assume right."

"Thank you for your candor, Ms. Simoneau."

She barely inclined her head. "If you find out more, I shall be interested in knowing. Believe me when I say my curiosity is without rancor."

"I can't promise anything," the detective said.

"I should think not," Ripkin added. "That avenue would have to prove relevant before we pursue it."

"Every avenue is relevant until we know the truth," his subordinate asserted.

"Thank you, Lorraine," Ripkin said. "Under the circumstances, I think we should have Josh's mother make the official identification."

"I see. I must admit, that at least is a relief."

"Thank you for your time. We'll get to the bottom of this, Lorraine. Again, I'm sorry." He opened the door for her.

She stepped outside and moved away from the field house.

"Ms. Simoneau..." Detective Turner had stuck his square head outside. "If I may ask, would you let us know if you receive any sort of communication from your ex-husband?"

"What, do you mean like a seance, a voice from the casket, what?" she asked, finally irritated by his manner.

"One never knows," he said.

"I can't make any promises," she said, recovering enough spirit to throw that line back at him. She walked back to her car.

Patti was glad to see Lorraine work her way back to the car. She appeared thoughtful, but not distraught. She had wondered if Josh's body was inside the field house, that close to Lorraine, being photographed and poked and prodded for any residual information it might reveal, or had it been in the ambulance that pulled away? She shuddered at the thought of it all, and was ready to leave this behind. She got out of the car.

"Hi," Lorraine said. "That was hellish enough. Did they tell you anything?"

"Robb told me a little. I'm so sorry, Lorraine."

Lorraine nodded, looking like some of the shock had worn off, but at the same time, still dazed by the events. Patti stepped over and hugged her. "How are you holding up?"

"Not great," her friend admitted. "But you know, it will probably get worse, when I start to realize that he is really gone. And I don't want to be within a hundred yards of a television camera when that happens." Even as Lorraine said this, they both noticed they had caught the attention of one of the television crews.

Of one mind, they walked to the car, Patti still intending to drive. She looked around as she opened the door, and saw Lorraine watching her.

"What's the matter, Patti, have you lost something?"

"No." They got in, and Patti started the engine. As she shifted into reverse and looked back, she saw Robb Turner approaching from the rear.

"Is that what you didn't lose?" Lorraine asked.

Patti shifted back into park and rolled her window down, saying to Lorraine as she did so, "You think you're smart, don't you?"

"I'm darn near sure of it," Lorraine answered.

The young cop leaned down into the window opening. "I can't tell you how sorry I am, Coach," he said to Lorraine. "We'll find out how this happened."

"Thank you. I'm in the phone book if I can help in any way," she said. She nudged Patti. "What about you? Are you in the book if the officer has any questions for you?"

Patti willed herself not to blush, and succeeded partially. "I sure am. PJ Lewis, officer, if you need any help with crowd control."

"I'll keep that in mind. It was wonderful seeing you again, Patti." He withdrew from the window and Patti shifted into reverse again.

Lorraine stared at Patti. "Wonderful seeing you, he said. Interesting."

"Okay, I'll tell you. We went steady for a while back in school."

"Who broke it off?"

"I don't remember."

Lorraine smiled. "Honey, if you don't want to say, that's fine. But I don't believe for a moment you'd forget something like that."

"I broke it off," Patti said.

"Why?"

"Darned if I know. He looked good, didn't he?" They both laughed. More seriously, Patti said, "I'm afraid I was a bit obvious. What must he think of me?"

"I think we both know what he thinks of you. He was a bit obvious, too, as you put it. There's no harm in letting him know you might be interested, is there?"

"I suppose not. I didn't like feeling as though I was back in high school, though. I'd like to think I've outgrown that."

"Believe me, child, I've outgrown it, and I don't wish it for you."

They were quiet for a half-minute, long enough for the mood to grow serious again. Lorraine roused herself.

"They argued right in front of me."

"Who did?"

"Sam, the police chief, and the detective in charge of the case. It seemed like a good cop, bad cop routine, except it wasn't being used to string me along. They were sniping at each other."

Patti shivered, and Lorraine noticed. "What's wrong?"

"I just got a chill. Robb said it might have been an accident or suicide or, and I'm sorry to have to say this, but he also said it might be murder."

"He said that?"

"Yes, he presented it as a possibility." She remembered his attraction for her. "I don't think he was supposed to tell me."

"They glossed over that with me. They talked about an accident, a struggle over the weapon, and suicide was brought up by the detective, even though Sam didn't approve. But murder? They didn't stress that."

"Maybe it is unlikely."

"Sure, but you'd think they would have talked about it to me. What if I am a suspect, and they wanted to put me off my guard?"

"I'm sure that's not it."

"How can you be sure? I'm probably Josh's beneficiary for his insurance;

I'm probably still in his will, if he has one."

Patti shrugged. "Still, the idea that they suspect you is incredible."

"But not impossible."

Patti didn't have a response for that. She drove on, as the car filled up with silence. Lorraine's apartment house came into view.

"Oh God." This was practically a sob.

"What's wrong, Lorraine?"

"I can't go in there. The phone will be ringing off the hook. His cronies might even show up there. I can't play the grieving widow, but they'll all expect it, despite the divorce. I can't do it. It was bad enough that Josh acted like we were still married."

Patti signaled and pulled over. "What do you want to do?"

"I'm not sure. I guess if I'm possibly a suspect, I'd better not leave town."

"That's not even funny. Why don't you stay with me for a couple of days?" Patti suggested.

"That's sweet of you, but I should be at home if the police call or show up, or relatives."

"Then I'll stay with you. I can answer the phone and the door and screen out some of it for you. That'll work."

"Maybe, Patti, but it's a lot to ask."

"You're not asking; I'm telling you." Patti checked for traffic and pulled ahead.

"It's a hard offer to resist. Park right there, in the space with a star on it. Those are for residents."

"Wow, you're a star," Patti joked weakly. "Lorraine, why did Josh stay in the house while you moved out? If you don't mind me asking."

"A lot of reasons. I didn't want to try to keep him out, for one. Plus, the house meant more to him than it did to me. Whenever something needed fixing I always wanted to call someone who knew what they were doing. But he loved doing the work himself, even if it meant that he'd make things worse. So I thought it would be less traumatic for him if he lived in familiar surroundings. It backfired on me, though. It allowed him to pretend we were just separated for a while, even through the divorce."

"He must have loved you a lot. I mean-" Patti wasn't sure what she meant. It seemed a slam at Lorraine, and she hadn't intended that.

"Yes, he did, in a man's way. They want it both ways. They want to be independent a lot of the time, but when they're needy, we have to be there for them, center our world around them. When the need ends, we have to turn it off or risk pushing them away. He loved me even more when he knew he couldn't have me back."

"Does it have to be that way?" Lorraine saw Patti's expression.

"Don't listen to me, Patti. Here I am babbling and male bashing, with you potentially getting interested in that young peace officer back there. I'm talking about Josh and me. Don't let me get away with vast generalizations about men. Besides, I don't pretend to be blameless over my divorce."

Chapter 5

They climbed a short flight of stairs, and Patti placed her hand on a large ceramic flowerpot containing annual wildflowers while Lorraine unlocked the door. "Pretty," Patti said. "But those daisies look out of place in captivity like this."

"That's approximately how Josh used to describe me when we were first married, pretty, but out of place in captivity. I had told him about my life on the street by then." She half-turned after the door swung open. "I have to warn you: I am only one generation removed from a woman who roped off rooms and put plastic on furniture. Living with a football coach all those years cured me of a lot of pickiness, but now that I'm living alone, I do ask that you take off your shoes, please."

"You're making me nostalgic," Patti said, "my mom made us do that."

"Good. In that case, make yourself at home."

Patti slipped off her Birkenstocks and looked around. This door opened into an immaculate kitchen, with bright yellow wallpaper and the usual conveniences: toaster, coffeemaker, microwave, toaster oven, food processor, dishwasher, blender, can opener, plus a pasta maker, a rotisserie oven and a couple of devices unfamiliar to her. There was something odd about the room, and it took her a moment to identify it.

"Lorraine, everything in this kitchen looks brand new."

"That's because everything is brand new. I went a little crazy when I moved in. See, I left everything behind for Josh when I moved out. I figured he would cope better with familiar household appliances around him. Not that he ever operated them much, mind you, but I wanted to increase his chances of survival living on his own. I didn't want to be the reason he starved to death in his own home. Oh, God," she added, a hand to her face.

"Are you all right?"

Her friend shook her head. "It's funny what comes out sometimes without thinking. He's dead, Patti, and I don't even know why."

Patti wasn't sure what to do. Lorraine didn't seem the type for emotional hugs, as Patti would be in the same situation. She compromised by putting a hand on Lorraine's shoulder, who made a lie out of that thought by turning and hugging her.

"I know," Patti said. "I'm trying not to say something dumb like, 'I know how you feel.' I've never been where you are, Lorraine. I realize I've never lost anyone really close to me, except my mom in a way, so I can't pretend to know what you are going through."

Lorraine stepped away as they released each other. "I hardly know myself. I'm walking in a dream world, aware of what's going on around me, but unsure of the connection between events. That probably sounds over the edge."

"No, it makes sense, actually. I felt a little of that after I got home from the hospital."

The phone rang. Lorraine looked up at the ceiling. "Here we go."

"Yes, and here I go, time to do my appointed job. I'll get that. Are you going to be okay?"

After the second ring, Lorraine replied, "Yes, I'll go take a hot shower."

Lorraine left the room, and Patti stepped over to the wall by the glass dining table and picked up the phone. It was Joe Justice from the local newspaper. That wasn't his real last name, but rather the name he took on to reflect his image. He usually reported on the injustice he found in stories of everyday misery, and if Patti could have picked one reporter for Lorraine to speak to, he would be it. Patti respectfully declined an interview for Lorraine at this time, and she also passed along a minor news flash, that Lorraine was no longer married to Josh Simoneau. You'd think working at the newspaper he'd know that, she thought as she hung up.

Patti found a pad of paper on the counter, and dug around in her purse for a pen. She played the messages on the answering machine and wrote down the names and a brief summary. There were five calls. Two were from local television stations, who both referred to Lorraine's husband, not ex-husband; two more were from coworkers at the high school, and a call from Ned Turner, the guy who had written that large check to the chapter. Patti realized his last name was the same as the two policemen she knew, Robert and Robb.

Patti passed through the dining nook attached to the kitchen, and walked through the living room to a hallway that apparently led to the bedrooms and bathroom. She continued partway down the hall. There was a small bathroom off to her right, but the door was open and it was dark. She heard water running, though, so she assumed there was another bathroom attached to the master bedroom. She returned to the living room. The walls were beige, as was the plush wall-to-wall carpeting. She began to understand the no shoes policy. The carpet looked just as new as the kitchen appliances. She knelt down next to the brown leather couch and browsed a bookshelf there. Mostly there were thrillers and glossy oversized travel books, with a few textbooks on physical fitness on the bottom shelf. Patti removed a book on Ireland and sat on the couch. She sank into the soft cushions until she thought it would swallow her up. The idea occurred to her that perhaps Lorraine felt just as swallowed up and absorbed by her tragedy.

Several minutes later; Patti was unsure how many, the book lay closed in her lap again. She heard the hum of the refrigerator in the kitchen, and the faraway splash of water. "Long shower," she said out loud, and then felt worry wash over her. She set the book down beside her and walked back to the hallway. This time she kept following the sound of the shower. The bedroom door was open and, from where she stood in the doorway, she saw that the bathroom door was not quite closed. She walked to that door and rapped lightly with the knuckles of her right hand.

"Lorraine?" She pushed the door open wider. The mirror and a small window opposite the sink were steamed up, and the shower curtain was bulged out towards her in such a way that she knew Lorraine was sitting there on the side of the tub. "Lorraine?" she repeated. She heard a sob, and pulled the curtain slightly to the side. Despite the steamed up glass, she could tell the water had cooled off. She reached for the controls and turned off the water.

Lorraine held her head in her hands, and her shoulders shook in a long shudder, evidence of emotions too big, Patti thought, for this small room and her own meager powers of sympathy. She reached above and behind her for a towel. She held it up so it unfolded, and then draped it around Lorraine's shoulders as best she could, standing beside her as she was. Lorraine took hold of the towel and finished wrapping it around herself. She sniffed and raised her face, and Patti glimpsed the sheen of tears.

"Are you okay, Lorraine?"

"No, I'm not," her friend said, in the smallest voice Patti had yet heard her use. "But I'm getting there. I haven't cried like that for ten years, when my mother died. Thank you, PJ Lewis. I'll be out of here in a few minutes and we'll talk some more before bed."

Patti left the bathroom and went back to the living room. After returning the book to its place on the shelf, she considered calling Tom to ask him to bring a change of clothes from her place. But no, she'd either have to take the clothes from him in the doorway and send him off, or invite him in for a few awkward minutes. She'd survive wearing the same clothes for a while in the morning.

Lorraine came out a few minutes later, wearing a luxurious thick robe and a purple towel wrapped around her head, not the towel Patti had given her. "I didn't mean to get my hair so wet. Oh well. So tell me, what was the score on the answering machine? I thought I heard you listening to them just before I started the water up."

"Yes, I did. There were five messages, plus the call that came in when we got here. Just a second. I wrote them down." She fetched the pad from the kitchen counter, and then read through the list.

"Joe Justice, huh? I'm in the big time, aren't I, in the realm of human suffering. And old Ned, too. Bad news travels fast. What did Ned have to say for himself?"

"Oh, just that he was sorry to hear of your loss, or rather ex-loss, he said. He was making a joke, trying to cheer you up, he said."

"Ex-loss, huh? The only thing that joke lacks is humor."

"That was my thought. He tried, I guess. Have you seen him since that day you met him?"

"No, we talked on the phone briefly one day, and made noises about getting together, but we didn't set anything up."

"Maybe you should call him. It might be just the thing to cheer you up."

"I'm not ready to be cheered up. I might start blubbering, and I always want to have the upper hand when I deal with him. I'll call him tomorrow. The others too, I suppose. I'll have to call Josh's mother to see what sort of arrangements she has made, and whether she needs any help. For now, I'm just going to go to bed and unplug the phone. Feel free to ignore it yourself. Thank you for doing this, Patti. You're a life saver." She came over and hugged Patti, as much as the bulky robe and the towel on her head allowed.

"Tit for tat," Patti said. "You rescued me the day you came to visit me in the hospital."

"Did I? I wonder. I think you are much stronger than you realize."

Patti thought about it. "I do feel stronger than I did a month ago."

"Amazing what major surgery can do."

"And a real friend."

"I see you are determined to give me some credit, so I'll just accept it humbly and move on."

"Lorraine, you don't do anything humbly. That's one of the things I like about you."

Lorraine moved towards the doorway leading to the bedrooms. "Thank you, I think. And while we're dishing out praise here, child, I see a sweetness in you, a heart of charity, my mum used to call it, that I dimly recall from my own younger days and wish I still possessed. But never mind, I'm making you blush. I'm off to bed. When you're ready to crash, just down this hallway a bit on the left is my exercise room. There's also a twin bed with clean linens on it. If you're peckish or thirsty, my kitchen is your kitchen. Help yourself, please. Make yourself completely at home."

"Good night, Lorraine. Don't forget to unplug the phone."

"I won't forget. Bless you, child. Thank you again for all this."

"It's nothing, Lorraine. Less than nothing."

"Really? Less than nothing? If that's true, I'd like to hear your definition of 'something.' Good night, Patti Jo."

"Lorraine? What about your cell phone? Is that set up to get messages?"

"God yes. I have left it in that mode. It's on the counter if you can figure out how to retrieve them. If you can't, that's okay too."

Lorraine left the room. She seemed more lively to Patti now than before, though it felt like a shadow still lay across her face. Of course, there was a shadow there, cast by a dark cloud Patti couldn't even imagine. Married to him all those years. What if Dad died, Patti thought, or Tom? How would she cope with something like that? Could she cope with something like that?

It was unanswerable. She went to the kitchen. She liked the idea of going to bed and letting this day end, but she knew she was in no frame of mind to sleep. Not yet. So rather than lie in bed tossing and turning, she picked up Lorraine's cell phone and spent a few minutes figuring it out. There were six more messages. Three were from relatives, who seemed more inclined to ask questions than offer sympathy. Two were from coworkers, and a quick "I'll call again later" from Josh's mother. Patti dutifully wrote them down as she retrieved them, and then set the phone back down. She then opened and closed cupboard doors until she found a mug and some herbal tea with a sleepy bear on the box. She filled the mug most of the way with tap water and set it inside the microwave. Standing there, tea bag and spoon in hand, she watched as the timer counted down. She tried to imagine what the next day would be like for Lorraine, but her imagination failed her.

The timer hit zero and the microwave dinged four times. Patti removed the steaming mug, set the tea bag into it, and placed her spoon on it to push the bag to the bottom of the mug. She remembered how years ago her brother rolled his eyes and told her that the tea would steep just as well floating as it would submerged. A lively yet not entirely serious family argument ensued, ended by their father making a typical observation that what difference did it make, and meanwhile her tea was getting cold and they were all going to be late for work. Patti sensed that Lorraine would be remembering a thousand such anecdotes over the next several days, or weeks, or however long she mourned the death of an ex-husband she had still cared about.

She removed the tea bag, threw it away in the small trash pail she found under the sink, and returned to the living room. For the first time, she noticed the picture window behind the couch. She opened the curtains and then shut off the lights. The window gave a good view of the street below.

Patti sat twisted sideways on the couch so she could see outside. There was a squat green candle on the windowsill, and a book of matches nearby. "She wants me to feel at home," Patti said to herself, "I'll feel at home." She struck a match and lit the candle. The flame wavered and then flared up. After a moment, the aroma reached her. "Green apples." She glanced around, as if expecting Lorraine to be standing there witnessing her solo conversation. But of course she was alone.

Sipping the tea, she noticed some activity in the back of a sport utility vehicle below in the apartment building's parking lot. Someone must have left their dog in there, she figured, and she wondered if she should call someone. But the single shape became two shapes, and she realized what she was seeing.

"Oops," she said as she moved the left hand curtain over enough to block that portion of her view. She wondered who owned the vehicle. It had been nine months since her last kiss, even longer since she had rolled around with anyone, in the back of a vehicle, a bed, or otherwise. That kiss had come from Greg Ritchie at the garage. They had dated a few times, never quite rising above the awkward fact that Patti was technically his boss. Greg decided to get back together with his ex-girlfriend, now pregnant and due anytime. He still flirted with Patti, though, a fact that only seemed to strike herself as odd. "I'm hooked, but I'm not in the boat yet," was Greg's explanation. Mostly, Patti thought she was the one that had gotten away and that his girlfriend was sunk. And she had been that close to getting serious about him. Beware the men with easy charm, was her lesson from that experience.

Now Officer Robb Turner, there was a man lacking such flirtatious glibness. During her more honest moments since meeting him again, Patti admitted to herself that a year or two before, she would have felt him not to be exciting enough. Now, however, his apparent shyness held an attraction for her, especially coming from a cop. Would he call? At the time, searching the expression in his face, she had felt sure he would. Each passing hour made her less sure. Immersed back in his life, perhaps the idea of renewing an old flame would seem less appealing. His father probably wouldn't approve either. Then again, he didn't get along with his father apparently, so that could work in her favor.

She shook her head. Why obsess over it? He would either call or he wouldn't. She knew one thing, she was in no hurry. The idea of sex while wearing the pouch scared the heck out of her. She had admitted as much to Lorraine on the phone once, unable to talk about it face to face. Lorraine had replied that, believe it or not, you forgot about it a lot of the time. Patti didn't believe it. Using a far-fetched cooking metaphor, she saw the post-surgical equipment and resulting body image change as the equivalent of an elephant in the kitchen. You might be able to work around it and cope with it, but you always knew it was there.

A few minutes later, Patti finished the cup of tea, blew out the candle and closed the curtain back up. The scent of apples still with her, she found the exercise room with its twin bed. She undressed and folded her clothes, setting them on a stack of weights on the floor at the foot of the bed. She slipped in between the sheets, expecting satin or something expensive, but instead feeling the familiar cool smoothness of percale. She hadn't turned the light on, so even when she first lay down, her eyes were adjusted to the near darkness. She convinced herself that the arms on the exercise equipment, raised towards the sky, were protecting her from bad luck such as had befallen Lorraine, and then she fell asleep.

It wasn't until she was in the shower the next morning that Patti remembered she had broken the cardinal rule of life as a new ostomate: she didn't have any spare equipment with her. She had gotten into the habit of putting something in her car, but of course her car was at her place now. She hoped she wouldn't need any of it, even if her hostess might have something she could use, and she vowed to buy a bigger handbag and take a further step towards preparedness.

She climbed out of the shower, dried off quickly, and put on her clothes from the day before. "Sheesh, I'm a bachelor," she said to her reflection, "smelling my clothes before I put them on." Towel around her head, she left the bathroom. It was going on 7:00, but she heard Lorraine moving around in the kitchen. She headed in that direction. Lorraine was already dressed and leaning against the counter. She inclined her head towards the coffeemaker.

"Decaffeinated, I'm afraid, but freshly ground. Or would you like some tea?"

"No, coffee's fine," Patti said, stifling a yawn. "How did you sleep, Lorraine? I hoped you might sleep later than this."

"No, I'm an early riser, in the best of times and the worst of times, apparently. Once I finally dropped off, I slept just fine. How about you?"

"Well, I'm not an early riser, usually. But I woke up a few times during the night and never slept for long. I never sleep well my first night in a strange bed. Who can that be?" Her question came about when the doorbell rang.

"At this hour," Lorraine said, "the apartment building better be on fire."

Patti drifted over to the door behind Lorraine, thinking it might be a reporter, and she wondered if she should offer to answer the door alone, But Lorraine seemed herself this morning, which is to say, a force to be reckoned with.

Lorraine opened the door, revealing three boys on the small landing. Three young men, Patti corrected herself, for these were big boys. Football players, she guessed, judging from the shortage of necks among them.

"Hi Mark," Lorraine said. "Boys. This is kind of early for a social call, isn't it?"

The middle one removed his baseball cap. "I'm sorry, Coach, but this is important. We'll only be a minute."

"I see. This is my friend, Patti."

Patti murmured a hello and absorbed their interest in her. She looked down at herself briefly, clothes plastered to her still damp skin; why wouldn't they stare at her?

"What's up?" Lorraine asked, getting Mark's attention back, if not the others.

"We brought you something from Coach," he said. "Joey Kallas was going to give it to you, but he asked us to."

"Why did he do that?"

"He's kind of in the hospital, in Portland or Boston or somewhere."

"Why is he in the hospital?"

One of the other two players giggled. Mark turned to him. "It isn't funny, Steve."

"It is, kinda," Steve disagreed. Patti didn't like his smirk, though she supposed it was a normal expression for a teenaged male athlete. "He grew tits," he explained to the women in front of him. "And him always thinking he's so tough."

"Thank you, Steve," Lorraine said ironically, "but perhaps you could let Mark do the talking."

Mark reached into his jean jacket pocket and pulled out a small package. He held it out. "Anyway, we snuck into Joey's room and got this. Coach told Joey he was to give it to you if anything happened to him."

Lorraine took it from him. "It looks like this has been opened and resealed again."

"Not by us, ma'am, I swear. Maybe it was Joey; I don't know."

"Why would Josh think something might happen to him?"

"I don't know," Mark said, staring at his shoes.

"I see. Did the cops talk to you yesterday, Mark?"

Mark snorted. "That Turner guy spoke to the whole team, and then they pulled some of us aside. He's an asshole. Excuse me, ma'am. He talked like Coach offed himself, maybe, and that ain't how it is."

"You're sure about that?"

"Damn straight," Mark said, using one of Josh's expressions. "Coach said he was going to fight to the end, go to the wall to keep coaching us. He wouldn't have bailed on us."

"Who was he fighting to stay on as coach?"

"I don't know. The school board was giving him crap about something. They always were." Mark's shoes were proving to be interesting to him again.

Lorraine crossed her arms, looking at the packet she held in her right hand. "Mark, does anyone else know you're giving this to me. Or that Joey was supposed to?"

"I don't think so."

"Do me a favor, and don't tell anyone. Don't lie if that cop asks you, but don't volunteer the information. And tell me if he does ask you. Can you do that?"

"You can count on it. We owe them nothing. Are you going to find out what happened to Coach, Ms. Simoneau?"

"I'm curious to know the truth," she admitted. "Though I might not get far if you guys aren't willing to tell me the truth." Mark squirmed a bit under her gaze. "Never mind right now. Thank you, gentlemen." They left a moment later.

Lorraine closed the door behind them, pushing on it until the latch clicked. She tapped the packet absently against her other hand. "Josh, Josh. What were you up to?"

"Lorraine, what happened to that boy?"

Lorraine looked at her, seemed to pull herself out of her own thoughts. "Which boy?"

"The one in the hospital. That awful thing that boy said. Did Joey gain too much weight or something?"

"No. Steroids, it must be." She slapped the countertop with the palm of her free hand. "Damn it, Josh! You fool!"

"What's going on, Lorraine?"

Her friend shook her head. "It's not hard to guess. That was always Josh's line in the sand. He'd bend a rule here or there, get a player off probation whose grades were suspect, but he was never going to let his boys take steroids."

"Maybe he didn't know anything about it."

"I don't know. It would be hard not to notice if players started bulking up too fast. I wish I'd paid more attention."

"You were divorcing him," Patti reminded her. "Maybe they were taking them all along."

Lorraine glanced at Patti. "Maybe. He prided himself at knowing what was going on with his boys, though. I've got to try to find out."

"Lorraine, I hate to keep bugging you with questions..."

"That's all right, Patti, you're helping me think this through. What is it?"

"Why did you ask them not to tell anyone they gave that to you?"

"Just a hunch. I'm irritated that Detective Turner asked me to let him know if I hear from Josh, and then to find the next day I get something. I hate coincidences, and I don't trust this one."

"What do you mean?"

"I don't even know what I mean. Here goes." She unsealed the small manila envelope and a cassette tape slid out into her hand. "God, all the video equipment he has bought for the team, and he uses this."

"You probably want some privacy to listen to that," Patti said, "would you like me to leave for a while?"

"That's sweet, thank you, but I don't think so. This may sound weird, but I know just where I want to listen to this. Maybe you can hang out here just a bit longer for me. I want to listen to this out in Brett Hill. Josh and I both lived out there when we met, back when the world was new, I used to tell him. There's a spot I go to when I need to relax."

"Sounds great, if you're sure. Go ahead. I'll amuse myself here until the next phone call."

Lorraine pulled a travel cup out of a cupboard. "I'll just take some of this coffee with me and some health food." She opened a box of toaster pastries and took a packet out. "That spot in Brett Hill is just ten minutes from here, so I should be back in less than an hour, depending on how long the tape is. Help yourself to cereal, toast, pancakes, omelets, whatever strikes you. And feel free to screen the calls; don't feel like you have to answer them, unless maybe if it's the police or someone like that."

"Gotcha. Go."

"I'm gone. Bye."

Lorraine left the apartment and drove out of town. She drove through the

University of Maine/Hancock campus and took in the rural countryside at its best. Within minutes she was in neighboring Brett Hill, which was named after one hill but which contained many. She and Josh were middle schoolers in Brett Hill when they met, and even though they hadn't liked each other until they dated at Ellsworth High School, the hills of Brett Hill were dear to her. She especially liked parking on the north side of the hill for which the town was named, on a dirt road near an apple orchard with a great view of the town in the valley and the surrounding hills. She had first come here as a girl to pick apples, but the view drew her back as an adult. She found it stunning all year round, with the new greens of spring, the lushness of summer and the stunning beauty of apple blossom season. And then forward with the fragrance of the apple season itself, with the accompanying colorful splashes of the foliage. Even winter drew her back here, when the snowstorms carved a Currier and Ives sculpture out of the valley below. She got to know the owner, an old-timer named Dick, who joked during every conversation with her that he didn't know dick about apples. He had mildly come on to Lorraine, but had the decency to know what the word no meant first time out of the gate.

Lorraine parked in what she had come to consider her spot, and shut off the engine, leaving the key switched on so it would operate the cassette radio. She smiled at the passing thought that she was glad she hadn't traded the car in for that new one with the CD player. She rolled both front windows down. The apples were coming on toward ripe now, and she only hoped Dick recognized her car if he saw her, and didn't mistake her for an apple poacher.

Lorraine drew in a few deep breaths, almost as though she were taking part in a ceremony. "Here we go," she said as she pushed the 'play' button.

"Hello Rainey. I can't believe I'm doing this."

Lorraine pushed the pause button with a gasp of surprise. It wasn't just because he used her old nickname, which he stopped using after they separated. It was also the tone of his voice, so measured and in control. No, don't mince words, she thought. He's cold sober, that's the difference. She started the tape up again.

"I wanted to tape a message to you in case something happens to me. Yes, I know how that sounds. Very melodramatic, but on the other hand, if you are listening to this, then something probably has happened to me. This is strange, like a sci-fi movie. I am healthy and hearty as I tape this, but if you are listening, I'm not either any more. I feel like I am existing in two different places in time at once. But I'm stalling. Let me cut through the crap I'm spreading here.

"I screwed up, Rainey, big time. I could sit here and make excuses, but I'm the head coach, so it stops with me.

"You see, I inherited the problem. That much I can say with total honesty. The people involved were pretty entrenched in what they were doing when I got here, when we got here, from Vermont. Anyway, it's all about steroids. Some of the older players were using them when I got here, and they were apparently passing on their information and techniques to the freshmen and sophomores. I slowly realized how elaborate the setup was. They were stacking the different types and running them in pyramids to avoid detection. But it went beyond that. I came to believe, and I still do, that they were given timetables of the random testing, to help them avoid getting caught. The system of what they took and when, and where they got it from, ran much too smoothly for it to have been the brainchild of the players. Someone outside was running the show.

"I say all this now, but I have to point out how long it took me to figure all this out. At first all I had were suspicions, and isolated ones at that. I saw only a little at a time, or picked up snippets of locker room talk, or else I might never have found out at all. It was that well organized. And even when I felt sure, I had no idea who was behind the operation or how they did it. Or, for that matter, how to prove any of it. The coaches who've been here longer had nothing to say on the subject, except for Paunch. We've argued long and hard over it. You've heard of circumstantial evidence; well mine was more like hearsay and educated guesswork. Since I couldn't prove any of it, I put off blowing the whistle on it."

"Oh, Josh," Lorraine said in the short gap he left there.

"Of course," he went on, "what didn't occur to me was that by putting off telling what I knew, or even suspected, I was implicating myself deeper and deeper. But I told myself I could root out the problem and purge it from my team, without harming any of the boys. It turned out not to be that easy."

"No, it wouldn't be," Lorraine muttered. She caught the pure notes of a nearby chickadee before Josh's calm voice took over again.

"I became quite vocal in my opposition to steroid use, without looking at any of them or giving any sign that I knew who they were. At the same time, I made it clear I knew it was going on. I told them it wouldn't be tolerated, and that if I received any proof any of them were using it, I'd throw them off the team.

"I felt like there was an improvement after that, but then I realized I'd just driven it farther underground. They were more careful. On top of that, it drove a wedge into the team, because of course, most of the players knew what had been going on. The players who were using thought I was betraying them, because they believed it had been winked at before. The players who weren't using were torn, thinking I was trying to have it both ways, expressing my opposition while allowing it at the same time. I was in a no win situation. I couldn't shake the feeling that someone close to the team was involved."

"An assistant coach, maybe?" Lorraine said.

"I was in a bad place. I still don't know who the suppliers were. The next thing that went wrong was predictable. We started losing a few games. Dissension will do that every time. I started having those days when I wished I had what it took to do myself in, throw myself on my sword like a dishonored warrior. Hell, I still have those days."

He paused again, until she wondered if he had finished abruptly. The chickadee hastened to fill the brief silence. Lorraine tried to pick it out of the nearby apple trees before Josh started up again.

"Now one of the players has developed side effects, potentially serious ones, and his parents are starting to ask loud questions.

"The sources have cut and run, and the players still won't talk to me, the ones who know what was going on. I think I'm being set up to take the fall. There is one player I can ask about all this, who I can trust to tell me the truth, if I can convince him to talk about it. He has refused to talk to me so far, out of loyalty to the team, loyalty to me, I think. If I can convince him to tell me what he knows, maybe I can break this thing wide open. If he tells me nothing, then I'm stuck. I'll be caught holding the bag. Maybe it's nothing more than I deserve, but I'd love to take a few others down with me, if I knew who they are.

"I feel mighty silly making this tape, even though I have received a few anonymous threats. I guess most threats of that sort are anonymous. And who knows, maybe I'll find the intestinal fortitude to off myself. That would solve a lot. But even then, I'd want you to know the truth, that I didn't start all this, and tried to stop it. I am guilty of bad judgment, but nothing worse, I hope. So, this tape will do that for me. I'll be ready for anything.

"Well, that's enough, too much probably. God, I need a drink."

The voice ended, and only the hiss of the tape running remained. Lorraine pressed the 'stop' button. "I'm with you, lad, I think I need a drink right now, too."

She thought of Josh as he made this tape, sounding more like the man she married than the one she had divorced. She lay her left arm across the top half of the steering wheel, and then rested her forehead against her arm. These tears were not borne of the fierce sorrow of the night before; they did not burn as they trailed down her face. They were selfish tears: she mourned the man she had married, the camaraderie of those early years, the shared interest in their students. She also mourned for the future that would not be, the years of friendship she had anticipated with Josh, after he got over the divorce once and for all. Nature was not immune to her tears; now a mourning dove took up an answering lament in the area. Lorraine raised her head, smiling at the coincidence, wiped her cheeks with her left hand and started the car with her right. She ejected the tape, slid it into her pocket, and drove home.

When Lorraine walked into her apartment, Patti sat on the couch with a book in her lap. "Any excitement while I was gone?"

"Not really, unless a call from Joe Justice makes your heart flutter."

"He's persistent. I hope he doesn't think there's a Pulitzer Prize nomination in this sordid story."

"I don't think he is sympathetic to you or Josh at all. I hung up on him. Is it a sordid story, Lorraine?" Patti asked.

"After listening to the tape, yes, I'm afraid so. It has to do with steroids, like I thought. I don't know if dear old Josh did anything criminal exactly, but at the very least, what he didn't do will be held against him, I think. He knew about the steroid use going on, and didn't act on it nearly quickly enough, or to the authorities."

"So there must be others who were more actively to blame. What about them?"

"Exactly. My remaining hope is that the police nail them, too. If they bother to try. Sometimes it seems like overzealous prosecutors are only too willing to settle all the blame on the bird in the hand, or am I just cynical?"

The phone rang, preventing Patti from responding. Standing near the caller ID, Lorraine leaned over to glance at it. "Anonymous. This can't be good." She picked it up. "Hello?"

There was a slight pause. "I know why your husband killed himself," a rather neutral sounding voice said. A young voice, she thought, trying to sound old.

"Do you now?" Lorraine replied. "Well, listen closely. First, he was my ex-husband. Second, he didn't kill himself. You got any more revelations for me? I didn't think so." She hung up with gusto. "Finally, someone I can take my anger out on," she said to Patti.

"Who was that?"

"I didn't recognize the voice." The phone rang again. She glanced at the ID and grabbed the phone. "I'm sorry. I thought we were done."

"That was rude," the same voice said.

"Yeah? You did sort of set the tone for the conversation. Who is this, by the way?"

"That's not important."

"Why does it seem important to me?"

"Listen, I have a notebook that belonged to Coach Simoneau. I know why he killed himself."

"I told you, he didn't kill himself."

"Are you sure?"

That was a tough question, except that Lorraine didn't feel obliged to answer this man. "So you have Josh's notebook," she said instead. "What do you want me to do about it? Mail it to his mother. I'm not married to him any more."

"I thought you might want to purchase it, to keep it out of the cops' hands."

It was tempting. What if this notebook held names in it, or more information than Josh had divulged in the tape? But her intuition was screaming against it. "Call the police," she said. "They have a bigger operating budget than I do." She hung up again, with less gusto this time. "I have to sit down and figure out what I'm going to do about this tape."

"What do you mean? You have to give it to the police, right?"

"Do I?"

"Why wouldn't you? You have to help them figure out what happened to Josh."

"I think Detective Turner has already figured it out, or so he thinks. I'm not sure I want to help him."

"Well, give it to Ripkin, then. You said he was nicer to you. And he's Chief of Police."

"Ripkin? I can tell you a story about Sam Ripkin. One he probably doesn't remember himself, or at least, to remember it was me. Your experience with the police has probably been a little different than mine, child. If your bike got stolen, your parents called Officer Friendly, and they checked into it for you. At one time, I would have let them do the same for me, before I ran away from home when I was fourteen."

"Why did you run away?"

"Why? The typical teenage reason, because I wanted everything my own way. My parents were in their forties when they had me, and when adolescence kicked in, I felt particularly alienated from them. I thought I knew everything and they knew nothing. They didn't understand me, the whole package. So I left. I lived on the streets in Bangor for a while. But it was kind of rough for me there. I first learned to avoid the police on those streets. Eventually I made my way back up here. I tried the Ellsworth streets. Less dangerous, I thought. Once I got into this abandoned car to spend the night. This guy was there, high on something, and he assaulted me. It would have been rape except he was pretty ineffectual and useless. He did hit me a few good ones, though. I'd seen the guy around town, so I went and reported the assault to a young beat cop, none other than Sam Ripkin."

"What did he do?"

"He ran me out of town. He had to bust this local drug lord, and he needed this guy who attacked me to nail him. So he turned it around, made me feel like the criminal. Said he was going to call my parents, but I took off. I think he wanted me to run. Easier for him. So I stayed out of town for a while, and laid low. Trust in my local police was not a big thing for me after that."

"What happened to you, Lorraine? Did you go back home again?"

"Yes. Since I was avoiding Ellsworth, I haunted the small suburbs. Even Brett Hill some, my home town. Mom saw me once. What a moment that was. I had changed, as you might guess. Thinner, I'm sure. She had changed too. She looked a decade older. She burst into tears when she saw me. I had never seen that woman cry."

"Lorraine..."

"It was quite a scene. I started backing off. I trusted no one, if the truth were known. All she said was 'Come home, baby,' over and over. She was pleading, not ordering. My skin was pretty thick by then, but I knew on the spot I had broken her heart. I started bawling myself. It was messy."

"So you went home?"

"Yes, but not at that moment. I called home a couple of days later. I told her I was different, that they wouldn't want me now. She said they did want me, under any terms at all. Only come home. So I turned up at their door a few hours later. I stopped at a McDonalds first, tried to clean myself up a bit. But I still looked pretty rough. After she hugged me for thirty seconds, like she was never going to let me go, she led me to the tub and filled it with hot water. I stayed in that until my skin wrinkled, crying my eyes out at the sheer comfort of it."

Lorraine was crying now, and reached for a tissue. "Sorry, this is all coming back to me, vivid and fresh all over again. Anyway, to make a long story a little less long, it took a while but I slowly settled back into a semblance of my old life. Everything felt strange to me. Even though I felt better off by far, I was still tempted to run because of the strangeness of it all. My parents handled me the only way that would have worked. They only loved me. I mean, the old strictness was gone. I was pretty hideous at times, but their patience with me was bottomless. I learned to trust them, but oh, did it take time. It was nine months before I went back to school. I wouldn't have stuck with that, except I got involved in sports. I spent hours running. Hours every day, I mean. I felt alive and in control when I ran. I was on the track team and the basketball squad. Their love and sports, that's what reclaimed me."

Lorraine blew her nose and smiled. "But I still distrust the police a little."

"No kidding," Patti joked. More seriously, she added, "Thank you for telling me, Lorraine. Did Josh know about all of that?"

"Most of it, except for the beat cop being Ripkin. I didn't know Sam's name for all those years, until we moved back here and we met him. You should have seen me. I practically ran when we were introduced."

"I bet."

"Well, that's my story." The phone rang. "Oh-oh," Lorraine said. "I'm going to work out for a while. It's time for you to punch in and earn your keep." She left the room, and Patti went for the phone.

Chapter 6

Patti's new role, screening incoming calls for Lorraine, became easier as the day progressed. After a flurry of calls in the morning, just two calls came in from noon through mid-afternoon. The first was from Josh's mother, phoning to let Lorraine know what the funeral arrangements would be. Patti offered to fetch Lorraine, who was having what she called a quick lay down, but the woman declined the offer. She'd catch up with her tomorrow. So Patti wrote down the information instead, and left it in a prominent place on the counter.

The second call was from a fellow gym teacher at the high school, who had just heard the news, he said. He was shocked and offered his deepest condolences. At least he seemed to know that Josh and Lorraine were divorced, a rarity for these calls.

Lorraine came into the living room at nearly four p.m., wearing sweat pants and a pink t-shirt that read "I Survived the Ice Storm of '98." She walked past Patti and said, "I'm going to make some coffee. Are you interested?"

"I wouldn't turn it down. Were you able to get some sleep?"

"Sleep? Oh, I dozed a little earlier. But I was working out for the past half-hour or so. I'm afraid this is all quite boring for you, isn't it?"

"Well, a bit," Patti admitted.

Lorraine erupted with her old booming laugh. "Bless you for your honesty."

"I'm still glad to be here," Patti insisted, "but it was more interesting when Joe Justice was calling every few hours."

"Yes, it would seem that the muckrakers have lost interest in me fast. I think it's time I drive you home so you can resume your life again. I need to start calling people back, and you don't want to be around here for that."

"Okay, but if I can do anything else for you, don't hesitate to ask me, Lorraine. I mean it."

"Do you? Let's see how fast I can make you regret saying that. Have you got your stuff handy?"

Patti grabbed her purse and followed her friend out the door. Lorraine waited until she was driving to explain what she wanted Patti to do. "You could do two more things for me, if you have the stamina."

"I'm just getting my second wind. What are they?"

"The first is easy. If you could get today's and tomorrow's newspapers and save the stories about this business for me. I'm not ready to read them yet, but I want them available to me."

"That's easy. Next?"

"There is an executive meeting tonight for the ostomy group. Just the officers. I'd like you to attend for me, and take this check old Uncle Ned gave to me. I left the regular meeting so fast I didn't give it to our venerable treasurer. A few questions are bound to come up. I love that group, but I'm not ready for their sympathy and searching questions."

"How much should I tell them?"

"Not much. Check today's paper and mirror that. We don't want to hurt tomorrow's circulation of the home town newspaper."

"All right. That sounds pretty easy, too."

"Obviously you've never been pumped for information by a crowd of people who are really good at it."

It seemed manageable to Patti as she drove to the meeting, to be held in the same medical building where the chapter had met, could it have been just the previous day? She'd go in, deliver the check and escape again into the night. No problem.

To start off, however, she had trouble finding the meeting room. She assumed it would be held in the same room as before, but she burst in on another meeting altogether, where about twenty men and women sat around the table, all dressed in suits or dresses. One man stood at the front with a flip chart and, by the looks of things, somewhat less than their undivided attention.

"I'm sorry," she stammered, "I'm looking for another meeting."

"If I don't finish up soon," the man in the front said, "some of these people may want to join you." A titter ran through the group. "But you might try upstairs; there are smaller conference rooms up there. The stairs are off to the left."

"Thank you, and forgive me."

"I should thank you. I believe we are all awake now."

Patti closed the door softly and aimed for the stairwell. She went up the stairs and tried a few doors. They were all locked until she found the room with the small group she sought. She stepped inside and closed the door behind her. This meeting room was indeed smaller, more suited to the size of this group. There was a full fireplace on one side of the rectangular table, and a gallery of grim, unsmiling portraits along the wall on the other side. Neither the fireplace nor the people in the portraits had seen action in a long time.

The three people seated at the table greeted Patti. There was Clay, the venerable treasurer, as Lorraine referred to him; Julia, the woman whose story at the first meeting had put Patti at ease; and Hal, whom she remembered as a wisecracker. They were waiting for Cliff Royce, the president, and the lovely secretary, his wife. Apparently they had been discussing the violent nature of Josh's death. Hal, apparently used to being the center of any conversation, waited for the greetings to be completed, and for Patti to express Lorraine's regrets, before he launched back into their conversation.

"I tell you, don't listen to those reports that say the incidence of violent crime is going down. The world is turning into a violent video game, an R-rated movie playing to different audiences everywhere, over and over. I'm thinking of becoming a recluse and just not answer the door or the telephone. The more people you know, the more likely it is you'll get murdered in your sleep. The more you show your face in public, the more likely you'll get rubbed out, along with half a dozen other strangers, by someone who's having a bad day. If it weren't for their sleeping outdoors in the winter, I'd say the homeless people have it right. Form no attachments, avoid the bullets that will fly sooner or later. "

"You don't really believe that, do you, Hal?" Julia protested.

"I sure do believe it. But I'm willing to leave it on the table. Show me the flaw in my reasoning. I tell you, I tremble for my grandchildren."

Julia sat back and smiled. "I've always had trouble picturing towheaded children running after you calling out, "Grandpa, Grandpa!""

"You and me both. Apparently it's a package deal. You have kids, then grandchildren will follow. Like death and inheritance taxes. I'm settling into the role. Good thing too; Sarah is cranking them out, begetting right and left. Three so far, Chastity, Felicity, and Entity."

"He's trying to be funny," Julia explained, as if there were some chance Patti might think him serious. "Don't let him fool you; he dotes on his grandchildren."

"That's only because I'm in my dotage. Do you have any children, Patti?"

"She's not married, Hal."

"That doesn't signify these days. It hasn't mattered for a long time, come to that."

"No, I don't have any kids, just a spoiled cat."

"A cat," Hal said. "When you say cat, you don't have to say spoiled. It's assumed. I have the most arrogant cat in New England. I'd trade him in tomorrow for a dog's unconditional love."

"Cats can be quite loving," Patti protested, but, remembering her brother's similar criticism of her cat, she did not feel overly confident about her argument.

"Not my cat," Hal went on. "I think Ugly Schnoz only tolerates me because I can operate the can opener and the light switches. And now that I think of it, judging from the feline Olympics that go on every morning at four o'clock, maybe he'd get by fine without the lights."

Feeling more comfortable with the small group, Patti said, "You named your cat Ugly Schnoz, and you're wondering why you don't get unconditional love?"

Hal's response was cut off by the arrival of Cliff Royce and his wife. Cliff formally inquired into Lorraine's well-being, which led to the barrage of questions and comments about Josh's death, as Lorraine had predicted.

"Was it suicide or murder, is what I want to know," Hal said. "The police are acting pretty coy so far."

"It may have been an accident too," Patti went so far as to suggest.

"I don't buy that. Is that what Lorraine thinks?"

Patti kicked herself for even opening her mouth. But Hal didn't wait for an answer.

"I heard he had troubles with the football team. One of his coaches quit on him a year or two ago. Very messy, though they covered it all up. Makes you wonder, don't it?"

"Makes you wonder, maybe," Julia said. "I've never seen anyone who circulates rumors like you do, Hal."

"It's my hobby. I collect them and pass them along to my friends."

"Well, I hope you don't harass Lorraine like this the first time you see her. Stop putting Patti on the spot. Shouldn't we talk about something else?"

"Like chapter business?" Cliff suggested with a hint of a smile on his face. Patti was grateful to both of them. "If our lovely secretary can take notes," Cliff said, "perhaps we can get started, so we can leave and Hal can go rustle up more rumors for his rumor mill."

"I'm just a curious individual," Hal muttered.

Cliff ignored him. "Let the record show the President and Secretary are present, albeit a little late. Sorry, folks. As I get older, I find I have to dress slower to go out, to avoid putting clothes on inside out or backwards and what have you. Plus we burst in on the wrong room downstairs, where we have the normal meetings." Patti suppressed a smile. What the man with the flip charts must have thought! "Julia Mannix, the Visiting Coordinator, is present, as is Hal Trent, the Program Coordinator."

"Visiting Coordinator?" Patti repeated. "So I can thank you for sending Lorraine to visit me in the hospital?"

"That's right. She was hand-picked for you from our legion of fully trained visitors."

"You're teasing me, right?"

"A bit," Julia said. "We try to match the visitor with the patient, as to age and gender and such, but we have a small group to choose from and no one as young as you are. I was going to come see you, but I had a flower show in Boston."

Patti liked Julia, but she said a brief prayer to the goddess of chance that had sent Lorraine in to see her instead.

"To continue..." Cliff nudged the group. "Clay is also present."

"Treasurer for life," Clay added, clearly the oldest of all of them.

"Or until senility."

"I'm already past that."

"And Lorraine Simoneau, our erstwhile vice-president, has sent Patti; I'm sorry, I don't remember your last name. I do good to remember my own."

"Patti Jo Lewis," she said.

"Exactly. Patti Jo Lewis is here in her place."

This reminded Patti of her desire to avoid staying for the entire meeting. "I'm sorry. Lorraine wanted me to deliver a check for her, mainly. I can't stay. I'm on my way to visit my brother and deliver a care package of blond brownies I promised him for watching my cat while I was in the hospital."

"Leave some of them with us, and we'll let you go," Hal said.

"I could leave a few of them," Patti said.

"That won't be necessary," Cliff said, motioning to a side table. "I see the coffee is ready, and that someone has brought us some delicious looking chocolate chip cookies. Let's not deprive Patti's brother of any of his just desserts, so to speak. What is this check Lorraine sent you to deliver?"

"Lorraine received it as a donation from a man and his niece she visited."

Patti retrieved the check from her purse and slid it across the table. "I guess it goes to the treasurer." She almost had to bite her tongue to avoid saying 'venerable treasurer.'

Clay picked it up and looked at it, pursing his lips. "My, my, what did we do to deserve this?"

"How much is it for?" Julia asked.

"Is this supposed to be anonymous?" Clay asked Patti.

She shook her head. "No, I'm sure Lorraine wouldn't have shown me if that were the case."

Clay looked at the check again. "It is for a thousand dollars."

There was a low whistle from Hal, and appreciative noises all around the table.

"Let's hear the rest of it," Hal said. "Who is it from?"

"Ned Turner." Hal made a face.

"Do you know him?" Julia asked.

"I've had dealings with him. Let's just say I always count my fingers after I shake hands with him. Which brings us back to Clay's original question. What did we do to deserve this? Or what will we be expected to do? Everything is an investment to that guy."

They all looked at Patti. "All I know is that Lorraine said he had read an article about your group sending kids to a youth ostomy camp, and he wanted to help."

"Our group," Julia corrected.

Patti smiled. "Yes, our group. Didn't I say that?"

"I guess his money is as good as anyone's," Hal said, "but I reserve the right to be skeptical later. He strikes me as one of those characters who never gets caught, but who always gives the appearance of being shady. And we were speaking of Josh Simoneau: didn't Ned Turner get in trouble over the football team a while back?"

That caught Patti's attention. "What was it about?"

Hal made a dismissive gesture. "Oh, he was warned by the school committee, but not too harshly, mind you, about fraternizing with the players. He was having them over at his place. There is no law against that, mind you. There were rumors of gifts, though, which are not allowed. But football is king in this town."

"Did anything come of it?"

"No, a lot of sound and fury from a few sane voices, but his wealth and position insulated him from any real harm. That was years ago. He has kept a lower profile since then. Why do you ask?"

Patti wasn't sure. "It's a big coincidence, isn't it? Him turning up when-" She'd said more than she wanted to say. She stood up to forestall followup questions. "I have to leave so you guys can get something done. I have my mission of mercy to perform for my brother."

"Is your brother one of those bachelors who can operate a microwave but who can't bake?" Julia asked.

"Something like that," Patti said, keeping her fingers crossed over her fib, but not wanting to launch into a longwinded description.

"One last thing," Cliff Royce said. "We are going to talk about fundraisers tonight. Do you have any ideas we might use, just in case thousand dollar checks stop falling out of the sky?"

Patti stood with her hand on the doorknob. "I've run car washes at my Dad's garage for charity before. It usually only raises a couple of hundred dollars, though."

"We wouldn't turn our noses up at that," Julia said. "We've made less on bake sales and such. How long would you need to set one up?"

"I could do one with less than a week's lead time. I might need a few volunteers, although I can usually dig up a few in the neighborhood."

"Sounds like fun," Julia threw in. "Sign me up."

"No offense," Hal said, "but I think teenagers in halter tops and shorts would get the healthiest tips."

Julia put her hands on her hips. "Have you ever seen me in a halter top and shorts?"

He raised his eyebrows now. "I withdraw my last comment, with apologies. In fact, my car could use a wash, I think."

Patti opened the door. "Good save, Hal. We'll talk, Julia. See you guys around." Waving at their farewells, she finally escaped from the room.

She drove across town, the aroma of the blond brownies strong in the car. She'd have to call Lorraine when she got home, if it wasn't too late, and tell her what she'd heard tonight. Patti lifted the clean hand towel protecting the blond brownies, broke off a corner of one, and popped it into her mouth. They had come out the way Tom loved them, soft and doughy in the center. Dad liked them cooked clean through. "Might as well finish cooking them," was how he put it to her. So, as with most things, father and son didn't see eye to eye.

A few minutes later, Patti stood in the entryway of her brother's apartment building. Balancing the tray of brownies on her right hand, she pressed the buzzer with the left. Tom's voice came through the intercom.

"Declare yourself! Friend or foe?"

"You tell me. It's your darling sister, with baked goods."

"Leave them at the door and go away," he said, but the answering buzzer sounded almost immediately.

Patti pushed through the door to the stairwell. Tom and Kelton were on the fourth floor, and Patti was puffing from the exertion by the time she reached their door, left slightly ajar for her. It was a reminder, more rare for her now and more subtle than her other reminder, that she had had major surgery a while ago. Her stamina seemed to be the last thing to come back. She entered the kitchen. It struck her that this place was the opposite of Lorraine's apartment. Most of the appliances had been rescued from yard sales and flea markets, and there wasn't a stitch of carpeting in the whole place. It would probably look like a bachelor pad to most people, except that it was neat, at least.

"Okay, what smells delicious?" she asked.

Kelton walked into the kitchen. "Eggplant Parmesan and broiled asparagus. You hungry?"

"I am now."

He took the tray from her, giving her a hug as he did so. Tom followed him into the kitchen, so Kelton uncovered the tray and showed him. "One of these days," he said to Tom, "she's going to take you up on it and go away when you tell her to."

Tom came over and hugged Patti. Pulling away, he said, "As long as she leaves the goodies, what's the problem?"

Patti shook her head. "Good thing I know you're kidding."

Kelton set the tray on the counter, and helped himself to one of the brownies. Tom took one as well. "Is this going to be enough? Maybe you should come eat dinner here twice a week, Sis."

It was a pleasant fiction between them all that the two men couldn't bake worth a darn, and were dependent upon Patti for treats. They knew their way around the kitchen, though, and could manage on their own. But she liked bringing something with her, and appreciated the appreciation.

Kelton and Tom seemed to be physical opposites to each other. Kelton was tall, slim, and light-haired, while Tom was a bit shorter and stockier, with jet black hair. Emotionally and mentally, however, they were aligned with each other. They seemed completely compatible.

"So how are you, Patti?" Kelton asked. "You look a lot better than the last time I saw you. The last few times, actually."

"Yes, I'm feeling quite well. I'm beginning to realize now how long I'd been sick. I mean, I was sick all along there, but it had peaks and valleys, and I tried not to let it slow me down, right up until it flattened me. When I woke up in the hospital with this pouch attached to my body, I thought my life was over. Turns out it was just beginning. I don't have to be constantly aware of where bathrooms are when I'm out in public. None of those little ailments I suffered through."

"Great," Kelton said. "You look wonderful, almost pretty enough to make me go straight."

They all laughed. "Don't let our Dad hear you say that," Patti said. "He'd wish the same for our Tom. Anyway, I still have my moments of fear and insecurity about this equipment I wear now, like the other day, at Super Bargain Mart."

"I always have moments of fear and insecurity at Super Bargain Mart," Tom threw in. "It's the naked frenzy of capitalistic glee, the onrush of the teeming masses of bargain hunters..."

"Hush, love," Kelton said, "this isn't about you. Go on Patti." As he said this, he switched on a coffeemaker, another small ritual of these visits.

"Anyway, as I was saying, I was at Super Bargain Mart, and I ran into this woman I knew. I mean, I knew I knew her from somewhere, but I had no clue where. So at first I'm thinking she must be someone I met at the garage."

"Doing my job," Tom said.

"You can have your old job back anytime. Just talk to Dad about it."

"That's unlikely."

"Well, so is my getting this story told, it seems. So I got to talking to this woman, and it turned out she was a nurse at the hospital when I was there. So she asked how I'm doing."

"This story does have an end, doesn't it?" Tom teased.

"I haven't decided yet. Now shut up. She asks me how I'm doing, and I'm trying to say fine, because I am doing fine. I'm not sick anymore, and I can eat what I want to eat. I'm doing fine."

"Okay, so you're fine. We got that part, I think."

"I'm warning you. Let me finish."

"If only."

She shook a fist at him. "So I'm standing there trying to form the word 'fine,' but I felt my eyes fill up with tears, and I couldn't say a word. I was bawling almost, so I finally stammered that I am doing well."

"Not fine?"

Patti smiled. "I do love you brother. I love you so much I may help the authorities find your body later."

"Okay, I'm through talking; finish your story."

"Why thank you. I managed to say something to her, only looking like half a moron, and I staggered away from her, wondering what all that was about."

"And what was it all about?" Kelton asked.

"I've thought about it since, and I have a theory. Most of the time I do really well adjusting to all this. I used to have a chronic illness, and now I don't. In and out of the hospital over the years, and now I won't be- well, hopefully. Some might argue the point, but I find already it's not a bad tradeoff. But I cope better in public when I feel certain no one else knows about it."

"That seems natural," Tom said, more serious for the moment.

"I suppose it does. So here is this nice nurse asking me how I'm doing, and suddenly this irrational fear overcomes me that everyone in the store suddenly knew about it like she did. I tell you, I exited from there in a hurry. If I had been holding something in my hand, they'd have nailed me for shoplifting. So, except for moments when I feel exposed and convinced that everybody must know about it, I'm okay."

"Whenever I feel exposed like that," Tom said, "I look down and zip up."

Patti laughed. "Enough about me, and my occasional massive insecurities. Let's talk about something else."

"How's your dad doing?" Kelton asked.

They all laughed. Patti wasn't even sure what was funny about it. "You guys are awful."

"Sorry," Kelton said, "I couldn't resist. Tom told me how your attempt to smooth the waters went. Have you spoken to your father since that scene?"

"No. I've had a lot going on. Should I be concerned, you think?"

"Someone should," Tom said. "But it won't be me."

"Tom..."

"I'm serious, Sis. He is going to have to meet me halfway next time, or a third of the way, or a quarter of the way..."

"Okay, you've made your point. Hey, are we going to have coffee, like, in this century?"

Tom grinned. "I take it that's a subtle hint to change the subject again." He walked over to the cupboard and pulled out three large mugs. Tom and Kelton had this quirk where they like to pour one large cup each with no refills and, while in their place, Patti went along with it. Tom poured into the huge cups.

"Speaking of parental units," Tom said, "are you looking forward to your time with dear old Mom?"

"Yes, more or less. It's a ways off yet, I imagine, depending on how long- what?" She interrupted herself when she saw Tom's expression.

"Hello?" her brother said. "Next weekend?"

She stared at him. "That's not funny."

"It's not meant to be. I just talked to her today. I assumed you had, too, since she said she was going to call you."

"I've been at a friend's house. Her ex-husband was killed, or killed himself, or who knows what."

"The football coach?" Kelton asked.

"Yes, but let's get back to Mom. Please tell me you're yanking my chain here. I can't go to southern Maine this soon. I want to be closer to my friend, just in case."

"Well, you're in luck, sort of. It is next weekend; you know Mom once she gets an idea into her pea brain."

"Tom, you're going to make me angry. Please fight with just one parent at a time."

"I'm sorry. That was a cheap shot. We're getting along now, really. Anyway, she decided it didn't have to be Kennebunk, or wherever it was when she stayed with you in that camp and split on Dad. She has settled on Bar Harbor. And instead of a week, it boiled down to a long weekend."

"Long weekend? This weekend?"

"Yes. I love seeing you on overload. You make the cutest faces. You really should check your phone messages more often. Here, have your coffee."

Patti took it from him and sat at the table. "Either that or not check them at all. On top of all this, now I have to tell Lorraine about Ned Turner."

Kelton and Tom exchanged a look.

"What?" Patti asked.

"What about Ned Turner?" Tom asked.

"Oh, Lorraine is almost involved with the guy, and I heard tonight he had been in some minor trouble over the football team, you know, the team coached by her ex, who is now dead. Oh my God..." She shook her head, and then glanced at them. "Why did you ask, after giving each other that look?"

"It's just that Kelton used to work for the guy," Tom said.

"That's right," Patti said. "You worked for the pharmacies." She waited for Kelton to give more details. He was just sitting down with his coffee.

"Yes. I worked for him for four years. Worked my way up to peon, second class. That was before I discovered the exciting career of medical sample delivery service. Actually, I still deliver for him sometimes, when he has something he wants transported in a rush."

"How well do you know him?"

"Hell, we're on a first name basis. He calls me Kelly, and I call him Mr. Turner."

"He calls you Kelly?"

"It's close. It's too much of a commitment for him to learn the correct names of his flunkies. He's kind of a jerk a lot of the time. I mean, his heart is in the right place; it just doesn't beat like yours or mine."

"I don't want to hear this about someone my new friend might be dating." Would she be able to pass this along to Lorraine? Patti stared into her cup, but the answer wasn't there.

"I may be exaggerating a bit," Kelton went on, "you know, the rantings of an embittered former employee. But dating might be the wrong word. The last I knew, the guy was quite married to a trophy wife right off a beer commercial. You know, gazoongas out to here, like straight guys love."

"Just great," Patti said. "It gets better and better."

"He might be divorced by now," Kelton offered. "He was never that exclusive anyway. Maybe the trophy got tired of it."

"Okay, stop talking for a while," Patti said, holding a hand up in the air. "I have to try and take all this in. Could you pass me a large brownie, please?"

Tom reached for one and stepped over to give it to her. "Here you go, but save room for dessert, eggplant Parmesan."

"Don't worry, stress makes me hungry." She chewed for a minute, and came to a minor decision. "Can I use your phone? I can't sit on all this until I get home. I need to call Lorraine and unload some of it."

"Of course," Tom said.

Patti walked over to the phone. "Maybe I should check my own messages first, and make sure there aren't any more surprises."

She did, and there weren't. Then she punched in Lorraine's number.

Chapter 7

Lorraine hung the phone up. What Patti told her hadn't surprised her as much as Patti seemed to expect it would. Lorraine remembered her own skepticism at the time when Harold Lynch had resigned as assistant coach, giving health problems as his reason. In her experience, coaches rarely left one job unless they had another one lined up, or got themselves fired. Josh had heard that the man had expected to get the head coaching job upon the death of the previous longtime coach, Hamilton Cameron, only to see Josh ruin his expectations. Lorraine assumed, without asking Josh about it, that Lynch had been strongly asked to resign or face dismissal.

Ned had already mentioned being involved with the football team, so that aspect of Patti's call wasn't alarming either. As to his being married, that wouldn't surprise her too much. At this stage of the game, she figured it was his problem if he was. She'd have to ask him straight out. She had a feeling he was capable of cheating on a wife, but she couldn't picture him lying to her about having one. Not that she'd give him a chance to cheat with her. He intrigued her, but if there was a wife in the picture, that would be an end to it, whatever 'it' was at this point.

Lorraine turned her attention to her pseudo investigation, as she called it in her mind, wondering if she should turn the tape over to the police and let them handle it. On the positive side, she could forget about the whole business and hope they get it right. On the negative side, they might not get it right. Lorraine knew she had a self-interest in the result of the investigation. Part of the reason she didn't want Josh to absorb all the blame was because it would reflect poorly on her. Maybe she should flip a coin: heads, she'd turn over what she knew, and tails, she'd keep pushing forward in her investigation. She smiled at the thought of it, but it wasn't in her to make a decision by chance. Instead, she decided to give herself a week to learn what she could. After that week, she'd turn over what precious little she might have to Sam Ripkin, not that detective who gave her a minor case of the creeps. Then if they settled on Josh as the convenient and main culprit, with the suicide as the ribbon to tie the case up neatly, at least she will have tried.

There were two things she knew about herself, for which she had been endlessly teased by Josh. She thrived on making lists, and she always needed to form plans. Of course, when he gave her a hard time, she gave as good as she got, pointing out that he never entered one of his team's contests without a game plan in place; why didn't he do the same in his day-to-day life? It wasn't the same, he always told her. But Lorraine decided she wouldn't proceed any farther without a plan of some sort. She located a notebook, and turned to the first blank page after some notes she'd written for the new school year. Oh yes, she thought, there's that looming ahead of her too. She began writing:

What I Know

1) *Josh is dead*
She felt stupid writing that, but she had to start somewhere.

2) *It was either an accident, suicide, or murder.*
"Brilliant," she said sarcastically.

3) *At least one of the investigating detectives believes it is suicide. (why?)*
4) *Some of the football players were using steroids.*
This was a bit of a stretch, she realized. She didn't know it was true, but both Josh and the players who gave her the tape suggested it. She left it in.

5) *An assistant coach (Lynch) left the team suddenly two years previously under a cloud of muffled controversy.*
6) *Ned Turner was involved with the team somehow.*
Then she added:
   Note: he owns a chain of pharmacies (hello, steroids?)
It wouldn't do to overlook obvious possibilities, just because she was potentially interested in the guy. She went on.

7) *Someone tried to sell me a notebook supposedly belonging to Josh.*
Why didn't I buy it? she asked herself, just because I felt a burning need to hang up on someone?

8) *Josh thought something might happen to him, to the extent that he recorded that tape for me.*

9) *Something did happen to him.*

Another brilliant deduction, she thought. It was getting a bit harder to take this list seriously. She read what she had written and muttered, "I don't know much, do I?" With a small burst of optimism that she'd need the space to write down further knowledge, she skipped a page and wrote at the top:

What I Think I Know (and why)

1)   *Josh didn't kill himself. (he wouldn't)*
Not too convincing, but there it was.

2)   *The steroid problem didn't start with his reign as coach, and he tried to stop it. (his tape must be true, I hope)*
3)   *More than one player has had to seek treatment for side effects of steroid use.*
She looked at the lonely looking entries and wrote facetiously:

4)   *I know more than I think I do. (I hope!)*
This is ridiculous, she thought, but she pressed on. She skipped another page and wrote at the top:

What I Don't Know
She suppressed an urge to write "Everything."

1)   *How Josh died.*
2)   *How deeply he was involved in the team's steroid use.*
3)   *Who else was involved (supplier?)*
4)   *How long it has been going on.*
5)   *Why the assistant coach resigned.*
6)   *Whether Ned Turner is involved.*
7)   *How much Josh knew. (notebook?)*

Lorraine began to realize she could keep writing all night listing what she didn't know. She skipped to the next page and wrote at the top:
Plan of Action.
She underlined it twice. This was more like it; just writing the words made her feel better.

1)   *Search in the house for anything pertinent Josh left around.*
2)   *Talk to Harold Lynch.*

*3)	Talk to some of the players.*
*4)	Buy that darn notebook if I get the chance again.*
*5)	Try to find out more about Ned Turner and/or get to know him better.*
A little self-serving, that one. Oh well, all in a day's work.

*6)	Kick butt for a week or so looking into this, and then meekly Give It Up.*
She read her action plan again. Pretty skimpy. Maybe two or three days
will be enough after all. Under number 6, she crossed out the word "meekly."
Might as well be realistic about this. The action plan wasn't as neatly laid out
as one of her lesson plans, but it was a start. And speaking of starting, she
went for the phone and punched in the number for Josh's mother.

"Katherine, this is Lorraine," she said, when the soft-spoken woman had
picked up and said hello. "I'm sorry it has taken a while for me to return your
call."

"That's all right, dear. I have been having trouble functioning myself since
it happened."

Lorraine doubted that; Katherine oversaw a flea market for the church
auxiliary a week after Josh's father died, but the woman was being polite.

"It was quite a shock," Katherine went on.

"Yes."

"Did your friend pass along the arrangements?"

"Yes," Lorraine replied, "but let me double-check." She found Patti's note
on the counter. "The wake is tomorrow night at 7:00 at the Wakefield's
Funeral Home?"

"Yes, rather a bad pun, isn't it? The funeral will be the next day, at 1:00.
Juniper Cemetery."

"Right. I've got it." The last Lorraine knew, Josh had wanted to be
cremated, but it wasn't her responsibility any more.

"I'm glad you called, dear," Katherine went on. I just spoke to Anthony."
Anthony was Josh's lawyer, who had reluctantly steered them through the
divorce. "We're going to waive a formal reading of the will. The house goes to
you. The money from his life insurance, his retirement assets, all of that, will
be divided three ways for the most part, one-third to you, and a third to a
scholarship he wants to set up at the high school in his name."

"A scholarship?" Lorraine repeated. She decided this wasn't the time to
point out that if Josh was found to be a suicide, the insurance money probably
wouldn't come through, and if he was found culpable for the steroid use, his
name wouldn't be connected to any scholarship. "And the other third? To you,
Katherine?" That seemed natural, even though Katherine was financially

comfortable after her husband's death.

"No, I talked him out of leaving anything to me. Anthony said...that is, um..."

Lorraine took the cordless phone into the dining room and sat down in one of the chairs. The woman was rarely flustered or tongue-tied. "Yes, Katherine?" Then an idea occurred to her. "He left it to his son, didn't he?"

"You know about him?"

"Not really. I've heard rumors, and the subject came up when I spoke to the police." And how much did you know about him, Lorraine wanted to ask. But Katherine saved her the trouble.

"Anthony sprung that on me just before the police asked me, fortunately. I'm afraid they would have found my expression rather comical otherwise. Do you know the boy is in high school, Lorraine?"

"Yes, I gathered that. Do you know who he is?"

"No, it's a blind trust. We can't find out unless the boy or his mother want us to know."

Lorraine thought of the steroid mess, and now this. The local media would have a field day when it all started coming out. There was already a hint of the steroid problem underlying the news reports, Patti had told her. "Katherine? I called for a different reason. I wondered if I might go to the house and look around."

"Of course. It's as good as yours now. The police have been through it already, you know."

"They have?" Even as she asked, Lorraine thought, of course they have.

"Yes, early this morning. It was just a few hours after I went down and identified Josh. They had papers, search warrants and such. As if I would have stopped them."

I might have tried, Lorraine thought. Her former mother-in-law went on. "They tramped through the place pretty thoroughly." The first sign of strong emotion had seeped into her voice.

"Are you okay, Katherine?"

"I'm all right. They just- they have a talent for making you feel like you've done something wrong, that everyone is guilty until proven innocent. I guess to them, everyone is."

"I know. Did they turn the place upside down?"

"Not really. I mean, the house was cluttered already, and it's worse now, but they were pretty respectful that way."

"Did they act like they found anything?"

"I couldn't say for sure. They kept me busy with their eternal questions while it was going on. They took his computer away, but overall they seemed disappointed, and looked at me like it was my fault. They kept asking me if he had a safety deposit box and lord knows what all."

"Oh my God," Lorraine said.

"What's wrong?"

"I'm sorry. I just thought of something I had forgotten all about. Will my keys still work then, Katherine?"

"Yes, of course. You know Josh kept hoping you'd just move back in. He kept nearly everything the same, except for the clutter."

Lorraine tried to tell if there was a mild reproach buried in that answer, but she couldn't hear any.

"Thank you. I'll see you tomorrow night."

"Yes dear. Good night."

Lorraine hung up. When Katherine brought up the police inquiring into a safety deposit box, that had brought to mind a locker Josh used in the boys' gym. It had been his locker when they went to school there themselves, and it had tickled him to reclaim it after all the intervening years. She didn't know what he kept in there, except he had mentioned keeping the originals of his team's playbooks there, but she knew he had kept it locked. She added it to the short list of things she wanted to check into.

Lorraine went to the house first. She strongly suspected that after the police had been there she wouldn't find anything useful. For that reason, as well as because of the memories it would drudge up, she wanted to get it out of the way first. This brought up an interesting question in her mind on the drive over: if she did inherit their old house, would she want to live in it again? She had received a cash settlement with the divorce, in lieu of any share in owning it, so she had not given any thought to living there again. Interesting, she mused, how the universe can shift and cause such an odd, circular path.

She pulled into the driveway and sat in her car for a moment. Then she sighed and got out. Finding the right key, still on her key ring after all this time, she let herself in. Katherine had been kind, Lorraine quickly decided, to describe the house as cluttered. Lorraine's take on it was that it was a mess, compared to when she lived here and kept it up. Still, despite the clutter, mess, whatever, she saw what Katherine referred to: Josh hadn't changed any part of the house in any basic way. The furniture was the same, and in the same places, as were the pictures and other decorations. After Katherine's reminder of why Josh had kept it all as it was, Lorraine felt strange to be standing here taking it in.

She decided to be methodical about this, for what little good she expected to come of it. Methodical, that is, without conducting a full-fledged search. She stood in the doorway of each room, then, and mentally checked her memory for any little hiding place or catchall corner where Josh might have left some scrap of paper or other. That was the point; she didn't even know what it was she was seeking. Josh didn't keep a diary, and he tended to throw away old appointment books. He didn't do e-mail, as far as she knew, and the computer was gone anyway, she reminded herself, when she saw the empty space it had occupied on the desk in the study.

In Josh's desk she did find some newspaper clippings, mostly local ones about him, such as when he was first hired out of Vermont, or those covering the results of big games. There was one column from the Bangor Daily News describing the resignation of the assistant coach, Harold Lynch. The article implied there was more to it than health problems. Funny the police didn't take this, she thought. Then again, they probably had this and more already. Perhaps the newspaper morgue was the first place they went to in these cases.

Lorraine locked the door as she left, and drove to the high school. There were a lot of cars parked along the road. "What now?" was her first thought. Then she saw the football team scrimmaging, with fifty or so onlookers. The team would miss practice the day of the funeral, no doubt, but otherwise, the show must go on. She could picture the interim head coach intoning with gravity, "That's how Coach would want it." As if he knew. Lorraine had lived with Josh all those years, and she didn't pretend to know how he'd have wanted it. She was pretty sure he wouldn't have wanted to die. She thought the tape showed that, at least.

She parked her car and walked towards the gymnasium, the shouts and whistles of the coaches, the hut-hut-hut of the quarterbacks, almost painful to her due to their lifelong connection to Josh. It seemed football had always been a large part of her adult life, and a larger part of Josh's life. Now he was dead and the football went on. She felt very mortal as she entered the gym. The outdoor football noises were replaced by the squeak of sneakers on the waxed floor, and the shouts of a basketball game. It seemed early in the year for that, with school not yet underway. She glanced up. That explained it: faculty, horsing around. One of them yelled to her to come show them how it was done. She waved the offer aside, though she was grateful for its sense of normalcy in a time when all she had been hearing were condolences.

She descended the stairs leading to the locker rooms, the frenetic squeaking of sneakers fading to a dim rumble of steps racing up and down the court. Since it was the boys' locker room, she knocked loudly and called out before pushing through the swinging doors. Only one boy sat on the long bench, fully dressed, thank heavens, she thought. She didn't need to be written up for harming the sensibility of a jock.

"I'm sorry," she said, "I need to check for something in here. Is anyone in the shower?"

The boy shook his head. "No."

Lorraine remembered him. Terry. Terry Clark? No, Clewley. That was it. He was one of Josh's favorites. She recalled the scrimmaging going on outside. "Aren't you on the football team, Terry?"

"No. I mean, not any more. I just quit the team." He got up and walked past her.

Why, she wondered, out of loyalty to Josh? She'd have to catch up with him later. She sensed this wasn't the time to question him about what had been going on with himself and the team.

She found Josh's locker, and was saddened to find it hanging open. It looked forlorn, another indignity thrown upon the head of her dead ex-husband. All that remained inside the locker was a baseball cap on the top shelf, a team jersey hanging on a hook, a pair of cleats, and scattered papers strewn in the bottom. She scooped up the papers: diagrams of plays, a training schedule, nothing of interest to her. She dropped them back inside and reached for the jersey. She held it up to read the name on the back: 'Simoneau.' For no particular reason, tears stung her eyes. This was his uniform from when he played for the school. She draped it over her left arm. His mother would want this, no doubt. She noticed that the baseball cap was one she'd given him, the simple words 'Coach (GOD)' stenciled in gold. She took that as well. Then she closed the locker and left.

During her drive back home, Lorraine wondered why Terry had quit the team. This train of thought led her to the realization that she had followed one of her action steps and already added to the list of things she didn't know. Some investigation. "I need coffee," she said as she pulled into her driveway. She prepared the coffeemaker once she stepped inside the apartment, and set it to brewing. While it bubbled and gurgled, and in a fit of pessimism over her investigative progress, she found a blank tape and her double tape player, and used its high speed dubbing feature to make a copy of Josh's tape. Then she addressed an envelope to Chief of Police Samuel Ripkin and set it on the counter. She'd mail the damn thing out and get it over with. She had probably broken a law for withholding it from the police anyway. Maybe, she thought as she poured out a cup of the fresh coffee, I should just give up and let the police handle it. She picked up the phone to call Patti. Talking to her always cheered her up somehow. The line was busy. "Figures," she said.

Patti was on the phone with Julia Mannix. The first words out of Julia's mouth were, "I'm calling about the car wash. You didn't think we'd let you off the hook once you suggested it, did you?"

"I was hoping." Patti joked.

"Well, abandon all hope. You said you could set it up pretty quickly. Would this weekend be too soon? The long-range forecast looks promising. I assume weekends are better."

"Yes, much better. Saturdays especially. This weekend is doable. I can go down and have the sign put up today. A lot of the business is spur of the moment, but it doesn't hurt to let people know in advance either."

"Are you sure this isn't too much trouble? Listen to me, I wait until you agree to do it before asking if you really want to, but what I mean is-"

"Really," Patti interrupted, "you don't have to explain. I've gotten these things down pat. I can set it up standing on my head. It'll help keep me occupied while I'm waiting to go back to work and school."

"Okay, Patti. I'm glad to hear it. I have two nieces who have already volunteered. They can't resist the urge to be seen scantily dressed in public, I assume. It's a stage they're going through. If they're like their aunt, it will only last fifteen years or so."

"God, I skipped that stage."

"Did you? Good Lord, I owned more bikinis and halter tops than J.C. Penney's, up until my surgery anyway. So you'll let me know the where and when?"

"I can let you know now. The when will be Saturday, from ten to two; it is best to keep it short, I have always found, and the where is at Lewis's R&R, on Crescent near the traffic circle."

"R&R?"

"Yes, repair and reconditioning, though I keep telling Dad that he can't blame the mechanics if they think it stands for rest and relaxation."

"Your father won't mind? It doesn't interfere with business?"

"No. It makes the parking situation a bit worse, but he doesn't mind the place looking even busier than it already is. Plus he goes out and chats with the owners while their cars are being washed. He has picked up a few new customers that way."

"Really? Everybody wins, then. That's great. Unless I hear otherwise, I'll see you on Saturday."

They said goodbye and Patti hung up. It took a few minutes for her to realize she had just scheduled the car wash on the same weekend her mother would be flying in. She picked up the phone's handset to call Julia back, but then she stopped herself. Her mother was flying in Friday, so maybe by Saturday they would need a break from each other. She could ask Tom to spend that time with Mom, and stun two birds with one stone. She'd wanted to arrange for him to see Mom too. It would work. She put the phone back. She could call the garage and ask them to put the banner up, but she decided it was a good excuse to stop by and see how things were going.

It took just a few minutes to drive to the garage. In fact, during the summer she had walked to work almost as many times as she had driven. She parked her purple Neon away from the bay doors and walked over. The guys greeted her with "It's about time you came back to work!" and variations on that theme. Her father came out of the office.

"I hope you're not planning to work today."

"No, Dad. I stopped by for a different reason. I'm going to be supervising a car wash here this Saturday. Don't look at me like that; I said supervising. I was hoping someone could put up that banner we made."

"Sure. Greg can do it. He has been useless to me today anyway. His girlfriend is due this week and he's jumping every time the shop phone rings."

"I bet. Let me know when she goes in to the hospital, Dad, so I can arrange to send her something. Do you remember where the banner is?"

"I remember," he replied. "Don't I have to step over it every time I go in back to get a muffler?" He moved to get it.

Patti grinned. She had offered to move it many times, knowing each time he'd rather have it there to complain about than have it moved to a more convenient spot. "Thank you, Dad."

Patti stood outside and thought about the onrush of events: the surgery, meeting Lorraine, Josh's death, her mother coming to visit. Who'd have thought that she'd come to think of her pre-surgical life, filled with illness as it was, as rather dull by comparison?

Greg interrupted her musing, showing up with the banner and a ladder. Patti held the banner and made small talk about his impending fatherhood while he set the ladder up on the left hand side of the garage. She passed one end of the banner up to him and watched him secure it. She'd have to get the ostomy group's nonprofit ID number, just in case someone asked on Saturday. Other details flitted through her mind. Greg stepped down off the ladder and moved it to the right hand side of the garage. Patti passed the other end of the banner up to him, and he finished the job.

"Thank you, Greg."

She looked up at it. It seemed straight. It read "Car Wash Saturday, 10:00 to 2:00."

At that moment a short burst of a siren jumped Patti. She turned and saw a cruiser pull into the small parking lot. "What now?" she said, her immediate thoughts calling back to Lorraine's troubles. Then the cop took off his sunglasses, and Patti realized it was Robb Turner. He rolled his window down as Patti approached.

"I'm sorry Officer," she said formally, "but this isn't a donut shop."

He grinned. "I've arrested men for less than that."

"Have you? Sounds like a training issue. I'll speak to your father about it." She leaned down closer to his window.

"My, my," he said. "You are hard today. This is my punishment for not calling you, I suppose. I thought about it a lot, believe me. I was on duty when I met you, you see, and I'm not sure how proper it would have been."

"Okay, I admit I haven't heard that one before. Are you on duty right now?"

"Ah, yes."

"Then we're in a bit of a fix, aren't we? What should I do, call you when you're off duty? Commit a crime? Come on, give me some direction here, officer."

"Here's some direction," he said. "Four inches towards you." He leaned forward. The kiss surprised her, not in an unpleasant way, but enough so that she lifted her head to get a better look at him, and bumped her head on the window frame.

"Ow. Kisses aren't supposed to hurt."

"The next one won't."

It didn't. "I think I swallowed my gum," she said.

"Lean closer and I'll get it back for you."

"Cheeky, as my American British Mum would say."

There was a low whistle from the garage. Patti shielded her eyes against the sun to look, and saw Greg grinning at her.

"Hey Greg," she called out, "the heat here wants to know if you want to keep your vehicle inspection license."

Greg raised his hands in mock surrender and went back into the garage.

"Actually, we don't oversee that," Robb said.

"Yes, I know it's the state police, but it got rid of our spectator."

"You know that? Do you work here?"

"Yes. I'm the service manager, and the owner's daughter. See on the sign, Lewis's?"

"What a coincidence."

"What's that supposed to mean? That I'm manager only because I'm his daughter? This from a cop who is also a cop's son?"

"It was a joke," he protested. "Revenge for the donut comment. So you've worked here for a long time, I take it."

"Yes. I started out playing here as a girl. Then at some point, I stopped playing and complaining about being bored, and started working instead."

"I'm impressed."

"You should be. So now are you going to call me?"

"Yes. PJ Lewis, in the book. I remember."

"Good. It's my turn now."

"For what?" he asked.

She leaned into the car and kissed him, longer than the previous two kisses had been. "For that," she said when she pulled away. She held out a hand. "Where's my gum? You promised."

"You caught me by surprise. Give me one more chance."

"No, it's half-digested by now. That was a nice kiss, though. I feel a little bad about the donut comment now."

"Don't. We cops love a good donut joke. In fact, use one the next time you're stopped for speeding; it works great."

"Thanks for the tip. I'll tell all my friends, too."

He looked at her more closely. "You're not really that naive, are you?"

"What do you think?"

"I don't know. I can't remember. It requires further study."

"How romantic. Listen, maybe you'd better go. You're on duty, and my dad is giving us strange looks. You'd think he'd never seen his daughter kiss a cop in uniform."

"Has he?"

"Oh, dozens of times. You're the last one on the force I've kissed. Now I've completed the set."

"Very funny. How did you like kissing my dad, then?" he teased.

She giggled. "Okay, so you saw through that one. Maybe I haven't kissed too many cops in uniform. But I'm developing a taste for it."

"Good. I'll call you in a day or two," he said, "for sure this time."

"Right."

"No, believe me."

"Oh, I do. But I'm naive, you know. Hey, maybe you can swing by here on Saturday." She motioned to the banner. "You can practice your crowd control."

"Sorry, I'm off duty Saturday. But I can stop by and practice something else, like gum retrieval." He waved as he drove off into traffic.

She saw her father watching her. "Might as well get this over with," she muttered, and walked towards the garage. "What?" she asked when she saw his expression.

"I can't believe what I just saw. How long have you known him?"

She was peeved enough at her father not to mention the old high school romance. "Oh, let's see. A couple of days, I guess. Well, a few minutes, real time. He threatened to arrest me if I didn't kiss him. What's a girl to do?"

"That's not funny."

"No? Not even a little? Look at the bright side, Dad. At least I was off duty." She turned and walked to her car before he could respond. She listened for him to call out a parting shot, but nothing came.

"Wow, I got the last word," she muttered as she started her car. "Imagine that." She took a sharp left out of the parking lot, enjoying the look of surprise on the face of the driver she cut off doing it.

"What a weekend I've got looming ahead of me," Patti said on the phone to Lorraine a few hours later.

"Why do you say that, Patti?"

"Oh, I'm obsessing over it, I guess. My mom is flying in on Friday. Who knows how that will play out. I have a long weekend with her. And Robb's going to drop by the car wash. I made a fool out of myself over him today, with Dad watching me, too. I'll look a mess when he sees me; the girls always wet everything down at these things. I'm looking forward to seeing him, but it's so awkward at first, isn't it?"

"My dear girl," Lorraine said after a moment's pause. "I'll tell you what. I'll visit with a mother who loves me enough to fly thousands of miles to see me, and then I'll suffer through some awkward kisses from a handsome young cop, and you can attend an ex-husband's wake and funeral."

Patti's eyes widened. "Lorraine, I'm sorry. They don't compare, do they? It's petty of me to go on about my so-called problems, I know."

"No, Patti, it's me who should apologize. My day didn't go too well, and I'm taking it out on you."

"What happened?"

"Nothing. That's just it. I started checking into this steroid business of Josh's and got nowhere. I think I lost ground. Let's talk about something more pleasant, like plagues or epidemics, or kisses from young cops."

"Well," Patti said, "it just so happens I'm an expert on one of those subjects, so I'll tell you the whole story."

Chapter 8

The following Friday proved to be a day of reckoning for both Patti and Lorraine. The big event was anticipated in Patti's case: the arrival of her mother from England. In Lorraine's case it was unexpected, coming as it did in the shape of a policeman at her door.

It was a light knock that brought her to the door, not at all the peremptory summons of a cop who means business. Lorraine poured her last cup of coffee of the morning and carried it to the door. She figured it was the newspaper carrier collecting for the week. Instead it was Chief of Police Ripkin who stood there.

"Sam," she said, her surprise making her feel a bit slow. "This is unexpected."

"Yes, I should have called. May I come in?"

Lorraine stepped aside. "Of course." Remembering that he had always periodically flirted with her when she had been married to Josh, she asked, "Is this business or pleasure?"

"Business, I'm afraid, except that it is always a pleasure to see you, Lorraine."

"Very smooth, Sam. Can I offer you some coffee? Though I must warn you, this is my last cup, so it might make me irritable to have to give it up. Or I could make more, which would make me less irritable, I think."

"I'm fine, Lorraine, thank you."

"How about orange juice? Can I tempt you with that? Yes?"

At his slight nod, she went to the cupboard and pulled out a small glass. As she found the juice in the refrigerator, she said, "I guess this is a compliment you came yourself on business. Don't you have drones you can send on your errands? Flunkies in uniforms? What good is it working your way up to chief of police if you have to run around doing all your own leg work?"

He took the glass she held out to him. "You sound wound up. Maybe I should take your coffee from you." He sat at the small kitchen table, and she dropped down into the chair opposite him.

"No, it's not the coffee. It's decaf. Though didn't I read there is a trace of caffeine even in decaffeinated coffee? Maybe we make it worse by starving our body of the drug, except for teasing it with such a trace amount. What do you think?"

She watched him stand up and move around the table. His actions seemed disconnected from her, until she felt his hands on her shoulders. She looked straight up at him as he leaned down close to her face. She didn't know what to do with her hands as he kissed her from that odd angle. He moved around beside her, and she stood up and wrapped her arms around him. "Is that a gun, or are you glad to see me?" she joked.

"Actually," he said, "it is a gun. I'm not as young as I used to be."

Lorraine kissed his neck. "Who is?" she said.

After another brief kiss, they sat down. "I've wanted to do that for a long time, Lorraine."

"It wasn't completely unwelcome, Sam, though you picked a crappy week for it. I went to the funeral of the man I used to love, who died God knows how; maybe you can help me there. School starts in a few days, and for the first time in my life, I'm not looking forward to it. Why are you looking at me like that?"

"I've never seen you like this, Lorraine."

"I'm discouraged. I don't discourage easily, so I'm not good at it."

"Then I picked a bad week to be hot for you," he said.

She smiled, and he added, "That's more like it."

She pushed the cup of coffee over to him. "Here, take this. Do you take cream and sugar? I don't have cream, but there's a convenience store down the street. It'll just take a few minutes to run and get some."

"I think you're serious."

"Sure. It'll buy me time. I'm trying to figure out if you're going to kiss me again or arrest me, and which one I'd prefer."

He laughed. But he took the cup and, twisting his body, poured the coffee down the sink.

"That solves that," Lorraine said.

"I'm not here to arrest you," he said.

"But you are here on business," she prodded him.

"Yes, but nothing that dramatic." He downed the rest of his juice. "Sorry, now I'm having a little trouble focusing."

"My kisses do that to men."

"I can't argue with that."

"Why are you here, Sam, if not to arrest me or kiss me? What is the main purpose? Are you going to run me out of town again?"

He sighed. "I always wondered if you'd bring that up."

"Then you do remember."

"Of course. You weren't easy to forget then, any more than you are now. Plus, I was a real jerk; how could I forget? I protected a real piece of crap druggie because I thought I could use him to make a few busts. A week later he skipped town anyway. All I could think about was my next promotion."

"And look where it got you," she teased, "Chief of Police."

"Yes, but not believing your story, or rather choosing to ignore it, I tried to make that the last time I forgot why I had the badge on in the first place. You know, sometime after that I put the word out that I wanted to find you. I thought I could somehow make it up to you, hook you up with some services- God, I don't know what. I just felt like a class one creep."

"Yeah? Well, if I heard you were looking for me back then, and I don't remember whether I did, it probably made me hide all the more. But that's all ancient history now, Sam. That kiss may have wiped any remnants of that day away."

"I wonder what the next kiss will do?" he said.

Lorraine smiled. "Who can say? But I think first you should tell me what brought you here. We ruled out arrest, as I recall."

"They tell me that you have received some sort of communication from Josh."

"How did they know about that, I wonder."

"Then it's true?"

"Sure."

"Lorraine..."

"Don't Lorraine me, I was going to send it to you. "Did 'they' tell you what sort of communication it was?"

He shrugged. "A cassette tape. It was a football player, Lorraine, just so you don't start seeing police conspiracies. One of the players that dropped it off to you gave us a call."

"It's on the counter over there." She pointed.

He twisted around and reached for the envelope.

"See, I addressed it to you and everything. But I got all lethargic and never did anything about mailing it. I've been in a nostalgia-induced coma most of the week, since the wake and the funeral. I had planned to do all sorts of investigating into Josh's death by now, but it slipped away from me. I guess I'm not a very good detective."

"Neither am I," he said bluntly. "But I don't have to be. What I do is manage a department, deflect the politics away from those who report to me.

Now Robert Turner is a good detective, even with his lack of people skills."

"I still don't believe Josh killed himself."

"It's a viable theory."

"He didn't, Sam. Look right at me and tell me you think Josh was capable of doing that."

He sighed. "Look, I don't believe he did," he admitted, "but Turner does. He's good at what he does, so I have to respect his opinion."

"What is his theory based on?"

"I can't discuss that with you."

"Don't give me that. If you weren't willing to discuss it, you should have sent him. He wouldn't have kissed me, at least."

A small smile crept onto his face. "That's true enough."

"I'm sorry," she said. "That was a cheap shot. What did the autopsy reveal?"

He considered his answer. "It was inconclusive."

"Well then..."

"Lorraine, if his theory were based on hard evidence, I couldn't tell you about it anyway. As it is, he has a strong hunch, and circumstantial evidence seems to support it."

"A hunch!"

"I'm not depicting it very well. Turner is from the old school. He works well with evidence and tracking down information, following leads, all which is 98% of a policeman's job. But he has an extra 2% he brings to his job, an intuition built on all his years of experience."

"He didn't strike me as the intuitive type."

"Maybe not about some things. But when it comes to an investigation, he is just that. And I have learned to respect it, because he is so often right." He held up the envelope. "What is on this tape, Lorraine?"

"What, didn't your source tell you that?"

"Lorraine..."

"Okay, I'll be good. Josh talks about a steroid problem on the team, but you probably know about that." He didn't take the bait, so she went on. "He is pretty vague, but he mentions the possibility of something happening to him, and I can just see Turner using it to support his precious cop's intuition about suicide. You can't let it stop there, Sam."

"Come on, Lorraine, you make it sound like we're going to railroad someone to the electric chair. Josh is dead, and that leaves us with two questions. Well, a lot more than that, but two main ones where Josh is concerned. How did he die, and what was his involvement with the problems on the team?"

"The tape won't answer either of those questions conclusively."

"It doesn't have to. It's just one more piece of the puzzle. I can speak for myself and for departmental policy, that we are more interested in finding out the truth than in closing a case for the sake of closing a case. But I can't guarantee the findings will please you, or me, for that matter. And if we can't prove what happened to him conclusively, then the cause of death will be recorded as unknown."

"Thank you for your candor, Sam."

"You're welcome. I mean, I won't pretend that cops aren't biased themselves sometimes at the outset of a case, but their performance is evaluated. If they screw up, it affects their performance ratings. Well, I'll say no more about it. I think I've made my point." He stood up and moved past Lorraine towards the door, caressing her shoulder as he passed her by.

She stood up and followed him to the door. "Thank you for coming yourself, Sam. And for not arresting me," she added. "And even for the kisses."

"Lorraine..." he leaned forward and kissed her forehead. "When this is all behind us, I want to look you up."

"Fair enough," she said, "but watch out if you screw up the investigation. I might run you out of town this time around." She closed the door behind him.

She felt relieved to have turned the tape over to him, but was still uneasy about the direction of the police investigation. Perhaps it was unfair of her to suspect Turner might settle for the simplest explanations, resting all the blame on Josh, and tying it up neatly with a verdict of suicide, but she couldn't shake the feeling. "I have intuition, too," she said to herself.

She wished she had Patti here now to talk to. There was a mixture of innocence and straightforward thinking in the girl to point a body in the right direction. What would Patti suggest she do? Keep asking questions, or let the police go their methodical way?

"Listen to me," Lorraine muttered. It reminded her of a neighbor they had in Vermont, who, he claimed, lived his life around the question, "What would Jesus do?" Invariably, Josh would walk away mumbling something along the line of, "Get up on the cross and take it like a man, that's what." Which always gained him a poke or a sharp word from Lorraine.

Lorraine shook her head. If she didn't watch out, she'd become as wildly imaginative as Patti was. Maybe it was rubbing off on her. She wondered how Patti's weekend with her mother would go, and sent a mental hug her way.

At about this time, Patti was at the Bangor International Airport picking up her mother. As the arrival time came and went, she studied each cluster of passengers as they disembarked. Finally she spotted her, chatting with a fellow passenger, male, of course. Patti would have known her walk even if she hadn't seen her face: still that regal bearing, those long legs she knew how to display- not with short skirts, she told Patti once. Sometimes less is more. Men have imaginations, make them use it, she said. As little as her father had in common with Mom, he liked those legs. On one of the few occasions she had seen him drunk, he had disparaged her mother for leaving him, but then said, "she has legs all the way up to her neck, damn her."

Patti looked to see if her mother looked older than the last time she'd seen her, but if there was a difference, it was minor. Her mom glanced up finally and waved, placing her other hand on the man's arm and saying something. Patti sensed the words were preparatory to launching herself away from his company and into Patti's. He was persistent, though, and stayed with her, looking up to see who was greeting his new companion.

Patti saw a look pass over her mother's face, and knew even before the man spoke that her own age had been misrepresented to him.

"Hello," he said. "Is this her? I say, she seems quite mature enough to stop and have a cup of coffee with us. I'm buying, of course."

Her mother turned to him, once again placing a hand on his arm. "Richard, be a dear and retire gently here. I only let my husband pay for my refreshments, and I need to get reacquainted with my daughter in any case. There's a sweet man."

The man left, defeated under silent protest.

Patti tried to take on a British accent. "I say, he seemed a pretentious ass."

"He was, a bit," her mother admitted. "He had his nose in the air when we first boarded and sat down. I said something to him, and he looked down that long patrician nose of his and said 'quite so' or something. Cold fish. He warmed up a little when I crossed my legs and showed him a little more skin, I can tell you."

"Mom, you're a shameless flirt."

"Yes, I guess I am. I don't like being ignored." They started towards the baggage claim area. "Chad says he almost feels sorry for the moths that get singed when they venture too close to my flame. He says it's like a traffic accident: he can't help but watch. I think he enjoys it. I'd stop in a minute if he made a noise against it."

"You never stopped when Dad asked," Patti said before she could stop herself. She quickly added, "I'm sorry, Mom. That was rude."

"A bit rude, but true, dear. I didn't love your father to distraction, and we had less than nothing in common. Surely you see that now, don't you?"

"Oh yes, mother, or should I say moth-er," she said, stressing the first syllable. Her mother didn't seem to catch the pun, so she added, "You were right to leave him."

Her mom looked over at her. "You're getting harder to read. I don't know if you're serious or not. I admit I could have handled it a lot better. But I was deeply in love, for the first time, I might add. I would have walked off a cliff for Chad, I think."

"Luckily he didn't ask. Would you still?"

"A small one, maybe."

They laughed. "Once I got to know him, though, I knew I wanted him. But I waited until I was sure he wanted me."

"And wrote a best seller."

"Ooh, someone has been whispering in your ear. Shall I guess who? I would have lived in poverty if he had asked sooner. I follow my heart, Patti, but I didn't learn that until I met him. He brought it to life."

"I'm glad, Mom, but it all reflects poorly on Dad. Perhaps we should change the subject." Patti had heard versions of this before, and recalled Tom's bitter comment, that the old money in Chad's family didn't hurt either.

"I'm sorry," her mother said. "There are my bags, the black ones." She pointed.

They moved into position to grab them. "Mother, they're huge. It's just a long weekend."

"I know. But I remember Maine weather. I don't plan to swelter one day and freeze the next. Leave them, dear. You shouldn't be lugging them so soon after surgery, should you?"

"Technically, no, I suppose."

"I've got them. Lead us to the car."

"I can't get over your British accent, Mom."

"Chad claims it was pretentious of me to take it on, but really, I did it for my sanity. The first thousand times I didn't mind being asked if I was American, but it wore thin. Where are you parked?"

Patti pointed to the left. "Over this way. That purple plaything illegally parked with all the other illegally parked vehicles."

"Oh, it's adorable, but will the boot hold these?"

"No, but the trunk will," she teased. "Here." She fished her keys out of her purse and opened the trunk. Her mother tucked the suitcases inside.

"It's a bit of a drive to Bar Harbor," Patti said as she unlocked the doors. "I thought we could stop somewhere on the way and get coffee and whatever."

"That sounds marvelous. I suppose there's not a decent cup of tea to be found anywhere."

"Please mother, don't sound so continental. I'll get confused about who I am."

She started the car and eased into traffic. "Do you know I've never met Chad?"

"Of course you have."

"No, not formally. I mean, of course when I was a kid, in that camp, before you left. And I've spoken to him on the phone since, But otherwise, no. He was off on assignment the times I came over to stay with you. I don't even remember what he looks like, except he was very handsome."

"He still is," her mother said. "Hold on, let me see if I have a recent snapshot." She fished around in her purse. She found a wallet and riffled through a few small pictures in plastic holders. "No, just you and Tom, I'm afraid. And they're rather old, too. I shall have to rectify that when I get back. But of course, everyone over there knows Chad from the telly, so I never have to haul a picture out. And you'll have to come over when he's home. You've never come over for Christmas, have you?"

"No, Dad never allowed it."

"Maybe this year?"

"Maybe."

"Lovely. We'll talk about it some more. So how are things with you? You look robust."

"I'm really good, Mom. I wish I'd had the surgery years ago."

"I'm so glad."

"Um, I've sort of met a guy."

"Wonderful. What is he like?"

"He's a cop. Dad's a bit miffed. I - well, he saw us kissing, and Robb was on duty. I felt like I was sixteen again. It's strange. We went together for a few years back in school, but now it's almost like we're strangers again, in a way."

"Robb Turner," her mom said.

"God, Mom, are you psychic?"

"Don't sound so surprised. Just because I was living across the ocean doesn't mean I wasn't paying attention. Besides, I knew his father. Does he know?"

"I doubt it. There isn't much to know yet. Why?"

"Oh, just that no daughter of mine would be good enough for his son."

"Oh God, Mom, now that you say that, his Dad's disapproval might have played a part in my breaking it off with him the first time around. I had forgotten that."

"Well, it doesn't have to matter now. He could be your Chad, dear. Be careful, love, but follow your heart."

"Dad would want me to follow my head."

"That's true. You have to try to balance the two most of the time. But believe me, there are no real regrets when you listen to your heart. When will you see him again?"

"This Saturday, briefly. I rather absentmindedly arranged to run a car wash for charity at the garage, and he's to meet me there. I've arranged for Tom to drive out and spend some time with you while I'm gone."

"You didn't have to do that, Patti. I am capable of amusing myself for short spurts, you know."

"Don't be difficult, Mom. I figured you'd want to see him, so it seemed expedient. You do want to see him, don't you?"

"Of course. To quiz him about you, if nothing else. Has he met your new bloke?"

"God, no. I mean, yeah, back in school, but not lately."

"How did you meet up again?"

Oh God, Patti thought. She didn't want to go into Lorraine's troubles. "It was an unlikely way to meet," she hedged. "He was on duty, and he fell for my quiet charm."

"I hope he's a nice boy. I read somewhere that policemen are rather high on the list of men that, um, don't treat their women very well."

"I wonder where reporters fall on that list?" Patti opened her mouth to apologize, but her mother laughed.

"Point taken, dear. I'll say no more. If you love him, I'm sure he's okay."

"It's too soon for love, Mom. I'm still dangling him in front of me, wondering what to do with him."

"Maybe some of my blood does course through your veins after all."

"Cut it out. You're scaring me, Mom."

Her mother smiled and rested her back. They were both quiet for a while, and Patti saw her mother's eyes close. She must have had to get up early for the flight, she realized. She let her sleep, if that's what it was.

Twenty minutes later, her mother stirred. "Sorry, I'm terrible company already."

"Please, mother. I'm glad you were able to rest a little."

"Where are we now?"

"I'm not sure. I haven't been paying attention. Not Bar Harbor yet, though." She saw her mother smile. "What?"

"Oh nothing. You were teasing me about my accent earlier, and listening to you makes me realize I shall probably start dropping my 'r's while I'm here."

"You might as well," Patti said. "They are rather useless when winter arrives."

They both laughed. "I don't even know why that's funny," her mom said.

"The best humor is often unexplainable. You just roll with it."

After another, shorter silence, her mother said, "Okay, now for The Question. How is your father doing?"

"Well, he has taken up golf. I know," she added, when she saw her mother's expression. "It surprised me, too. He seems to enjoy it."

"Good. I always thought he needed some hobbies. Maybe he and Chad can play a round someday." She laughed. "It sounds funny just saying it. I do wish he'd remarried, though. Say what you like about me. but I am happy now, and I wish that for him, too."

"I know, Mom. And I don't think poorly of you. I once did, I'll admit. It was easy to blame you. I think the golf is a good sign. It is the first new thing he has taken on, really. It brought him to life, in a way." She sighed. "But I wish he and Tom would get along. It's a big gap in his life, in all our lives."

"They have a lot to overcome," her mother mused.

"It's not that much. Dad needs to get a grip. Homophobia is passé, and inexcusable."

Her mother looked over at her. "Yes, you're right about that part of it. But that's just one layer of their antagonism. Even in the best of times, theirs was an uneasy truce. If you think back, you'll see it. I could see it from across the water, from Tom's letters and phone calls."

"I suppose you're right. Tom's coming out overshadowed it, but they've been fighting since Tom was in high school. Not unusual for a family, I suppose, but it doesn't make it any easier for me, in the middle."

"There's only so much you can do."

"Yes, but I'll keep doing it. All I can."

There was another brief silence. Patti thought of something she'd wanted to ask for a long time. "Mom, where are those paintings?"

"What paintings? Oh, you mean the ones I painted that summer at the camp?"

"Yes. I know you didn't take them with you. I remember looking at them after you left, while I was waiting for Dad to take us home."

"No, I pretty much took just the clothes I had with me. Did you ask your father?"

Patti realized her mother never said his name, just 'your father.' "He doesn't appreciate talking about that summer."

"I bet. I asked him once. He claims he didn't destroy them, but in the same breath he said he doesn't keep them in the house where his children are, like anything I created would have contaminated you two. That was a long time ago; maybe I should ask again. Perhaps he keeps them in that horrid garage."

"No, I'd know if they were there. And it isn't horrid, mother."

"I'm sorry. I never liked that place, or the time you've spent there. Or spend there now, for that matter."

"Yes, you've never kept that a secret."

"You know me, love, always saying what I feel. There is nothing dishonorable about working in a garage, or owning it someday. I guess I pictured Tom taking it over, somehow. He always loved cars, whereas you just sort of fell into working there. I want you to try different things."

"I will. I'm a young puppy still, as Dad keeps reminding me. I started taking classes, didn't I?"

"You're staying with them, then?"

"Yes, I've got the bug. I took two courses over the summer. They were intense, whole classes packed into seven weeks. And of course I got sick near the end of them, but I managed to pass them with a reasonable grade before the emergency surgery came along."

"Have you decided on a major yet?"

"God, no. I've been thrashing around. I've thought about Communication, English, even Drama."

"Drama, really?"

"Yes. Why?"

"I majored in Drama when I started out, but I switched to Art in the end."

"Drama seems like a stretch to me," Patti admitted. "I've never been outgoing. But it would be a challenge, and maybe force me to break out of my shyness. Of course, it may not be very sensible from a career standpoint."

"Yes," her mother agreed, "it's like art that way. But my mother confided to me that the main purpose of college was to expose me to available college men. So she didn't even flinch when I majored in art. Of course, I upset her apple cart when I married a man who hadn't even finished high school. Maybe that's part of the reason I married your father. Funny I haven't thought about that until now. But to get back to you, love, any sort of degree will help you in a lot of jobs. So by all means, major in something that excites you. Of course, there's always the garage."

"Now you're teasing me."

"A bit. But I'm serious about aiming in a direction you can stay interested in. While we're talking about college, I have two things to say to you. Please give them both some thought, as a favor to a mother who loves you dearly."

"Good grief, with a buildup like that, you're worrying me. What are the two things?"

"No, they're good things, really. The first is that I'd like you to take at least one art course. It's egotistical of me, I know, but I'd like to know if I passed any of my modest talent to you."

"Okay, that's no hardship. What's the other one?"

"I want you to consider an idea. What if you went back to school full-time? Chad and I are in a position to help out financially. I'm sure your father would even approve. You are the only subject he and I can talk rationally about. You could work part-time in the garage, if you prefer, and you know how hard it is for me to say that."

"It's an intriguing idea, Mom."

"So you'll think about it?"

"Yes. It's kind of you and Chad." Her mother waved that off. They were quiet again for a while. Patti considered the suggestion. Sometimes she felt like she was missing a lot of the college experience: the extracurricular activities, hanging out on campus without having to rush around, and even the relative luxury of giving her assignments more complete attention. All that could be within her grasp. She knew Dad wouldn't stand in her way. Still, he might be disappointed to have his other child pull away from his business. She snuck a glance at her mother, hoping that getting her away from the garage played no part in her generous offer.

Patti made a small vow to herself. If she took them up on this, which seemed likely in the first glow of thinking it over, she'd keep working at least on Saturdays at the garage, so her father could still feel all right about taking his weekends off. And she could still keep track of the figures to hand over to their bookkeeper. As a final precaution, however, she'd talk to Dad before giving her answer.

She became aware of their surroundings. "I think we're getting closer," she announced. "The Bed & Breakfast is right on the main drag along here. I wrote the name down somewhere, something to do with a sea gull."

"The Artistic Sea Gull?" her mother joked.

"No."

"The Autistic Sea Gull?"

"Mother. It's alliterative, I'm almost sure. Like the Silly Sea Gull, but that's not it."

"The Sullen Sea Gull."

They were getting into it now. Patti said, "no, maybe the Slippery Sea Gull."

"How abut the Sojourning Sea Gull."

"Sullen? Sojourning? Maybe you should have been an English Major, Mom. How about the Sad-eyed Sea Gull?"

"The Slack-jawed Sea Gull."

"The Sleazy Sea Gull."

"No, the Slutty Sea Gull."

"God, Mom, you win. I can't top that one. Can you imagine if that was the name of an inn? Maybe on a Nevada strip or somewhere. People would ask us where we're staying and we'd be vague. "Oh, a homely little place down on the main drag. Do you know it?"

"And they'd be horrified and say, "Surely not the Slutty Sea Gull? I called there and it was all booked up with a 1-900 convention."

Her mother laughed. "I've always loved your imagination, Patti. That sounds just like something you'd see on the telly."

"Mom, stop being so British. Chad is right, it is pretentious. I say there chap, be a love and talk Americanese, okay, so I don't forget you're me Mum?"

"I'll try, but I refuse to drop the 'r's. I'll need them when I fly back home."

"Deal."

They found their bed & breakfast, but got off to a rocky start there. The proprietor wasn't sure what to make of them when they burst out laughing, just after he solemnly welcomed them to the Sleepy Sea Gull.

Patti's mother decided she needed to lay down for a bit. Remembering they had not stopped along the way for coffee after all, Patti found a cafe nearby and sat for a half-hour sipping French Vanilla coffee, and balancing her thoughts between full-time college, Robb's kisses, and wondering how Lorraine was doing. Her friend seemed to be teetering on the brink of what her mother would call a spell of melancholia. She tried to give this and the question of college her full attention, because thinking of Robb made her blush. She had been bold outside the garage, not at all like her. Maybe some of Lorraine's brashness had rubbed off on her, or her mother's boldness. "I could use some of that," Patti said, not realizing she was speaking out loud until a passing waitress reacted. She must have thought Patti was referring to a refill of coffee, and went and fetched the pot.

Chapter 9

A few hours after Patti wondered how her friend was doing, Lorraine was feeling better, in a more positive frame of mind. Giving Sam Ripkin the copy of the cassette tape had been a relief to her, despite how little it held in the way of hard information, and also despite what Detective Turner might make of it. And thinking of the personal side of the visit, it was gratifying that Sam remembered that incident all those years before and regretted his actions. Finally, she admitted to herself that his attraction to her had lifted her spirits again. Attracting Ned Turner hadn't felt like much of a challenge. To distract herself away from romantic speculation, she decided to refer to her action list. "I'm back in the game," she said to herself as she took the notebook in hand and sat down.

After consulting the action list, she picked number three to work on: talking to football players. She decided she would start with an ex-player, Terry Clewley. She knew what part of town he lived in, and so was able to find his family's listing in the phone book. Not wanting to give him a chance to turn down an interview over the phone, Lorraine drove to the house. She thought about what questions she might ask and how she might frame them. In the end, though, she decided to just play it by ear, like any good investigator, she told herself with a smile. Detective Turner wasn't the only one with intuition; as a woman working with teenagers for two decades, she must be dripping with the stuff.

When Terry's mother came to the door, she didn't seem surprised to see Lorraine. She confirmed this by saying, "I've been expecting you, especially after Terry said he spoke to you."

"Well, here I am," Lorraine said.

"Come on in, please. I won't apologize for how the place looks, because it's always a mess. I gave up the battle against the teenage tornadoes ages ago. I just fight dirt now, not clutter."

"I understand. I won't lie and say you should see my place, because I don't have a child, but I do understand."

Lorraine followed the shapely woman into the living room. Curves in all the right places, Josh would have said about her. Lorraine saw sports magazines on the heavily scarred coffee table, and baseball equipment in the corner of the room. "Do you have any other children, then?"

"Yes, another son and a daughter, both also teenagers."

"You have my sympathy."

The woman smiled. "It's not so bad." A nervous look crossed her face then. "It's Lorraine, right?"

Lorraine nodded.

"I'm Maria. You may already know that. This feels awkward to me. I've always wondered what I would say to you. Now it has all left me. This sounds stupid, but I want to assure you that Rachel and Kyle have a different father, okay? It wasn't Josh."

Lorraine felt a little stupid herself, and almost had to physically stop her jaw from dropping. Of course, this is why Terry was highly thought of by Josh, who normally didn't play favorites among his boys. "I see," she managed to say out of her surprise.

"I probably have no right to ask, but it has bothered me. Terry and I didn't have anything to do with your divorce, did we? Josh assured me we didn't, but I worried he was shielding me."

"No, Maria. It had nothing to do with you," Lorraine replied, even though she wasn't sure.

"Good. I mean, it was over years ago between us, almost before it started. But he has maintained contact for Terry's sake. I never asked for money from him, Lorraine. I want you to know that, too. When Terry joined the team, Josh helped him by buying weight equipment for here at home, and he helped out in other small ways-"

"Maria," Lorraine interrupted her. "I appreciate your telling me, but it's a non-issue, believe me." She wondered if Maria knew about her share of the estate. She supposed she did. "If you don't mind a question from me, Maria, how did you meet Josh?"

"It was at a basketball game at UMH. I was a cheerleader. He was refereeing a game. A ball hit me and he asked if I was okay. Then after the game, we talked for a while. He said he had always wanted to date a cheerleader."

"That sounds like him."

"I'm sorry. I knew he was married, but...well, anyway, six months later he was feeling wicked guilty and I was feeling wicked pregnant. He left it up to me what we were to do. I didn't want to make him leave you."

"No?"

"No. To be perfectly honest, by that time, I didn't think he and I were right for each other. He was rather obsessed by his job and by sports in general."

"He was that," Lorraine agreed.

"And I didn't think he really loved me. Oh, he did in a way. But it wouldn't have worked. I would have demanded a full-time father. Anyway, a while later he got that coaching job in Vermont, and then I met Carl. It worked out. I'm sorry, that was a dumb thing to say."

"No, Maria. It really did work out. Did you have much contact over the years, then?"

"Very little. Carl didn't allow it. That sounds bad. He didn't forbid contact, but he made it clear that he was going to be Terry's father. I was surprised when you guys moved back here. Carl had just died."

"I'm sorry."

"Thank you. It was lung cancer. I always told him those cigarettes would kill him. Sometimes I hate being right." She wiped at her eyes and attempted a smile. "I'm sorry. And now Josh."

"Yes." Lorraine wondered if she should go to hug Maria. She stayed where she was.

"Josh offered to help after Carl died, but Carl left us in good shape. Now that lawyer has called and said that Josh left Terry some money. That was kind of him. College might have been tight, with the schools he has had his eye on. But it'll be much easier now."

"I'm glad," Lorraine said. And she found she was. "Maria, is Terry here? I had a couple of questions for him, about the team, actually."

"Yes. He's in his room, listening to what passes for music nowadays. I pine for the relative innocence of the Beatles. I'll get him." She left the room.

Lorraine took a few deep breaths. "Now I can finally add something to the list of things I do know," she said to herself. "That's a good thing." Standing there looking at the school pictures on the wall, Lorraine decided to be blunt with Terry, and invite him to be the same. Chances are the police told him not to talk, so what did she have to lose?

"Hi," Terry said from the doorway, pausing before stepping through.

"Hi again. How are you doing?"

"Fine, I guess. Mom says you know."

"Yes. I didn't ten minutes ago, but I do now."

He laughed. "Mom was so sure you already knew. I tried to tell her you didn't, but I figured she'd spill it."

"I'm glad she did. Please don't tell her I didn't know, Terry. I don't want her to feel bad about it."

"I won't tell her."

Lorraine didn't see much of Josh in the boy. He seemed to favor his mother in looks. Dark complexion, jet-black hair. "Terry, I'd like to ask you a few questions if I may. If you don't know, please just say so, don't give me gossip, please. And if you think it's none of my business, just tell me. Okay?"

"Sure."

"Don't just say that. Here is a test. How's your love life, Terry?"

He smiled. "That's none of your business, Coach."

"Good. Terry, have you ever used steroids?"

"No. I might've been a starter if I did."

Lorraine heard a touch of bitterness behind the observation. "If that's true, why didn't you?"

He thought about it. "A few reasons. They're not safe. Mom read stuff about it. There was a player a year or two ago who got sick. Plus Coach told me not to."

"Josh?"

"Yes."

"Terry, this is where I don't want to hear gossip. Have other players on the team used steroids?" There was a pause, until Lorraine almost regretted advising against gossip. Wasn't gossip usually true, she asked herself?

"Yes, some were. I didn't witness it, ma'am, and they didn't talk openly about it, but it was obvious. They talked in code that was pretty easy to see through."

"What kind of code?"

"Well, they'd talk about stacking some jazz. Pretty transparent. One guy called it Red Kryptonite."

"That's from Superman, isn't it?"

"Yeah. I guess he was referring to it having unpredictable side effects."

"So they knew the risk of taking them?"

"In a way. They had heard about the guy who got sick too. They called him Mr. X. One guy said, 'Can't take too much jazz, or I'll turn out like Mr. X.' But they kept taking them even after someone got scared and stopped providing it to them. They got the stuff on their own. I think that's why they developed problems. No one there to regulate it. They figured it wouldn't happen to them, though. "

"That's the way it is with the young," Lorraine mused, almost to herself. "Then you get to my age, Terry, and you worry about everything happening to you."

"Yes ma'am."

Lorraine grinned. "Sorry, we adults aren't supposed to warn you about what it's like to get older. We don't want to spoil the fun of discovering it for yourself."

"I'll try to forget what you said," he teased.

"You're a teenager; I'm sure you'll manage it nicely," she shot back, both of them smiling now. "Seriously, I have just a couple more questions. If you don't want to answer, remember, just don't. I don't want to put you in a spot where you have to lie or humor me."

"It don't matter. The truth will come out soon enough. The lawyers for the guys' parents will see to that."

"The whole truth, or just part of it?"

He shrugged.

"See, that's what I'm worried about, Terry. I'm going to be totally honest with you, here. Maybe it makes you suspicious when an adult says that."

"A little," he said, smiling again.

"I don't blame you. You have the right to doubt my motivation. I loved Josh for a lot of years, so naturally I am biased in his favor, but here goes. You said someone stopped the flow of steroids; who was that? Who was providing it?"

"I don't know, ma'am. Really, I don't," Terry added. "You said you don't want guesses or rumor."

Lorraine sighed. "No, I don't. But I reserve the right to ask you for gossip later."

"And I reserve the right not to tell you," he said.

"Fair enough, Terry. Listen. More truth, as I see it. I think Josh made some serious mistakes after he took over the team. Mostly I think he ignored the steroid use. Well, ignored is the wrong word. He didn't pursue it aggressively enough. Maybe for what he felt were honest reasons, and maybe not. That's hard for me to admit, Terry. But I also don't think he killed himself, and I don't believe he was as responsible as others were for the problem. I don't want to see him take all the blame, just because he isn't here to defend himself. That's as plain as I can state it. I don't want to cover up his mistakes or his role in it, either. You said a few minutes ago that you thought the whole truth would come out. That's all I want, Terry. Not part of the truth, enough to nail Josh and no one else, but all of it."

He didn't seem to know what to say to that.

She sighed again. "I'm sorry. I said I had a couple more questions and then I blathered on. But it's important that you know one thing. I wouldn't be asking questions if I believed everything will come out naturally. I hate to say this in front of a teenager who should be taught to trust authority, but the police aren't perfect. They are people, and people make mistakes, or even-" She shook her head. "Listen to me. There I go again. Okay, questions, as promised. Have they been conducting drug tests, Terry?"

"Yeah, Coach Cameron started them, but they're a joke."

"How so?"

"They weren't as random as they were supposed to be. A few of the guys knew about when they would come up. And they were lax. I could have brought in cat piss- sorry, ma'am. But they were sort of set up on the honor system."

"I figured as much." She remembered something on Josh's tape about the tests. She'd have to listen to it again. "Okay, Terry, last question. Let me preface it by telling you that I'm not the least bit interested in punishing players. I'm interested in the people who arranged and provided the steroids, or who allowed its use by looking the other way. But I'd like to talk to a few players, if they'll talk to me. I can figure out a few of them by comparing the active roster of last year's team to this year's. That would give me the names of the ones who are sick right now. But you could save me a lot of time by giving me their names. Will you do it?"

He thought about it for several seconds. "I can give you the names of the three guys who are sick. But they won't talk to you, except maybe Damon."

"Damon Vachon?" She asked. He nodded. "Why do you think Damon will talk to me?"

"Just a hunch. He wouldn't let his mom talk to the lawyers the other parents brought in."

"I see. Who are the other two players, though, so I can try at least?"

"Earl Bethune and Kip Thompson."

"Thank you. I hate to ask, but are you sure you can't give me a name or two of players who have been using them who haven't developed symptoms?"

"No. It wouldn't do you any good anyway. They're running scared. They're not talking to anyone, not the police or each other, anymore. One of the co-captains made threats to anyone who breaks the veil of silence, as he called it. He heard that expression on television. The three that got sick, well, these guys figure they experimented too much and got what they deserved."

"I see. Well, I won't ask you to break the veil of silence either, then. What about the police?"

"What about them?"

She smiled. "Did they ask you for names? You don't have to tell me what you answered, but I'm curious about how hard they're pushing."

"They asked. And they know we're not talking. They tried to work a few of us against the others. You know, those of us who weren't using the stuff, but I'm pretty sure they came up empty."

Lorraine knew there must be more questions she could ask, but she couldn't think of any. "Thank you, Terry. Really. Listen, if you ever want to talk about Josh, or ask any questions, anything at all, please let me know. I mean it. I have no bad feelings about it."

"I might do that," he said. "I mean, Dad was my real father, is how I look at it. But I think about Coach sometimes too. I might take you up on it sometime."

"Fair enough. Thank you for your honesty, Terry. I'll leave you alone now. You take care, now."

"I always do that," he said, "for Mom's sake." He looked at his watch. "The game will be on the radio soon."

"There's a game already?"

"It's just an exhibition, but it's against Bucksport. We like beating them more than our regular season opponents."

"Oh yeah, the rivalry. Bye Terry."

She left, and hunted down a pay phone. The third one she ran across had a phone book. "It would have been just as quick to drive home," she muttered as she approached the phone. Of the three players, she was only able to reach Damon Vachon's mother. Damon was being treated at the local hospital, the woman told Lorraine, and she went on to say that it was okay with her if Lorraine visited him. No one else wanted to, it seemed, she added. He was in Room 310.

Lorraine stopped into the hospital gift shop and bought a small flower arrangement. She knew the hospital pretty well from her ostomy visits, so a few moments later she was outside room 310. She entered to find him sitting up in bed with no visitors, watching baseball. He muted the sound when he saw her.

"Hi, Coach Simoneau."

"Hi Damon. I hope I'm not bothering you."

He seemed a little nervous to Lorraine, but he said, "Nah. I'm just watching the Red Sox bounce balls off the Green Monster."

"May I sit down for a minute?"

"Sure. I'm really sorry about Coach. I know he's your ex now, but..."

"Thank you, Damon. I still hardly believe it."

"Tell me about it."

"How are you doing, Damon?"

"Not bad, considering. I'm going home in a day or two, if things go my way. I may still have some long-term problems, I guess."

"I hope not, Damon."

"Thank you."

"How are your parents taking it?"

"They read me the riot act, for sure. It scared the hell out of them. On top of that, Dad was laid off a while back. He'll get back in there next month, I guess, but in the meantime, no health benefits. They joked about it, and told me not to worry, but I'm not a little kid. I hate being a burden to them. Plus they're worried about the possible long-term problems. They don't talk about it in front of me, but I know. I feel helpless."

"I understand. Things will work out. Would your parents allow me to do some fund raising at school, do you think? It is done all the time."

"Well, actually, a friend of the family has already approached the principal. Given the possible scandal ready to erupt, he and the superintendent won't allow it anywhere inside the school."

"That's ridiculous!"

"I wasn't surprised. They don't want to show any sympathy, because they figure we're going to hire a lawyer and sue them any day now."

"Are you?"

"No. A few people have been whispering in Mom's ear about it, but this is my own damn fault. I couldn't lie and say I was misled or coerced into any of it. Mom and Dad agree."

"Other parents have lawyers, I've heard."

"I've heard that too, Coach, but they're not me. I couldn't do it. I'd have to drag all the coaches through the mud, and it probably wouldn't even touch anyone who made money from all of it."

"Who might that be?"

"I haven't a clue. We never knew where the jazz came from. Or the money to pay for a lot of it. We used to kid that the stuff dropped out of the sky and into our lockers. I mean, a couple of the guys knew a little more, but they kept their yaps shut about it. I didn't want to know. That could have been dangerous."

As if taking the drugs weren't dangerous, Lorraine thought, but he said he'd already gotten the riot act from his parents. "Damon, is Josh to blame for all this?"

"No. We knew what we were doing. Guys were doing it before Coach got here."

"I don't mean it that way. Did he find out about it and try to stop it?"

119

"He must have found out, because he lectured us against it. He didn't approve of it, he told us."

"But?" Lorraine asked, hearing a but in the way the sentence trailed off.

"It's just, I think he disapproved of it, but we were winning and using when he got here, and I got the feeling he didn't want to rock the boat too much."

Lorraine felt her last hopes of Josh coming out of this with his reputation intact fade away. Perhaps if it hadn't been his old school, where everyone else and himself held such high hopes, perhaps then he would have ripped the cancer out of the team, even if it cost them a couple of winning seasons. But he apparently didn't have it in him to try. Lorraine buried her sadness over the thought. Time enough to lament his fall from grace later.

"Damon, how do you think Josh died?"

"I assume it was an accident of some kind? Why?"

"The police didn't suggest anything different to you?"

"They didn't say squat about that to us. To me, anyway. They asked about his mood, and what we saw and heard that day, but they didn't tell us nothing. It was an accident, wasn't it?"

"They think it might have been suicide," Lorraine said.

"No way. Coach would never throw in the towel. He couldn't have."

"Maybe he was murdered," Lorraine said, just to see his reaction. His eyes widened.

"By who?"

"I don't know. By whomever was supplying the jazz, maybe. Josh was making noises about stopping the supply, even if he didn't do anything about it."

He shook his head. "You're just yanking my chain, aren't you?"

Unsure whether she was or not, she replied, "Sort of."

"I thought so." There was a brief silence, and then he roused himself. "I wish I could be at the game. Ma'am, I've heard they might pull the plug on the season. Have you heard anything?"

"No, not yet."

"I sure hope they don't. I'd feel even worse about all of it. Responsible, you know?"

"Yes, but you have to focus on getting better, Damon. Don't take too big a chunk of the world on your shoulders right now."

"That's what I've been telling him." A woman said this from the doorway. A young boy moved around her and walked to the bed, giving Damon a subdued high five.

"Brother," Damon said.

"Yo. How are you?"

"I've been worse, just not lately," Damon said, grinning, apparently a regular exchange between them.

The woman stepped forward with her hand held out. "You must be Lorraine. I'm Sarah."

"Hi Sarah."

"You were married to the coach."

"Yes, up until a couple of years ago, yes."

"I don't mean to be nasty, and I'm sorry about his death, but shouldn't he have done something about this?"

"Mom..." Damon cautioned from the bed.

"It's okay, Damon," Lorraine said. "Sarah, I was married to Josh for a lot of years, and he spent them all coaching. In all those years I would have sworn he never would have allowed his boys to put themselves at risk. I don't know what to believe anymore, but I'm trying to figure it out."

"Ask the police," Sarah said, her voice rising in intensity. "They seem pretty sure he allowed the players to use those drugs, provided them even, maybe."

From the bed Damon said, "Mom, I told you it wasn't his fault."

"I know what you told me, Damon, but I need to have someone to blame! It's all right to blame yourself a little, but somebody who knew they were putting you all at risk needs to pay. Am I wrong?" she added, looking at Lorraine.

"No, others are to blame. Josh might be one of them, but I don't think it stops with him. I'm worried he may take the fall, since he's conveniently dead, but I'm not trying to claim he had no part of it." She reached down and dug around in her purse. She pulled out her checkbook and a pen. Sarah watched her write out the check, but didn't react until Lorraine tore the check off.

"You don't have to do that. I just had to rip somebody."

"Well, someone has to start doing something. Damon told me what the principal said. I think it was pretty shabby. I'm going to arrange a collection outside the school. It's normal in situations like this," she added before Damon's mother could object. "In the meantime..." she passed the check to Sarah.

"Five hundred dollars; I can't accept this."

"You just did," Lorraine joked. "Now I'll leave you folks to yourselves. Take care of yourself, Damon."

Lorraine left in the middle of a further mild objection to the check, touching Sarah's shoulder as she passed by. "Don't be silly. And try not to worry."

Lorraine left the hospital and found her car in the parking lot. She would write another check for Damon's family after soliciting donations from others.

She drove to the high school stadium, counting on it being a home game. It was. She parked and paid the reduced admission fee, idly wondering if she could raise a sentiment among parents to have proceeds from the game benefit the Vachons. But should she separate them from the parents with the lawyers? She wasn't sure. Nothing seemed simple about this business.

The grandstands were fairly full, for an exhibition game, but she easily found a seat. She scanned the sidelines for Julian McLain, who had been named interim coach for the season. What a thankless job that would prove to be, Lorraine thought. In an interview with the local news, he had seemed to be uninterested in keeping the job beyond that season, which was probably just as well. The man who prowled the sidelines when all the scandal broke out would not stand much chance of enduring as coach, even if he was found to be blameless. Lorraine figured it wouldn't do any good to talk to him. Why should he open up to her, when he was perhaps as anxious as anyone to see the bulk of the blame settle on Josh's lifeless shoulders?

Sitting there staring at the sky, Lorraine realized two things almost simultaneously. She was too distracted to sit through a football game, and she was very hungry. She left her seat and descended underneath the grandstand to the concession area. She purchased a couple of hot dogs and a diet soda, and stepped over to the condiment table. She spooned some raw onions onto each and added some mustard, passing on the ketchup. As she stepped away from the table to allow another customer access, she noticed a familiar figure in the shadows, smoking a cigar. He was a big man, and shared a smile with everyone who walked past, whether they acknowledged him or not. He noticed Lorraine looking at him.

"Good game so far," he said. "Pretty intense, for a preseason game. But then again, it's Bucksport."

"Yes. I just got here, and realized I skipped lunch. I'm sorry. I know you..."

He held up the cigar. "I'm not easy to forget, with my big gut and my see-gars. Not many that still smoke these. I got chased down here by a nicotine Nazi up in the stands. It has gotten so you can't even smoke outdoors."

Lorraine didn't bother to point out there was no smoking allowed down here, whereas it was technically allowed up in the stands. "You're Coach Harold Lynch," she said instead, as her memory kicked in finally with a name.

"Yes, well, I don't get called 'coach' much anymore, except during little league season. You're Josh's wife, aren't you?"

"Ex-wife," she corrected. He looked confused for a moment, as if wondering whether Josh's death somehow had changed her marital status, so she added, "We were divorced a while back."

"Oh, I didn't hear. I'm sorry to hear that. I'm sorry to hear about the other thing, too."

The death thing? she wanted to ask, but she held it back. It would probably be lost on him anyhow. "Could I ask you a couple of questions, Harold?"

"Only if you call me Paunch. Don't worry about keeping a straight face when you say it. It has been my nickname forever, even before I was this big. The kids on the team always razzed me about it, but that was okay. I was always the funny guy, and Coach Cameron was the serious one."

"You didn't develop that relationship with Josh, did you?"

"No, we didn't work together long enough. Probably wouldn't have anyway. We were like oil and water, cat and dog, you know what I mean?"

No, give me a few more cliché metaphors, she thought. She found herself not liking the guy, and she wasn't sure why. Loyalty to Josh, maybe? "Paunch, was this steroid business going on while you were still an assistant coach?"

"You know about that?"

She let her silence answer the question. Watching him consider the question, she could read his eyes as he wondered how much, if anything, he should say. Finally he shrugged. "Sure, it's pretty common knowledge, ain't it? Cam and I, Coach Cameron, that is, had suspected it for a while. Cam was getting on, though, and he didn't want to watch it blow up at the end of his watch. I don't blame him, really. I might have done the same in his place. He retired pronto, I think, so he wouldn't have to face it. Then he croaked- I mean, he died. I guess retirement does kill sometimes. When they interviewed me for the head coach job, I hinted to them that they would do themselves a favor by keeping someone on who was familiar with all the problems. But they didn't want to hear about problems, I guess. They heard Simoneau promising the sun and moon and a state championship, and they went belly up for him. No offense, lady." He puffed on his cigar before continuing.

"So Josh came on board and I tried to tell him how it was. He said he'd check into it, period, end of report. I got the message; I was just an assistant. So I waited a while, and then I brought it up again. He said he wasn't sure what to believe, but that he didn't want to disrupt the team. I told him it would be even worse to let the problem take root, if it hadn't already. We won the regional title that year, but we lost to Winslow in the state game. A damn good team they were. Come the spring, I brought it up yet again. Still he was dragging his heels, so I told him if he does nothing about it, I was gone. He

123

talked for a while, and I realized he was telling me how much the team would miss me, so I quit. First time I ever quit anything in my life, but I wasn't about to stick around to watch everything go to hell in a bushel basket. I said it was for health reasons. I could hardly give the real reason. I washed my hands of the whole business."

"So you left the team just because he wouldn't do anything about the problem?"

"Well, I'll admit I was always second guessing him anyway. I mean, me wanting the head coach job and not getting along with him made it inevitable. But ignoring the problem, especially when one of our players got sick, that launched me out of there quicker."

"A player got sick because of the steroids back then?"

"You didn't hear me say it."

"You can't deny saying what I heard you say, Paunch."

"I just did. You gonna eat both those dogs?"

"I was planning to," she said, surprised at his bluntness.

"They look good. I've got to get me a couple of them. Are we done?"

Apparently, she thought. "Yes. Thanks for talking to me."

"No problem. Talk is cheap." He laughed at his own wit as he walked over to the concession stand.

"So are hot dogs," Lorraine said under her breath. She walked up the ramp leading to the seating, taking a bite of a hot dog as she did so. She stood in the opening, watching the game and eating. She wondered if Paunch was telling the whole truth. He had admitted that he had wanted the head coaching job. The most natural thing for him to do now might be to unload some of his blame onto Josh. On the other hand, Lorraine was nervous about giving Josh too much credit just because she wanted him to be less guilty. Somewhere in between the versions she had pieced together rested the truth, but where?

Lorraine ate the second hot dog. The scoreboard read 14 to 6, in favor of the home team, and it looked like they were getting ready to score again. If the steroid problem was as deep as she suspected, they might not get to play out the season, or be minus a lot of their players. What a mess. She walked towards the exit, drinking the soda. A roar erupted from the crowd over her head. She threw the cup, still half-full of ice, into a trash can. Enjoy this win, she said to herself as she walked out, the next one might be quite a while in coming.

When Lorraine arrived home, she found her action plan and glanced over it. There didn't seem to be much left to attempt. She hadn't heard any more about buying that notebook, if it existed at all. It had turned out, not surprisingly when she thought about it, that she hadn't learned a lot from asking questions, lacking as she did any authority to do so. She smiled when she saw the notation on getting to know Ned better. Although it was possible his drugstores were involved in the trafficking of the steroids, what were the chances she could learn anything about it from him? Still, she decided to give him a call. She had to admit she found him attractive, even as she was wary of getting involved with him. But she wasn't seventeen years old, and was unlikely to fall for him, so as she sat with her hand on the phone, she said, "Heck, I'll date him just for practice and anything I might learn from him about the team."

She punched in the number Patti had written down from her messages on the machine. She got Ned's secretary, who told her he was unavailable for the long Labor Day weekend. When Lorraine left her name, however, the woman asked her to please hold on for a moment. Lorraine listened to Vivaldi for thirty seconds until the secretary came back on.

"I'm sorry for the delay. I have just paged Mr. Turner, and as soon as he calls in, I'll put it through to you. Could I have the number where you can be reached right now?"

Lorraine gave her the number. Hanging up, she marveled that her name carried so much apparent weight with Ned. It was worth the call just to find that out. Five minutes later, her phone rang.

"It's about time," she said when she picked it up, but it was Patti.

"Lorraine, what's wrong?"

Lorraine laughed. "Not much. I'm waiting for a return call from Mr. Ned Turner, and I was preparing to bust his chops."

"That would probably do him good. It might be too little, too late, though."

"I think you're right, but it will be fun to try. How is the weekend with your mother going?"

"Lorraine, it has been lovely so far, much better than I expected. She's laying down for a while. For the first time since she left, all those years ago, I feel like we've made a real connection. I'm not feeling bitter or petty about what she did."

"I think I know why," Lorraine said.

"Please don't tell me it's because of Robb. I've had boyfriends before this."

"I wouldn't dream of giving a mere man credit, sweetie. It's you. I think your perspective has changed since undergoing that piece of surgery. You've grown, girl. Give yourself some credit."

"If that's true, I can thank you, too."

"Well, I'll let you do that. Hey, I should hang up in case Ned calls.

Anything else?"

"One more thing. I don't know if you've heard. I've arranged to oversee a car wash at my father's shop, to benefit some needy self-help group. A local ostomy chapter or something like that," she joked.

"Oh, I've heard of them. I'll swing by. I'll even try to convince Ned to bring his fancy car over. What's a few more dollars after that thousand dollar check?"

"Great. I hope I will see you there."

"Is Robb going to be there?"

"I think he'll stop by."

"I bet he will. I meant to thank you properly for going to that executive meeting for me."

"Oh, you're welcome. Funny how things work out. If I hadn't gone to that meeting, I wouldn't have volunteered to do the car wash, and I wouldn't have been at my father's garage when Robb drove by. I'll see you tomorrow then, probably."

"You got it. Bye."

Lorraine hung up, and the phone rang almost immediately. More cautious this time, she picked it up and said just "Hello?"

"First you call me and then you tie up the phone," Ned said, causing Lorraine to wish she'd answered the phone the same way she had when it was Patti.

"Sorry, pal. My days of pining over the phone waiting for a guy to return my call ended years ago, if they ever existed in the first place. How are you doing?"

"Not wonderful. It seems like a good day for problems. At least most of them are the sort of problems that go away if you throw enough money at them. I'm supposed to be going to Atlantic City for the weekend, too. Hey, what's this I hear about you following the cops around and asking all kinds of questions?"

"I thought you were in pharmaceuticals, not law enforcement," she shot back.

"I have friends in low places. It's just that it doesn't look great, since your ex-husband- well, it looks like you're trying to get him off the hook."

"I'm just trying to make sure no one sticks him on the hook unless he deserves to be there."

"That's fair enough," he conceded. "I'm just giving you a hard time."

This reminded Lorraine that she had planned to do just that to him. "Hey, I've been meaning to ask, are you related to Detective Turner, by any chance?"

"Not noticeably. I mean our great grandparents might have swapped dogs and made us distant cousins, but we never sat down and figured it out. Why?"

"Just wondering if he is your friend in a low place."

Ned chuckled. "He'd love to hear that. But a shrewd businessman never divulges his sources of information."

And a shrewd woman never gets involved with a man with something to hide, Lorraine was tempted to say. But it might not be a fair remark to make. Instead she tried to back into the steroid question. "Listen, you're a football booster, do you think they are going to cancel the season?"

"I've heard that rumor. That would be a damn shame. I think we can ride it out: fire a coach or two, expel a few students. All of them have hired lawyers anyway, so you know they're looking out for themselves."

"Not everyone has a lawyer on retainer," Lorraine said, taking a shot in the dark. She waited for an angry remark, but he proved he could surprise her by laughing.

"Ouch, that hurt. I suppose it's true. I would do the same in their place. But canceling the season would just drag the recovery process out."

"Aren't you interested in punishing the people who are responsible for providing the steroids?"

He paused. "That's a police matter. Besides, and I hesitate to say it, but that could lead to your ex-husband, and he's out of anyone's reach now."

He was blunt, she'd give him credit for that. She thought for a moment, and decided she could be blunt, too. "I guess I'm just concerned that others may be beyond reach if the police miss a step, or want to miss a step."

He whistled. "A conspiracy, eh? That's not too original. I can't buy it, Lorraine. It's too easy. I understand your wanting to protect Josh's reputation, but in the real world, people who look guilty usually are guilty. We should change the subject, shouldn't we?"

"Yes, we should, Ned. Let me ask one more question, not quite on the same subject, but I've wondered about this. Why are you so interested in the football team? I mean, a lot of high school teams have booster clubs, but the sort of attention that seems to be lavished upon them here is usually reserved for college teams. What's the payoff for you, collectively, I mean?"

"First of all, Lorraine, please don't believe everything you've heard about the boosters. A lot of it has been said in malice. No substance to it at all."

Lorraine felt this was a strong denial, since she had heard practically nothing about the boosters.

"Having a quality football team," he continued, "pays off for the kids, the school and the community. It's a source of pride for the community, one more reason to move here. The college scouts recruit the kids, and offer scholarships. I played high school football for four years and never had a whiff of a scholarship. We've changed all that."

"Okay, okay, Ned, don't send me the brochure, I got the picture. That sounds feasible, actually."

"It should. Even when I'm full of crap, I have a knack of sounding feasible. But listen, we're talking about everything except the important stuff. Are you going to go out to dinner with me next week?"

"Next week, is that the earliest you can fit me in?"

"Well, I think I mentioned I'm going to Atlantic City this weekend. I don't think you're ready for that. Separate rooms?"

"No, you were right the first time. How about Monday or Tuesday, then?"

"Monday works for me. Pick you up at 6:30?"

"Okay, it's a date. I feel a little strange just using that word. Oh yeah, one more question I've been meaning to ask. Are you married? I have sources in low places, too."

"Technically, yes. We're separated, though, and our divorce lawyers are doing the dance of death. You know what that's like. Marriage number two, down the tubes. If I'd known you four years ago, you probably would have warned me about marrying a twenty-two year old so soon after my first divorce."

"Or else I'd have warned her," Lorraine said.

"Oh, don't weep for her. She'll make out all right. As long as I am generous, we will part the best of friends, she assures me."

"Really? Give me her number. I'll get a reference from her before I go out with you."

"I know better than that, Lorraine. Until Monday, then."

"Yes, Monday." They said goodbye and hung up. Lorraine kept a hand on the phone, wondering what the man was really like. Sometimes he seemed clever and sympathetic, while other times she was convinced he was a rogue. She felt a burst of empathy for Patti and other young women, all immersed in the dating wars full-time.

Chapter 10

Patti drove back home the next morning to run the car wash, leaving Tom and their mother staring at each other across the breakfast table at Silly's Cafe. Neither of them had appreciated Patti arranging their time together, but Patti couldn't quite let go of her efforts to bring the scattered family closer together. For her own part, the weekend with her mother was going quite well. They had explored the Park Loop Road the afternoon before, stopping like tourists at Thunder Hole. Her mother had made Patti and a few bystanders laugh by announcing that the noise Thunder Hole made sounded like Chad when he couldn't find the shirt he wanted to wear.

When Patti drove into the garage parking lot, she saw that the guys had already moved the cars around to make room for the car wash. The buckets and hoses were ready also. She was impressed by their thoughtfulness before she spotted Julia Mannix, standing near the bay doors talking to one or more of the guys inside. Julia hadn't gone the halter top route, but decked out in shorts and a tank top, she had apparently inspired the men to set up the car wash. Julia waved as Patti found a place to park.

Getting out of her car, Patti saw it was her father Julia was talking to, rather than the mechanics. "Hi Julia. I see you've already got a head start on setting up here."

"Hi Patti. Yes, they've been very helpful. My nieces are off buying some donuts and bagels that your father has generously offered to supply for the chain gang."

"It's the least I can do," Patti's father said.

No, Patti thought, the least you could do is what you've done for past car washes. But she wasn't even tempted to say this. Her father was obviously interested in Julia, and Patti marveled at it.

Twenty minutes later, Patti had assembled a volunteer crew of seven, and the event was underway. Unlike previous car washes, however, she found she was expected to do little more than collect money.

"I can rinse cars," she protested to Julia, but she was waved off.

"You've had major surgery recently," Julia lectured her.

"Oh yeah, I forgot," Patti said, not quite true, obviously, but it had slipped her mind. She only thought about the surgery and her pouch once in a while, a minor miracle in itself. They occasionally let her hose down a vehicle, but mostly she fetched sodas from the vending machine for the workers, talked to the customers as their cars were exuberantly washed, and collected the donations. Several familiar faces from the ostomy chapter stopped by to have their vehicles washed, and Lorraine drove in around noon.

"Did Ned call you yesterday?" Patti asked as they watched the volunteers descend upon Lorraine's car.

"Yes. We appear to have a date on Monday."

"Well, well."

"I know. I hardly believe it myself. I'm not even sure I like the guy. But if nothing else, it will do him good to date someone who isn't in awe of his money. I'm afraid he won't be overpaying for a car wash, though. He's in Atlantic City for the weekend."

"And you didn't go with him?"

"Well, he did ask. I resisted the temptation, slight as it was. I wouldn't be shocked if I found out he was already bringing along a female friend, and only asked me because he knew I'd say no."

"That would be a good reason to say yes," Patti suggested.

"You think like I do, Patti. That would be my only reason to say yes, to see him wriggle out of it or ditch her. He moans about his failed marriage to a much younger woman, but I'd bet you dimes to dollars he is still dating sweet young things. But I don't know. He is sort of a question mark to me, and that's the real reason I'm going on a date with him. I'm a curious broad."

"I've noticed that. Most guys are question marks to me."

"Really, Patti, at your age? I would think they are all exclamation points. That young cop seemed to be."

"He could be," Patti conceded. "He is supposed to stop by here, too."

"Yes, well, good luck with that. I see Julia is really in her element here. I guess I'll go chat with her for a minute, seeing as they are nearly finished with my car. They are fast workers."

"They're operating on a diet of pure sugar."

"That'll do it. It'll catch up to them after they pass forty."

"Do people really live that old?"

"Very funny. I'll call you soon."

Robb turned up at 1:30. He chatted for a moment with the girls preparing to clean his car, and then walked over to Patti.

"You took your time getting here," she said as he approached.

"Actually, I gave it a lot of thought," he said. "I considered coming when your car wash first started. There would have been the advantage of seeing you that much sooner."

"A big advantage I would think."

"I don't deny it. But there is a disadvantage to that also."

"We might have put you to work."

"Exactly. No, I mean, that's not it at all. You guys were much busier earlier, and you were hobnobbing with the customers. My ego wouldn't have allowed me to be virtually ignored."

"I can believe that."

"I thought you'd be able to get your arms around that theory. You see, you are sort of on duty here, like I was the last two times we ran into each other. But you'll be off duty in a bit. I can help you clean up, and then we can go for coffee or something."

"Yeah? I know what going for coffee entails. I have a frame of reference for that. But what is the 'or something,' if I may ask? Could you elaborate?"

"Not really, I was being deliberately vague. I just wanted to leave other options open."

"I bet."

"No, It was completely innocent, just covering my bases."

"Wanting to get to second base with me, is more like it."

"I can see you're in a mood, aren't you? Not that second base isn't a pleasant thought," he added. "I have fond memories of circling the bases with you."

Patti felt herself blush, but she covered it up. "Oh boy, a sports metaphor. They always turn me on."

"Don't you have fond memories too?"

Patti weighed whether she wanted to give a flippant answer or be more serious. She glanced at Robb. He was smiling, just a little, but there was a serious quality to the tension he exhibited.

"Yes, though I'm not sure fond is the exact word for them. It was exciting and muddled and it was all new to me, to both of us, I mean, and exploring it all was a thrilling adventure."

"You make it sound like we were rock climbing."

"Don't make fun of me. It's hard for me to talk about sex. You know what I mean: learning how to make love, exploring the mystery of it, was mostly wonderful."

"But? I definitely heard a 'but' there."

"Well, looking back at it now, I also see how clumsy it all was. It was, I don't know, furtive."

"I agree, but that added to the excitement."

"Maybe. Like I said, it was wonderful. All I'm saying now is that there's a lot to be said for how it- I mean, how it could be this time. Not that I'm assuming- oh never mind."

"That sounds hopeful. So we've established that sex is good? Is that the thrust of this conversation? So to speak?"

"You're impossible."

"What? I'm just agreeing with you."

"Your choice of words was rather suggestive."

"Sorry, it just slipped out."

It struck Patti that he was still being suggestive in his choice of words, that he was about to follow it up with a further comment, but they saw Julia coming their way.

"It looks like they are finished with your car. It is time to pony up." Patti held out her hand.

"How much?"

"It's a donation. You need to decide that for yourself."

He pulled out his wallet and took out a five-dollar bill. "Is that good?"

"Almost," she said.

He took out another five, and she nodded. "That's very generous, kind sir. Are you sure you have enough money left for coffee, or something?" He said the last two words along with her, and they both laughed.

Julia listened to this exchange, wiping some suds from her cheek. "Things are slowing down here, Patti. Why don't you take off and let me close up and clean up here? Your dad has offered to help, and I think you might have better things to do." Julia smiled and raised her eyebrows before turning on her heel and going back to where the others were washing Robb's car.

"Well, that was fairly transparent," Patti said.

"Sounded like good advice to me."

"Or something," Patti added.

Robb shook his head, smiling slightly. A few minutes later, Julia returned and tossed a set of keys to Robb. "Your chariot is now clean," she announced. "I saw you paid the boss. Now please take her off our hands."

"My pleasure. Thank you."

"No problem." Julia turned to Patti. "Are you leaving in his car, then? We'd still like to wash yours." She glanced at Robb. "Were you really in uniform and on duty when you two kissed out here?"

"I can see Dad has been talking to you," Patti said, blushing.

"Almost constantly," Julia answered.

"I was on a donut break," Robb said.

"You're making it worse, buster," Patti said, handing Robb's donation to Julia. "Now kiss me or shut up, please."

"Tough choice." Robb bent down slightly and took Patti's face in his hands.

"You'll scandalize your father," Julia observed.

"God, I hope so," Patti said when the kiss was finished. "Come on," she said to Robb, "I just had this idea. Let's take your car, shall we?"

They climbed in. Robb started the engine and ran the wipers briefly before shifting into drive. "So it's coffee, is it?"

"Or something. Let's go to my place. I have both there. Go left here."

They didn't say much on the way to Patti's apartment, beyond her giving him directions. She realized she was feeling nervous about this. To help obscure the feeling, she forced herself to say, "You know, I believe my dad likes Julia a lot."

"You think so?"

"It's rather obvious. And she seems interested in him."

"Is that good?"

"I hope so. It's just that he hasn't shown much interest in women lately. He has never found one to replace Mom, even though he won't admit it. He has some emotional baggage, but I suppose Julia can take care of herself."

"That's the impression I got," Robb agreed.

"It's right there," Patti directed him into the driveway. He pulled in and shifted into park, but left the engine idling.

"You know, we can still go get coffee somewhere, and forget the 'or something.' If you're, I don't know, uncertain."

She put a hand on his knee. "Thanks. I think I needed to hear you say that. But let's go on up. I make totally awesome coffee. And my 'or something' isn't bad either, if all reports are accurate."

They got out of his car, and she led him to the porch on the front of the apartment building. She climbed the stairs and heard his footsteps behind her. She tried to remember what shape her place was in. It wasn't a mess, she knew, but she'd be mortified if she had left some underwear or even stockings laying around. After letting them in, she glanced anxiously around, and was gratified to see she had not left any dainties in plain sight.

She moved to the kitchen counter and pulled the coffee maker towards her. "Could you get the coffee? It's in the blue canister in front of you."

"Your place is nicer than mine," Robb said as he brought the coffee over to her. "Neater, too."

"You were always a bit of a slob," she said, grateful for the familiarity of this small talk.

"I'm better now," he protested. He motioned out into the living room. "Just not this neat."

Patti didn't answer. She was remembering what her mother had said about how she should follow her heart. But she wondered if her heart was running a close second to other parts of her anatomy. She blushed, and hoped Robb didn't notice. She thought about the pouch she wore on her body since the surgery. It wasn't even nighttime, no chance he wouldn't see it. What was she thinking? Even in the dark, unless she managed to keep most of her clothes on, he'd find out about it. Of course, even if she told him, it might be a shock to him when he encountered it. Patti thought about undressing in front of him and blushed some more.

Patti set up the coffee maker while these thoughts fell into place. As she poured water into the base, she saw his eyes on her. "What?"

"You didn't even hear what I just said, did you?"

"No, I didn't. I'm sorry."

"You're blushing like crazy. What are you thinking about?"

She snapped the cover of the coffee maker closed and walked over to the doorway to the living room, where he stood. "I'm just not sure I'm ready for this."

"You're not ready for coffee?"

"You know what I mean. The 'or something.' "

"Why aren't you ready?"

"It's hard to take it apart and analyze it," she fibbed, knowing exactly why, but feeling too shy to talk about it for the moment.

"It is? Well let me try."

"Robb, I'm serious."

"I can see that." He stepped behind her, placing his hands on her shoulders, and kissed the back of her neck. "Don't you like me?"

"Oh god, use a western word."

"What?"

She smiled, feeling his hand on her cheek. "Dad said that years ago, when I asked him if he still cared for Mom. 'God, use a western word,' he said. He got it from a Zane Gray book I bought for him. I never forgot it."

He kissed under her right ear. "Okay, that makes it sound like a western word would be even stronger than 'like.' So what's the problem? Is it that time of the month?"

"Robb!" She felt herself blush again.

"Don't Robb me. I had two sisters near the same age. They talked about periods more than paleontologists do. Besides, you won't give me any clues. You're leaving me out here groping in the dark for the answer to the riddle."

"Groping is right. What's your left hand up to?"

"Just trying to get to second base."

"That's not second base, that's third base. The right one is second base."

"This one? Are you sure?"

She spun around and wrapped her arms around his shoulders. "Yes, I'm sure. At least, if your hands were under my clothes it would be second base."

He slid his hands under her t-shirt.

She felt his hands on her back, and then they moved around to the front.

"Okay," he said, "where are the blasted hooks in this thing?"

"It's a sports bra, silly. There are no hooks. They're the latest rage."

"Great. It took me years to learn how to unhook those things. Another skill obsolete."

"Sorry. There, wasn't that easy?"

He lifted up on the t-shirt. She raised her arms, and he pulled it off her, taking the bra with it. He dropped them on the floor and kissed her neck. Then he dropped slowly to one knee.

"You better not be praying or proposing down there," she said. "Ooh, what was that? Do it again."

"Do what again?"

"That nibble thing you had going there."

"One nipple thing, coming up."

"Nibble, I said, and you know it. Ah, that's it."

He moved his head slightly. "I don't want this other one to get lonely."

"Third base," she muttered.

A moment later, he pulled his head back, and then kissed just above her belly button. "What's this humongous scar?"

"Oh God."

"What?"

"That's part of the reason why I'm not sure about this. Most of the reason, actually. Stand up here and hold me, so I can tell you without you looking at it or at me."

He stood up and held her close.

"I had surgery a while ago. Major surgery, actually."

He kissed her neck. "I can tell. Hey, if it's too soon after surgery, just say so. I'm not 16 any more. I won't whine about not finishing what we start."

"That's not it. The surgery was an ileostomy."

"Oh."

"You know what that is?"

"Sure."

Every one of her nerve endings tried to measure if he pulled away from her, even a little, but she detected nothing. "How do you know?"

"My Aunt Barbara had that done. Cancer."

"Great. Now whenever you close your eyes you'll picture your Auntie Barbara."

"Well, she's not a bad looking woman, now that you mention it- ow! What did you pinch me with, lobster claws?"

"Yes, I keep a set in my pocket for impertinent remarks like that."

"I was kidding. She was my great aunt, and she had to be seventy when she had the surgery done."

"I'm not sure I like that any better," Patti said.

"I can see there is only one avenue to forgiveness open to me."

"The nibble thing?"

"That's right."

He knelt down again, and in a moment Patti took hold of his head, tilted her head back and sighed. "You've learned some tricks since high school."

"No kidding. It was pretty much lunge and groan back then."

"Well, I hope there will be a fair amount of that going on in a minute or two," she said, blushing again despite her bold words.

"Now you're talking, Patti."

She felt his hands slide under the waistband of her denim skirt. She reached down and felt for one of his hands. "Robb, can I keep the skirt on?"

"What?"

"I'm sorry. I'm feeling shy. Not in general, but because of the surgery, the...result. Close your eyes."

"Patti..."

"No, please. Humor me. Just close your eyes for a few seconds, We can work around this."

"We don't have to do this now, Patti, if you're too nervous about it."

"On the contrary, pal, my body tells me we do have to do it now. I'm nervous but not too nervous. Be a good boy and close your eyes."

He obliged her, and Patti leaned down and lifted the hem of her skirt. Reaching up under the skirt, she tugged on the bottom of her panties and pulled them down. Robb opened his eyes in time to see her throw them behind the couch.

"I see your throwing arm is still in good form," he commented.

"You'll find other parts of my body are right where you left them, too."

"Are they? I just hope I can find them. It has been a long time."

"You're filling me with confidence."

He kissed her, lifting her skirt a few inches at a time until his hands were on her bare bottom.

"You found that okay, at least. Hold on, I'm falling behind."

"Oh, I'll hold on," he said. But he lifted his arms as she yanked up on his t-shirt.

"You've been working out since I knew you," she said as they combined to pull off the shirt.

"A little," he said, He threw the t-shirt behind the couch. "Now I can remind you where to look for your undies."

She undid his belt and then his pants. She knelt and pulled them and his underwear down. "Whoa, be careful where you point that thing, officer."

"I aim to please, ma'am."

"Very funny, sir. Do you want to look for a bedroom? I've got one around here somewhere."

He motioned with his head towards the couch. "What's wrong with right here? And let's take this silly skirt off. That bag doohickey won't bother me in the least."

"I- it won't be in the way, but I need to keep it on. I'm sorry."

"I don't like women apologizing when we're about to make love. It's a bad omen."

"Does it happen often?" she asked, and saw him smile. She bent down just a little, and raised the hem of her skirt. "See, easy access."

He helped her move over to the couch and lower herself onto it, following along with her.

"This is where the aiming to please comes in, I believe," she said, willing herself to give as good as she got and not subside into emotion just yet.

"Thanks for the stage direction. I am rusty." He reached between them. "There, I believe it's all coming back to me."

"Jeepers," she said.

"Jeepers? Use a western word, Patti. So what do I do now? Lunge and moan, you said?" A moment later, he said, "I bet the coffee is ready."

"No it isn't."

"I can smell it. "

"Don't stop doing that, or I'll kill you."

"Really. Here I am trying to be tender and loving, and you're threatening me with violence."

"Oh."

"Oh what?"

She didn't answer.

"This is all about rhythm, you know."

"God, I don't remember you talking this much. Oh that's-" She shifted slightly.

"That's what? Finish your sentences."

"You're one to talk about finishing," she shot back.

The phone rang, cutting off his response. Instead he said, "Do you want me to get that?"

"You stay where you are. The machine will get it."

It rang again. "It might be important."

"No, this feels more important. Don't move."

"Not at all?"

"You know what I mean. Keep moving the way you were."

It rang a third time and then stopped. "There," she said. "I told you it would stop."

Suddenly a voice came from the answering machine on the corner table by the lamp. "Patti, Tom just left for home, and I'm going to lay down for a while."

"Who's that?" Robb asked.

"My mother."

"Great."

Her mother had paused, but now went on. "So if you haven't left to come here yet, please don't call. I'll meet you in the lobby for supper at seven. I hope your car wash went well. I love you. Ta."

"Now I'm really out of the mood," Robb said.

"Well, I did offer the bedroom," Patti pointed out. "Besides, I can change that." She reached with her right hand and changed that. "Now this is much better than a silly car wash."

"Don't be so sure, Patti. You don't know what I can do with a soapy wash mitt."

"Oh my."

"Patti?"

"Robb, I swear I'll go into the bedroom and finish without you if you don't stop talking. This is serious business here,"

"Just one more question?"

"Oh, all right. As long as you keep up what you're doing. What are you doing, anyway?"

"That's a trade secret. But you tell me, who the hell is Zane Grey?"

Chapter 11

"Last day," Patti said at the breakfast table. She spread a map of Maine onto the table, folding it so that the right section faced up.

"Don't remind me," her mother replied from behind her newspaper, sounding miserable enough that Patti wanted to hug her.

"As if Mondays aren't bad enough," she said. As she said it, Patti realized neither of them were working full-time right then, but Mondays sucked in general, so she let the comment sit there. "What do you want to do today, Mom?"

"I want to call the airline and reschedule my flight for tomorrow."

"That's sweet," Patti said, "but we've already covered that ground. You have that thing Wednesday, that thing that can't be postponed, that thing you've been looking forward to for months. What was it again?"

"You know very well. You're trying to provoke me. I told you, a few of my friends are being exhibited at this showing, and I need to be at the opening."

"They must be good friends," she teased, "to drag you away from your daughter."

Her mother lowered the newspaper. "Well, actually..."

"What?"

"I didn't want to say. This weekend is about us."

"Mother, you're showing some paintings there too, aren't you?"

"A few. It's a small studio, love, and I know the curator. It's not a big deal."

"It is so a big deal," Patti said. "Do you know how many people in the family have displayed artwork in a studio showing?"

"Two or three?"

"Very funny. You'll have to tell me how it goes."

"Of course I will. Now tell me what we're going to do today."

"We could go to Schoodic Point." It was more of a question than a statement.

Her mother folded up her newspaper. "Show me where it is."

Patti pointed on the map. "Right there. The problem is, what with wending our way along the coast, it will take about an hour to get there."

"An hour? Forget it, love. We don't want to be car-bound that long. We'll have enough of that on the drive back to the airport. It looks like it would be quicker to take a boat over there."

"Yes, but to charter a boat? How expensive would that be?"

"Okay, but roll with the idea. There are plenty of whale watch cruises here."

"Good idea. I saw where one of them guarantees whale sightings."

"I'm not sure I want to go on a boat that guarantees anything. It sounds too organized and predetermined. I'd rather go on one where the unexpected is always possible. Probable, even."

"I see. What do you define as unexpected: a shipwreck, mermaids?"

"Come on, Patti, where's your sense of adventure? All I'm saying is that there are smaller boats available to rent, too. Why settle for being elbow to elbow with the huddled masses, just because the crew can trot out a semi-tame whale on cue?"

"Mom, you're being ridiculous. I can tell you have something on your mind. Just come out with it."

"Okay, I was talking to a boat owner yesterday."

"I knew it!"

"Let me finish. His craft has the intriguing name of Late for Work Again. It's a lovely boat."

"Let me guess; he's a hunk, isn't he?"

"He's cute, in a way. But that's not the point."

"Isn't it? Well, how can we be sure he won't rob us and feed us to the sharks?"

"Patti, really. Sometimes I swear your vivid imagination is a real hindrance. It's not like he skulks up and down the docks, opening his jacket and selling watches and one-way cruise tickets to nowhere. He's a member of the Chamber of Commerce. His wife sells the tickets. You watch too many bad movies."

"Are there any other kind? Okay, you win, mother. Let's go find this paragon of small business."

Patti's mother downed the last of her tea. They left the cafe and walked along the waterfront. Patti noticed they were getting looks from the men they passed. She was about to comment on it when her mother spoke.

"It should be up here, yes, there it is."

Patti saw the boat her mother pointed out. The distinctive dark blue stripes along the guardrail and the name, "Late for Work Again II." She saw an old woman in a lawn chair on the dock, knitting. A little old man leaned against the guardrail and talked to her, motioning with his head towards the boat. Patti turned to her mother. "Okay, you got me, Mom."

"I said he was cute, didn't I?" She waved to the man, just as there was a chirp from her handbag. She reached in and drew out a small cell phone. Unfolding the phone, she started to walk slowly along the dock. Patti heard enough to realize she was talking to Patti's father.

Patti walked over to the woman in the lawn chair. "Are you going out very soon?"

"In five or ten minutes, dear. Are you coming along?"

"Yes, me and my mother over there."

"Is that your mother?" the man asked. "She looks more like your sister."

Patti said, "Mom would appreciate it if you say that again when she is listening."

"No hardship at all," the man said.

Patti turned back to the woman. "I'm Patti."

"I'm Elizabeth," the woman said, "but you can call me Beth."

"That's my Mom's name, too, except she goes by Liz." She read the small sign next to the chair, and paid their fares. She stood aside so as not to block the sign from view of passersby, and glanced around. There were a few others standing nearby, apparently also waiting for the cruise to begin.

A few minutes later, Patti's mother folded the phone and placed it back in her handbag. The old man called out something that sounded like "Let's be off!" and they all followed him. The captain's wife folded the lawn chair, picked up the sign and boarded behind them.

Patti found a seat near the rear of the boat. Her mother came and stood nearby at the railing.

"That was your father."

"So I gathered. How did it go?"

"We had a good chat, the first good one in ages. Who is Julia?"

"She is a new friend of mine. Dad met her at the car wash Saturday."

"Older friend?"

"Yes, older than I am, why?"

"She has made quite an impression on your father. I mean, he only talked about her briefly, but in an odd way, the whole conversation revolved around her."

"Really?"

"Yes. There is something there, for sure, or at least he hopes there is."

The old captain, dressed in a dark blue shirt with insignias and epaulets designed to let tourists know he was a sea captain, came over to the passengers and waited until he had their attention. "Hi, folks, I'm Captain Vic, or just Vic, if you have lingering problems handling authority figures. We're heading out into the open water. With God's grace, we're going to see a whale or two, maybe some seals and dolphins or who knows what all- maybe a Hollywood star with a yacht paid for eight dollars at a time by us in darkened movie theaters. In my younger days, I would have talked your ears off, but the older I get, the more I seem to have to concentrate on keeping us afloat. I hope y'all don't mind that. My lovely wife, Beth, can answer any questions you might have. If she can't answer it, she'll come ask me. If I don't know, then at least you've got a lovely view out here, so maybe answers aren't what you're paying for. The life jackets are along this wall behind me. The bathroom is just below. We have a limited supply of drinks, anything you care to add, Beth?"

The woman shook her head. "No, Vic. Hurry up and show us something memorable out there."

He put on his cap. "Any questions before we hit the high seas?"

A thirtyish man in jean shorts and a tie-dyed t-shirt asked, "What happened to "Late for Work Again I?"

"Vic don't like to talk about that," Beth said. "If we don't see anything interesting out there," she motioned to the open water, "maybe I can tell you that story."

"In that case, we'll see plenty that's interesting," Vic promised. He retreated to the cabin.

As the boat pulled out into the bay, Patti joined her mother at the railing. "Look how the water is sparkling," her mother said.

"It's beautiful," Patti agreed.

Her mother dug around in her purse and pulled out a small camera. "It's not much of a camera," she said, "but it might capture just enough of it so I can paint it later."

Patti watched her mother take a couple of pictures, and then replace the camera into her purse, still staring at the water. "That'll be tough for me, to capture that glittering on canvas. It'll be fun trying." She turned to face Patti. "Your father approves of your going back to school full-time."

Relief almost made Patti's knees weak, "I'm glad," she said after a moment. "I would have done it anyway, but it's so much better this way."

"Yes. And he liked that you're willing to still work Saturdays. Keeping your hand in it, as he called it. But that's not the best part."

"There's more?"

"Oh, yes. Hang onto your fedora. Your father has spoken to Tom about coming back into the business."

"Mom, how did you manage that?"

"I wish I could take credit. I gather Julia doesn't tolerate intolerance. She...Patti?"

Her eyes blurring, Patti had groped a few steps away from the railing to sit down. Her mother reached into her purse and located a lacy handkerchief.

"Don't be fooled," Patti managed to joke, "these are tears of bitterness because I wasn't responsible for bringing them back together." She took the offered handkerchief.

Her mother sat down next to her. "Well, lust is a wonderful motivator. No, I'll be fair, let's call it the stirring of potential love. I do wish it for him, really. But, Patti, forgive me for being realistic for a moment. This is wonderful, but some men are able to compartmentalize issues like this. They can be against homosexuality, but conveniently overlook it in their own children. He's not cured."

"Yes, I'm sure you're right, Mom. But you don't know what I've been through since Tom left the garage. This is like Peace in the Middle East for me. Tenuous, with pitfalls at every step, but worth celebrating all the same."

"Yes, I don't mean to lessen its significance. It's wonderful, even if I didn't have anything to do with it."

Patti laughed with her mother. Then they stood up together and stepped over to the railing. Patti was vaguely aware of a resemblance between herself and her mother. Mostly, however, she thought about how the various members of her family had never been as close to each other, all told, than they were at this moment.

Lorraine sat at her desk with one hand on the phone and the other under her chin, when the phone came to life and rang. She jumped, and then picked it up to cut it off. "Hello?"

"Hi Lorraine."

"Patti, I think you cost me one of my nine lives, and at my age I can hardly afford it. I was just getting ready to give Ned Turner a call when the darn thing jumped me out of my skin."

"I'm sorry," Patti said. "It sounds like an unpleasant sight. How is the Nedster doing, anyway?"

Lorraine laughed. "The Nedster? I bet he'd just love that nickname. I have to try it out on him."

"Do you still have a date with him tonight?"

"Yes. Actually, though, I was thinking of calling him and canceling out."

"You're having second thoughts, then?"

"And third, and fourth. It's occurring to me that I'm seeing him for the wrong reasons."

"What's that, lust?"

"Are you kidding? Lust is a fine and noble reason for two persons to spend time together."

"Whew," Patti said. "I've been feeling my share of lust lately."

"I've felt a little myself," Lorraine admitted.

"Lorraine!"

"What? You think you're the only one who can kiss cops?"

"Gosh, I thought you didn't like Robb's father."

"Very amusing. If you even suggest such a thing again, I shall have to reevaluate our friendship. No, I have neglected to mention that Sam Ripkin paid me a visit."

"I see."

"Do you? Then you must explain it to me. It turns out he remembers that incident years ago when he was a street cop and I was a-"

"Street person?"

"Yes. He claims it was some kind of a defining moment in his career, if you can believe that."

"Oh, I believe it, but I'm a horrible romantic sometimes. And now he's ready to lay his heart at your feet. It's straight out of a romantic movie."

Lorraine caught herself rolling her eyes. Bless Patti and her imagination. "Except that he's no romantic lead and I'm no femme fatale. But I must admit, I like the idea that the event was an epiphany in his life, if it's true. It makes that part of my life seem, I don't know, less wasted, I guess."

"And even better than that, now you two are hot for each other."

"Patti, really."

"Sorry. I just thought one of us needed to cut through the deeper nuances of your relationship and get at what's important. It's a public service I'm glad to perform."

"I see. Well, there is definitely chemistry between us, I'll give you that. And then there is Ned. The Nedster. He is curious about me, attracted to me, I can almost say with confidence, but I don't feel any emotion behind it, only, I don't know, curiosity maybe. I wonder if he is seeing me for the same reason I'm seeing him: because I'm a challenge and because he wants to get information out of me over this business with Josh."

"God, Lorraine."

"What?"

"Things are a bit of a mess with me right now. I'm not sure how much of what I feel for Robb is love, and how much is a twisted combination of nostalgia and good old fashioned lust. But my love life seems simple and straightforward compared to yours."

"Well, sweetie, wait a few days and everything will change again. That's what love is all about. It's never so messy and complex that it can't get worse. If love were easy and straightforward, everybody would want some."

"Lorraine, I believe you're a philosopher."

"That explains the lousy pay I've been getting."

Patti laughed. "So what are you going to do about the Nedster? Call and cancel?"

Lorraine hesitated, and then sighed. "Oh, I'll go out with him, I suppose. Why should I deprive him of an evening with a femme fatale?"

"Seriously, Lorraine, you seem indecisive tonight. It surprises me."

"I guess Josh's death has upset me even more than I realize. But listen, enough about me and the cheap thriller that has become my life. How is your weekend with your Mom going?"

"Oh, Lorraine, it has been lovely. She is still in her room packing. I think armies have traveled with fewer clothes than what she brought. But I hate to see the weekend come to an end."

"I'm glad to hear it, Patti. I hate to sound like an old busybody, but you've let her know this, haven't you?"

"Are you kidding? I think crying during our last meal together gave her some indication."

"Just checking. I guess I need to get ready for this date, if I'm going. We'll get together soon, okay?"

"Yes. Have fun tonight."

"Fun?" Lorraine mused, "how likely is that?"

"Don't be so negative," Patti commanded. "Goodbye."

"Bye, Patti."

Lorraine took a quick shower and came out of the bathroom into her bedroom wearing a flannel robe and a towel wrapped around her head. She walked into the kitchen, standing trying to decide what she wanted to drink, when she noticed the light on her answering machine blinking. She hadn't checked it when she returned from running errands that morning. Then again, she usually didn't hear the phone when she was in the shower either. She leaned over to check the number of messages. Two.

She pressed play, and the computerized voice she called Ronnie, after the late President Reagan, announced that the call had come in at 9:23 that morning, during her errands. It was a Miss Santana at the local library. "We'll be happy to help raise money for the Vachon family," she said. "One of our part-time girls is very artistic," she went on, though her accent was such that Lorraine thought for a moment she'd said autistic, "and I have her working on a notice to post with the donation can." The woman left a number where she could be reached at home, which Lorraine jotted down. The smooth electronic voice of Ronnie came back on, but rather than saying, "my fellow Americans," it announced another call at 10:22 a.m. There was another beep.

"Hi Coach, this is Damon Vachon," the voice began tentatively.

"What a coincidence," Lorraine muttered, thinking of the first call.

"Coach, I wanted to thank you for giving that check to Mom. And I wanted to say that I-" he paused. "I was the one who called you about that notebook. I found it in Coach's locker. I was looking for something he had offered me but I didn't accept. A hat," he added. "Anyway, I was mad when I made the call. I wanted to try to raise some money for Mom to pay the bills."

"I'll be." Lorraine nervously drummed her fingers on the counter top.

"But I'm giving it to you now, to do what you want with it. I've arranged for it to be left at the school for you. Thank you again, Coach Simoneau."

Lorraine rewound the tape, shaking her head. She'd have to go back and see Damon after she reviewed the notebook. Or would he rather not see her after this admission? She'd give it some thought.

The dinner with Ned was not a success. They were both distracted, Lorraine figured: Ned by heaven knows what, and herself by thoughts of the notebook and what it might contain. They agreed at the outset not to talk about Josh's death, but that only seemed to narrow their options rather than broaden them. Lorraine tried to salvage the evening by asking him to hike with her at Shadow Lake State Park the next day, an annual event for her just before school started.

"My hiking days are behind me, Coach," he said brusquely. Then he added softly, "After tonight, do you really want to spend more time together? I'm sorry. I'm not good company right now. A few walls seem to be closing in on me, and I haven't worked out the solutions I need to yet."

She touched his arm at that moment, surprised by his apology. "Hey, I know about walls shifting around on a person, though with me it was more like the floor falling away underneath me. I don't mean to be pushy, Ned, but I'm not talking about mountain climbing here. This is a pleasant walk along some trails. It's very relaxing. It'll do you good. "

"Maybe it will at that," he said with a sigh. "Thank you for being a little bit pushy.

Back at her apartment, he kissed her cheek when he dropped her off, but neither of them suggested he come inside. "I'm afraid it's not in the cards for us, Nedster," Lorraine muttered as she let herself in. She took off her sweater and hung it up just inside the door. She walked to her bedroom and wasted no time getting her dress off. She wanted to get comfortable and cozy and maybe watch some television before going to bed. She was hanging the dress in the walk-in closet when the phone rang. She stepped over to the extension by the bed. "Hello?"

"Lorraine, this is Ned."

From the background noises, she could tell he was driving. "God, Ned, can't you let me finish getting undressed and settled in before you call?"

"Oh, are you naked, then?"

"I'm too old for phone sex, Ned."

"I'm beginning to think I'm too old for anything else."

"Well, at least pull off the road so you don't kill yourself."

He laughed. "I don't know but that might be the way I'd like to die. But seriously, Lorraine, there is something I didn't tell you tonight. I didn't want to throw a wet blanket over the evening. Not that-" he cut himself off.

"Don't worry, Ned," Lorraine said, "I'm aware the evening wasn't a smashing success."

"It didn't go as well as I hoped," he admitted.

Lorraine laughed. "Thank you for that massive understatement. You've inspired me to add blind optimism to the mix. It'll be better next time."

"It's bound to be," he added, and they laughed together this time.

"What was it you didn't tell me?"

"I've heard that the Vachon boy is back in the hospital. In Portland or Boston this time."

She felt an urge to ask how he knew, but she let it pass. "I thought he was doing better. I just had a message on my machine from him this morning."

"What did he want?"

Lorraine paused. She certainly didn't want to tell him about the notebook, so she settled on half of the truth. "He wanted to thank me for giving his mother a check to help cover their bills. You know, there's a good project for the booster club: raising money for his family. They are the ones who haven't hired a lawyer."

"That's an idea. I can bring it up."

Lorraine didn't think he sounded quite sincere. She set it aside. "So how is

Damon doing, Ned?"

"I'm not privy to that information. He may have taken more pain pills than he should have."

"On purpose?" She could almost see him shrugging on the other end of the line. "That doesn't sound like him," she added.

"It doesn't? I don't know the boy."

"I suppose I don't either," she conceded. "But my impression was that there's no quit in him."

"It's only what I heard. Street gossip, practically."

"I hope so. But thanks for telling me, anyway."

"You're welcome. I should have brought it up earlier tonight. That pact of ours not to talk about the case was rather hair-brained. Whose idea was that?"

"Yours, actually."

"Oh."

"Don't feel bad. I jumped at it. Listen, I'm sitting here in my skivvies."

"Describe them for me."

She laughed. "That's where this conversation started. Good night, Ned."

"We're still on for tomorrow? Shadow Lake?"

"Sure. Why not? I could think of worse people to spend time with." That at least is true, she thought.

"Stop it; you'll turn my head." They both laughed and said their goodbyes before hanging up.

Two hours after speaking to Lorraine on the phone, Patti was driving her mother to the airport. This time they did stop for coffee, but still the trip passed much too quickly for Patti. As they crossed the Penobscot River from Brewer into Bangor, Patti saw her mother watching her. "What?"

Her mother laughed. "You look stricken, like one of us is going to the gallows. We've had a wonderful time, beyond all my expectations, and we'll be together again fairly soon. Christmas at my place, remember?"

"I know. I can't help but feel sad. It's selfish of me to want more. You have your life waiting for you back there."

"Don't make it sound like I'm anxious to leave you, love. If it weren't for the art show and Coronation Street, I'd figure out a way to stay longer."

"Coronation Street?"

"Don't ask. I can't explain it. But listen to you. I'm not the only one with a life waiting for me. You have to get ready to go back to school; you've got Robb waiting breathlessly for your return, a father and brother getting along, for now, at least. So don't make it sound like your life will be empty; I'm not buying it. Oh, speaking of buying it..." She reached into her purse and pulled out a cell phone, not the one she had used before. She set it on the seat next to Patti, dug around in her purse again, and brought out some paperwork.

"This is for you. Tom helped me pick it out Saturday. The first six months are paid for, unless you make more calls than the plan allows. The paperwork there tells you about the plan and the warranty and all that. This is the number."

"Mother, you should have told me you were coming up with a parting gift. I feel wretched."

"Oh, fiddlesticks. This isn't a gift at all. You're going back to school full-time, and I'll feel better about you tripping around campus alone if you have one of these. Besides, your father and I are sharing the cost."

"You and Dad are getting to be pretty thick lately."

"Yes. God knows if it will last. I think your friend Julia might be the linchpin to the whole detente. If it doesn't work out between them, I wonder what state he might rebound to."

"I hope it works out then," Patti said, declining to mention Julia's romantic history as related at that first ostomy meeting. "If it goes back to how it was before, I may have to emigrate to Australia and work on a sheep farm to get away."

Ten minutes later, walking with her mother at the airport, Patti felt something warm on her upper leg. "Oh-oh," she said.

"What's wrong?" her mother asked.

Fortunately, they were near a rest room. Just a minute, Mom." She ducked into the rest room and into an empty stall, grabbing a few paper towels on the way.

"Are you all right?" Her mother had followed her into the rest room.

"Not exactly," Patti said. "It's like that awful joke about the wino with a flask in his pocket. He falls downs and feels something wet, and prays that it's blood.' Well, what I feel isn't blood or booze. Could you wet a couple of paper towels for me?" Patti had wiped up what she could. It wasn't as bad as it could have been. The clamp had worked partially loose from the ostomy pouch, but not completely. She reached into her purse and dug around for a spare. Wiping the end of the pouch, she reclamped it. Wet paper towels appeared under the door of the stall. Patti cleaned herself up further, cleaned the clamp that had come loose, and dropped it into her purse.

"Are you doing okay, love?"

"Yes, Mom. I'm almost done."

"What happened?" I mean..."

"You don't want to know. I'll spare you the details, but when I used the restroom at the cafe where we stopped for coffee, I guess I didn't secure my equipment, shall we say."

"Equipment problems? You make yourself sound like an airplane. If you're all set, then, I'll go back out with my suitcases before someone makes off with them."

"I'm fine. Thank you, Mom."

She heard her mother leave as she straightened herself up. No one else had come into the restroom during all this, for which she was grateful. She joined her mother outside in the hallway. "All set. Luckily, it was minor. I try to carry emergency supplies with me, but I'd need a handbag the size of the Hindenburg to hold everything I'd like to carry. The surgery was a blessing to me, healthwise, but it is quick to punish carelessness."

"It's like love that way, then," her mother said.

"I'm not sure what that means, Mom, but it sounds deep, so I won't question it." By now they were approaching the proper airline desk. "It reminds me of something Dad told Tom after he started working at the garage. He told him there were two times when it was dangerous to use heavy equipment: once when you aren't used to it, and then again when you are too used to it. Here we are."

Patti stood by while her mother checked her luggage in. She came back over to where Patti stood. She reached down for the carry on bag Patti had carried for her, but then stopped herself. "Maybe we should part here and now, rather than waiting around until they board us. I hate long goodbyes."

"Yes, I think I know that about you," Patti said, but she was smiling.

Her mother smiled back. "For the first time in my life, Patti, I feel like you've almost forgiven me."

"I guess I have, Mom. How about that?"

"You don't know what that means to me, love. I don't know if I've come out and said this, but even though I've never regretted what I did, I deeply regret how I did it."

"I know, Mom. You have said it, many times, back when I wasn't ready to hear it. Let's say no more about it. Call me when you're safe and sound back on your estate, ordering your servants around."

"I'll never hear the end of having a maid and a gardener come in once a week, will I?"

"No. Why should you? You go now, before I start crying. I love you, Mom."

"I love you, too. I'll call." After a long hug and a kiss on the cheek, her mother turned and walked towards her gate. She turned and blew a kiss, but otherwise she didn't hesitate. Patti watched as long as her mother was in sight. Then she sighed and walked to the exit and back to her car.

Patti drove into downtown Bangor, back across the Penobscot River into Brewer, and followed Route 1A to Ellsworth. She thought about Robb and listened to an oldies station most of the way home, turning off the radio only when she was entering town. She picked up her new cell phone and dialed Robb's number. It rang four times before the answering machine came on. She waited through his message and the beep.

"Hi there. This is the love of your life, or lust of your life, whatever. You fill in the blank. I wanted to try out my new cell phone, given to me by my mother, who is now winging her way back to London.

"I've been thinking about you on this drive home. I was just thinking about when we dated back in school, neither of us had a car of our own, at first, and now we both have cars, apartments, answering machines, jobs and the whole package. And I was thinking about why we broke up. Oh-oh, you're thinking. But I'm not going to pick a fight. It happened in the summer, right? After our junior year? I saw you with that girl, the same girl you had your arm around in that yearbook picture. I may have overreacted, but you sure acted awful guilty yourself. What was her name? I won't rest until I know, so I can torture you with it. Hey, if you're not alone, turn off the machine and listen to this later. If you are alone, lean in a bit closer." She lowered her voice. "Listen, you were my first lover, you know that, right? What we did on Saturday, I want to do again. I want you, and I pray your father isn't standing there as you listen to this. I had a marvelous time with my mother this weekend. And with you. Call me, okay?" She hung up, still blushing. She'd meant to say even more, but she couldn't bring herself to say the things that popped into her head.

Instead of going home, Patti drove to her father's place. There was an extra car in the driveway, Julia's, no doubt. She found them kneeling in front of the flower bed near the porch. After exchanging greetings, her father said, "Julia is giving me advice about fall bulbs."

"Cool," Patti said, and she meant it, so grateful to Julia for the truce between her father and brother that she swallowed the twinge of hurt his statement might ordinarily have caused her. He had never shown much interest in her own gardening efforts here.

Julia proved quickly, however, that she knew the score. "Judging from his ignorance about what he has planted here," she said to Patti, "I assume you're the one who has done all the work up to now."

"Yes, but I'm glad to give it up. I don't have a green thumb. Something tells me your efforts will be more greatly appreciated than mine were anyway." She started up the steps of the porch. "I stopped by to look at my old yearbooks."

"Your stuff should be in the attic," her father said.

"Thanks." Patti went inside and upstairs. Although her father had made it clear she could move back in at any time, he had turned her old room into a den. Tom had always used the attic room as his bedroom and that was kept more or less the same, so what her father referred to was not the attic itself, but rather the crawl space. Patti went partway up the attic stairs and stopped at a small door in the wall. Since the cellar tended to leak unpredictably, this was the family storage space.

She opened the small door and reached in to the left. She groped and found the small flashlight he kept there. Her father was nothing if not a creature of habit. Patti leaned inside, turned, and sat on the lip of the opening. Then she twisted her body around and pulled her legs inside. There were several boxes just beside her, with her name written on them. The first one she reached for also said "Stuffed animals," so she passed it by. She could picture her father packing these boxes, handling each item and remembering where they came from. She had been miffed when he had packed her room up, seeing it as punishment somehow for her moving out. When she had commented on it, however, he had stated simply, "What I've done I can undo. Meanwhile, I'm getting some use out of the room. I can be as sentimental as the next guy, Patti, but there is nothing sentimental about wasted space."

Patti pulled the next box towards her. It read simply "Books" under her name. This seemed promising. She opened it up. A moment later, she was rifling through the yearbook in question, from her junior year. She quickly found the page she sought. There they were, a boyish Robb with an arm around a blond girl. She was beaming for the camera, while he seemed to be surprised by the picture, as if already anticipating his girlfriend's reaction. His jealous girlfriend, Patti added in her thoughts. She checked the caption. Peggy Robichaud. That's right. Her family owned Robichaud's Furniture. Patti suddenly remembered the cruel jokes about the girl being like a piece of furniture in the back seats of cars, and she felt less inclined to tease Robb about her. She slid the yearbook back into the box and folded the flaps closed. She'd pack them off to her apartment another time, or not; she didn't have much room there.

When she picked up the flashlight again, it shone upon some shapes off in the corner of the crawl space. Though they were covered with a blanket, she realized with a lurch what they were. She got onto her hands and knees and moved closer. She tugged at the blanket. The dust it raised made her feel like sneezing. There were three paintings stretched onto crude frames leaning against the pitched roof, and several rolled up canvases nearby. They were her mother's paintings from all those years before, she was convinced of it.

Patti set the blanket aside and reached for the framed pictures, tilting them so she could shine the flashlight on them. The first two were beach scenes. "No glittering water," she said under her breath. The third framed painting was of Patti herself. She decided she wanted to keep this one. But who would she have to ask, her father, mother, or both? She moved it over closer to the opening.

Patti reached for the rolled up paintings. The first one she unrolled was an unfinished water color of the camp where they stayed. The next one was of Tom, though it looked a bit off to Patti. She moved it closer to the opening, to take advantage of the natural lighting it afforded. Of course, it wasn't Tom, as he was a child when this was painted, and this painting featured an adult. The idea crept into her mind that this must be Chad, and Chad in turn must be Tom's natural father. This explained why she hadn't been shown pictures of Chad. It even explained Tom's repeated and rather cryptic explanation of why he and their mother didn't get along very well: "It's genetic."

Patti pushed most of the paintings back into the corner of the crawl space, except for the one she hoped to keep, and the rolled up canvas of Chad. She struggled over next to the opening and stuck her feet out. Ducking her head, she slid though the small door, pulling the paintings behind her. She put the flashlight back in its spot, closed the door and went downstairs. She left the portrait of herself near the crawl space door, but carried the one of Chad with her.

Her father and Julia were in the kitchen. He was shaking a quart of orange juice when she entered the room. He saw the rolled up canvas, and she thought she could read in his expression what it meant. "Why wasn't I told about this?" She unrolled it enough to show a smiling face, the Tom but not Tom face.

He poured orange juice into two small glasses. "Would you like some?" he asked.

Patti shook her head, and he put the quart back in the refrigerator. "The short answer," he began once that was done, "is that I didn't feel it was my place to tell you. I did enough sniping about Liz without taking the pleasure of being the one to tell you that."

Patti sat down at the kitchen table, setting the canvas down in front of her. "That's a good reason," she said, "but I'm not sure I buy it completely."

"That's up to you," he went on. "I've always wished I didn't know myself. I certainly tried not to let it make a difference with Tom."

"No? Not even when he came out to you last year? Are you sure it didn't make it just a bit easier to push him away from you?" Patti regretted the words once she uttered them, but her father didn't give her time to take them back, even if she wanted to do so.

"I don't blame you for lashing out for being kept in the dark, but you're attacking the wrong person. If I'd told you, you would have questioned my motives for doing it."

"Maybe so, but at least I would have known. Meanwhile, I've barely forgiven Mom for what she did to us twelve years ago, and now I've got this staring me in the face."

He drank his orange juice and set the glass on the counter. "Be careful how much you read into all of this. Someone should have told you, I agree. But otherwise, it doesn't have a lot to do with you. Since the divorce, it has been a matter between Tom, Chad and Liz."

"So it doesn't concern me? I guess you're saying that you're sure I'm your daughter, then?"

"Perhaps I should go," Julia suggested, her orange juice untouched.

"No, you've heard the worst of it. Patti didn't mean that, did you?"

"No, I suppose I didn't."

"You're my daughter, and in every way that counts, Tom is my son. I knew about Chad, almost from the start. Even saying what I have about Liz, she has never lied to me. He showed up in Kennebunkport, ready to commit to something long-term, and she made up her mind fast, like she always does. She called me and asked me to come get you. I refused."

"I didn't know that," Patti said.

"No, well, I've never talked about it, have I? I guess I figured I could keep her from leaving. Finally she sent me a telegram and told me what time she was leaving there, and said that I'd better show up there to pick you up. She said I was a fool if I intended to jeopardize your safety just to try to hang onto her when she didn't want to stay. I was angry at her, but she was right, and I saw that, eventually. I appeared at the appointed time. You were cutting pictures out of a magazine when I got there."

"Why didn't I end up with her? Didn't she want me? Or Tom? He is Chad's son."

Her father smiled. "She wanted both of you, but she resisted the urge to try. She was pretty straightforward about it. She said she knew I would move heaven and earth to keep custody of both of you kids, and she admitted that even though Chad was the better husband for her, I was the better father for you two. Apparently the traits that disqualified me for one role worked to my favor for the other. Chad was always traveling. She didn't mind that; she looked forward to traveling with him, but she readily admitted it wasn't as stable for raising kids. Like me, Chad didn't have a say in the matter."

"You poor men," Julia said. "Twigs blown around in the gusts of wind produced by women. It's an American tragedy."

"And a British one," Patti added. She stood up and picked up the rolled-up canvas. "I can see you're in good hands here, Dad. I'm going now."

"Are you all right?"

"Yes," Julia joined in, "Are you?"

Patti hesitated in the doorway. "I don't know. It's a lot to take in. I need to think about all this for a while. I'll see you. Bye, Julia."

Once in her car, Patti realized she'd forgotten the painting of herself. Another time. She decided to drive to Tom and Kelton's place. It took just a few minutes to get there. Only Kelton's car was in the driveway, and Patti contemplated whether she still wanted to go inside. She really wanted to speak to Tom, and they might even be out somewhere together. As she mulled the choice over, however, Tom's car pulled into the parking space beside her. She saw that Kelton was driving. She turned off her engine and got out. Someone she didn't know rode in the passenger's side with a twelve-pack of beer in his lap. They both climbed out of Tom's Toyota.

"I figured it was Tom who was out."

"No," Kelton said, "my clunker has a noisy fan belt. Patti, this is Jacob. We worked together back at the Pharmacy."

"And I'm still stuck there," the man said. "Nice to meet you, Patti."

"Same here." She thought of Lorraine. "Hey, Jacob, what's it like working for Ned Turner, anyway?"

"It kind of sucks. You kind of have to keep your head low to get through the day without low level abuse. Of course, Turner is keeping his head low himself nowadays, what with that coach's death and his own involvement with the team."

"I see," Patti said. "Did Turner have anything to do with all that?"

Jacob shrugged. "How should I know? But dudes with money like that always have crap to hide. And old Ned baby didn't like it one little bit when the cops beat a path to his door over that business."

"Jacob," Kelton said, "why don't you head upstairs with the brew. I need to talk to Patti for a minute."

Jacob tapped the twelve-pack with his free hand. "Good deal. One of these babies has my name on it." He went inside, and Kelton sighed.

"More than one, I'll wager. But I thought I'd stop him before he started in on government conspiracies and Elvis being still alive and working in a Dubuque supermarket. He's a nice enough guy, but ever since he went back to night school and learned to read, he has believed everything he sees in print."

"Kelton, I believe that's the most uncharitable thing I've ever heard you say about anyone." Patti jumped up and sat on the hood of Tom's car.

"Yes, that was excessive. It's just that I've just seen him cause some grief with his gossip. Never mind him. How did your visit with your mother go?"

Patti raised a hand to her face. "Oh, God."

"What's wrong?"

"Why didn't Tom ever tell me about Chad being his father?"

"Oh. It's true, then."

"What's true?"

"Tom has always figured you already knew about it, but that it was one of those things no one wants to talk about. But recently you said something that made him think you didn't know. So your mother told you this weekend?"

"Oh, no, I found out by accident just a few minutes ago. But I'm sure she has a good reason for not telling me, like Dad, and Tom."

"And me?"

She shook her head. "No, I can't fault you. It should have come from one of them."

He smiled a bitter smile. "Because I'm not family, because I can never be family."

"Kelton, it isn't like that at all. That's unfair."

"Yes, it was. This isn't about me; I'm sorry."

"That's all right. How long have you known?"

"I don't know, nine months, maybe."

"And they've known- God, there's no comparison. One of them should have told me long before this. Who knows, if they had been able to talk about this, maybe they could have discussed other topics rationally, like sexual orientation, that sort of thing. Maybe Tom wouldn't have had to wait so long to come out."

"Why do you suppose they didn't tell you?"

"What?"

"No, really, think about it. Why haven't they told you?"

"Cowardice, I suppose."

"Your father is a lot of things, but he's no coward."

"You're right. He claims he didn't want to seem like another attempt to discredit Mom in my eyes. I'm not sure that's the whole reason."

"Maybe not," Kelton countered, "but even if it's just partly the reason, it's not such a terrible thing. I think it is similar with Tom. He didn't want to take cheap shots at your mother. You got along better with her than he did, after all. Plus, he wasn't sure if you already knew about it. Maybe he was kidding himself, but he wasn't sure. What about your mother?"

"Mom. Well, she's the one who really should have told me, I guess. Maybe she chickened out every time she thought about it."

"You think so? She told your father and Tom about it. Does that sound chicken?"

"What are you getting at, Kelton?"

"She felt she couldn't tell you when you were young. After a while, she assumed your father succumbed to the urge to tell you. She has withstood your father's bitterness and Tom's standoffishness, but she has been absolutely petrified of losing you. Why risk it all by bringing up such a touchy topic if you didn't mention it? In a way, they all kept it from you for the same reason."

"Because they love me and didn't want to hurt me."

"It sounds lame, but it's true. They aren't that great at loving each other, but you have to admit they all love you like crazy." He reached into his jeans pockets and produced a tissue. "Now, me, I would have told you in a heartbeat, because I'm hateful and can't stand you."

She dabbed at her eyes and blew her nose. "Good. I need a little balance in my life. It's stressful being loved so much by everyone."

She slid off the hood of the car and threw her arms over Kelton's shoulders. "Thank you. I feel a lot better."

"I'm glad. Do you want to drop in on our little party?"

"That depends. Are there any really cute straight guys?"

"There's no such thing. Besides, aren't you off the market?"

"I suppose I am for now. I'll go home and unpack and do some laundry. Tell Tom I know now, will you? It's time the family learned to talk about this stuff."

"I'll tell him. Is it my imagination, or have you grown up some over the past few weeks?"

She thought about it. "Maybe I have. Tom and Dad always helped me through my illness, but I've been on my own since the surgery. Thanks, Kelton." She hugged him again and then got into her Neon.

"Take care, Patti. Come over again soon, with or without baked goods." He waved as she pulled out of the driveway.

Chapter 12

Most of the schools in the area opened the next day, but Lorraine's high school opened on Wednesday. On Tuesday morning the staff and administration held meetings, and in the afternoon the teachers reported for last minute instructions and information. The previous year, Lorraine had used the morning to hike in Shadow Lake State Park, and she had arranged to do the same with Ned this year.

She wasn't meeting Ned there until 9:00, and it was 8:15 now, so she decided to stop at the high school on her way and pick up the notebook Damon had said he'd leave for her.

She found a parking space on the street and went in the main entrance. She stepped into the first office on the left. Jayne Chappelle looked up from a file open in front of her. A stack of files rested on the right hand side of her desk. Jayne was the administrative assistant for the principal, but was also working her way into a guidance counselor position.

"Hi Lorraine," she said. "What are you doing here? You're either confused or very dedicated, neither of which will get you far in this school system, I can tell you from personal experience."

Lorraine stepped over to the mail slots. "If you're confused, Jayne, then we're all in trouble. You're the only one who knows what's going on around here. I just stopped by to see if anything was left here for me over the last day or so." She checked her mail slot. A few notices, and a packet of materials for her afternoon workshops, but nothing that looked like it could be a notebook.

"No, just the usual, as you can see," Jayne informed her. "You can check your desk, but I'm pretty sure your office has been locked all along, except when maintenance was in there cleaning."

Lorraine checked her office and, as usual, Jayne was right. There was nothing on or in her desk. She locked up again and walked down the hallway, past classrooms where staff persons were meeting. She realized she could tell by the buzz of conversation that these weren't students in the rooms. She wondered if she could tell what grade were in classrooms just by walking by. She'd have to test it sometime. She left the school through a side entrance and jogged to her car.

Okay, she thought as she started up the car, what if Damon hadn't managed to arrange for her to get the notebook before he ended up sick again? Should she try to talk to him? It could be awkward if others could hear his side of the conversation. And did he really take too many pills on purpose? She felt a sneeze coming on, and opened the glove box. Maps, papers and toiletry items spilled out onto the floor. "Holy Fibber Magee's closet," she said. She grabbed a tissue and blew her nose. She pulled onto the shoulder of the road to scoop the items back into the glovebox, and saw her copy of the cassette tape Josh had made. She couldn't remember why she had wanted to listen to the tape again, but she popped it into the cassette player. After a pause, the tape began.

"Rainey, I can't believe I'm doing this."

His use of her pet name jarred her, just as it had the first time she listened to the tape. He must have felt melancholy or nostalgic to go back to the name he'd discarded when they separated. Of course, if he had killed himself, he must have been a lot more than melancholy. People under the spell of melancholia write poems and sigh deeply.

Lorraine only half-listened to the tape as she drove through town. She caught his reference to the random blood tests being a joke. One of the players had told her that too. Lorraine froze when she heard a name. She rewound the tape a little. "even when I felt sure, I had no idea who was behind the operation or how they did it. Or for that matter, how to prove any of it. The coaches who have been here longer have nothing to say on the subject, except for Paunch. We've argued long and hard over it."

Lorraine tuned the voice out of her mind. She hadn't known the first time she listened to this tape that Paunch and Harold Lynch were the same person. But Paunch resigned a long time ago. Why would Josh be arguing with him recently? The answer began to form when the tape reached the part where Josh mentioned the player who got sick. Player, not players. There were a few sick players now, but when this tape was recorded, back before Paunch quit, back when Josh still called her Rainey, there was only one sick player. And so, if this tape was recorded a couple of years before, it couldn't be held up as supporting evidence for a suicide theory, could it? She drove to the police station.

She asked for Sam at the front desk, but she was ushered in to see Detective Turner instead.

"I'm sure Ripkin would have loved seeing you, Mrs. Simoneau-"

"Ms. Simoneau," Lorraine threw in.

"I'm sorry. One never knows nowadays." He motioned toward a chair near his desk.

He had a talent for rubbing her the wrong way, she realized. It was in her mind to say she had been Ms. Simoneau even during the marriage, but it seemed pointless.

"Anyway," he continued, "he would have wanted to be here, but he is a servant of the townspeople, after all."

Lorraine sat down. The room smelled of tobacco, even though smoking wasn't allowed in public buildings. "I guess I should be grateful that the townspeople can spare you for a few minutes."

"I'm always available to anyone with information that might help me on a case. What have you got?"

"Do you have a transcript of the tape Josh made?"

He seemed wary. "Why?"

"It would be quicker to point out what I'm talking about if we had a hard copy."

He made a vague motion with his arm. "I'm sure we transcribed it, but I don't know if I can lay my hands on it this minute."

"I see. Can I take that to mean you're not going to try?"

"What is this about? Did you remember something on the tape that you'd like to confirm?"

"Not exactly. I listened to it again, and-"

"You have a copy of it?"

"Yes. I made it just after I got it."

"You didn't tell Ripkin that when you gave it to him."

"No, I guess I didn't. Is it that important?"

"Everything is important, or could be. One copy might be of better quality than the other."

In other words, Lorraine thought, you'd rather have all of the copies.

"Did we at least get the original?" Turner asked.

"I'm not sure, I was rather upset at the time."

"Not too upset to make a copy of the tape and start questioning our witnesses," he pointed out.

"That's true enough, though I think the reason I started talking to people is because I was upset, and wanted answers."

"We want answers too, and taxpayers shell out a good sum of money for us to get them. We spent a fair bit of time and effort analyzing that tape, and obviously it would have been time and effort better spent on the original rather than the copy."

"I can understand that. Could I ask a question?"

"You can ask."

"Did you know about the tape right from the start, back when you asked me to hand over any sort of suicide communication?"

"Why do you ask?"

Lorraine shifted her position slightly, feeling irritation creep over her. He obviously was not going to give out any information. She wanted to get away from here, but she had to say what she'd come to say. "Never mind. As I was saying earlier, I listened to the tape again, and a few things jumped out at me."

"Like what?"

Lorraine was irritated at the way he kept asking questions rather than letting her talk, as if trying to maintain control of the conversation. But perhaps that was what they taught you in the police academy. "Josh talks about arguments he had with Paunch, the assistant coach. When I first listened to the tape, I didn't connect Paunch to his real name, Harold Lynch." Lorraine paused, and waited for the question she knew would come.

"So?"

"So then I ran into Paunch at an exhibition game. We started talking. He said he had argued several times with Josh about the team and the steroids."

"What do you know about that?"

"More than you want me to, I expect, but less than I'd like to know. The point is, he was talking past tense. He argued with Josh while he was still assistant coach, so that means the tape is a couple of years old."

"That's your interpretation. They could have renewed the discussion recently, in bars and such. They were both fond of their alcohol."

Lorraine felt he was trying to provoke her, but she realized that part of her heart didn't ache as badly as it had before. Stick to the point, she thought. "Something else bothered me. Two things, really. Josh also refers to the player who got sick. Not players, plural, but player, singular."

"He might have recorded the tape a few weeks before his death, after hearing about the first of the second set of players. What's the other point?"

"It's personal, a gut feeling. It bothered me the first time I listened to the tape, though I chalked it up to sentimentality. He calls me Rainey on the tape, and he hasn't called me that since before the divorce. If he recorded the tape a couple of years ago, it would makes sense he'd be calling me that still."

Turner grunted. "Or if he's sitting there, stone sober for the first time in ages."

"Was he sober when he died?" Lorraine asked.

"I was referring to when he recorded the tape. He doesn't slur his words like he does when he has had a few, or more than a few. So he's sober when he makes the tape and realizes what a mess he has made of his life and his marriage, which he wouldn't even admit to friends was over, and feeling depressed and nostalgic, he calls you Rainey."

Lorraine admitted to herself that he could be right, but it wasn't pleasant to have all her thoughts thrown back in her face. A little angry, she said, "Just because the idea of an older tape doesn't fit your theory, doesn't mean it's not true."

"I don't have a theory, singular. I have theories, plural."

Lorraine felt, perhaps irrationally she knew, that he was using her words of a moment ago to show disdain for what she was saying.

The detective stood up and leaned forward over his desk towards her, and as he started speaking, part of her felt he was using body language to take control of the conversation, as if he had ever relinquished it. "I'm more than willing to listen. In fact, I've been thinking of calling you in for questioning ever since you developed your practice of following us around and muddying up the water by nosing around. Did you take anything out of your ex-husband's locker at the school?"

The question surprised Lorraine. Perhaps that was partly why he asked it. "Yes, I took a baseball cap I had given him, and his old football jersey from his high school days. I gave that to his mother. I thought she'd want it. You can ask her."

"She has told us. Some people willingly volunteer information."

"I was surprised to find the locker hanging open," she said, choosing to ignore his dig, "and I certainly wasn't going to let them get stolen. Your people didn't leave it open like that, did they?"

"Hardly." In a rather startling admission, he added, "we didn't find out about the locker until after you raided it."

"Then I wasn't the first to 'raid' it," she stated.

"As you say."

"Jesus, Mary and Joseph," Lorraine said, her irritation bubbling over, "you don't let up, do you?"

"I try not to," he said, almost looking like he was suppressing a smile. "Was the jersey and the cap the only things you removed from the locker, then?"

"Yes." She sat up straighter, and Turner noticed her movement.

"What's wrong?"

Lorraine covered up the idea that had just occurred to her by looking at her watch, grabbing her handbag, and standing up. "I'm sorry. This has taken longer than I expected. I'm meeting someone at Shadow Lake. I have to dash, unless you are going to hold me for questioning like you suggested."

He brushed his hand in what seemed to be a gesture of dismissal. "No, but thanks for coming in. I'll tell Ripkin you were here. And make sure we get that other copy of the tape, soon, please." The word 'please' seemed to have a different meaning when he said it.

Lorraine realized as she left that here Sam and Detective Turner worked fairly closely, especially on this case, and yet they referred to each other by their last names. Men.

Even as she started the engine and shifted into drive, Lorraine groped in her handbag for her cellular phone. She thought she knew where the notebook had been dropped off. Obviously, whoever Damon sent with it wouldn't have wanted to leave it at the front office. What had she been thinking? It had been removed from Josh's old locker, so it made sense it would be returned there. She was already late meeting Ned, so she punched in Patti's number. Patti lived close to the high school.

Patti didn't pick up until after the third ring, so Lorraine was half-expecting the answering machine.

"Hi, Patti, you're there."

"Yeah. How are you?"

"I'm okay. I'm rushing from one guy named Turner to another guy named Turner. Maybe I should be running from both of them, I don't know. But I was wondering if you would do me a big favor."

"If I can, Lorraine, I will. What is it?"

"I'm on my way to Shadow Lake State Park, to meet Ned. You live near the high school, right?"

"Yes, it's a stone's throw away, if you have a strong arm and a mean disposition. Why? What do you need?"

"Well, somebody dropped something off to me there, and I just figured out where."

"You mean they didn't tell you?"

"No."

"Are you sure they want you to have it?"

Lorraine laughed. "It sounds weird, I know. It has to do with this business with Josh. It's a notebook. But not just any notebook."

"That one you got the call about? The blackmail?"

"Hmm. When you say it like that, I'm having second thoughts about sending you to get it."

"Is it dangerous? I have Robb here with me. I could send him."

"In some ways that makes sense, especially since I think it is in a locker in the boy's locker room, but what with his father and all..." Lorraine let the sentence hang there.

Patti's voice was more guarded. "I see what you mean."

"I could come back and fetch it later," Lorraine suggested. "It will probably still be there."

"I'm not sure of that. Never mind, Lorraine, I'll get it for you. What locker is it in?"

"Number 235."

"All right. Do you want me to bring it to Shadow Lake?"

"That's a lot of trouble."

"Please. You're talking to a postoperative gal with time on her hands."

"Yes, but still...I'll tell you what. You check to see if the darn thing is even there. If it is, call me on my cell phone. Okay?"

"You got it. Oh, I have a new cell phone myself." They exchanged cell phone numbers and hung up.

Lorraine glanced at her watch as she maneuvered through traffic. She'd be late, but waiting for her wouldn't hurt Ned a bit. She kept it at five miles per hour above the speed limit, though, to keep close to the appointed time. When she pulled into the park access road, she saw his Cadillac parked near the closed gate. Ned leaned against the gate with an arm resting on it. Lorraine parked next to his car and got out. "Ready for a hike to get to the hike?"

He slapped his hand on the gate. "Why didn't you tell me the park was closed today? I might have been able to arrange something with the uniforms that run the place, to have them keep it open for us."

"Oh my, stop hinting about how much money and influence you possess. I might swoon and fall down and hit my head on the pavement. Then where will we be?"

"The emergency room, I guess," he said.

"Do you have connections there, too?"

They moved around the gate and started walking down the access road. "Joke if you want, but some women have admitted to me that my money was a main attraction for them."

"If a woman said that to you, then you must not have been trying very hard to win her over." She pointed. "The best trail starts up just past that Park Ranger shack."

"I'll be tired out by the time we get to the trail," he complained. Then he returned to their topic. "Are you going to tell me with a straight face that a lot of women would find me attractive without my money?"

Lorraine thought about that. If Ned was a sometimes boorish, sometimes charming janitor at the school, would she be curious enough about him to accept dates? "I'm not sure," she said finally, "but I wonder if you want to get me thinking about it that way."

He laughed, inappropriately, it seemed to her. "It's your fault," he said. "This habit of yours, of always saying what's on your mind, has rubbed off on me. Let's face it, when people start seeing each other, dating, or whatever, they're always on their best behavior, telling each other what they want to hear. It's fake, in a way. You're seeing me, the good, the bad, and the ugly. No surprises later on. It's quite liberating. I should thank you."

"Great, but what am I getting out of it?"

"What do you mean?"

"What you say is all well and good, but when you say my bluntness, saying what is on my mind, has rubbed off on you, maybe you're only telling me what you think I want to hear. Maybe you are on your best behavior, and you will get worse from here on out."

He laughed. "Now you're getting in a little deep for me."

That didn't take long, she wanted to say, but she resisted the urge. Instead she said, "I don't always say exactly what's on my mind. I'm not without discretion, and maybe you shouldn't be either."

"Fair enough," he replied, sounding like he wanted to change the subject.

They walked in silence for a moment. She didn't like the idea that she might not have shown this much interest in him if he wasn't so well off financially. It seemed an inescapable conclusion, however, perhaps mitigated somewhat by his involvement in the football team, and Lorraine wanting to learn what he knew about Josh's death. "Maybe I should thank you, too. You've given me something to think about."

"I don't know if I like the sound of that."

You shouldn't, she thought, for as the Ranger shack came into plain view, she decided not to remain involved with him. The decision made her feel more charitable towards him. She slipped her right arm though his left one. "Step it up, Nedster, we have a lot of ground to cover this morning."

"You should have seen the expression on my secretary's face when I told her what I was doing this morning. She talks to people every day who leave messages asking me to take a hike, but now I'm doing it."

She felt a twinge of guilt, having just decided to tell him to take a hike figuratively, but she was also determined to try to enjoy the morning in the breeze and the fresh fall air. Her cell phone rang, and she drew it out of her purse.

"No fair," he said. "I turned mine off."

"This is Patti," she said, "I asked her to call. She's doing me a favor. It'll just take a minute." She opened the phone. "Hello?"

"Hi Lorraine, this is Patti."

"Hi, did you find the notebook?"

"Yes, it was there in the top of the locker. Do you want me to run it out to you?"

"That's a lot of trouble."

"I don't mind. Robb showed an interest in this little errand, and I'd just as soon get it off my hands if it has to do with the case."

"You have a point. I'll give it to the police soon enough, but I can't resist the urge to see it first. It cost me five hundred dollars, sort of."

"You're kidding."

"Sort of." She noticed Ned was taking advantage of this opportunity to make a phone call of his own. He walked away from Lorraine as he spoke.

"So I'll bring it out to you?" Patti said. "It won't take long with the traffic this time of day."

Lorraine's curiosity got the best of her. "All right, if you're sure. Do you know where the park ranger shack is, where you pay to get in?"

"Sure. That's where you'll be?"

"Yes. We'll walk a short trail while we're waiting. So if we're not there when you get here, hold on a second. Oh, and the gate is closed, so you'll have to walk a bit yourself."

"Great. That'll be my exercise for the day. See you soon."

"Bye." She disconnected. Ned was finishing up also.

"Sorry," he said. "I couldn't resist checking my messages."

Lorraine thought he had been talking, but she shrugged. "Fair is fair. We'll do the White Birch Trail first. Patti is going to meet me back here in a bit. She's dropping something off to me."

"Can't it wait?"

"It can, but it doesn't want to."

"Can I ask what it is?"

"You can ask."

He smiled. "What is it?"

"It's a modern day Rosetta Stone, I hope, and that's all I'll say."

"You've lost me."

"As long as I don't lose you on these trails, we'll be all right."

A few blue jays shrieked as they started out. "Sounds like my first wife," he commented.

Hiking the White Birch Trail took longer than Lorraine expected. They stopped twice, the first time to watch a garter snake move across their path, and the second time to enjoy the sight of five playful chipmunks rolling and running down the slope, chattering like kids at recess.

Lorraine figured they were keeping Patti waiting, but when they emerged from the woods near the ranger shack, it was Detective Robert Turner, the elder, who waited for them. His car was parked nearby. He must have driven around the barricade. "Why didn't we think of that?" she asked, not bothering to explain what she was talking about. She glanced at Ned, and he seemed angry. He confirmed it when he spoke to the detective.

"I told you I'd handle it."

"That's fine," Turner said, matching his tone, "except, of course, I don't believe you. I know what you're up to with my boss."

"You don't know anything," Ned replied.

Robert Turner looked at Lorraine. "I need to talk to your boyfriend here for just a moment."

"He's all yours," Lorraine said, with more feeling than she had intended. She only wanted to get away from both of them right now, especially before Patti arrived. She should have met up with her later, rather than letting her curiosity get the best of her. She began to walk away from them, towards the tree line.

"This is serious," she heard the detective say to Ned.

"Listen, calm down. You're going to blow it."

"Me? You've already blown it, cousin. Where are you going?"

Lorraine realized the last was meant for her, so she stopped and half-turned. "You said you wanted to talk to him. I came here to hike, not stand around."

"I'd really rather you didn't." The detective drew a pistol from inside his jacket.

"Christ, Robert," Ned said, "what are you playing at here?"

"This isn't a toy, Ned, and the game is nearly over. Please don't leave," he said to Lorraine. "Aren't you expecting company?"

Lorraine realized that Ned must have phoned the Detective earlier, when he'd said he was getting his messages.

"I really need to see what her friend is bringing, and I need to see it first."

"Well, for God's sake," Ned said, "just order her to turn it over to you. Show your badge and give an order."

"Ordinarily that is good advice, but Ms. Simoneau has this nasty habit of not listening to the police."

"We can do this another way," Ned said. He turned to Lorraine. "What is

Patti's-" As he said this, he reached in under his light jacket, in a motion Lorraine recognized despite not knowing him long. She'd just seen it a few minutes before.

Detective Turner must not have recognized it, or chose not to do so, as he fired his gun. Lorraine shrieked as Ned fell to the ground, his cell phone clattering onto the pavement.

"I thought he was going for a weapon," the detective said, "you saw what he did."

Lorraine didn't feel inclined to agree with him, but it occurred to her that not agreeing with him at this moment might be dangerous. She walked towards the ranger shack, hoping to put it between her and the armed officer. She glanced over as she reached the point where it would shield her, and saw he was bending over Ned. As she jogged towards the trees, she fumbled in her purse for her cell phone. She had it in her hand when she reached the tree line. Glancing back, she saw the detective leaning into his car, talking on the police radio, it appeared. Lorraine moved deeper into the trees and called 911, and tersely reported what had happened. She didn't stay on the line for a longer explanation, however, but rather disconnected and tapped in Patti's cell phone number.

When Lorraine phoned the first time, Patti had been sitting on the couch with Robb. He was leaning towards her, his hands under her t-shirt, and she had said, just before the phone rang, "See, I told you that you'd get the hang of these sports bras." She jumped when the phone rang. "God," she said between rings, "this reminds me of high school." She reached for the phone, an image of them fumbling on the couch of her father's living room fresh in her mind. Robb removed his hands from under her t-shirt, sat back, and used the controller to cycle through muted television stations as she talked. He turned off the TV when Patti hung up.

"What are you sending me to get?" he asked.

"Nothing, actually," she replied. "That idea was nixed." Patti realized she didn't want to explain much of the conversation to him, and that bothered her a lot. "I need to swing around the corner to the high school and pick up something for Lorraine."

Robb stood up. "There were a lot of cars parked there when I drove by. Let me drive you. A police car comes in handy when you want to park close to a public building."

She couldn't think of a good reason to decline, and it would be easier for her. "All right," she agreed. They didn't say much until they were in the car.

"Does this have anything to do with the case?" he asked.

"What case?"

He smiled. "I see. It's a good thing you're so cute when you play dumb."

"I'm cute all the time."

"I can't argue with you, but you didn't answer my question."

"No, I didn't. Listen, I didn't quiz her about it." That was true enough, but this felt more than awkward to her. What did it mean that she didn't quite trust Robb on this? She consoled herself with the thought that it really was Lorraine's place to tell or not tell people. "Park by the gym," she said as they drew up to the high school. "Please," she added with her sweetest smile.

"Anything for that smile."

"You mean that?"

"Try me."

"I'll think on it," she said as she got out of the cruiser. She jogged to the entrance to the gym and pushed the double doors open. She made her way to the heavy door to the boys' locker room and hesitated. I don't believe this, she thought, visualizing a half-naked football team hooting upon her entrance. But no one was in sight. She hurried to the locker in question. The door was closed but not locked. She opened it and looked up and down. She saw it in the back of the top shelf. By standing on the bench and stretching, she reached it. It was a five by seven spiral notebook. She tucked it into her purse as she retraced her steps. Just before exiting the gym, she looked out the door windows. She saw Robb talking on his police radio. She elbowed the doors open and hurried over to the car. She climbed in.

"Are you on call?" she asked, partly because she wanted to know, but also to deflect any questions from him about her mission. "I saw you talking on the radio."

"In an undermanned small-town police force, you're almost always on call. Did you find what you were looking for?"

"I found something. Lorraine will know if it is what she is expecting. Please don't ask me any more about it, okay?"

"But if it's evidence..."

"I don't know what it is, and I'm not going to try to find out. I'm just going to give it to Lorraine. Drop me off at home. I should deliver it in my own car."

"I can take you," he suggested.

"That's sweet of you, but no."

"I'd feel better if I were there with you."

"I'd feel better if you weren't. It sounds like only one of us is going to feel better here, so I'm afraid I must insist on it being me."

He pulled into the driveway and shifted into park. He glanced at her. She gave him another dose of her smile.

"I hope you're not going to be this pushy every time I am involved in a murder."

"We don't know it was murder, and I just-"

"Robb," she interrupted, "I was just kidding." She leaned over and kissed his cheek. "Call me tonight." She got out of his car and got into her own. She dug into her bag for her keys and the cell phone. She talked to Lorraine for the second time, and agreed to bring the notebook to Shadow Lake. It was a quick call, and as she backed out of the driveway, she saw Robb was still parked where he had pulled in. She waved and shifted into drive. He waved back, halfheartedly. Poor guy, she thought. We've placed him in a tough spot. With any luck, this would be the last time she brushed up against this whole ugly business.

Patti thought about her mother on the drive to Shadow Lake State Park. Her mother had called that morning, but Patti let the machine pick it up. Her mother sounded so tired that Patti nearly picked it up, but she hadn't felt like talking to her so close on the heels of finding out about Chad and Tom. Her mother reported an uneventful flight, described how much she had enjoyed the weekend, and looked forward to talking to her.

As Patti turned onto the access road, She decided she wasn't going to let the revelation about Chad tear down what the weekend had built up between her and her mother. It hurt that no one told her, but, as Kelton pointed out, the reason she wasn't told wasn't a terrible one. No one wanted to be the one to cause her any pain. It would be different if Chad were her natural father rather than Tom's.

There were two cars near the park gate, Lorraine's and a Lincoln Towncar that had to be Ned Turner's. Patti parked next to Lorraine's car and got out, slinging her pocketbook strap over her right shoulder. She went around the gate and walked on the grass alongside the access road. It was a mild day, in the 60's, the radio had announced, but the breeze that rustled her hair whispered of the long winter still to come. Patti had lived in Maine all her life, and had learned to listen to that whisper. She decided she would do some hiking herself soon.

As Patti came around the slight bend in the road, she saw another car up ahead, parked near the ranger shack. A few figures stood nearby. Not quite close enough yet to be sure, she thought it was Lorraine and two men. She saw one of the men collapse, and less than a second later, she heard the delayed sound of the gunshot.

She screeched out Lorraine's name before she could stop herself. She saw her friend moving away from the remaining man. Who was it, Patti wondered, and did it have anything to do with the notebook she was carrying? She wasn't sure if she had attracted attention to herself by calling out, but she half-walked, half-stumbled towards the trees. She heard the sound of a car approaching. She turned her head in time to see a police car spin its tires slightly moving around the gate. She saw Robb's profile as it sped past her, but he didn't appear to see her. He must have followed me, she thought.

At that moment her cell phone rang, muffled in her small handbag. She opened the bag, thinking wryly, "That better not be Mom." The second ring was louder with the purse open, seeming to reverberate through the trees nearby. She opened the phone and said "Hello?"

"Patti!"

She realized who the hoarse whisper came from just as she identified herself.

"This is Lorraine. Where are you?"

"I'm here in the park, near the access road. I saw what happened, well, sort of. Are you all right?"

"For the moment, but I can't say the same for Ned. Detective Turner shot him."

"My God, Lorraine, why?"

"He claims Ned was reaching for a gun, but I think there was more to it than that. I think they were both involved with the mess with Josh. Is that Robb in the police car?"

"Yes, it is. I think he followed me here. He heard more about the notebook than I wanted him to hear."

"Jesus, Mary and Joseph. It's the notebook Turner wants, I bet. Patti, if you can see the detective, get behind cover. He's waving his gun around again."

Patti heard two more shots. She felt sure one had come within yards of her, or was it just her heightened imagination working under stress? She moved into the trees. "Lorraine? Are you okay?" She was talking into a disconnected line. She felt a strong urge to run for her car, but she could hardly leave Lorraine here alone with the detective roaming around. And she hated to admit it, but she didn't know what Robb's intentions were either. She tried to walk carefully through the trees, but it seemed the forest floor was covered with dry leaves and twigs, which snapped and exploded with every step. She heard movement in the woods off a ways, and dearly wished she knew whether it was Lorraine or someone else. She resisted the urge to call out Lorraine's name.

There was another gunshot. "God, Lorraine?" she said, but too softly for anyone to hear. She tried to figure out what she should do now. It seemed useless to call the police, as two of their officers were already here. The phone rang in her hand, almost making her cry out. This time she kept her voice in whisper. "Lorraine?"

"Patti. I'm all right. But that last shot was for me. I can't tell if he has followed me in here. One of those shots before was in your direction. Can you see anything from where you are?"

"No, I'm in the woods. Do you want me to-"

"Don't show yourself. Stay on the line, Patti."

The line grew quiet, though Patti could hear Lorraine moving along. She got down on one knee and pressed the phone against her ear to hear better. There was another whisper, not a winter wind this time, but Lorraine.

"Patti, go back to the car. I'll try to work my way out there."

"Lorraine?" Patti heard movement off to her left, but it was hard to judge how far away it was. "God," she said, and began to work her way back the way she had come. Surely she wouldn't make as much noise this time, she thought, as she must have broken every loud twig there was between her car and here. She heard a shout, a male's voice, but not Robb, she figured. Then there was another gunshot. "Lorraine?" Patti repeated. This time a whisper came back to her.

"Patti, do you trust Robb?"

She agonized over the question for a moment. "I think so, Lorraine, but if he thinks he's doing his duty...I don't know."

There were two more shots, close together. Something about the sound they made convinced Patti they weren't fired from the same gun. "What's going on?" She asked into the phone.

All she got back was "Wait."

Patti must have strayed a little bit, for she saw a trail off to her right. She hadn't seen that on her way in. She could make better progress on it, for sure, but where did it lead? She remembered some sort of trail coming out of the woods near the gate, but was this that trail? It was a risk, but she welcomed the chance to make faster progress. She stumbled over to it, and in the process she disconnected the phone. "Damn it." She didn't dare call Lorraine, in case the shooter was near her friend. Or was it shooters? I'm in a bad action film, she thought, except neither Arnold Schwarzenegger nor Bruce Willis would be bursting out of the trees to help them. She'd settle for having Robb on their side, if he was, that is.

Her phone rang again. She answered halfway through the first ring. But it wasn't Lorraine. "Patti, where are you?"

Surely Robb wasn't a threat, but his voice sounded anguished, and she remembered him being on his radio to the police station, and now people were here possibly shooting at Lorraine and herself. "Sorry, Robb," she said softly, and disconnected. She hated to do it, but she needed to keep things simple right now, if that was possible, plus the line needed to be open for Lorraine. A moment later, the woods ahead of her grew thinner, and she saw the cars by the gate. Her phone rang again.

"Oh, God." She had no choice. She opened it and brought it up to her cheek. "Lorraine?"

"Yes, Patti." Then her friend asked the same question Robb had asked. "Where are you, Patti?"

"I'm back at the gate with the cars, Lorraine."

"Praise the goddess. I tried to make it look like I was heading deeper into the park. Good thing I know these trails. Hold on for a second. I need to think." The wait was excruciating. Finally, Patti had to say, "Lorraine?"

"I'm sorry. I'm just getting my bearings. Listen, get in your car and take a left onto the main road. I'm closer to the main road than I am to you. Drive along slowly until you see me come out. Okay?"

"Okay, but stay on the line, please, Lorraine."

"Don't worry. Hearing your voice is a comfort to me, too."

Patti started her car and backed up to turn around. As she drove towards the main road, she expected to see Robb's car speeding along the access road behind her. But she made it to the main road without seeing anything in her rear view mirror. She drove slowly along, the phone still held in position to speak. "Lorraine, I don't see you."

"I'm almost there. Do you see a big old white birch tree? I'm aiming for that."

Patti saw the tree on the fringe of the woods. She crossed over the left lane and drove into the field between the road and the trees. She pulled up near the wide white birch just as Lorraine emerged from the trees. Patti stopped and leaned over to unlock the passenger side door. Lorraine threw open the door and got in.

"Floor it, girl."

Lorraine didn't have to tell her twice. The wheels spun for a moment on the grass before they caught.

"I'm going to come back and kiss that birch tree after this is over," Patti said, maneuvering them back onto the road.

"I may join you," Lorraine agreed. They heard the siren coming closer.

"They'll be coming from the other direction," Lorraine said, twisting her body around to get a look. "Never have I ever been so glad to have a cell phone."

"Amen," Patti said. "I'll kiss Mom next time I see her, too, for giving me mine."

"Speaking of kisses," Lorraine began, leaning over to plant a kiss on Patti's cheek. "Bless you, girl, for having a clear head and throwing yourself into God knows what here for me. If I'd known, believe me, I would never have asked you. I wasn't thinking very clearly."

"Bosh, Lorraine. How could you have anticipated any of this? Where are we going, anyway?"

"Let me think. Not towards town. We'll be spotted and pulled over before I have a chance to think. Turn left here on the Wing Road. We'll head for Brett Hill. I know the area."

"You got it." Patti took the left. She glanced at her friend. "I don't know if you're ready for it, but the notebook is there in my pocketbook next to you."

"Oh, God," Lorraine said, but she picked up the bag and placed it in her lap.

Chapter 13

Lorraine opened the pocketbook and drew out the spiral notebook. She set Patti's handbag back down on the seat and began flipping through the pages of the notebook, about one page every thirty seconds. "We'll stop off at my favorite apple orchard for a few minutes," Lorraine said. "Take the right hand fork at the top of this incline. When you see apple trees on the left, just pull over and enjoy the view.

Patti did as instructed while Lorraine continued to peruse through the notebook. After she pulled off the road and shut the engine off, Patti said softly, "I'm going to stretch my legs." Lorraine didn't reply, but Patti didn't expect her to, so intent was her friend's concentration.

Patti walked away from the car several yards, and then stopped and looked down into the sloping orchard. She wondered about Robb. What had happened back at Shadow Lake between him and his father? Had he gone there to help him, or to help Patti, or did he show up just out of a sense of duty? It was unanswerable for her at the moment. One minute she trusted him completely, and the next minute doubts would surface and sweep away her faith in him.

She saw figures down in the orchard among the trees, picking apples. They must work for the orchard, for they were using ladders. Perhaps this orchard didn't allow people to pick their own, for it seemed too early in the season to send employees in to clean up the trees. Or did they perhaps pick the apples higher up to prevent them from falling and bruising? She knew nothing about running an orchard, of course, just as they presumably knew nothing about running an auto repair facility. If she had been born to different parents, it could be her working down there right now, climbing the ladders. "Deep," she said to herself, smiling.

Then she thought about what she had just been through, and the smile faded away. Wasn't it only a week or two before that she had merely read about shootings and violence in the newspaper, or saw them on television? Now here she was involved in them, nearly a witness to a shooting. It struck her how it would be, married to Robb and panicking if any kind of story ever broke about a shooting involving a cop. Of course, thankfully there were precious few shootings in Maine, especially in this part of the state, but they were increasing all the time.

Patti sighed, and made her way back to the car. She felt they should be doing something. She opened the driver's door and got back in. "Lorraine, maybe we should take this notebook directly to Sam Ripkin. You know him. We can stop and make a copy of the pages if-" She saw the tears on Lorraine's face and interrupted herself. "What's wrong?"

"Don't mind me, Patti love. I grieved for Josh before, and now I have to grieve for his integrity. I don't know which feels worse."

"Oh. The notebook implicates him, then?"

"You could say that. It's pretty clear that he was guilty as hell over this steroid business. Mind you, he is cagey here, using numbers instead of names. Not jersey numbers like you'd expect, but some other kind of code."

"I don't get it, Lorraine. If he was guilty, why did he keep a notebook that shows he is guilty, especially with what he said in that tape?"

"I wondered about that, too. First I figured it was because he was so obsessively organized. But maybe not. And then I found in here that others seem to be involved, helping him. He isn't quite as careful about them. R Turner isn't hard to figure out."

"Robb or Robert?" Patti said softly. Lorraine looked surprised.

"Good Lord, Patti. After what I just witnessed, I feel sure it is senior, not junior behind all this. Josh must have kept this to use against Turner if he felt threatened. Looks like he didn't use it in time."

"Or maybe he did," Patti offered. "Robb's father seemed awful anxious to get his hands on it."

"You have a point, Patti."

"So what do we do now?"

"You had the right idea, I think. I trust Sam Ripkin. Let's bring this to him. But I liked your other idea too, though, making a photocopy of it before turning it in."

Patti started the engine and drove back into town. "You know, Patti, when he made the tape, maybe he still wasn't guilty."

"Why? When did he make it?"

Lorraine didn't answer. She dug into her purse for her cell phone and phoned Sam's work number. She asked to speak to him, and half-expected to be asked to leave a message, but she was put straight through to him.

"Lorraine, are you all right?" he asked after picking up. It did Lorraine's heart good to have him start off with that question.

"Yes, Patti and I are fine. Shaken up, but fine."

"I'm glad. So Patti's with you? You know, you shouldn't have left the scene."

"Please, Sam. Don't make it sound like we irresponsibly left the scene of an accident. I saw a man I know get shot, and got shot at myself. And I called the emergency number."

"Yes, I take your point. I'm sorry. Detective Turner's initial radio report said that he shot Ned Turner accidentally."

Lorraine laughed without humor. "That's odd. At the time he said he thought Ned was reaching for a gun. As if all citizens carry hidden sidearms. What does he think this is, Texas?"

"He said that about Ned?"

"Yes, and you know, after it happened, he didn't seem to show one ounce of remorse, as if he has killed someone else in cold blood before, recently, maybe."

"Lorraine..."

"Yes, I know. He's a police officer, so he can't have done anything wrong."

"I didn't say that. Did Patti deliver a certain item to you during all this?"

"Yes, and she got shot at for her trouble."

"Is that true, or are you trying to get my goat?"

"Both, maybe. It's hard to be sure, but it was a very real possibility. Patti, pull in here," she interrupted herself, pointing to a photocopy shop. She covered the phone mouthpiece with her hand as Patti drove into the small parking lot. "Be a dear and photocopy this for me. I'll set up a way to give it to Sam while you're in there." Patti got out and walked towards the building with the notebook. Lorraine spoke to Sam again.

"Sam, I have to see you right away."

"I've been waiting a while to hear that from you."

Lorraine laughed. "Don't flatter yourself. I want to turn this damn notebook over to you. It seems you already know I have it."

"Yes. We knew of its existence."

"Well, I can see why your detective was anxious enough to get his hands on it to start shooting people for it. It shows that Josh was as guilty as hell in the steroid business, but I'm afraid it puts Detective Turner in the middle of it as well. But you know, finally, I don't care about all that. This will wrap up the case, then after the internal investigation finds the shooting justifiable, and pins the steroid business all on Josh, we can put this nuisance behind us."

"Lorraine, you're upset, and I can't blame you. But there are a few things you're not aware of at this point."

"Well, enlighten me."

"In good time. Why don't you bring the notebook in to my office?"

"No, I was rather thinking I could meet you in a public place."

"Lorraine, don't be ridiculous."

"I know. I sound like a character in a Hitchcock movie. Being shot at by a cop does that for you."

"You don't trust me?"

"If I didn't trust you, we wouldn't be having this conversation. I just don't want to walk into that building with a notebook someone has been killed to get. Being near Detective Turner again would make me nervous."

Sam chuckled. "I think he'd say the same about you."

"Yes, but he's armed, as we know. Can we meet at the Korner Kafe, right on Center Street? It's near the police station."

"All right. Do we need a secret password?"

"Sam, you're making fun of me. First I get shot at, and then I'm the butt of your jokes. I wonder which is worse? Can we meet at one of the outside tables, then?"

"Okay. I'll be wearing a rose in my lapel."

"Very funny."

"And Lorraine, Ned isn't dead, by the way, though it is touch and go right now. He's in surgery."

"I'm glad, Sam. Thanks for telling me. See you over there." Lorraine disconnected and waited.

A minute later, Patti came out of the shop carrying the notebook and a thin sheaf of loose papers. She tossed them onto the seat as she got in. "All set."

"Thanks." Lorraine stuffed the loose papers under the seat, but left the notebook where it was. "I've turned us into extras in a bad movie, Patti. Drive us to the Korner Kafe on Center Street. You know where it is?"

"Sure." She started the engine and eased her way into traffic.

"I'll get out and give the notebook to Sam. If I get gunned down in a hail of bullets, you can drive off and don't look back."

"Lorraine, you don't really think something like that is possible, do you?"

"Not really. In movies, the conspiracies always go straight to the top, so I guess I'm just nervous. I dearly hope Sam is not involved, for personal reasons in addition to matters of my own health."

"I know what you mean," Patti said, thinking about Robb, the other R Turner. She turned down a one-way street. "It's on the other side of the YMCA, isn't it?"

"Yes. Just around the corner up here on the right." Patti took the right.

Lorraine pointed. "There's a parking space. You can see the cafe from there."

Patti tried to drive into the space, moving back and forth to better align the car. "Parallel parking was never my strong suit," she explained. "Tom says my skills are unparalleled."

"Well, there is Mr. Ripkin." Lorraine pointed him out to Patti. He walked towards the cafe and took a seat at one of the sidewalk tables. A few other people sat outside, but he sat as much to himself as he could. Lorraine picked up the notebook. "You know, he carries a gun too. You wouldn't think he'd have to. Can you imagine being married to a cop?"

"Very funny."

"Sorry, I forgot who I was talking to for a moment. But it would be strange to be married to someone who carries a gun on the job."

"Yes, I'll have to deal with all that before I consider such a move. But it's way too soon to worry about it."

"Ain't that the truth. Well, I'm off." Lorraine got out of the car, fed a couple of quarters into the meter, and quickly jogged crossed the busy street towards the cafe. Sam stood up as she drew closer.

"Hi Lorraine."

"Hi yourself. Here." She tossed the notebook onto the table.

"Well, that was accomplished without any ceremony."

"I told you I wanted to get rid of it."

"Did you make a photocopy of it?"

"How did you guess?"

"I'm beginning to know how you think."

"That's dangerous," Lorraine said. She sat down, but he remained standing a moment longer. He pointed.

"What are you doing, Sam?" She twisted her body around and saw a woman approach Patti's car. "Who is that? I know her."

"That is Officer Mills. She is asking Patti to join us."

"I didn't want to get Patti in any deeper than she has to be."

"She is in it as deep as you are, as far as today's activities are concerned. Do you trust me, Lorraine. The truth, now."

Lorraine thought about it as Officer Mills and Patti crossed the street. "Yes, I do."

"But you don't trust Detective Turner."

"Right again."

"Good. I don't trust him, either. I haven't for a while now."

"So what's going on?"

"Just a second. I only want to do this once." He stood up again as Patti and the other woman approached.

"That's right," Lorraine said. "Officer Mills, with the volleyball player for a daughter. I spoke to you on the day Josh died."

"On the day Josh was killed," Sam corrected.

Lorraine stared at him. "That's the first time anyone has said that in my presence. I-" For a reason she couldn't quite fathom, she felt tears coming on. Sam found a tissue in a pocket and passed it over to her.

"Who killed him?" Lorraine asked.

"Please," he said. "Let me look at this first." He picked up the notebook and thumbed through it.

"You're a fast reader," Lorraine commented.

"I've been told about a lot of what's in here. Damn. The players are represented by three-digit numbers. I assumed it would be their jersey numbers."

"I would have expected that too," Lorraine agreed. But then a thought struck her. "Those are locker numbers, Sam. I'd bet anything on it."

Sam smiled. "Lorraine, maybe you would make a good detective. Is there any way of knowing which player has which locker?"

"Well, they're not assigned, if that's what you mean. I doubt there is a formal list."

"Yes, well, I'd hardly expect any part of this case to be that easy. We can figure it out."

"Excuse me," Lorraine asked, "but could you please tell us a little about what went on back at Shadow Lake? What have you found out today, besides the fact that those three-digit numbers are locker numbers?"

Officer Mills smiled, and Sam laughed. It occurred to Lorraine that Detective Turner would never have laughed at himself that way. "I've found out a little bit more than that. Here's my version, as much as I can tell you, at least. Josh Simoneau was shot and killed. It could have been in a struggle over the weapon, or suicide, or even accidental death. Due to circumstantial and hard evidence, Detective Turner reported to me that he leaned towards suicide. In recent days, without much in the way of evidence to support a change, he switches to where he thinks the death was accidental. Now Turner is bullheaded. He would never change his theory without some kind of evidence. So I became suspicious."

"So why did he change his theory?" Patti asked.

"Because Lorraine here was putting pressure on him, is what I figure. Okay, fast forward to today. He hears that Patti is bringing something to Lorraine, something to do with the case. He has a pretty good idea what it is."

"Robb told him that," Patti said, blushing angrily.

"Well, why not? It was police business, as far as he could see."

"He might not have," Lorraine said. "Ned made a call, while I was talking to you the second time, Patti. Detective Turner showed up after that. And they spoke to each other like they were both involved in the steroid mess."

"In front of you?" Sam asked. "I'm afraid I misread the intensity of the situation. So Robert Turner shoots his distant cousin, Ned Turner. At first he says it was because the other man was making a threatening gesture, right, Lorraine?"

"Yes."

"Later, on the police radio, he says it was an accident. Still later- but I'm getting ahead of myself."

"Why did he shoot him then?" Lorraine asked. Sam didn't answer immediately. Lorraine added, "He made it sound like Ned was weakening somehow. Wait a second, it'll come to me. He said that he knew Ned had been talking to his boss. You, Sam?"

"Yes, we were talking to Ned. I can't go into it, so don't ask."

"Ned was trying to cut a deal. That's not a question," Lorraine said, "but I'll let you rush in and disagree if you like."

"I'm not in a position to agree or disagree," Sam said. "Before I go on, I'd like to hear what you two went through back at Shadow Lake. Anyone want to start?"

"I will." Patti said. "I probably have less to tell." Patti succinctly related her adventure, the phone calls to Lorraine, feeling that one of the shots came near her, almost getting lost on the way back to the car. "It doesn't seem as dangerous now as it was when it all happened," she concluded.

"It was dangerous enough," Sam said. "So you heard six shots in all?"

"If that's what it added up to, yes."

Sam looked at Lorraine.

"Starting from when? Ned and I getting there?"

"The moment Detective Turner arrived at Shadow Lake will do for now."

"Okay. Well, like I said a minute ago, Ned and the detective had a brief argument. Ned pretty much told him to keep out of it, that he'd handle it."

"Keep out of what?"

"Good question. I took it to mean getting their hands on the notebook, but they weren't specific about it."

"Okay, go on."

"Well, Detective Turner insinuated that Ned was talking to his boss, meaning you. Ned denied it, I think. Then I was asked to give them a little privacy, which I was only too happy to do about that time. I started walking away. The detective said, 'This is serious.' I can't remember exactly what Ned said, but the detective asked me where I was going. I had it in mind to get out of there, you see. I was quickly deciding that being Ned's date was not as promising as he'd led me to believe." Sam smiled, but waited for her to continue.

"I gave a semi-wiseass answer, believe it or not, because I know the detective likes them. In fact, he likes my wit so much he pulled out his gun and said he'd rather I didn't leave just then. They talked about getting the notebook- do you want me to try to remember every word?"

"Not just now. We'll go back over it later."

"Fine. At some point Ned said there was more than one way to handle this, and he reached in his jacket for his cell phone."

"How do you know that?"

"How? Because when he fell down after he was shot, the cell phone fell out of his hand."

"That answers that," Sam said. "We found the phone in Detective Turner's pocket."

"In his pocket?" Lorraine realized that for Sam to phrase it like that, something must have happened to the detective. But she went on. "I walked over to put the ranger shack between me and Detective Turner. I saw him using his car radio. Then I aimed for the woods. When I made it to the trees, I called for an ambulance. I caught another glimpse of Detective Turner. By then Robb was there, too. He was yelling at his son. He saw me, I think, because he aimed in my general direction and fired a shot. I think he saw Patti too, because he shot in her direction, it seemed like. I could be wrong. I hightailed it. Of course, I was talking to Patti on the cell phone also. Oh, it's hard to get the sequence of events right. It's such a muddle."

"That's all right," Sam said. "Just keep going."

"There's not much more to tell. I made some noises to make him think I was going deeper into the park, than I doubled back. Silly thing to try, I suppose. I realized I didn't want to appear in plain sight on the access road, so I asked Patti to meet me in her car out on the main road. By that time she was back at her car. So that's what we did. After that, you know more or less what happened."

"Yes, thanks, both of you."

"So are you going to tell us anything about what happened after I left the scene?" Lorraine asked. "To Detective Turner, for instance?"

"Why do you say that?"

"Oh, I don't know. Something about the way you said you found the cell phone in his pocket."

"You're quick, aren't you?"

"Menopause has made me intuitive. Makes up for the hot flashes, but never mind. What can you tell us?"

"Okay, prepare yourselves. It isn't pretty. To start with, Detective Turner is dead. Robb shot him."

"Oh, my God," Patti said, "he shot his father?"

"We're pretty sure of that, yes. Detective Turner died in surgery. Before he lost consciousness for the last time, he cleared Robb of all wrongdoing. He said he tried first to goad him into shooting, by threatening to shoot you two ladies- the wild shots aimed at you that you both described. He aimed his gun at Robb, but Robb stood there, Turner said. So he went over and made a convincing case that he was going to finish off Ned. Finally Robb shot him."

"Do you believe the story?" Patti asked.

"We tend to take what amounts to a deathbed confession pretty seriously."

"What does Robb say about it?" from Lorraine this time.

"There's the rub. He hasn't reported in. Like you two, he left the scene. I don't know why Turner would force Robb to shoot him, rather than turn the gun on himself. Pride? I can't explain it yet, and I never trust what I can't explain."

"You're going to hate being in love," Lorraine joked.

"It's okay so far," he replied.

"You know," Patti said, "Robb's dad was always testing him. Maybe this was some sort of final test for him to pass or fail."

Sam shook his head. "That's a scary thought. All the more scary because it could be true."

"How is Ned?" Patti asked.

"Still in surgery. They think he'll make it. The ambulance got there just in time."

"Thank God for cell phones," Lorraine said, barely above a whisper.

"Wendy," Sam said to Officer Mills, "why don't you phone in and see if there is any word on Robb or Ned yet?"

"Right," she said, and left the table.

"Can I go now?" Patti asked. "This has been quite a morning. I think a hot shower and a quiet afternoon are in order."

"Yes. Thank you, Patti. I'll be in touch with you. And speaking of being in touch, if you hear from Robb, encourage him to report in, would you?"

"Sure. Bye, Lorraine."

"Bye love." Patti came over, hugged Lorraine awkwardly from her standing position, and crossed the street towards her parked car. While this was going on, Sam spoke to the waitress. Then he turned back to Lorraine.

"Do you have a few more minutes? I've ordered some coffee."

"Sounds lovely," Lorraine said, glancing at her watch. "I'm going to be late for work. I'll bet they haven't heard this excuse yet."

"I think you'd be justified in not going in for a while. If you thought Josh's death caused a lot of talk..."

"I see what you mean, Sam. Maybe I need to take a leave of absence."

"I think you should." He reached over and put his right hand over her left one. "How are you feeling?"

Lorraine paused before answering, to allow the waitress to set down the two cups of coffee and several half-and-half packets. It gave Lorraine a chance to consider her response. She prepared her coffee. "I don't know, Sam. In a way, today seems unreal to me, like it couldn't have happened. Things like this don't really happen to people, do they?"

"If they didn't, my sort would be out of a job."

"I'm sorry I dragged Patti into it. My God, if I had thought for a moment...well, it's done. There is one thing that I don't understand, Sam. More than one thing, really, but one big thing. Giving steroids to high school students is lamentable, and somewhat scandalous, but this business seems all out of proportion to it. The shootings; surely trafficking in steroids isn't so serious as all this."

"I was wondering if you'd tumble onto that. Let's just say a lot more than steroids were trafficked by the operation."

"God, Sam, please tell me Josh wasn't the ringleader of that as well."

Sam shook his head. "No, he was set up to be the fall guy. Convenient. If there was trouble, they could nail him for both. I wondered if he found out about the other drugs, and that was why the whole mess blew up. It is hard to tell with all the lawyers involved, but I think some of the players' health problems could be due to the drugs and not the steroids. This case will be in court for a while."

"What about Ned?"

"I don't know how deep he was in it. A few of his people were used as couriers, but beyond that..."

"Where do you think Robb has got to?"

Sam shook his head. "I would have bet he'd have gone to see his mother. We have somebody there and at his apartment."

"What about at Patti's place?"

Sam smiled. "Damn. I didn't think of that, because Patti was also there at Shadow Lake." He stood up as Officer Mills approached. He listened to something she said and said a few words himself. He sat back down, and she walked away. Lorraine sipped her coffee as he did all this.

"No more word on Ned or Robb. I'm sending Wendy over to Patti's place," he said. "Robb doesn't know his father is dead, though he may suspect it. I didn't mean for Patti to have to tell him."

"She could be the best one to tell him," Lorraine pointed out.

"You may be right. You have a good track record so far."

"I sure haven't felt like I've figured much out up until today. Hey, my car is still over at Shadow Lake. Any chance of me getting a ride out there?"

He drank down the rest of his cup of coffee. "Sure. I'll take you out myself. I'd like you to retrace your steps for me if you can."

"It's a date. The strangest first date I've ever heard of."

"I should have asked Patti to come out, too," he mused.

"It can wait," Lorraine said firmly. "Three's a crowd. Besides, she needs to see Robb so she can send him in to report to you."

"You're pretty sure of yourself now, aren't you?"

"I am, at least when I'm not dodging bullets."

"I'll file that information away," he said. "Finish your coffee, lady, and let's get this hot date under way."

Chapter 14

Patti slowed her car to a stop as her apartment building came into view. She stared at Robb's car in the parking lot. She thought she saw a figure on the driver's side, but she wasn't sure, as there was no movement. With her cell phone in her purse, calling Lorraine right now was an option, to put Sam Ripkin's mind at ease. But could she put him at ease? She wished the figure behind the steering wheel would move. A terrible premonition washed over her, that Robb had done something to himself out of overwhelming feelings of guilt. This was a heck of a time for her imagination to kick in, she thought as she pulled into the space beside his car.

As she got out of her car, keeping her eyes on him, she saw him shift his position a few inches. That was something. She drew in a deep breath as she moved around his car to the driver's side, stopping by his door. She didn't want to jump him, but he wasn't noticing her either. Worried that knocking on the window would be too sudden, she took a few steps towards the front of the car and boosted herself up on the hood. She remembered that she used to do this back in high school, on his very first car, testing his love for her against the love of his car's paint job. She usually won. Shifting her weight, she rocked the car slightly. He glanced up finally, and she wiggled her fingers in a playful wave. He leaned over and unlocked the passenger side door.

Not much of a greeting, she thought, but then chided herself remembering what he had just been through. She slid off the hood and walked around the front of the car. She opened the door and got in. She saw that he had been crying, and why not? Then she noticed the pistol on the seat between them. "Can we move that?"

"Don't touch it," he said. "The damn thing might go off."

"The last time I heard that, I was in the back seat of your old Malibu." She tilted her head to get a better look at him. "I guess you're not in the mood for jokes. But if you don't move it, I sure as heck will."

That seemed to rouse him a little. "It needs to only have my prints on it." He took the pistol by the muzzle and lifted it over the back of the front seat. He set it on the rear seat. "Did they tell you what happened?"

"A lot of it."

"The part about me shooting my father, who was also a fellow officer?"

"Yes, that part."

"He's dead, isn't he?"

Patti wondered if a blunt yes would be kinder, in a way, than softening the blow. During the scant seconds she used to consider this, he spoke again.

"I know he is. The EMTs didn't seem too hopeful, like they were with Ned."

"He made it to surgery," Patti said.

"He was a tough old bird."

"He exonerated you in the shooting," Patti added. "Before he went into surgery. He cleared you."

"Did he?" The two words were charged with bitterness. "Do you know why I shot him?"

"He made you, I guess," she replied. "He shot at Lorraine and me, and threatened to shoot you, and Ned again, I gather."

"Don't dress it up with too much heroism. He fired those wild shots towards you two and told me to shoot him. He cited code at me. But I knelt down and worked on Ned instead. He hit me with the butt of his piece, told me he was serious, to listen to him for once in my life. As if I haven't always listened to him more than I should have. He told me his life wouldn't be pleasant for an ex-cop in prison, but that suicide wouldn't help Mom out with insurance either. He pointed the gun at Ned, near Ned, I should say, and fired into the ground.

"I took out my gun and pointed it at him, told him to drop his weapon. He was putting me down, saying if I didn't have the guts, that was fine, but for God's sake I should get my sorry ass off the force and go flip burgers for a living. He said I should watch closely while he finished off Ned, or maybe he should shoot me instead. Something like that. Then he fired his gun past my ear, it seemed like. I reacted, instinctively, I guess, and shot him. I could hear the ambulance by then."

"You had to do it, Robb."

"Did I? I wonder. I've replayed it in my mind fifty times since it happened, and I still don't know."

"You don't know what?"

"Whether he would have shot Ned, or me. Whether I should have just called his bluff. But I've never been good at that."

There was a silence for a minute. Patti weighed asking him a question on her mind. This wasn't a great time, she knew, but she had to know. "Robb, can

I ask you a question?"

"Sure."

"When I came out of the gym, and you were on the phone; was that call about the notebook I picked up for Lorraine?"

"Yes. It was important evidence. I mean, we already knew about it."

"Well, did you think about me? I felt betrayed."

"Betrayed?"

"Yes. You tell your father I've picked up the notebook for Lorraine, and then he shows up at Shadow Lake and starts taking pot shots at us."

"Is that what you think? I wasn't talking to my father; I was talking to Ripkin."

"Ripkin? Then how did your father find out? Did Ripkin tell him?"

"I doubt it. He was having his doubts about Dad. I'm surprised he trusted me, actually."

Patti remembered something Lorraine had said at the cafe, which Patti discounted at the time. "Maybe Ned did call him, then. If so, that was a big mistake on his part."

"Or Dad might have been following Lorraine."

"I suppose I should go inside," Patti said. "A hot shower waits for me, and you need to go report to Sam."

"I'd rather report to you in the hot shower."

Patti smiled, but didn't respond. Robb drummed the steering wheel with his fingers.

"So where do we stand, Patti, really?"

"I honestly don't know, Robb. I guess I really need to know more about what happened today, and I need time to react to it. I'm all confused now. I'm relieved as all heck if it was Sam Ripkin you called."

"If?" he asked, but he was smiling.

"I'm sorry. I don't mean to doubt you. But I'm feeling paranoid still. Give me time. I feel I want you in my life, Robb with two 'b's. I just can't imagine sliding effortlessly back into how we were, though. Is that enough for right now?"

"That will do for now, Patti with two 't's. So we'll be in touch."

"Yes, please. You know what you need to do now."

"Head for Canada?"

"Very funny. But it's good to see you smile again."

"That was just for you."

"That's a start. Call me later. I want to know how it goes."

He pointed to his cheek. "I will, as long as you plant a big one right here."

She moved towards him, half expecting him to cheat and move his lips into position. But he sat still as she kissed his cheek. She touched where she had kissed with her left hand before sliding back over and opening her door. "Call me."

"Now I know we're still dating."

"I mean it. Say you will, or nod your head or something."

"I'll call. Maybe from a jail cell, but I'll call."

She matched his flippant tone. "Hey, just tell Ripkin that if they issued you a gun, they must expect you to use it." She opened her door.

"Thank you. That will settle everything."

"Are you okay?"

He looked out through his windshield, until Patti glanced in that direction. There was a car exuding loud music fifty feet away with teenagers gesturing to each other, but nothing more.

"I still have to face my mother, my whole family."

"They won't blame you once everything comes out."

"It would almost better if they did."

"I can come with you if you like."

"Thank you, but I don't think I want your seeing Mom for the first time in years to be under that cloud."

"Whatever you think best." She got out of the car. "Bye Robb. Remember, call me."

He seemed not to hear. "I guess I'll be running my own life from now on, from in prison or out."

He seemed inclined to delay leaving. She closed the door and stepped back. She blew him a kiss. He started the engine, and she waved when he glanced over before backing out of the parking space. As she let herself in, she heard her phone ringing. She jogged up the stairs and unlocked the door. As she came through the inner door, she heard the machine picking up. She switched it off and grabbed the phone when she saw Tom's number on the caller ID.

"Hi, Tom."

"Patti, are you all right?" At first she thought he had heard something, but he added, "You don't sound too lively."

"I'm out of breath. I just ran up the stairs. I guess I forgot I'm not 100% after the surgery."

"How can you forget you've had major surgery?"

"You know what I mean. How are you doing?" She almost felt silly asking, considering the kind of day she just had, but it seemed natural to ask.

"I've had better days. I came home early from the shop. Kelton was taken down to the police station to answer questions."

"Oh no. Why?"

"It's because of his working for Ned Turner. He has talked to them before, but they seemed grim this time, like they were naturally assuming Kelton had something to hide."

"Well, they would seem grim," Patti explained. "Ned was shot at Shadow Lake today."

"Ned was involved in that? They didn't give out any names. I figured it was a drug deal gone bad or something like that."

"Actually, it was something like that, in a way, now that you mention it."

"How do you know so much about it?"

"You aren't the only one who hasn't had a great day. I was there at Shadow Lake, and got shot at myself."

"Always trying to top me, aren't you?" Then serious, he added, "You're not joking, are you?"

"No. I don't think it came close to me. It was unnerving all the same."

"I bet it was. Who fired the shot, Ned?"

"No. I don't know if I'm supposed to talk about it, but it was most likely Robb's father, if you can believe that."

"Wait a minute. Isn't he a cop? Isn't he supposed to shoot at the bad guys?"

"Yes, he is, I mean was," Patti added. "He's dead."

"God, Patti, Who shot him, Ned? Kelton? You maybe?"

"I can't take credit." She hesitated, wondering how many times she'd have to explain all this. She'd talk to her father and mother, and then stop answering the phone, she decided. "It was Robb. His father sort of made him do it. It's a long story, and not one I feel like going into right now."

"You're not going to make me read about it in the paper, are you?"

"I'll tell you more if you promise to call Mom and Dad and tell them, so I don't have to."

"My dad or yours?"

"Tom, this isn't the time for comments like that."

"I'm sorry, it just slipped out. I must have a deeper well of bitterness than I imagined. I'll talk to them both if you like. What do I tell them?"

"First tell them I'm fine. And don't tell them I was shot at. I'm not a hundred percent sure, and it will only worry them."

"You think so?" he asked sarcastically. "Now here is where you tell big brother more about it, like you promised."

"I'm not going to give you the full Monty, as Mom calls it."

"My mom or yours- I'm kidding; go on."

"It has to do with the business Lorraine's ex-husband was involved with, the steroids and the football team."

"I've been meaning to talk to you about your recent choice in friends," he joked.

"Very funny. May I take a moment to remind you that, besides helping me get past the surgery, Lorraine led to Julia, who has led to family harmony?"

"Okay, so it was maybe worth getting shot at."

"That's it; I'm done talking to you about this. You're impossible."

There was a knock at Patti's door. "Listen, someone is at the door." She covered the phone. "Come in!" she called out.

"It's probably an agent, wanting to set up a book deal for you."

"Bye, Tom."

"Bye, Sis. Listen, stay out of the way of people with guns, okay?"

"You have always enjoyed spoiling my fun. Besides, Robb carries one sometimes. I'll call you back. Bye."

She disconnected the phone as she walked towards the door. She thought it might be Robb, somehow, but that guess was disproved violently when the door was kicked in. Three young men spilled in through the door.

"What do you want?" Patti tried to sound more forceful than she felt.

"I dunno," one of them said. "Guys, what do we want?"

"Just a little cooperation," another one of them replied. The biggest of the three, he walked over to the window overlooking the street. He turned around and leaned against the windowsill.

"Since you asked so nicely, how can I refuse?" Patti saw no weapons in plain sight. The boy who had spoken first sat down on the couch. The third one stood by the door. She realized these were young men, not mere boys. She moved slowly towards the door to the kitchen. She could always make a dash for the back door, which connected to a hallway and doors to other apartments.

"What did that cop want with you outside?"

It flashed through her mind that these were football players. The one by the window, who had just asked the question, seemed to be in charge.

"He warned me about football players breaking into apartments," she said, amazed at her own bravado.

"Joe," the one by the door said, confirming through his concern that they were players, at least.

"Shut up," the one on the couch said.

"Why don't you tell me why you're here?" Patti suggested.

"Fine. We heard that you picked up something for Coach Simoneau's wife, and we want it. It's simple."

She thought of the copy under the seat of her car, but they probably wouldn't leave quietly without the original, and she wasn't sure how far they'd go. "You're kidding, right?" she asked to buy time.

"Yeah, we're kidding," the player on the couch said, "except you forgot to laugh when we opened your door just now, so maybe you can tell us what the joke is."

"I can tell you two jokes," she said. "The first is that you're way too late. We gave the Chief of Police what you're looking for at a cafe a half-hour ago. The second joke is that my door was unlocked when you kicked it in."

"We wanted to make a statement with our entrance," the young man by the window said.

"Did I hear someone say they wanted to make a statement?" Patti glanced over and saw Officer Mills standing in the doorway, with another cop behind her. The player nearest the door took a few steps further into the room.

"We're just talking to the lady here," the one on the couch said defiantly.

Mills stepped into the room to allow her fellow officer room to come in. "Really? She must have been anxious to speak to you to break her latch opening the door for you."

"She did seem a bit anxious," the one by the window joked, but his veneer of toughness seemed to be wearing thin, Patti thought.

"Actually," Patti said to Mills, "it's Sam Ripkin they want to talk to. They seem to be mighty interested in what Lorraine and I delivered to him just now."

"I guess they should come with us, then."

"Have they threatened you or done any personal harm to you?" the other cop asked.

"No, they hadn't gotten around to anything like that. The threat was subtler than that."

"Good, Then we'll just remove the threat, subtle or otherwise. Come along, boys. Your parents will be proud of you all." The male officer swept the young men out through the door. Mills stayed behind. Patti listened to the footsteps descending the steps, the closing of the entryway door behind them downstairs.

"I don't think they would have hurt you," Mills said. "But I shouldn't wonder if it wasn't pretty frightening all the same."

"Yes," Patti said. "I mean, I was scared, as any sane woman would be around three males who are looking for trouble. But it wasn't like over at the lake, where I was petrified. I did feel there was a limit to what they would do, so I felt a measure of control over the situation. I might have been kidding myself."

"Fortunately, we'll never know," Mills said. She stepped over to the door, and tested it by closing it and pulling on it. It opened back up. "You'll have to get this fixed, I'm afraid. I hate to sound like a cop, but I'd suggest a dead bolt this time around. If you don't think the landlord will spring for it, we can whisper in his ear."

"Oh no, they're a dear little old couple, and they do anything I ask. I almost feel guilty sometimes. I'm sorry, should I call you Officer Mills?"

"If any male cops are around, yes. Otherwise, Wendy is fine."

"Okay, Wendy. How did those players know about the notebook?"

"Well, I'm sure I shouldn't discuss this too much with you, but considering how fast everything took place today, I'd guess it had to come from one of two sources."

Patti thought for a moment. "Robb or his father."

The woman officer shrugged. "Best guess, yes. And I'd be quick to rule out Robb."

"So would I," Patti agreed. "He was here just before the boys showed up, and they asked about him. They aren't smart enough to play it that cool."

"Robb was here?"

"Yes. Well, down in the driveway when I got here."

"That's why Sam sent us here, Patty. Your friend Lorraine suggested Robb might come here."

"Did she? Now I owe her one. She probably saved me from something worse. I had to tell Robb about his father's death. I don't think it was a shock to him, but someone else should have told him. Family."

"Maybe so. But I'm sure you handled it all right. Where is he, by the way?"

"If he listened to me, he's reporting in to Sam Ripkin."

"Well, if you managed that, I'll come back to thank you. Robb was put in an impossible situation, and reacted the only way that made sense. But, of course, the unbelievable fact that he had to shoot his father because he discovered him to be a criminal was quite a double whammy. I think he'll be vindicated, but it looks worse the longer it takes him to come in. Do you need anything else, Patti?"

"No, I'm fine. But I think I will stay somewhere else until my door is fixed."

"Good idea. I'll go now. Take care, Patti."

"I will. Bye."

Patti walked over to the window facing the street as Wendy left. She saw the police car down in the driveway. The players were packed into the rear seat. She watched Wendy get in on the passenger side. The car pulled out of the driveway and drove out of sight down the street.

Patti settled down and watched some mindless afternoon television for two hours. She was standing at her kitchen counter, trying to decide whether she wanted coffee, tea or cocoa when the phone rang. She checked the caller ID and picked it up.

"Hi Tom."

"Actually, it's me," Kelton said.

"Oh, I'm sorry. I told Tom I'd call him back, but I forgot."

"Yes, I know. He told me."

"So you're back from the police station. Obviously," she added when she realized how dumb it sounded. "Don't mind me. I guess I'm still a little shaken up from having my door kicked in by three rather large football players."

"Wait a minute. You had your door kicked in? Tom told me about the shooting. I thought it took place at Shadow Lake?"

"It did. This is a more recent atrocity."

"Good Lord, Patti. You do live an exciting life. Are you okay?"

"Yes. Luckily Wendy the lady cop showed up in the nick of time, just like on TV."

There was a slight pause on the other end of the line. Patti heard Tom ask a question. "I don't know," Kelton said to him. Into the phone, he said, "Patti, I think I enjoyed talking to you more back when the only excitement you reported was the occasional major surgery, or finding out your brother has a different father than you do. It was easier to keep up with."

"Tell me about it, Kelton. If this continues, I may have to start packing heat."

Kelton laughed. "I'm trying to picture it. Just a second, Patti, your brother is on the verge of throwing a full-fledged fit. Yes, dear, what is it?"

Patti couldn't make out what her brother said, but heard the tone bordering on a whine.

"I'm not ignoring you, love," Kelton said, "I'm just not responding. There's a difference. I'm working up to it. Don't worry, I'll give you credit. Patti," his voice got louder as he spoke fully into the phone again. "Tom is suggesting, and I agree with him, that you must come here and spend the night. We haven't had anyone kick our door in for- I don't know, at least a year or two. It should be safe."

Patti had been thinking more along the lines of staying with Lorraine, but then again, with her friend becoming romantically involved with Sam Ripkin, maybe this would work out better. "All right, I'll pack an overnight bag and come over. Put the kettle on for cocoa."

After hanging up, Patti went into her bedroom and pulled her carry-on suitcase from under the bed. Two minutes later, the bag was full. She hardly remembered filling it up. She double-checked. A couple of t-shirts, jeans, a skirt and two tops, five pairs of stockings, an equal number of panties and bras, and her nightgown. Under the clothes, extra ostomy supplies. "Close enough," she said out loud, flipping the suitcase closed and zipping it up.

She phoned the landlord's property manager and left a message about fixing the lock and installing a dead bolt. She offered to pay for the work, but she had a pretty good idea they wouldn't take her up on it.

During the drive over to Tom and Kelton's place, she felt like her hands were shaking, but when she held a hand in front of her face, she couldn't tell. She let herself into their building's entryway and rang their bell. She waited for Tom to holler, "Who goes there?" or "Friend or Foe?" or one of his variations, but all that crackled over the little speaker was, "Come on up, Sis." The buzzer sounded and she went upstairs.

The guys were in the kitchen, trying hard to look casual, it seemed to Patti. Tom came over to hug her, then Kelton. She looked at their faces as they each pulled away. They seemed strained. Sitting at the kitchen table, she asked, "What's wrong, guys?"

"Nothing much," Tom offered, "except we're worried about you. For instance, you didn't happen to get run off the road on the way over here, or have your tires shot out from under you, did you?"

"No, it was an uneventful trip. You don't have to worry, really. I was just in the wrong place doing the wrong thing, acting as courier with a vital piece of evidence. I'm out of the picture now."

"Good," Tom said, nodding his head. He sighed. "Don't mind me, but it's a bit unnerving to have both my sister and my main man involved in this scandal, even if it is on the fringes of the case. Not as stressful as being shot at or dragged down to the police station like you two were, but it ranks up there somewhere. By the way, here's the cocoa you ordered." He brought the mug over and set it in front of her. "Oh yeah," he said, "I called Mom and Dad. They both pretty much freaked out, as you'd expect. I am under orders to tell you to call them and reassure them that you're all right. I did stall them off, so you can wait until after supper."

"Thanks for the reprieve."

"Don't mention it. But speaking of fathers and that sort of thing..."

"What now? You haven't come up with another real father, have you?"

"No, it's not that earthshaking, but almost. You haven't forgotten Chad during all the excitement, have you?"

"Chad?"

"Which rhymes with Dad," Kelton threw in.

Patti glanced at both of them. "Why? What's up with him?"

"It's just that he is in Maine right now."

"What's he doing here?"

"Working, mostly. He's in Kennebunkport. He covered the Bush presidential campaign eight years or so ago, when he conquered Mom's heart, and now he's back covering the younger Bush campaign."

"Okay," Kelton said, "tell her the punch line. She's already sitting down."

"I'm working towards it," Tom protested. "The punch line, as Kelton puts it, is that Chad will be in town on Thursday. Now that Mom's secret is out in the open, he wants to have dinner with the extended family. I took the liberty of reserving a table at the Shark's Tooth."

"That's a bit pricey, isn't it?"

"He's a world trotting journalist, Patti. Only the best for him."

"Tell her the other part," Kelton said.

"There's more?" Patti held up her right hand. "Hold on, let me take a sip of my cocoa." She raised the mug and tried to figure what was coming next. Was Julia pregnant, or Mom? No, both were unthinkable. "Okay," she said, grateful that her imagination could still crank out alternatives that were bound to be worse than the reality, "tell me."

"It's just that on Thursday afternoon, Dad, Chad, Kelton and I are going to play a round of golf."

She stared at him. "Dad is going to play a round of golf with Chad?"

"I swear on my mother's empty grave, it's true."

"Now I get it," she said finally. "A bullet grazed my head back at Shadow Lake and I'm lying comatose on a hospital bed. This is all a feverish dream."

"No," Tom said, "if this were one of your dreams, you would have given me a much sexier body."

"And I'd have a job that doesn't suck," Kelton added.

"And I wouldn't be wearing this pouch on my body," Patti agreed. "So this is real." She sipped at her cocoa. and looked up at Tom. "Maybe Dad's playing a deep game here, waiting to get Chad in front of him. Golf clubs make good weapons, don't they?"

The two men laughed. "Honestly, Sis, this romance of Dad's, as much as I scoffed at it at first, seems to be doing wonders for his personality. The man's in love, and it has stripped a lot of the bitterness away. He joked about beating the pants off his ex-wife's future ex-husband. He already spoke to Chad on the phone. Either we've slipped into a bizarre parallel universe, or it's true."

"Amazing," Patti said.

"Isn't it? Listen, we have to start supper. Do you want to lie down for a while? You've had quite a day."

"Ain't that the truth. I think I will. First I need to call Lorraine and let her know where I am."

"There's a phone in our bedroom. You can crash there if you like. You'll wake up to delicious aromas, guaranteed."

"Sounds lovely. Thanks for taking me in." She downed the rest of the cocoa and headed for the master bedroom. She briefly considered calling Lorraine's place and leaving a message. But she called her friend's cell phone number.

"Hello?"

"Hi Lorraine. How are you doing?"

"I'm just fine, Patti. How about you? I've heard you had some more excitement."

"Wow, news travels fast."

"It's a fringe benefit of hanging out with the chief of police. Wendy said you seemed okay. I'm more sorry than I can say to have dragged you into all of this."

"Don't be silly. If someone had to be dragged into it, I'm glad it was me."

"Thank you. You're only saying that because the bullets have stopped flying your way. But in that case, I'll drag you into every scandal I'm involved with."

"Lorraine, did Robb report in?"

"Yes. He's still being debriefed, or whatever you want to call it. What about you and him now, Patti?"

"I honestly don't know. Earlier today I was convinced he had betrayed me, from a sense of duty, of course. Then it turned out it was probably Ned that called Robb's father. But still, I'm not sure it will be the same between Robb and me. I mean, he has to deal with what happened today. I may be a complication while he does that."

"That doesn't wash with me, Patti. If you need to step back because of your own feelings, that's fine. But we both know you're a lot more than a complication to him. Of all the places he could have gone, he was waiting in your driveway to talk to you. After seeing you, he came in to make his report. Do what your heart tells you, girl, but I don't know how he'd get through what he has to get through without you."

"If that's true, I won't abandon him, Lorraine. I can promise you that."

"Great. But don't promise me, promise him next time you talk to him. I can just picture you two, tongue-tied, each assuming the other wants to back off. Don't let that happen unless you both agree on it and say so. Okay?"

"All right. I promise to talk to him about it. Sheesh. What about you and Mr. Ripkin? Are you two a hot item?"

"We're pretty warm. He seems serious about me."

"Lorraine, already?"

"Yes, but he is walking careful. There has been something between us since Josh and I moved back here from Vermont. Sam's obviously worried I'll run like a jack rabbit. I'll let him swing in the breeze for a while, but I like his chances in the long run."

"That's great, isn't it?"

"Yes. In a way, he has made my knees weak for a while, but I thought we had this ancient undisclosed secret in the past that would come between us once it was revealed. But he knew who I was all along, and felt bad about it, too. We'll see how it goes. I have to run, Patti. It looks like he's done, finally. We're going out to dinner."

"Okay. I wanted to let you know that I'm staying at my brother's apartment until the lock is fixed at my place." She gave Lorraine the number and they hung up. Patti lay back on the bed. She really didn't think she'd be able to nap, but it would be nice to just lay here and listen to the sounds of supper being cooked, the thin shrieks of kids playing outside, and just think about what had happened and what might still happen.

Chapter 15

Two days later, on Thursday, Lorraine walked into the hospital to visit Ned Turner. She had decided to arrive shortly before the evening meals were served, so that she could excuse herself gracefully when the food showed up. She felt a little guilty coming like this, as her main objective was to let Ned know they were through as a couple, to whatever limited extent they had been a couple to begin with. It was awkward, but she figured telling him was better than letting the silence build up any hope in him that he had a chance. That was if he even cared if there was a chance. Like she told Sam Ripkin before he left for work that morning, it was tricky breaking off a relationship if you weren't even sure you had a relationship.

Lorraine took the elevator to the third floor, and upon exiting, passed the nurses station on her way to room 364. Sam had told her the room number, and about when Ned was less likely to have guests. Like she had told Patti, there were pragmatic advantages to being involved with the chief of police. He knew stuff, and what he didn't know he could find out quickly. Her one concern was that a reporter or a city employee might find a conflict of interest in his interest in her. He wasn't worried, telling her he'd love an excuse to retire early, buy a camper and travel the country with her.

It wasn't hard to find room 364. Sam had posted a cop outside the room from the start.

Lorraine didn't know the cop, so she passed by without a word, pausing in the doorway. Strictly speaking, it wasn't a private room, but the other bed was unoccupied. She wondered if the city was paying to keep it empty. "Tax dollars at work," she muttered as she entered the room.

His eyes were closed, but he opened them when he heard her come in. "Still alive, I see," she said.

He looked smaller and vulnerable, as even imperious people do when in the hospital.

"Yes. Sorry to disappoint you."

"I'll get over it," she shot back. "I'm younger than you are, so sooner or later you'll go first."

He smiled, not as robust a smile as she was used to from him. "How are you, Lorraine?"

"Better than you are."

"That's not saying much."

"I'm fine, Ned." She moved over and sat in the chair near the bed. She thought about all of the ostomy patients she had visited over the years in this hospital, maybe even in this room. "I can't seem to stay out of this hospital."

"I've managed pretty well, until now. Is it as pleasant outside as it looks?"

She sighed. "I didn't come here to exchange pleasantries, Ned. I have something to tell you."

"I've always admired your bluntness."

"Well, if that's true, you can't admire it for much longer. I don't intend to see you anymore. I can't put it any plainer than that."

"That's plain all right," he said. "So it's true what I've heard, that you and Sam Ripkin are a couple. Or are you going to tell me that you're dumping me because you think I'm guilty? Neither explanation is very noble."

She had vowed not to lose her temper at him, but she felt her face getting warm. "Then it's a good thing I'm not striving for nobility. It's happiness I want. I loved a man for years who turned out to have an unsteady moral compass, and I'm not going to let it happen again. So yes, I guess that means I am convinced that you're guilty of a lot. You brought me into danger by calling Robert Turner to Shadow Lake. I'll give you credit in that you tried to defuse the situation, and got shot for your trouble. That's why I'm here. I owe it to you to say what I've said. Besides, I didn't enjoy our dates very much."

He started to laugh, and gripped his abdomen. "Please, don't undo the hard work of several good surgeons. So tell me, does that mean if I'm found guilty, and mind you I don't expect to be, but if I am convicted, you won't visit me in jail?"

"No."

"That tears it, then. My lawyers will just have to get me off. While I have my freedom, I at least have a chance, slim though it may be."

"You don't know how slim," she said, standing up. She was tired of being here. "I've said what I came here to say." She moved towards the door.

"Aren't you going to wish me well?"

She stopped in the doorway, and looked back at him. "I don't think so. You have lawyers and former wives on your payroll to do that for you."

"That's cold, Lorraine. What's more, it's beneath you."

"Life is cold, Nedster, old boy. I'll tell you what; I'll wish for you what you deserve. That way, whether you're as innocent as the driven snow, or guilty as sin, I'm covered. Bye."

She thought she heard a response from him, but she couldn't make it out as she strode back down the hallway. He can have the last word, she thought, as long as I don't have to listen to it. Surely there was another twenty-something lady out there waiting for the Nedster to show up in her life.

Outside in the brilliance of the setting sun, it wasn't difficult to find her car in the parking lot. Sam was leaning against her car. "Why Sam, are you stalking me now?"

"That's not even funny. I had one of the guys drop me off. I wanted to be here when you came out."

"Why?"

"It's hard to explain."

She smiled. "Nevertheless, I think I'd like you to try. Were you afraid I'd try to sneak him out and run off with him?"

"Hardly that. But I guess I still can't help but think of him as competition."

Well, don't."

"Not at all?"

"No."

"Fair enough. Then I'll ask. How is he doing? You weren't in there as long as I expected."

"It was long enough for me. He's all right. Sweet talk and protestations of innocence, as you'd expect. He seems to be the sort that always expects a soft landing."

"I guess piles of money provide a big enough cushion. It may not be enough for him this time."

"I almost feel mean enough to hope that's true, Sam."

"I'm more than mean enough to hope it. Would you like to go for a drive?"

"Sure. Where?" She glanced at him. "Let me guess, Shadow Lake."

"You are quick. I've got a spot for you on the force."

"You just happen to have an opening." She shuddered. "Nothing to joke about, I suppose."

"Two openings, if Robb Turner leaves."

"Has he decided?"

Sam shook his head as he opened the driver's door for her. "Not yet. Would you like to drive?"

"Sure. Thank you." She got in, and he closed the door after her. He walked around and got in beside her. She had started the car by this time, and backed out of the space as soon as he buckled his seat belt.

"Have you heard the latest about the football team?" he asked her.

"I'm out of the loop now. Have they canceled the season yet?"

"That's still to be decided. They may strike a deal and play all the games as exhibitions. No, McLain, the interim coach, has quit."

"Why?"

"Why? Let's just say the guilt for the steroid business runs a lot deeper than just Josh. Don't say it. I know you've thought so from the start."

"I won't gloat. I'm past that. So who will they get to replace him?"

"That's a good question. They need to find someone above reproach, and not involved in the program right now. But who'd want to jeopardize their career taking on this huge headache? It won't exactly shine on a resume."

"I see your point," she said. An idea occurred to her. She rolled it around in her mind. "I can think of someone," she said after a half-minute."

"Seriously?"

"Yes. Harold Lynch."

"Paunch?"

"Yes, otherwise known as Paunch. Think about it. He was sounding alarms a couple of years ago, and was pressured to resign for his trouble. He has come out looking pretty good in all this, but he hasn't landed anywhere else. He's flamboyant enough to take the pressure, but hard up enough for work to take on a thankless job like this."

Lorraine glanced over at Sam. He seemed to be considering it seriously.

"Good old Paunch," he said softly. "You may be onto something. He looks clean; God knows we checked him out closely during all this. I'll ask him about it. If he's willing to take it on, I'll whisper into the ears of some on the school committee. They are desperate for a way to lead the team back to respectability. You just may have provided a public service, Lorraine."

They rode along in silence for a minute. Lorraine rolled her window partway down. "We have precious few weeks left of this," she observed. Then we'll need to keep our windows up and winter will be right around the corner. Do you ski?"

"No. I don't ski, snowmobile or ice fish. All I do for winter recreation is shovel snow, and stare out the windows and will it to melt."

"I'm glad to hear that," she said, "because all I do is stare out the window and will it to melt. It will be nice to have someone around to shovel. Hey, what are we going to Shadow Lake for? Not another reenactment like yesterday, I hope."

"No. I just thought you might like to go for a hike, like you originally planned. Is that okay?"

"It sounds lovely. What about you? You've been spending a lot of time with me. Don't you have work to do? Detective Turner told me you are a servant of the townspeople."

"You're a townsperson."

"Oh, I see. You service us one at a time, and this is my week."

"That's right. I'm all yours."

"This could catch on, Sam. Firemen, dogcatchers, all at our beck and call one week a year."

"Or longer," he said.

She looked over at him. "Why Sam. If I were more self-confident, I would think of that as some sort of half-baked proposal."

"I'm just working up to it. You'll know the real thing when you see it. And speaking of work, have you decided when you're going back to work?"

He was referring to the leave of absence Lorraine had requested just after the shooting. "Actually, I'm toying with the idea of not going back."

"Really? Why?"

"I was having trouble getting myself fired up for this school year anyway, and this whole business with Josh has soured me even further. I think it's time for a change."

"Maybe you can come down and work at the station."

"We're almost there," Lorraine said, making a left turn. "I couldn't be a cop. I don't have a proper respect for authority, as Detective Turner must have told you."

"Yes, that came through in his reports. But I was thinking more of a job as a dispatcher, taking emergency calls. We always need good people for the position, and it's part-time."

"Too stressful for full-time, is it?"

"Oh, we have a couple of full-time people, but most prefer to remain part-time. It is a demanding job in some ways. You have to keep a cool head and be an excellent listener. There is training, of course."

"It sounds intriguing. I'll think about it." Lorraine turned onto the access road to the park. "What's this? The gate is open."

Sam made a small gesture with his left hand. "Oh, we and the State Police have been in and out of here so much the last couple of days, I've arranged to keep it open. What's so funny?"

"It's an inside joke," Lorraine replied. She had been thinking of Ned's boast to open the park up for her on Monday, and here another man in her life had done just that.

As she drove down the access road, Lorraine saw the police car parked near the park ranger shack. The car door opened as they approached. "I believe I know him," she said as she glimpsed Robb Turner.

"He didn't want to sit at a desk during the internal investigation, so I put him here to keep out the general population."

They got out of the car. "I'm sorry, sir, I'll have to see some identification," Robb deadpanned. "You're all right, ma'am, though I'm afraid I have to question the company you keep."

"Don't I know it," she responded.

Sam shook his head. "No respect." He looked around. "It looks like the state boys are done?"

"Yes. They packed up their toys and left. I was just calling in to see if I should take off."

"Yeah, go on. Close the gate when you leave. We'll drive around it when we go. Is your shift nearly over?"

Robb checked his watch. "Yes, in a half-hour."

"Fine. We'll find something even more dull for you to do tomorrow."

"Desk jockey, that's me," Robb said. "Good night, sir. Ma'am."

He went over and got into his squad car. He drove off back toward the main road.

"He seems fairly upbeat," Lorraine observed. "Or is he covering up his feelings, as men do?"

"He probably is covering up to some extent while he's on the job. But we have him receiving some informal therapy, and in a way it has helped him to see the level of his father's guilt being revealed. He could have gone on a leave of absence, but he wants to keep busy."

"Makes sense."

"Yes. I think he'll do all right. Which trail do you want to take?"

"The Big Loop Trail," she suggested. "I like the boardwalk bridges over the marshy areas."

"Great. Let's go." They started out.

"Speaking of how people are doing," Lorraine began, "I haven't been able to find out how Damon is lately, since he went to the hospital in Portland." She noticed his smile. "What?"

"Damon is fine," Sam said. "It's just that this is going to sound like something out of a thriller. He never went to the hospital. He went to stay with family in Massachusetts."

"Why the cover story? Was he in danger?"

"Maybe, maybe not. About the time we found about the notebook, we learned he was the one who had it. But he'd gotten rid of it by the time we spoke to him. I suggested to his mother that Damon leave the area for a while.

It felt like the stakes were getting higher, judging by how nervous Ned was becoming."

"It does sound like something out of a thriller," she said. "While we're on the subject, there is something I don't get. Robert Turner shooting Ned Turner. Setting aside his stories that he thought Ned was going for a gun, or that it was an accident, I don't understand why he did it. Everything unraveled because of it."

"I've wondered about it myself, believe me, Lorraine. I don't think it was any one thing, but I figure he felt everything closing in on him. He might have sensed I was suspicious of him, and of course, Ned was talking about a deal to us too. The players' parents were getting their lawyers, and-" he interrupted himself.

"And I was putting pressure on him, too, is what you were going to say," Lorraine finished for him.

He shrugged. "Like I said, there was a lot closing in on him. My big problem was that I was pretty sure they were both guilty of something, whether it was murder, blackmail, running the drug operation, or what, I had no idea."

A blue jay screeched and flew past them. They watched it swoop into the trees overhead.

"It's trying to tell us something," Sam suggested.

Lorraine slid an arm through his. "Yeah, like shut up and enjoy the hike. Oh, shoot."

"What?"

"Nothing much. I meant to call Patti after I visited Ned. I forgot all about it. Having my boyfriend waiting by my car threw me off."

He looked over at her. "Good Lord. Do you know how long it has been since I've been called a boyfriend?" Then reverting back to what she had said, he added, "You can use my cell phone if you'd like."

She held his arm tighter. "No, I'm fine. It can wait. Everything can wait except this."

At that moment, Patti stood by her car outside the Shark's Tooth Restaurant. She scanned the parking lot for a car she recognized. Instead she saw Julia getting out of her car two rows away. She waved, and Julia waited for her.

"I thought I saw you drive in," Julia said. "How are you, Patti?"

"I'm doing fine. A couple of calm days have done wonders for me. I just hope tonight goes smoothly. Imagine Dad and Chad at the same table."

"I think it will go well. By all accounts, the golf game was a success. But I'm glad I caught you out here. I have something to tell you."

"Why do I get nervous when I hear that? You're not dropping Dad, are you?"

Julia placed a hand on Patti's arm. "No, quite the opposite. We're sort of living together."

"Julia!"

"Sorry to spring it on you, but I have a feeling he plans to announce it at dinner tonight. You've had enough shocks for one week, so I thought I'd give you advance warning."

They walked towards the restaurant. "I feel silly even asking this, Julia. I mean, I love the idea, but are you sure you know what you're getting with Dad? I love him dearly, but..."

Julia laughed. "Do we ever know what we're getting in a relationship? Patti, Martin is crazy about me. In my life, I've always been the one more in love. He is trying really hard, which is a nice change for my men. It's hard to explain, but it's just what I need this time around. That, and a rabbit's foot, with my history and his."

"I really am pleased, Julia. I was beginning to think I'd be the last woman to live with Dad." They stopped and hugged a few feet from the door to the restaurant.

"I just hope I'm the last," Julia said. "Now let's go inside and make the men talk about something other than golf."

They entered the restaurant and were guided past the bar to the table where the men waved and waited. As they approached the table, the waitress came over. "I knew four handsome men like these wouldn't be eating alone. Which one of them is yours, Julia?"

"Any one of them I want, Peggy," Julia joked.

Patti smiled at Tom and Kelton. The waitress didn't realize how funny that was.

The woman laughed and guided them the rest of the way. "Would you two like a drink, or do you want to settle in with these smooth talkers for a while first?"

"You know me, Peggy," Julia said. "Bring me something dark and foamy."

"I'll have a diet soda," Patti said.

Chad and Patti's father remained standing until Julia and Patti sat down. Patti looked at Chad. The resemblance to Tom was not as pronounced in person as it was in the painting. Apparently her mother had taken some artistic license. Chad leaned over and kissed Patti's cheek.

"Good evening, Patti. It is a pleasure to see you again after all these years. You are a little taller than you were the last time I saw you."

"And you are a little older."

"Aren't we all," her father said.

"Speak for yourself," Julia said. "Armed with thousands of dollars worth of cosmetics, I stare down Father Time every morning."

"She does, too," Patti's father said. "I can hear the old man whimpering from where I lay. It's a terrible sound."

"Father," Tom said with fake surprise, "you don't mean you two are living together in sin, do you?"

The group laughed at this. Their father took a sip from his glass of beer. "When I know what I want, I know. It was that way with your mother," their father said, looking like he wished he'd swallowed the words, especially when Tom responded.

"And look how that turned out."

The awkward tension and brief silence were broken when Julia laughed and slapped the table top with her hands. "You asked for that, Marty," she said after catching her breath.

Tom looked across at Patti and mouthed a one-word question. "Marty?"

In the minutes leading up to ordering, they talked about the golf game just completed, Patti's classes, and George W. Bush's chances of following his father into the presidency. It was the sort of conversation, Patti realized, that ordinary adult families shared. Inexplicably, she felt like crying. She blinked back the tears that threatened and glanced around to see if anyone was noticing. Julia was looking at her, and Patti feared she would ask what's wrong and thrust her into the spotlight. But Patti forced a smile and Julia winked and said into a brief silence, "It's not like we're getting married or anything. We're going to shack up. I'm going to dent his straight-laced reputation. It's all part of a long-range plan to break his spirit."

Martin lifted his glass in a mock toast. "It will be quite a ride, boys. Here's to it."

Patti realized that Julia and Mom had one thing in common: they could both keep Dad on his toes.

Chapter 16

Three weeks later, Patti walked through the main entrance of the hospital. Just inside the door, an old man was pushing an apparently even older woman out in a wheel chair. Patti stepped aside and turned slightly to watch them pass by. She could have sworn she'd seen him somewhere, the sparkling blue eyes, thinning hair and wire-rimmed glasses. She watched him stop outside and help the woman rise out of the chair. When the old woman was assisted into a car parked at the curb, the old gentleman pushed the empty wheel chair towards the entrance. Maybe the old guy worked here. Maybe that's why he was familiar. She must have seen him when she was here for her surgery.

Patti boarded the elevator and pushed the button for the third floor. She wasn't yet an official ostomy visitor, but Lorraine knew this patient, who wanted to see someone young and fairly new from surgery. They didn't get much younger and newer than Patti.

Patti knew the patient was in room 312, and her name was Alicia. A few yards short of the room, Patti looked down and checked herself out. She had wavered between wearing her knockout strapless red dress and jeans. Her mind went back to her own experience, when she realized Lorraine had the same surgery she did, and yet could still wear jeans. It had been quite a moment for her. But Julia had said the woman was gentile, which stuck Patti as an odd description. "You know, feminine," Julia corrected herself. So in the end Patti went with the dress. It sure turned a few heads on the way to the room.

Patti was a few minutes early. She didn't hear any conversation in the room, just the hum of the television, so she went in. The bed on the right hand side of the room was empty, though with plenty of personal belongings scattered about to indicate occupation. The curtain was drawn partway around the bed on the left. Patti stepped far enough to see the woman reclined there. She looked bored, but tried to sit up farther when she saw Patti. The woman looked to be in her early thirties.

"Let me," Patti said. She stepped to the side of the bed and helped maneuver pillows behind the woman.

"Are you here for me, or Mrs. Akers over there? They've taken her for an ERCP, poor thing."

"What's an ERCP? It sounds ominous."

"It's putting a scope down your throat. They're looking for tumors, or something, in her stomach. You'd have thought they were wheeling her off for torture, though, the way she moaned about it. Mind you, I don't blame her. She's eighty if she's a day, and she has been through a lot. But I hope she sleeps a while after the procedure."

Patti thought of her own hospital stay. She could have benefited from more peace and quiet herself. Thinking about it made her realize that the old gentleman wheeling the lady out had been Cal Briggs, the husband of her own unfortunate roommate. He must work or volunteer here now, unless he was an unlucky elderly bigamist with multiple ill wives.

Patti set the frivolous thought aside. "Well, if you're Alicia, I'm here to see you. I'm Patti Jo Lewis. Did anyone tell you I was coming?"

"I think it was mentioned. But I'm confused. I just saw that nurse- what's her name, Carole?"

"Yes. Isn't she great?"

"Yes, I can see where she's a good person to know in my situation. So what kind of nurse are you? Or are you a social worker? I was a little foggy when they told me."

"Believe me, I understand. My first couple of days were like a bad dream." She stepped over closer to the windows. From where she stood, she could see some of the acres of parking lot, but she imagined from the bed Alicia mostly saw trees and Crittenden Hill beyond Main Street. "You have a better view than I did."

"It's okay," Alicia agreed, but then she amended it. "I prefer the view from my back yard, though."

"Ain't that the truth," Patti said. She took a few steps back towards the hospital bed. "I'm not a nurse, Alicia. I was asked to come see you by representatives of the local ostomy chapter. Someone visited me when I had the surgery, and now I'm visiting you. It's sort of like a human chain letter, when it works like it should."

"You've had the same surgery I just had?"

"Yes. Not all that long ago, either. You'll get through it, believe me."

Patti tried not to primp under the other woman's scrutiny. "Maybe I will get through this," Alicia said, to Patti's great relief. "I've been having my doubts."

This Patti could relate to. But she realized she was still standing. She could have just sat down, but it became a point of honor to be invited. "May I sit down?"

"Of course. Where are my manners? Back home with my dog, I guess."

Patti moved the chair a little closer and sat down. "You have a dog? You must miss him. Her?"

"Her. Aspen. Yes, I miss her. In a way, I feed off her energy. Some days I feel like I wouldn't even get out of bed, except that her energy and excitement about the new day put me to shame, and I get up."

"Maybe I should get one," Patti remarked. "I might need two dogs to get me up."

"My uncle said he'd try to smuggle her in, just to see if it could be done, but he can't right now. Of course, he would have had to muzzle her, and I wouldn't have liked that. She's quite a little yapper."

There was a brief silence, and Patti wondered if Alicia was dwelling on the absence of her dog. "Alicia, were you very sick before your surgery?"

"Not as bad as before. Remission. Just a matter of time, though. I'd rather be sick like I was than how I feel now."

"You'll feel differently when you get through the worst of it, Alicia. The surgery has turned my life around. For years, I have had trouble with what I eat, and how far I dare to venture away from bathrooms. I guess Carole told you about the ostomy group?" Alicia nodded, beginning to look tired. "I hope you'll let us help you, Alicia. Moral support at the meetings, and before that I can get materials for you: brochures and such, that discuss the day-to-day details of living with an ostomy."

"Oh, I probably have most of that stuff. My uncle got it for me."

"Oh yeah, through Lorraine."

"You know her? My uncle wanted to know her better, but he's in the hospital right now too."

"I'm sorry, is it serious?"

"You could say that. He was shot."

"Oh my God," Patti said. "Is your uncle Ned Turner?"

"Yes. You've heard about it on the news, I suppose? And that tabloid," she added, with disdain in her voice.

Now it came together for Patti. Lorraine had visited Alicia and gave her the ostomy materials, meeting Ned in the process. She was about to tell Alicia that she had more than heard about it, that in a way she had lived it, when she saw the other woman's expression.

"Sure, but if you don't want to talk about it, we don't have to. I'm here for a different reason."

211

Patti read the relief sweeping over Alicia's face. "Thank you, Patti. I'm all talked out over it. The nurses and the police can't seem to get enough. I almost postponed this surgery because of it. I'm relieved to have it behind me, even if there is a struggle ahead of me. Having it loom ahead of me was the worst."

"I didn't have much time to think about it," Patti said. "I was so sick; it was pretty much an emergency surgery."

"I almost would have preferred that," Alicia said. She glanced at Patti. "I'm sorry. I don't mean to trivialize your experience. It was probably horrible for you."

Patti smiled. "That's okay, Alicia. I was just thinking how we have a different experience surrounding the same surgery, and here we are each envying the other. It's human nature, I guess."

Alicia played with the fringe of the two-tone purple afghan resting on her legs. "I don't how I'm going to manage. I'm all thumbs. That nurse was positively bristling with confidence and encouragement, but I can't even thread a needle."

"Neither can I," Patti assured her. "Don't get me wrong, you'll run into problems, and it's harder at first until you get used to it, but it's as easy as falling out of bed once you're used to it, and less painful."

"I hope so. Especially a bed as high as this one." Alicia sighed, continuing to run her fingers through the yarn fringing the afghan. It occurred to Patti that Alicia was nervous about something.

"Do you have a significant other, Patti?"

Patti thought about it. Did she? "Sort of," she said finally. "I mean, we're not married or engaged, but we..." She let that sentence drop, unsure how to finish it off.

Patti took a new direction. "Are you concerned about intimate moments, then?"

"What a subtle way of stating it. Yes, I guess I am concerned. I was dating this guy. When he found out about this surgery, the details, I mean, he tried to stop me. At first I thought he was worried about me. But it became clear he just thought the whole thing was repulsive. I mean, I guess I don't blame him."

"You should blame him," Patti interrupted. "He obviously believes beauty is truly skin deep."

Alicia looked at her hands. "Oh, I came to realize that I was well rid of him, for a multitude of good reasons, but it hurt all the same."

Alicia didn't seem approachable enough to Patti to want a hug at that moment. She reached out, however, and touched one of her hands. "Lorraine" she said, "who first visited me after my surgery like I am here now, gave me the definitive answer on the question. She said that this type of surgery is the ultimate jerk detector. It can save you months separating the wheat from the chaff, the deep from the shallow."

"She's probably right," Alicia said, smiling. "But being the contrary creature I am, sometimes I want to have the right to make a lousy decision."

"I know what you mean," Patti said, withdrawing her hand. Alicia yawned. "Perhaps I should leave you now," she added. "Some of my favorite moments after surgery were when I was sleeping."

"When you put it like that," Alicia said, "I can't help but agree. I don't want to be rude, but I would just love to take a nap while my roommate is gone, and before my family starts flowing in."

Patti stood up. "Of course. That's a good idea. Would you like me to come see you again before you are discharged?"

"Actually, I'm not supposed to be here much longer."

It almost sounded like a brush-off, but Patti persisted by pulling out a handwritten card she had made up. "I'll just leave this with you, then." She placed the card on the woman's bedside stand. "Call me when you feel up to it, for anything at all."

"Thank you, Patti. I appreciate your coming."

Not exactly the rapport she'd developed instantly with Lorraine, but Patti felt okay about the visit. "Take care, Alicia. I'm sure you will be feeling much better soon."

"Bye, Patti."

Patti waved and left the room. On an impulse, Patti decided to drop in on Ned Turner while she was here. She couldn't say why she wanted to meet him, except that she never had laid eyes on him, and perhaps it would help her gain some closure to the whole mess. Of course, if there was any kind of a trial, perhaps true closure might be fairly elusive. She knew he was on this floor, so she walked down the corridor past the elevators until she saw Officer Wendy Mills sitting outside a room.

"This must be the place," Patti said under her breath as she drew closer. They exchanged greetings, and Patti motioned towards the room. "Are you guys worried that he might make a run for it?" she asked, only half-joking.

"Stranger things have happened. With my boss off on a sin tour with Lorraine, he didn't want any nasty surprises when he got back. Turner likes the idea too. It seems to support his claim that he is still in danger if he cooperates with us. Plus we're a built-in screening service in case any more tabloid people show up. How is Robb doing, anyway, after his fifteen minutes of fame?"

"Pretty good. When it all came crashing down on him, he wavered between wanting to be a thousand miles away, and wanting to hang around out of sheer stubbornness. Even though the tabloid and CNN made him out to be a hero, shooting his own father, a bad cop, in the line of duty, the attention was pretty unwelcome."

"I can imagine. Some of that attention shone on you as well."

"A little of it," Patti admitted. "A tabloid photographer, or a guy claiming to be one, offered me $5,000 to pose in something scanty."

"Sam said something about that," Wendy said. "The femme fatale of the scandal. Is it true an agent called Robb?"

"Not exactly. Some guy called and asked Robb for an interview so he could write a screenplay, or present an idea to someone who would write a screenplay, or something like that. I told him to hold out for six figures, but Robb wasn't amused."

"I bet. Did you want to see Turner?"

"Yes. I don't even know why. It's like a car accident. I'm passing by, and I can't help but look."

"He'd like that," Wendy said. "Say what you like about him, he is able to laugh at himself. Hold on a second." She ducked into the room and came right back out.

"He said gorgeous women are always welcome."

"Well, I don't have time to find one of those, so I'll go in."

Ned was propped up in bed, a few magazines in his lap. "Hi. I'm Patti."

"Finally we meet," he said. He didn't extend his hand, so Patti stayed where she was. There was no IV pole nearby.

"You look ready to go home," she observed.

"Or to jail," he countered. "Once Sam Ripkin gets back from his vacation, the lucky sod, he gets to intervene with the prosecutor to decide which it will be for me. Sit down, please."

Patti sat. Ned picked up the magazines and set them aside.

"So I finally meet the gal who gave me that nickname, the Nedster. I used to hear a lot about you from Lorraine. No more, sad to say. Did I hear they went to Niagara Falls?"

"Yes, when she turned down his marriage proposal, she said she'd give him the honeymoon at least."

"She turned him down?" he asked, and Patti almost winced. Why had she told him that. Would that only give him hope?"

"Women often say no the first time," she threw in carelessly. "Just to increase the desire and improve the proposal."

He didn't seem to be paying attention. "I could have taken her to Paris," he said, pouting just a little, she thought. Then he shook his head. "Or the visitor's room at the local jail," he added. "She's better off, obviously."

Patti decided to redirect the conversation. "So you're doing all right?"

"Yes, I guess so. I'm hoping for probation, obviously, since I got shot and all. The prosecutor's a hard nose, though, and is newly elected, so we'll see."

"Well, I was talking more physically and emotionally."

He waved his hand in a dismissive gesture. "Oh yeah. The food isn't up to my standard, but I'm lucky to be able to eat at all, or breathe. It was a near thing, the doctor tells me. The bullet danced around and tore me up inside."

A silence quickly developed as Ned seemed to lapse into deep thought. Patti decided she wanted to work up towards leaving, but not while he was in this frame of mind. "I just saw your niece," she offered as a more positive topic.

"Alicia, yes. They let me see her briefly. How is she today?"

"She's doing well. I think I was able to give her more reason to feel good about where she is at."

"If you did, I'm grateful. I tried to talk her out of having that kind of surgery."

You and everyone else, apparently, Patti thought. But she said, "You're lucky to be around to see her at all."

"I know it. A friend of mine said that if the surgeon had ever had business dealings with me, you could be talking to a dead man right now."

"The question is, would I notice?"

He laughed. "Now you're starting to sound like Lorraine. I miss talking to her. She had a way of putting me in my place and making me like it. The next time you talk to her-" he interrupted himself and stared in the direction of the windows. "No, I guess we both know she won't want to hear from me. Listen, Patti. Thanks for stopping in. And thank you especially for visiting Alicia. You'd better go before I start getting maudlin and embarrass myself."

"All right. Take care, Nedster."

Ned smiled, and Patti left the room. Wendy looked up.

"How is he doing?"

"He seems pretty good. His mood jumped around. Is he really going to go to prison?"

"Your guess is as good as mine. It looks like most of the blame for the harder drugs rested with Robert Turner, but the prosecutor thinks it's bad politics to place too much blame on dead people. He's convinced Ned knows who the drug suppliers were. Sam disagrees. I don't think Sam will push it too far, though. He lost some credibility when he got involved with Lorraine. That's working against Ned, in a way."

"In more ways than one," Patti said. "Ned had his own hopes where Lorraine was concerned."

"I had heard that. A strange business all around."

"Oh well," Patti said after a brief silence. "I confess, I won't shed too many tears over Ned's fate. I do like his niece, though, and I feel bad for her."

"Yes, this has hit her hard. She barely spoke to him when he was allowed to see her. I think that even though she knew he was a tough businessman, she assumed he was tough but honest."

"Sort of like Robb with his father," Patti commented. "Well, I'll take off. I'm having company tonight."

"Young male company?"

Patti felt herself blush, just a little. "A gathering, really. But yes, Robb will be among them."

"How are you two doing?"

Patti thought about it. "It is strange. When we first got back together, it seemed natural, almost like we took up where we left off. But now, in an odd way, it's awkward. It's like we started all over again, through the dating process, becoming close for the first time all over again. It's hard to explain."

"You did pretty well at it. Tell him his badge is waiting for him whenever he wants it back."

"Sam has made that clear. Bye, Wendy." Patti walked down to the bank of elevators, reflecting that it seemed odd to be calling police officers by their first names. After waiting twenty seconds, she decided to take the stairs. She jogged down the stairs, hardly puffing as she emerged into the main lobby. Of course, jogging up stairs would be a different matter, even this long after the surgery. The stairwell opened into the main lobby, and Patti saw that Cal Briggs was still there. She moved in his direction.

"Mr. Briggs," she said, when she was near enough to be heard.

"Hi Patti. You're looking much better. I hardly recognize you."

"I feel much better." She didn't quite know how to ask about his wife, in case the news was very bad, but he saved her the trouble.

"Kate is in the White Pine Manor," he explained. "She is worse, I'm afraid. Stable, they tell me, but I'm not to expect her to come home ever again."

"I'm sorry, Mr. Briggs."

He shrugged. "It is the way it is." He motioned around them. "I've been coming in here most days, just a few hours a day. I keep people company mostly, or make myself useful in small ways. Kate suggested it. It was practically the last coherent discussion we had. It occupies my mind for a while each day. Well, it looks like they want me for something. You take care of yourself, Patti."

"You too, Mr. Briggs." She watched him walk over to the main desk, and then she left the hospital. She located her car in the parking lot and got inside. She had planned to stop at the supermarket on the way home, but when she saw the time on the radio face, she reconsidered. She could start supper with what she had, at least until Robb showed up. He had said he would arrive early in case she needed help. She could prepare the chickens for the oven and send him to the store for the salad makings. He was a man, but he would have to do. Kelton and Tom were coming for dinner, as were Dad and Julia. She'd have to try to get them out through the door by nine o'clock so she could work on her Philosophy paper for an hour before Lorraine phoned. It seemed unlikely, though, that the dinner party would break up that early, so perhaps she'd be working on the paper after the call, or in the morning.

Patti let herself in and climbed the stairs to her apartment. She remembered to slide the dead bolt into place.

There were two messages on her answering machine. Tom and Dad, she guessed. She was close. The first was from Julia.

"Hello Patti. How are you? Listen, We went to the public market this afternoon, and I bought bags of stuff. I'm going to bring a garden salad. Nothing fancy: lettuce, tomatoes, cukes, radishes, avocado. Do you have cheese to grate? I'll bring some just in case. I know when I have a few people over, making the salad is my least favorite part. So don't worry about that, okay? I'm looking forward to seeing you."

Well, that took care of the salad. Now if only Tom was offering to bring over two roasted chickens. But it was Kelton's voice that came on.

"Hey, kid. We were wondering if you need us to do anything to make this soiree a success. We could bring along some broccoli spears or dress in drag, whatever you like."

"Don't you dare," she said under her breath.

"Just let us know," Kelton went on. "See you in a while."

Patti shook her head as she put on an apron and went to work on supper. The cross-dressing joke grew out of something Dad said when Tom first came out, like he expected that would be a natural step for Tom to take. Patti turned the oven on to preheat and took the chickens out of the refrigerator. She put the livers and hearts aside to fry up later, and washed the chickens. She sprinkled pepper and lemon juice on top of them and popped them unstuffed into the oven. Both Tom and their father preferred the boxed stuffing cooked on top of the stove, and the chickens would cook faster this way.

She had toyed with the idea of making scalloped potatoes, but she decided to stick to baked potatoes, which the men in her life loved. She'd make up a sour cream and chive topping when she delivered them. After washing the biggest potatoes she had, she set them aside and shifted gears to dessert. Home made ice cream, she figured, again, a family favorite. She plugged in her blender and dug out her dog-eared recipe for chocolate ice cream. No other flavor would do for this bunch. She poured and spooned in the ingredients and turned on the blender. She was pouring it into a plastic container when the doorbell rang.

"Come in!" she called out as she sealed the container, but then she remembered the dead bolt. Whomever it was fumbled with the handle. "Just a minute!" She left the ice cream mixture on the counter and walked over to the door. She released the dead bolt and opened the door.

"That's a mean trick to pull," Robb said as he stepped inside.

"Sorry. I've gotten so I remember to lock it when I get home, but when someone comes, I forget it is there." As she explained, she went back to the small kitchen. "You're early. I mean, I knew you were coming early, but you're even earlier than I expected."

"Yeah, I planned it. I thought maybe we could fool around on the couch for a while."

Patti let the suggestion, half-serious yet hopeful, hang in the air between them. Actually she savored it. They hadn't done much more than kiss since the day at Shadow Lake, at first out of the feelings of betrayal she had felt, and perhaps his feelings of guilt over the shooting. More recently it seemed to be attributed to the feeling of renewed awkwardness between them and their busy schedules.

Patti picked up the ice cream mixture and put it in the refrigerator. She decided to buy a little time to think about his amorous offer. "How is your new job going?"

"It's a project and a half."

"I can't believe you're working for Ned Turner, after all that has happened."

"In a way, I'm not at all. I haven't even spoken to the man. I interviewed with his controller and deal with him mostly. I know Ned's behind it, of course. I realize he wanted me partly for the PR value. He doesn't have a great public image right now. But it's also true that his drugstores need a better security system. One of his branches was broken into and some painkillers stolen. It will keep me busy while I decide what I want to do with myself."

"I spoke to Ned today," Patti said, turning and leaning against the counter. "It turned out the woman I made the ostomy visit to was his niece. Isn't that remarkable? Wendy Mills was there. She said there's a place on the force whenever you want to go back."

"Yes, Ripkin told me the same thing."

"Now that he's cozy to my best friend, you're going to have to start calling him Sam. Are you giving any thought to going back to the force?"

"Why, would you want me to?"

"Not really, though there is something sexy about a man in uniform."

"I've always thought the same about a woman in an apron," he said, moving closer.

She snaked her arms over his shoulders and they kissed, the longest kiss in weeks. As they pulled away slightly, Robb said, "I could flip burgers somewhere. They wear uniforms."

"They wear aprons too, don't they? We could work there together."

He took her hand and led her towards her bedroom.

"You're in luck," she said, smiling. "I'm wearing one of those old fashioned bras. You can strut your stuff."

"Good, my stuff needs strutting badly."

"I sure hope you're the only guest who is way early," she said as they stepped into the bedroom. They made love for the first time since the shooting. As she told Lorraine later, it was better than a poke in the eye with a sharp stick, but..." and the ellipsis carried a world of meaning, they both realized.

As Lorraine hung up the phone, she took the tissue Sam held out for her.

"This is the first time I've seen you cry," he said, a smile playing around his mouth.

"Well, get used to it. I'm poised on the leading edge of menopause, so my emotions may resemble a roller coaster."

"I've always enjoyed a good thrill ride. What brought it on? I gathered you were talking to Patti."

"It's just me being sappy and sentimental. Patti and Robb are still going through a rough patch. Patti talked about giving it time, and she said a few of the right things about her feelings for Robb, but I can read between the lines. I'm not sure I see a real future for them. When I think of what that young lady has lived through. Even as a child: virtually losing her mother at an early age, her long-term illness, and now the surgery and finding out her father isn't

Tom's father. And of course this mess I got her into. What a lot she has had to wade through."

"As opposed to you," Sam said. "Homeless for a year or more as a teenager, your ex-husband killed and dishonored. You've had it easy, I suppose."

She smiled. "Yes, and run out of town by a belligerent cop when I was homeless. You left out that part."

"I also left out the part about the same belligerent cop that now loves you to distraction."

"Does he?" she asked, more seriously than she had intended. She stood up and walked over to the hotel room's picture window. She stared at the far off Canadian falls, lit up by floodlights. "I've been here a half-dozen times, and I never get my fill of it. Some people are drawn to Florida or Las Vegas; I run here year after year. Someday I want to live near moving water."

"We can arrange that," he said. "Would you settle for a river instead of Niagara Falls?"

"I'd settle for a stream, as long as it never dries up." She sat down in one of the two chairs near the window. "So much like love," she said softly.

"What's that?"

She rested her head on her arm, which rested on the arm of the chair. "With Josh. I settled so long for a trickle of love. All I asked was that it didn't run dry."

"But it did."

"Yes."

"Maybe you shouldn't settle for a stream," he suggested. "Why don't we move here? Not on the Canadian side of course, but somewhere within a five minute drive of the falls."

"Oh, don't even joke about it."

"Who's joking? We could pull it off. Just say the word."

She sighed. "I swear, you seem to propose in one way or another in every other sentence. I would like to know the sound of that watery roar is not too far away."

"When I'm with you," he said, "I always hear the sound of water rushing in my ears."

She smiled. "I'm not sure what that means, but it sounds like a compliment." She continued staring out the window. "Have you seen that statue down there in the courtyard?"

"No, not to remember it, at least."

"You can see the shape of it from up here. It's a statue of some local wealthy businessman, who died around fifty years ago. He made piles of money for decades, went blind at the age of sixty, and died shortly after that. In that period after he went blind, he gave away a lot of his money. There are buildings and parks around here with his name on the signs."

"I can't wait to hear what this has to do with anything," Sam said. "Where did you learn all of this about him?"

"They talked about him on a local TV channel. But think of it, all that money and still he went blind. On top of his small world, but now transformed into a pillar of stone, reduced to eavesdropping on snippets of conversations from passing tourists. The babbling and whining of the children, and the tiny arguments of their tired parents."

"You're in a strange mood tonight."

"I suppose I am."

"What brought this train of thought on, Ned's plight?"

"Hardly that. Patti's plight, to be alliterative."

"She'll be all right."

"If I moved here, I'd be leaving her behind."

"She'll be all right," he repeated. He kissed her on her upper shoulder and walked over to the bed. Lorraine glanced at him as he picked up some tourist brochures they had gotten at the visitor's center. Then she turned back to the window view. She thought about Ned's final comment to her, left on her answering machine while he was in the hospital. He said he was surprised she would be with the one man who could have helped Josh but who had refused to do so. Of course, Ned would probably be the first to admit he had spoken out of bitterness. But how much of it was bitterness, and how much truth? Did Sam have the opportunity, years before, to prevent the tragedy that overtook Josh? If so, did he have any inkling the opportunity was there? There was a big difference between missing an opportunity and ignoring it. She never told Sam about it. She didn't want him thinking that was why she hadn't accepted his proposal. Especially since she didn't know exactly why she had turned him down.

She looked up and saw Sam watching her, another thing Josh never did. She sighed.

"What?"

"I don't know, nothing, everything. I want to be happy for a while."

"I can manage that, for a long while, I hope."

"I think you can, Sam Ripkin." She looked for the statue in the courtyard again, now disappearing into shadow. Perhaps the spirit of the blind man encased in that stone only cared to hear the snatches of conversations from passersby: the shared laughter, the small intimacies, even the mild complaints. She thought, that is the stuff of life, the framework of love. Why dig deeper?

Peter McGinn works as a business writer for an insurance company, because someone has to do it. He and his wife have raised a special needs child and faced adversity large and small together, including his own ostomy surgery many years before. They live in Maine with their MINI Cooper, even though they have discovered there are warmer places.

Printed in the United States
60680LVS00004B/41